DEMON CHRONICLES

DEMON CHRONICLES

The Chaos Prophecy

AERUM DELEVAN

Ingram Spark

Contents

Acknowledgements

Generally, the words of *Demon Chronicles* flowed freely—the result of inspired ideas that were received and cultivated over a lifetime. Throughout the writing process, family and friends provided love, support, and editing assistance. To them, I am deeply grateful.

Life brings hardships and heartbreak to all. However, it also provides us with gifts that enable us to cope. I believe the greatest gift I have received is that of a far-reaching imagination. I am also grateful for freedom of the mind, with which we are all blessed and without which this book would not have been possible.

—Aerum Delevan

Prologue

The universe, a giant mass of energy in which the powers of both light and darkness collide and divide, contains an infinite number of galaxies which spin and spiral as they travel through the void of space and time. Great beings, wielding unlimited power, create and destroy these galaxies on a whim. Most mortals call these beings, "gods."

Most gods are of light and love, yet a select few choose to dwell in darkness. The powers they use balance as well as complement each other, for without darkness there could be no light. However, the reverse is also true; if light did not exist, then even darkness would fade into nothingness.

Untold eons passed where peace reigned between the gods of light and darkness, but then one of the greater gods of darkness grew weary of the light receiving the majority of souls. Skath, the darkest of gods, shattered the peace; he disrupted the balance. All of existence suffered for his choice. For the first time in the eternities, the gods of light and darkness were at war. Existences were extinguished as the gods and their demon allies devoured each other's souls in a transcendent war.

The war has now long ended. The gods of light—the true masters of creation—have returned to their ways of creating light and life, giving birth to souls, and testing their mortal children. The time of balance swiftly approaches as one of the grand gods of light places a single life form, which is now ready to be born to mortal parents, on a planet called Earth. This one tiny act will set into motion a chain of events that will affect all life.

I

Insight

Many onns have passed since the Skath were driven from our galaxy. The majority of our outlying systems have suffered devastating losses. Entire races and cultures have been destroyed. I am hoping that my galaxy's two groups of Verse (the power of the universe) users will heed my counsel and fully join the Marcisian Empire. I have already sent envoys to the Ja'Shari on Firax and the Zaharaj on Zharaj. I pray to God for good news upon their return. Otherwise, I fear another storm will soon be upon us.

—Marcisian Emperor, Barren Marcis

Only the brave walk the path of shadows. Only a few will truly master the path. Only the foolish fully embrace it, and only the weak allow it to consume them.

—An excerpt from Lord Baltrix's discourses on the Zah'harrim form of the Verse

Two different sources rule our lives. The first is what most beings call fate, or destiny, and the second is choice. Just how much of our lives are ruled by destiny? How much choice do we really have? Though I am now old, I have yet to find the answer.

—Lord Baltrix

The Zah'harrim form of the Verse is not always evil, just as the Jah'harrim is not always good. Every being who understands this is on the true path to enlightenment.

—Lord Nosfaren

We were supposed to thirst for knowledge, but knowledge also brings power. The Council has failed to acknowledge this. It is up to me to correct their erroneous ways.

—Lady Dreth

We are the chosen; we are power. There is only one truth, and that truth is Skath. Skath is the one true God. All must bow. All must submit, or all will perish. Only Skath will remain.

—Creed of the Skath Worshippers

The Verse is vast; the Verse is power; the Verse is Skath. Skath's power comes from the Zah form of the Verse—from darkness. We embrace the darkness. Darkness is eternal—it will devour all. This is the truth of Skath, and only this will please him. We will bring forth his truth. We are his children, and we gladly obey.

'—Oath of the Skath worshippers

2

The Calm Before the Storm

The young Korean woman normally had a beautiful view of the vibrant city of Seoul, South Korea from her apartment's kitchen window. However, the storm clouds, which had been ominously looming over the city for several hours, now gave way and obscured the view. Flashes of lightning intermittently burst from the sky and re-illuminated the city with brilliant colors of white and blue. Thunder cracked and echoed. Though the fierce cracking of the thunder startled the woman, she quickly regained her composure—and none too soon. She turned off the faucet and wiped her brow just in time to avoid the effect of a huge lightning strike. The strike narrowly missed her apartment complex, but a nearby skyscraper was not as lucky and took quite a hit.

"Wow that was a big one! I hope *our* building doesn't get hit!" Immediately another angry bolt launched into the heart of the metropolis.

I guess I should be grateful for the bad weather. At least it gives me the chance to catch up on my housework. Lucky thing I have a brother-in-law for a boss. That was nice of him to give me a few days off in advance of the storm. After letting out a sigh of relief that she had gotten the dishes done before the storm had fully hit, Kim, who was in her early thirties and rather tall for a Korean woman, turned to inspect the dinner table in the dining room, hoping to find that her son hadn't forgotten to thoroughly clear it. She smiled in satisfaction; he had not only cleared the table but had also wiped it down.

Kim's two older daughters were at school, and her husband, a destroyer captain, was deployed to the Gulf with the rest of the US Third Pacific Fleet. Only her youngest, Orran, was home with her. Because of his peculiar condition, he had to be homeschooled. Even though he was different, he loved to do his classroom studies and pour over the many books in Kim's small library. His curiosity and diligence put his knowledge level leagues ahead of that of his peers. He studied multiple languages and had quite the affluence in both his native Korean and in English. *I wonder what he's up to in there.* Kim walked from the kitchen into the living room and found Orran in the middle of reading yet another book. She bent over to wipe her still-soaked hands onto the leg of her pants, stood up, and swiped several strands of straight-black hair out of her face, pushing them behind her ears. Quickly refocusing, she peered anxiously at her seven-year-old. "Orran, you need to put your clothes on! We're having company this evening."

Orran peered back at his oma, his sapphire-blue orbs staring into her dark-colored eyes. He blinked several times before answering. "But Oma, I hate putting on clothes. Every time I do, they end up burned." His light-blue lips turned down into a slight pout. Kim let out a disgruntled sigh. It was true—her son would periodically burst into flames. Then he'd take off to no one knew where—though most of the time he ended up flying to his father's fleet out in the Pacific. Kim, for the most part, lived in fear for her son and his future. Ever since he was born, he had been a strange child—probably the strangest in the world.

Orran's hair was silver, and his skin was white as snow with blotches and patterns of azure on parts of his body; his ears weren't rounded but pointed; his fingers and toes ended with claws and talons instead of nails. However, his two rather bushy, silver, blue-tipped tails were definitely his most striking feature. Yes, his appearance was strange all right, but he was hers, and she loved him. That was all that mattered.

Orran lay on his stomach and peered up at his mother. He was clutching his book with both hands, his white-and-blue fingers gently caressing the cover. He didn't want to tear the delicate pages with his claws. His legs were crossed and swaying back and forth, causing both tails to swish from side to side. Kim couldn't help but smile, despite his disobedience. "I don't care—you can't run around the house undressed all the time. Now go put some clothes on!"

Orran grimaced before closing his book. With both tails swishing in annoyance, he reluctantly stood up, glumly walked past his oma, and made his way upstairs to his bedroom. Kim gave him another stern glare. "Don't you wag your tails at me!"

Orran turned around, flashed a toothy grin—which exposed his pearly fangs—and half-heartedly called back, "Yes, Oma."

What am I going to do with that boy, Kim thought while at the same time peering at the book he had been reading. After catching a glimpse of the title, she made her way over to the couch, sat down, and opened the book to a random page. By the time Orran got back downstairs, she had finished her second chapter. Orran, now fully clothed, had on a pair of blue jeans. All of his pants had been altered in order to allow his two tails to stick out the back. Luckily, most department store shirts fit him without any problem. His feet were still bare, since no shoes could accommodate his taloned toes. He seemed pleased when he noticed that his mother was reading his book. Kim grinned and then patted the cushion next to hers, inviting him to sit. He responded with a fang-filled smile before accepting the invitation. However, after taking only two steps towards the couch, he doubled over and fell to the floor. Blue-and-white flames engulfed his entire being. Kim dropped the book and rushed to her son's side. Without thinking, she reached and thrust her hand into the flames. Though she quickly withdrew from the scorching heat, her hand and wrist had already sustained severe burns.

Orran felt his mother's pain. He could hear her crying and see that she was clutching her right wrist. He was terrified that he might hurt her further, so he ran for the door and grabbed onto the latch. With his fire-engulfed hand, he threw open the door and bolted out into the darkness. Dark clouds were now completely obscuring the sky, and heavy rain pelted down onto his flaming body.

Kim was horrified when her flame-engulfed son fled his home. She had initially tried to grab him and hold him like she had always done in the past, but this time the flames were ferociously hot—much hotter than they had ever been—and they severely burned her hand after only a brief touch. Though wracked with pain, she managed to race to the doorway, but the only thing she could see was the thickly cloud-covered sky and the drenching rain.

"Orran! Orran! Come back! Please! I'm all right! I'm not mad! Orran!" The response—just the slapping sound of the rain. Though Kim anguished over the decision, she knew she had to get to a hospital. She had no choice; the burns were too severe. "Orran, I'll find you, I promise."

3

⚬⚬⚬

Preparation for Pickup

Lord Nosfaren was walking to his starship while his mechanized doll prepared for takeoff. After making his way up the ramp into the ship's cargo hold, he mentally crossed off every item on his pre-flight check-list. By the time he reached the ship's cabin, he was more than ready to slump down into the chair next to the one occupied by his TAD (Tactical Assault Doll).

The TAD turned his head towards his master and asked in a metallic voice, "Master Nos, is it true we are going to the forbidden planet?"

"Yes, Tri, we are," Nos replied, though he was simultaneously working the controls and pressing several buttons on the console.

Tri spoke quietly and with what sounded to Nos like a concerned tone. "Master, is it true that the inhabitants killed their own God?"

Nos grimaced before slumping back into his chair, pulling off the hood of his black cloak, and running his left hand through his messy-looking black hair. Normally, his hair was tied up neatly, but not tendronn. Tendronn, he was aggravated; he obviously had not had a good menronn. He straightened back up in his chair while his TAD launched the ship, sending it skyward. "Tri, there are times I wonder why I ever gave you artificial intelligence. But yes, the Earthlings did indeed kill one of our gods, and trust me, Eendril was not happy."

Tri processed Nos's response before asking, "So why are we returning to Earth?"

"Because we were ordered to! Now give me the controls—I don't want to have a personal relationship with one of those asteroids!" After he wrested the controls from Tri, he skillfully maneuvered the ship through the asteroid field until it safely emerged from the cluttered mess. At that point, he slammed the lever on the console forward and catapulted the vessel into hyperspace. The mission—to pick up a single life form, which Eendril had, for whatever reason, placed on Earth.

4

Encounter in the Rain

Night was settling in, and the rain was not letting up. Everything was wet and cold. However, despite the wet environment, Orran's blue-and-white flames had not yet quenched. The boy sat alone, clenching his legs tightly to his body in order to keep warm. Tears streamed down from his sapphire-blue eyes, causing small wisps of energy to arise when they hit the ground surrounding his bare, taloned feet. He began whimpering. "Why am I so different?" He searched the heavens for answers, only to hear the sizzling sound made by the raindrops when they landed on his fire-engulfed face.

Orran desperately wished to be a normal child. He peered at his two bushy tails; they were both wildly swishing about near his body. His silver-colored hair was floating about above his head as though it were underwater. The marks that randomly adorned his snow-white skin were now glowing in an angry blue color. His cat-like pupils were usually vibrant, but not today. Racing through his mind were thoughts of what had transpired. He had nearly burned down his apartment. His oma, in a desperate attempt to help extinguish his flames, had ended up severely injured in the process. Having felt her pain, he had fled out the door in order to prevent his uncontrollable "ailment" from causing any further harm. He had run as far as his stamina would allow, finally collapsing in the wooded area where he now sat. He was alone and on fire. When his flames danced onto the log on which he was sitting, the log itself was at risk of catching fire, but, luckily, was too rain drenched to do so. However, he was not so lucky. His clothing had completely burned away, including the jeans his grandmother had made for him. It was painful to watch them disintegrate into ash.

These episodes were now happening more and more frequently. Normally, the flames only lasted mere minutes, but today they *still* had not stopped. He was terrified! Because of his inability to control his body, he had nearly killed the one who loved him most.

I almost killed Oma! I don't want these flames anymore. Maybe I should go find Dad. Maybe he can help me. He knew his father loved him. At times, he had made several trips out to sea looking for him, unbeknownst to his oma. The first time he had taken flight, it scared both of his parents to death. However, he was not afraid; he also had the ability to sense where his parents were, no matter how far he had traveled, and, for this, he was extremely grateful. On the first trip to his father's ship, his father, who was the captain of one of the fleet's destroyers, had to beg the Admiral not to shoot down the blue fireball. Though his father was thrilled to see him, the fleet members weren't too happy about the boy flying into the middle of their carrier group and were more than shocked by his peculiar appearance. However, it didn't take long before everyone, even the Admiral, became totally attached to the little guy. The Admiral even jokingly conferred upon Orran the high honor of being the youngest pilot in the Navy.

***

Suddenly the rain stopped. *That's odd,* Orran thought before gazing skyward. "What on earth is that thing?" Once he realized that, instead of stopping, the drenching rain was being blocked by

the presence of a giant object, he was gripped with fear. He knew the object was a vessel of some kind, but he'd never seen anything like it before. "Maybe the Navy built a new aircraft?"

The vessel sat motionless, suspended in the air by some unknown force. Then, after what seemed like an eternity, a small opening appeared on its underside. Orran gazed on—still in relative shock—while a large, black-cloaked man stepped into the opening! The man stood above the child. He peered down at him for a moment before jumping from the platform to the ground and landing within a few feet from his new, awestruck, soon-to-be friend. The black-cloaked intruder studied the young boy for a moment before speaking. "Hello there, young one," he said in a voice that sounded muffled and metalicky, since his face was hidden behind a mask. The man spoke Korean, so Orran relaxed a bit and offered a slight nod. Even this small gesture caused the flames on his head to dance a bit.

In order to get to Orran's eye level, the man crouched. "I can't help but notice that you are having a hard time controlling that power of yours; I can help you learn how to control it better." He then arose and slowly closed the gap between him and the still flame-engulfed child.

"Help me?" Orran asked the stranger. "I don't understand. Who are you?"

"You will know in time," the stranger said, examining the child through the red-glowing slits in his metal mask. "Even though we don't usually get involved in disorganized planets like this one, your case is the exception to the rule. If we were to leave you unchecked, you could destroy Earth—or even the solar system."

Orran couldn't believe what the man was telling him. I don't want to do *any* of those things. He spoke softly. "I . . . I don't want to hurt my family. I didn't mean to burn my oma. I didn't want her coming near me. I tried to tell her to stay away. She . . . she was trying to help, but my fire was too strong, so she got burned and I . . ." Orran trailed off, his tears starting anew.

At that moment, the stranger reached the child and again bent down to Orran's level. Glowing-red eyes met sapphire-blue ones. Orran was now afraid. He screamed through sobs, "No, don't touch me! I'll burn you like I did my oma!"

The masked stranger balked at the child's protective demeanor. "My dear boy, the day your flames harm me is the day that gods don't exist," he said with a muffled chuckle. With that, the man wrapped his gloved hands around the desperate and crying boy and brought him in close, hugging him. Almost immediately, the seemingly unquenchable fire that was encompassing Orran's body died. Simultaneously, Orran could feel a dark—yet also light—energy emanating from the mysteriously dressed man.

"My name is Nosfaren, of the Zaharaj, and I have come to take you home with me. There, you will be taught how to control your powers so that you will no longer have to live in fear."

"I'm Orran; my oma is Kim and my dad is Tim. I don't want them to be mad at me. I don't want to hurt any being. Can you really teach me how to keep my flames from burning people, Mr. Nosfaren," he pleaded, still sobbing lightly. "I guarantee it, Orran, and please, call me Nos. Lord Nos is also fine, but you are now my friend and ber'nan. Orran, in behalf of those I represent, I welcome you to the Zaharaj." Nos then scooped up the no longer fire-engulfed child and flew back up to his ship.

Orran got a ride all the way to the bridge, where a metal man sat on what looked to be a copilot's seat. After setting Orran down in one of the passenger seats, Lord Nos removed his cloak so he could use it to cover the now unclad young demon.

"You can't burn this with your flames because it's fireproof. Trust me Orran, I've tried," Nos said as he lay the cloak over the child. Orran nearly floated in the much-too-big black cloak. The seams on the cloak were a dull red, and the inside had a unique rainbow effect that changed with the lighting. Orran wrapped himself in the cloak's comforting embrace.

"Where are we going?" Orran asked his new friend.

"We are going back to my home, the planet Zharaj, where you will learn more about us as well as yourself."

Orran was filled with both awe and glee "We're going into space!" he cried with wild excitement.

"Yes, indeed we are. The Firaxian Galaxy is our backyard, but Zharaj is our home world and final destination," Nos responded in almost the same excited tone Orran had used.

"I've never been to space before," Orran said, his excitement building as Nos and his metal copilot punched in coordinates for Zharaj. The ship moved silently through Earth's atmosphere, accelerating quickly as it ascended. Soon, the planet disappeared. The vessel had made its way into the blackness of space. "I'm sorry, Oma. I didn't mean to hurt you. I need to learn how to control my power. Please understand. I'm too dangerous right now, but if I can control this awful power, I won't have to be afraid anymore." He then began peering at the small dots, which he knew to be stars, as they turned into streaks of light.

Lord Nos smiled. *You don't know your own worth, my young friend. There is so much out here for you. If you had stayed on Earth, no one would have known what to do with you. On Zharaj, you'll be accepted.* Nos turned to his white-and-blue-colored passenger. Silver strands of hair were hanging out around the oversized hood, and the boy's clawed fingers clung to the fringes of the sleeves of the oversized cloak. Shallow breaths were now escaping in short intervals from his pursed blue lips. *"Orran, when you wake up, you'll be in a whole new world,"* Nos mused.

5

Introduction to Zharaj

Orran awoke. He rubbed his tear-stained eyes and wiped them off with his new friend's cloak. "You woke up just in time, kid. We're making our descent onto Zharaj. Come take a look at your new home." Nos's mask was hiding his wide grin.

After struggling a bit, Orran made his way out of his seat. His eyes went wide when he saw what seemed to be hundreds of asteroids overshadowing a red-and-black planet. At least he thought it was a red-and-black planet. However, he soon realized that the colors actually represented structures. The structures jutted out from large trenches, which zigzagged across the surface. The ship wove around the asteroids before finally heading for a particularly large, black, pyramid-shaped building. Atop the structure was a long spire, which protruded from where the four sides met at the top. "That is our main temple. It's where we teach the next generation of Verse users—like you," Nos explained to his cloak-covered friend. He chuckled at the two noticeably glowing blue eyes that peered out from beneath the boy's overly large hood.

"This is Platform Seventeen to *Recluse*. Lord Nos, is that you? Come in." The voice over the communication system came through loud and clear.

"This is the *Recluse*. I have a new ar'teth with me. I just picked him up from Earth—from the Regal Sector. Is my usual spot still open?"

"Yes, my lord, it is. But I'm curious as to why you brought an Earthling here when it is forbidden," the voice openly mused.

Orran appeared restless and sheepishly asked, "Is it wrong for me to be here, Lord Nos? I don't want to get you into trouble." Orran's two white-and-blue-clawed fingers clutched his new robe more tightly, causing the large hood to hide his face.

Nos laughed at the child and shook his head. "No, kid, like I've said, you're the exception to the rule." He then reached over and patted the boy on his hood-covered head before continuing. "Trust me, you belong here!"

Nos now maneuvered his ship in for a landing. It came to a complete stop before descending like a Harrier jet, its landing feet touching down onto the smooth, black, glass-like surface. After the vessel gave a slight moan, Nos pressed the button to activate the hatch on the floor of the cargo area. A small ramp descended, and he disembarked, followed by Orran. The boy was still wearing his cloak, which was dragging along the smooth, blackened ground.

Several beings watched the duo make their way towards what Orran thought was an incredibly large pyramid, which was the same color as the surface upon which he was walking.

The black cool stone under Orran's bare feet felt much better than the hard, rough, cement roads and sidewalks he was used to back home. It wasn't just smooth; it was also reflective. As the two beings walked towards the pyramid, Orran could see his and Lord Nos's distorted figures reflecting off the stone. Before long, the pair came upon two rows of giant stone beings. The beings were wearing great cloaks; masks hid most of their faces. They were all cradling strange, pyramid-like objects in their outstretched right hands. They also held great tomes, or giant books, which were partially hidden in the folds of their robes. They held them under their left arms while their hands clutched the ends of their spines. Just past the giant stone statues, the black, smooth pavement turned a striking violet or deep purple where the dull-red glow of the sun blanketed the area.

****

Nos stoically led Orran through a pair of giant burgundy-colored doors, which were open widely, welcoming all to enter. Orran was stunned by the grandeur of the building. Tapestries were hanging from every conceivable location. Black pillars, which were ornately decorated, jutted up from floor to ceiling. A second floor, guarded by a railing, jutted out from the edges of the walls and stopped after it met the first perimeter of pillars. Nos noticed the look of awe on Orran's face. "I know, it's beautiful, isn't it. And this is just the entrance," he said to his small friend, whose mouth was agape.

"Lord Nos!" A person dressed just like Nos ran up to the pair. A crowd of black-cloaked beings was already gathering around in order to witness the exchange. Nos sighed. "Yes, Lord Baltrix? What is it?" he dryly asked.

The man pointed at the bundled-up Orran with an accusing finger. "What in the Verse is he doing here!" he bellowed loudly enough to garner the attention of every being in the hall.

Lord Nos nonchalantly shrugged. "I was told to fetch him, so I did."

Lord Baltrix threw up both of his hands and challenged, "By whom!"

"By me," a female voice responded.

"Lady Riza, I have brought the Silvarian as per your request." Lord Nos gave the woman a slight bow.

The woman was unlike anyone Orran had ever seen. She had red skin with black, thorny-looking tattoos situated randomly on her body, and she wasn't wearing much—just a black-leather top and very tight leather shorts, which only came down to her upper thighs. Her hair was waist length and black that turned fiery red, but her most striking features were her eyes and wings. She had great bat-like wings, which were currently bent at odd angles at the joints. Orran also thought he saw a long red and black tail snaking around behind her. Her eyes were just like his, except for the color. His were a sapphire blue, but hers were blood red and very piercing. Orran just stared at the strange looking being. He felt very uncomfortable when she knelt down and looked him straight in the eyes.

"Hello, Orran, do you remember me?" the woman sweetly asked. Orran emphatically shook his head. At that point, another woman— who had all of the same features as the first except for her dark-blue skin and jet-black hair that turned dark blue about halfway down her back before ending at her thighs. The upper part of her hair matched the color of her own thorny-looking tattoos—entered the room. Orran noted that she also had much softer facial features than the red-colored woman, who was still kneeling in front of him. Both women were physically gorgeous to behold.

"Come on, Riza, he's not going to remember you. I don't think he even knows what he is," the blue-tinted woman said, wrapping her leathery wings about her body and turning them into a makeshift cloak.

Lord Nos spoke up. "Orran, meet your two fiancées, Lady Riza and Lady Vira." Both women started shaking their heads. Riza then put her clawed hand to her forehead and sighed. Vira's disdain was more evident; her dark blue and black tail thrashed rather wildly behind her.

"You didn't have to tell him that, Nosfaren!" Vira scolded the masked man, who was standing to Orran's left.

Orran blinked hard, staring at the three beings who were surrounding him and not understanding what exactly was going on. The other cloaked beings started murmuring, and Orran overheard one word that he thought he knew: "Silvarian." He wasn't sure who had said it, but he knew it had been directed at him. Riza finally broke the awkward moment.

"Orran, we have a lot to discuss. First, you are a Silvarian demon. In fact, you are the last Silvarian demon in existence. Secondly, though you most likely don't remember this, Vira and I were the ones who carried your spirit to your adoptive dar'nra, or what you commonly refer to as father. Thirdly, yes, we have been betrothed to you, thanks to your true dar'nra... and mine." Riza stopped, to glance up at Lord Nos, and gave him a death glare. *Why did you tell him that, Lord Nos!*

"Finally, we are demons. I'm a Meserino, and Vira"—Riza nodded to her blue-skinned friend—"is a Veserino. We are here to help you control that power of yours."

Orran stood silently. He was wide-eyed, completely dumbfounded by everything that Riza had revealed. He knew he was different. Back home, his family were the only ones who accepted him, other than the Navy guys. He had been called many names: strange, ugly, freak, monster. Monster was the worst! "But what about my parents back home? I thought Kim and Tim were my oma and dad," he said, peering at the red-eyed demoness with a confused look on his face.

Riza closed her eyes and thought for a moment before continuing. "Yes, Kim and Tim are your parents—your temporal parents. However, your spirit parents, or true parents, were the demon king, Arnen, and the grand goddess, Keldras!"

After Riza's revelation, murmuring could be heard throughout the crowd, but Riza just ignored it, and Vira put her hands out in one of those 'meh' gestures, like that used by Orran's aunt back home. "I take back what I said about the child not belonging here. Though you should have passed it by the whole council before picking him up, Lord Nosfaren," Baltrix declared in an accusing tone while pointing his finger at him.

The group was then joined by yet another cloaked figure. "He's correct, Lord Baltrix. Our numbers have been dwindling ever since the Ja'Shari opened their giant academy on Firax. Despite his home planet's faults, we need every Zaharaj we can get," said a cloaked woman, who had the same metalicky sounding voice as the other two mask-wearing lords.

"Ah, Lady Dreth, how very good of you to join us. I do apologize for any inconvenience I might have caused by going to get Orran. But, as you can see, my orders came from much higher authorities," Lord Nos said, gesturing to the pair of demonesses, who were standing in front of him. He was now grinning widely, his face hidden by his mask.

Riza stood up. She folded her arms and leered at the newcomer. "Chirras, wasn't it you who tried to prevent Orran from coming here?

Why are you suddenly all for it?" Riza asked the woman, harshly calling her by her real name rather than her more honorable one.

"That is my doing." Yet another feminine voice shot out from the on-looking crowd. Another red-skinned Meserino demoness made her way over to join the group. She had much longer hair that went to her knees it was a combination of deep black that turned fiery red. Her eyes burned brightly. Her fingers, ending with razor-like claws, were wrapped around two metallic cylinders, which were strapped to either side of her belt that wrapped around her black-leather, form-fitting pants. Her feet were bare, and her own black and dark red tail swayed back and forth hypnotically while she walked.

"Hello, husband, I see that things went smoothly on your pick-up-and-retrieve mission," she said to Lord Nos, who, at this time, was rubbing the back of his head and seeming a bit embarrassed.

Everybeing turned to Nos. He was now even more uncomfortable, thanks to all of his newly acquired attention. "Well, Ali'stia, at least I got him here, didn't I?" he quipped.

Ali'stia chose to ignore her husband's response. Instead, she had zeroed in on Lady Dreth, as Chirras was more commonly known, and was giving her an unmistakable glare. Chirras fidgeted under the demoness's gaze. Even Orran could feel her fear of the Meserino, and, despite her mask, he thought she was sweating a bit too much for such a mild climate.

"I don't like my judgments being questioned—especially by one who just got her crath accepted onto the council—not even a full onn ago." Ali'stia related in a snarky tone. Everybeing in the group nodded their approval.

"I think I'll take my leave!" With that, the woman abruptly turned, causing her cloak to give off a swooshing sound, before she quickly retreated.

"Chirras!" The woman froze in her tracks when she heard her name. "In the next council meeting, I will be taking your appointment under scrutiny. I don't like it when council members go back on their word and try to persuade others to do the same," Ali'stia stated loudly enough for everybeing to hear, even the ones up on the balcony.

"My wife is right. As the current ruling council member, I deem your actions to be questionable, if not treasonous. Furthermore, you might find yourself out of your position at the end of our next meeting, or"—it was now Lord Nos who was threatening—"expelled from the Zaharaj altogether!" With that, every being seemed shocked. Murmuring was rampant throughout the complex. Chirras stormed off. Stripped of all dignity, she left the entrance hall and headed for her quarters.

"Lord Nos, is this all my fault?" Orran was on the verge of tears. He had slumped to the floor and was hugging Nos's cloak, his head completely engulfed by the oversized hood. Ali'stia knelt down and pulled the hood off the young Silvarian demon. Placing her clawed hands on the boy's shoulders, she looked deeply into his sapphire-blue eyes. Her eyes took on a softer appearance, and every being in the hall fell silent.

"Orran, look at me." Once assured that the child was paying attention, she continued. "It is by no means your fault. Lady Dreth, or Chirras, has made several questionable decisions. This time she tried to turn the council upon itself. I don't know why, but she didn't want you to come here, even though this is where you belong. I can feel that this is your real home, can't you?" Orran looked at the Meserino demoness and could see and feel a great glow and warmth emanating from her, as well as from all those around him. With a smile forming on his face, he cautiously nodded his head.

"Yes, Miss Ali'stia, I think I do," was all he managed to say before a round of laughter and chuckling erupted throughout the great hall. Orran wondered why the beings were laughing but then noticed that the Meserino demoness was looking a much brighter red in the area of her face and cheeks that wasn't adorned with dark tattoos.

"Wow, iloni, I think that's the first time any being has addressed you as 'Miss,' her husband said, still chuckling slightly.

"I didn't think it possible to embarrass a demoness. I guess you do learn something new every deronn," Lord Baltrix chided.

Ali'stia let go of the diminutive demon and stood straight up with her tail thrashing wildly behind her. "Stop doing that!" she demanded, shutting her red-glowing eyes and crossing her arms in front of her in a defiant manner. The crowd only laughed more heartily.

"I don't think you could be any more cute, Ali'stia." Vira walked over to her disgruntled friend, put her arm around her, and gave the poor embarrassed demoness a quick squeeze.

"I'm sorry," Orran said sheepishly. He hadn't meant to embarrass Ali'stia. He just wondered why she was embarrassed. *Back home, I was taught to use honorifics for those who were older than I was, in order to show respect. I don't get it!*

Lord Nos read his young charge's mind. "Don't worry about it, Orran. Here, we use Lord or Lady. I don't think any being has ever called my wife 'Miss' before." After glancing over at his wife, he walked over and embraced her.

"He's only been here a few dironns and he's already embarrassed one of the most powerful demons in the galaxy. I think he'll fit in just fine," Riza said, giving the Silvarian a wink.

"Now that introductions are over, I think you ladies have something else to do," Lord Baltrix said, gesturing to Orran. After the two demonesses gave him a slight nod, he turned and caused his cloak to make the now-familiar swooshing sound before he strode off and left the group.

"We must also take our leave," Lord Nos said, turning his head to give a quick nod to the three remaining demons before he and Ali'stia left and headed for the inner parts of the temple. The three demons stood by and watched the Lord and Lady disappear into the crowd of black-cloaked beings.

Vira and Riza were still smiling from the "Miss" incident when they turned to their young companion. "We had better be off, too, Orran. And you're coming with us," Riza pronounced. Without further hesitation, and with no resistance from Orran, the trio also headed to the inner rooms of the temple.

6

Mark of the Vorihelcom

Orran was in awe. Lord Nos was correct: The entrance was grand, but the inner depths of the temple were breathtaking. The ceiling and the walls were a kaleidoscope of blacks, reds, and violets. The carpet was violet in the center with a deep shade of burgundy on either side. It felt soft and plush under Orran's bare feet. Both of his tails were in constant motion, causing the lower back of the over-sized cloak to dance around while he moved from one corridor to another. Black-clad beings greeted the trio when they passed through the hallways. It was hard to tell who they were or even what race they were since every being was wearing a metal mask. The only thing that stood out was that each mask was decorated with different-colored designs and patterns. *I wonder why Riza and Vira aren't wearing the same style outfit as the rest of the beings,* Orran mused.

Riza started laughing before turning around to face the young demon. "We don't wear the cloaks because of our wings. And most demons already have markings on their faces, so wearing a mask would be meaningless," she offered. She then returned to leading the trio.

When Riza and Vira made their last turn, they ended up in another hall, which was apparently the temple's center. At the end of the hall, there were rows of elevators and stairwells. Orran followed the two demonesses into one of the elevators. Then Vira pressed on one of the symbols on the glowing keypad, which was located on the left-hand side of the doors. The boy was nervous— even more so once the doors closed and the elevator started its ascent.

It seemed like forever before the lift stopped and the doors slid open once again. Vira stepped out first, followed by Riza and Orran. Orran tripped on his cloak. He flailed wildly, bumped headfirst into Vira's well-muscled leg, and had to grab onto her for support. Vira blushed; the places on her face that weren't covered with the black, thorny design turned a deep purple. Orran didn't notice. He was leaning against the demoness's upper thigh while trying to get his taloned toes dislodged from the robe.

Riza looked on, putting her right hand to her cheek and slightly leaning into it. *That's just cute,* she thought as her friend Vira peered at her. She was at a loss as to what to do. She knew that Vira was trying hard not to pick up the Silvarian and hug him to death. Vira took a deep breath and slowly released it before her face finally reverted to its normal dark-blue hue. Meanwhile, Orran was continuing to struggle at getting his foot unstuck.

"Here, let me help you with that," Riza offered, finally deciding to rescue both beings from their obvious embarrassment. She had to lean down in order to untangle Orran's foot but found that doing so took a little more effort than she had thought. When the Silvarian gave her a hug, she was so overcome by emotion that she was briefly paralyzed.

Vira was now the one who was looking on. *See. Not so easy now, is it?* she telepathically related, but Riza ignored her thoughts and put her own arms around Orran, hugging him in return. Riza's mind raced back eons. She reminisced about the time when she and Vira had taken a newborn soul to its new parents. She marveled at how that same soul, after taking possession of his new physical body, had made his way to Zharaj. However, she still was not fully aware of Orran's critical role in the future of the Universe. Tears welled up in her eyes, and she tightened her embrace, pulling Orran's warm little body as close to her own as she could.

He's the very last of a noble race who sacrificed everything in a war that wasn't their own. Now all hope rests on this single child, and I'll be damned if I let Skath's followers, or any beings like them, get anywhere near him.

"Um... Lady Riza, is something wrong?" Orran asked. Riza came back into the moment, let the boy go, and blinked a few times in order to clear away her tears.

"No, everything is fine, Orran. Here, let me show you something." She got up, took one of his cloak-covered hands, and led him to one of the windows that lined the hallway. Orran's eyes went wide while he looked out and took in the full view.

Asteroids floated in the sky like a great curtain, letting in only single rays of the sun's light or, rarely, narrow bands and streaks. The rays presented quite a spectacle; they splashed against the red color of the planet, the bright orange and yellows butting up against the planet's more normal dark-red coloring. In the distance, majestic black-and-violet mountain ranges mimicked the look of whales that were frozen in time after breaching the ocean surface. Other spires could be spotted jutting up from deep ravines and trenches in the distance.

Orran uttered only a single word from his lips: "Wow!" It was barely audible, but Riza and Vira heard it and, even more so, felt it. The pair flanked their fiancé. Even they stood in awe every time they came to the top-most level of the Zaharaj's main temple, and they knew that Orran would feel the same. They wanted him to have as much joy as he could, for soon he would know pain such as he had never experienced before.

For several dironns, the trio looked out upon the grandeur surrounding Zharaj and watched the star ships coming and going, weaving and spinning as they avoided the planet's asteroid belt. One of the ships got so close to the tower its three onlookers that the pilots waved when they flew past. Orran waved back enthusiastically, causing the sleeves of his cloak to wag and flop about like a flag caught in a massive gust of wind. Riza and Vira gave the pilots a more traditional salute. Vira then interrupted the group's entertainment. "Orran, we have important matters to attend to, but we can come back here later."

Orran smiled and nodded before he turned away from the window.

He and Riza then followed Vira down the hallway, turned left, and entered a very dark room. As soon as the doors opened, Orran could feel a strange energy flow out from the room. It didn't take long before three sets of glowing demon eyes adjusted to the darkness. Orran could easily see that there were four twelve-foot-tall obelisks jutting up from the floor. The floor itself was made of that same smooth cool stone as the landing area at the temple's entrance. Carved into it, and located between the obelisks, was a large, circular glyph; strange writings and patterns ran along the rim of the circle. In the center of the circle, there was a six-pronged star. Orran took note of the obelisks, realizing that they weren't as smooth as he had first thought. Embedded within each were designs and strange writings, and their tops were carved into pyramids. Even the sides of the pyramids were adorned with symbols. The walls of the room were smooth, and there was no source of light. If it weren't for Orran's demon eyes, he would have been unable to see.

Riza spoke, startling the boy. "Orran, please take off your cloak and step into the center of the room," she said, kneeling down to help him get out of the oversized robe. Naked once again, Orran obliged. As soon as he breached the pillars, a tingling energy washed over him. It grew in intensity the closer he got to the star-shaped center of the circular glyph. He noticed that Riza and Vira were also stripped of clothing and facing each other. Becoming more and more uncomfortable, he just wanted to leave. Then Vira spoke.

"I'm sorry Orran, but this is going to really, really sting." Riza mustered up a weak smile and shrugged.

Instantly, Orran fell to the floor, overcome with pain when the two demonesses chanted in some language he couldn't understand. Both the star glyph and the runes and patterns on the obelisks started to glow a dark purple and red. The pain escalated, and a surge of pure energy blasted Orran's body. He cried out, wanting the ordeal to stop, but his pleas were unable to clear his lips; the pain was too great. The glow intensified, along with his screams, while lightning bolts of energy danced from one obelisk to another. The energy was absorbed and redirected into the tops of each pyramid, then poured forcefully and fully into Orran's body. His entire body was wracked with pain, but the most excruciating pain was centered on his back. His bare white skin had been exposed and was being burned; a glyph pattern of his own was forming. Seven circles and seven layers of runes appeared partially on and between his shoulder blades, the greatest circle starting just below his neck and ending several inches above the base of his tails. The gold-and-yellow seal scorched and seared his white skin.

Orran could no longer scream. His mouth was agape as though he had been caught in mighty prayer. Though it seemed impossible, Riza and Vira started chanting with even greater fervor, resulting in an increased energy flow from the obelisks into Orran's body. The pain continued for several more moments before the chanting mercifully ceased. The glow of the runes and obelisks calmed and cooled while a child lay passed out in the center of room. Steam was issuing from his back.

Riza and Vira ran over to the prone figure. "Well, at least he's still breathing," Riza managed to whisper while she bent over and scooped up the motionless form.

"He's going to be seriously drathed off when he wakes up, isn't he?" Vira queried when she made her way over to the bundle of discarded clothing. After grabbing everything, she and Riza opened the doors and headed back to the lifts.

"Nah, he'll be fine. I actually like the new look," Riza said while brushing Orran's now black hair out of his face. She was putting up a good front, but inside she was a wreck.

"We'd better get him to the infirmary." Vira added. *I don't really care for his human form,* she thought behind a strong mental barrier. *He was much cuter in his Silvarian form...*

7

The Disguised One

Orran was screaming, his arms flailed about uncontrollably. By the time he had thrust his body into an upright position, a mechanical man and another black-cloaked being had rushed to his side.

"Whoa! Whoa! Whoa! Calm down Orran, you're safe," a black-clad woman said with that familiar metallic voice. She grabbed Orran's flailing arms and laid him back down on the bed. "Is it still painful? If it is, just nod and I'll let you up, but slowly," she said while she shined a bright light into each of his eyes.

Orran barely mustered up the nod; he was still panting heavily. With that, the woman put the light away and gently helped him sit back up. Despite the pain, he was able to survey his new surroundings. He noticed that he was in was some sort of hospital-like facility with all of the bright overhead lights and several rows of beds, each having their own monitors with the usual accompanying wires and cables. Several beings then entered the room. Since Orran's bed was only a few feet from the door, the beings were immediately at his side.

"I told you it was going to really, really sting." Vira gave him a conniving grin.

Orran winced in pain. "That was more than just a sting! That really,

really hurt!" he weakly retorted while the apparent doctor prodded his back.

"At least his mouth is working again, so that's good," Riza chimed while her red tail swayed in amusement behind her.

"Oh, would you two leave the boy alone. He just woke up." After admonishing the visitors and introducing herself to Orran, Rid'zela started studying the glowing screen that appeared from the green gem that she was wearing on her right wrist. Every now and again, she nodded approvingly at the readings displayed on the gem.

"So, Orran, how do you feel about your new human form?" Lord Nos asked while stroking the chin of his mask.

It took a while for Orran to process everything that had just transpired. He examined his body from head to toe. His skin was no longer white and blue but a cream color; his fingers had actual nails instead of claws. Opening his mouth slightly, he rubbed his tongue over his teeth, which were now blunt. His upper and lower fangs were gone, or, more appropriately, shorter and much less sharp. He checked out his feet and found that they were now those of a human. His toes had nails, similar to those on his fingers, as opposed to talons. Suddenly, several black threads popped into his vision. He batted them away before realizing that they were his own hair, which had turned a glossy black, the same black color as his mother's and sister's hair. Ignoring the pain on his back, he got off from the bed and stood, shakily. He soon realized why he was so shaky. Both of his tails were gone! After taking a few tentative steps and determining that his balance was off, he still managed to make his way over to the trio of onlookers.

"Don't worry, Orran, you'll get used to it—trust me," Riza assured the patient. Once Orran reached her, he stood on tiptoes in order to give her a big hug around her waist.

"Thank you! This is the best!" The boy then repeated the same grateful gesture with Vira.

The group simply looked on. Smiles were on every face. Though several were hidden behind masks, the chuckles were still audible. While Orran started walking back to his bed, still a bit shaky, he noticed that he had an unusual-looking tail hanging down from the lower portion of his abdomen. Cocking his head to the side, he soberly asked, "Do all humans have a stubby front tail like this?" A torrent of laughter erupted. Even the patients and doctors in the back of the room joined in on the hilarity.

Orran, that isn't a tail. It's normal human anatomy," Rid'zela explained while she attempted to maintain her composure.

"Oh, that's right, Silvarian male sex organs are internal," Riza mused.

"Until they're called for," Vira added.

"I think he's a bit too young for that." Nos gave Vira and Riza an accusing glance, causing the two demonesses to blush.

"I'd never—" Vira started.

"What kind of demons do you think we are?" Riza retorted to Nos,

"The good kind!" Orran blurted, after which the room grew quiet. Nobeing thought the child was being funny, but he had brought something with him from his home world that had been sorely lacking—a playful innocence.

Rid'zela broke the silence. "So, is your seal still bothering you, Orran?"

Orran was obviously confused. "Seal, what seal? Does this planet even have an ocean?" His question brought another round of laughter.

"No, a seal... like a seal that seals something up. Not that water-based mam—" Nos started to explain, but Rid'zela interrupted him, walked over to the group, grabbed Vira, and spun her around so that her back now faced Orran.

"What's the big idea?" Vira started, but she soon understood.

"This is a seal," Rid'zela said, pointing to a circular pattern on Vira's back. Vira's wings were somewhat in the way, but there definitely was a circular seal on her back.

"It's really pretty!" Orran was mesmerized by the intricate runes and overlapping series of circles on the seal. The circles were emanating a soft light blue color that turned gold toward the inner parts, causing the seal to stand out as it clashed against Vira's dark blue and occasionally black skin. "So I have a design like that, too!" the boy excitedly asked.

"Yes you do, but yours is even more unique," Riza said, prompting Vira to turn around and give her the evil eye. Riza responded with a shrug.

"So, Orran, turn around and show me." Lord Nos was anxious to make up his own mind about the uniqueness of the boy's new seal. Orran obliged. He spun around so his back was to the group, grabbed his mess of black hair, and laid it over his right shoulder. After getting a good look at the seal, Nos let out a whistle. "I've never seen a seven-point Vorihelcom seal before!" he remarked while he rubbed the metallic chin on his mask with his gloved hand. "That is quite impressive!"

Rid'zela, who wanted to see the seal and to assess her patient's condition, now joined the ogling group. The seal was indeed quite a spectacle: seven layers of ringed runes with a sideways eight, the symbol of infinity, located in the center. The largest rings emitted a very cool-purple glow on the outer layers. The purple glow turned to a light gold color when each successive layer got closer and closer to the central infinity symbol. The symbol itself was a striking silver color. "Does it still burn?" Riza asked the young Silvarian, who now looked like the other members of his human family.

"Not like it did when I first got it; I guess it feels how a sunburn might feel." The boy now allowed his hair to fall back down. A good portion of his new Vorihelcom seal was concealed behind the thick black curtain. Orran then faced the group gave them a victory sign while he flashed them a wide smile.

"At least you still recover quickly," Riza didn't even attempt to hide her smirk. After her comment, the group started to disband; Rid'zela went back to her duties. Riza and Vira headed out the door, waving slightly before it closed. Lord Nos then walked over to Orran and knelt in front of him.

"Orran, I have a few things to tell you before I take you to your new quarters. Now, listen carefully. From now on your name will be Visage." Orran was about to interrupt, but Nos shook his head. "There are many beings in this galaxy who don't care much for Silvarians, and, if you stick with your real name, they will eventually figure it out. There are already too many here who know the truth about you, but you need to try and hide your real identity as much as you can." Nosfaren placed his hands on the boy's shoulders and spoke authoritatively, but with compassion. "Do you understand?"

"I guess so, Lord Nos. But why do I need to hide what I really am? I thought you said I would be welcomed here." The boy's disappointment manifested itself when his brows knitted together before he frowned.

"It's not that you won't be welcomed here, Orran. Let's say that out there," Nosfaren gestured wide. "There are beings who would like to get a hold of a Silvarian for—various reasons," Lord Nos cautiously responded, trying not to upset the boy any further.

"Is it because I'm the last Silvarian?"

Nos sighed after letting go of Orran's shoulders. "Something like that," was the only thing he could offer.

"So, I'm 'Visage'? What does 'Visage' mean?"

"It means 'one who hides in shadow,' or 'the disguised one.'"

Visage looked himself over. It did seem appropriate. He was human, at least appearance wise, but there was no way to hide the demon blood that was coursing through his body. However, this new form should be more manageable—the Vorihelcom seal should help suppress the power that he had previously been unable to control. "Lord Nos, I won't burst into flames anymore, will I?"

Nos slowly shook his head. "No. With the Vorihelcom seal in place and the natural suppression of your human form, there won't be any danger of that happening. Now, follow me and I'll show you to your quarters."

***

Visage nodded and walked behind the Lord. The duo exited the infirmary and headed for the main hall where the lifts were located. Despite Visage's naked appearance, the beings they passed didn't seem the least bit unnerved. Oma used to yell at me if I left the house without wearing anything, even though, when I wore clothes, they always ended up burned. Lord Nos started laughing. *Did I miss something funny?* Visage thought, causing the Dark Lord to laugh even more heartily.

After catching his breath, Nos explained, "Sorry, Visage, but with the power of the Verse we can read each other's minds, especially if the being is thinking rather loudly—and your thoughts are screaming! Besides that, let's just say that being naked here isn't as big of a deal as it is back on your home world. I know that some Earthlings consider it obscene. There are many planets in the galaxy, and each planet has a different environment. In some places, wearing clothing can be a great inconvenience. Some beings, like the Skelaxians, even find wearing clothing to be offensive. Even the Twillans are scantily clad because of their sun's intensity. So, no, you don't have to worry about your nakedness."

***

Nos and Visage reached the main hall and then the lifts, which were on the righthand wall. After getting in, Nos pressed a sequence of buttons on the glowing keypad, causing the lift to ascend.

"I have a lot to learn, don't I?" Visage asked.

There were several other black-cloaked beings in the lift with them. The one in the back and to their left replied with the now familiar metallic tone, "You'll get used to it soon. Don't worry about learning everything all at once."

Lord Nos turned his head slightly to the right to speak to his fellow council member. "Lord Baltrix, we will be assembling right after I show Visage to his quarters."

"Visage. Hmm. Interesting choice of name, Lord Nosfaren: 'The one who hides in shadow.'" Lord Baltrix peered down at the seven-year-old and studied his new human form. "A seven point seal—intriguing," he said when he noticed the glow emanating from Visage's back.

Before Visage could respond, the lift doors opened. Lord Nos exited with Visage following closely behind. *I really like my new name. Thank you, Lord Baltrix,* Visage thought after turning and giving the two beings in the lift a slight bow.

I look forward to seeing you in class, ar'teth Visage, Lord Baltrix thought back. The child's sapphire-blue eyes grew wide, and he snapped straight up right before the doors closed.

While the lift continued its ascent, the two beings still occupying the cab started a silent discussion. *Was that really the Silvarian Demon, Master?* Lord Baltrix's Twillan apprentice asked. The young Twillan's red-and-gold eyes, hidden behind his mask, went wide with excitement.

Yes, it was. Baltrix answered nonchalantly.

Things are going to get more interesting around here, aren't they, Master?

You'd better stop thinking what you're thinking, my apprentice. After all, he is from Earth, so he has much to learn. I don't want you and your friends messing with him, Lord Baltrix warned.

You're no fun. The disgruntled Twillan thought behind a mental barrier. *Master,* he folded his arms indignantly across his bare chest.

8

❧

New Roommate

Lord Nos escorted Visage for some time, all the while answering a myriad of questions, before halting in front of one of the doors that was lining the left-hand side of a hallway. With the press of a button on the outside panel, the door slid open. Nos stepped inside the dimly lit room, beckoning his young charge to follow. Visage did as commanded, and the door closed behind him, making a soft thunk when it sealed. It took a second for his vision to adjust to the dark-red lighting emitting from one of several lights that were embedded in the ceiling. If the light had not been located just above her desk, which was located in the far-right corner of the room, Visage probably would have overlooked the presence of the strange looking being.

A pile of black leather-bound books, several scrolls of parchment, and three pyramidal-shaped black things were cluttering up the top of the desk and nearly hiding the being who was apparently studying one of the thicker books. In order to get the being's attention, Lord Nos put his right hand, which was covered with a black glove and had a strange, ovular, light-green gem embedded into it, to his mouth and loudly coughed into his fist.

Visage couldn't make out the being's distinct features, since she was wearing the same black cloak that every other being in the temple wore.

He did notice that her eyes were striking. They were darting between him and Lord Nos. *Wait. Did she say, 'Master'?* Visage wondered.

"Yes, Visage, let me introduce you. This is my apprentice, Azala. She's a Twillan, and she'll be your roommate for a while. Azala, this is Visage; he's new here, so be nice." Azala was obviously distraught. She was audibly grumbling over her master's mandate. "Don't worry. Visage is nothing like your last roommate," Nos chuckled at the look his apprentice was giving him. Nosfaren gave her a reassuring smile and nod before placing his hand on Visage's left shoulder.

"He'd better not be!" Azala shot back before going back to reading the large tome, which lay open on the cluttered desk.

Lord Nos turned around. "I'll leave you two alone to get better acquainted. Apprentice, don't forget we're heading out on our mission in a few deronns." Azala only waved her right hand in a dismissive manner while she continued to read. "Don't worry, Visage, she'll come around," Nos said as he opened the door, gave a wave, and exited, leaving the two beings alone.

When the brighter light of the hallway vanished, it took Lord Nos with it, and the Silvarian demon, disguised as a human, now looked nervously around his new environment. There was, to his immediate left, an unoccupied desk with an accompanying leather chair. Across from the desk a little way, there were two twin-sized beds, separated by an aisle that was several feet wide. The beds had layers of shelves at their heads. The bed covers appeared to be made of a black velvety material, but it was hard to tell in the dim light. Then in the left hand corner, on the side of the furthest bed, there was what looked like some kind of metal statue. Azala and the desk she was sitting at were backed into the right hand corner of the room. Directly to the right of the entrance was another doorway that was open, and, from what little detail Visage could make out, it looked to be a bathroom of some kind.

Azala spoke, startling the new occupant. "The bed and desk closest to the door are yours. Your new uniform was dropped off several dironns ago; it's on your bed." Azala nonchalantly offered the information without even lifting her head.

"Thank you," was all Visage managed to say while walking over to the large bed. When he picked up the bundle of clothing, he was unaware that Azala had stopped reading and was now focusing her full attention on him. When Visage turned to inspect his new attire, Azala noticed a soft-blue glow emanating from his back. Her amber-and-red eyes opened widely. Her mind had not yet caught up to her mouth, and she asked aloud, "Are you a—demon!"

Azala's abrupt question caused Visage to turn and stare back at her with his two sapphire-colored orbs. *So what if I am?* Azala's mouth hung agape at Visage's apparent, though silent, confirmation.

"Really! That's really a Vorihelcom seal on your back!" Azala was so flabbergasted that it took her a moment to compose herself.

Visage cocked his head to the side. *I don't believe it! Can she read minds, too?*

The Twillan let out a brief laugh. "Yes, I can," she matter-of-factly stated before she spun her leather chair around so she could face her new roommate. "And why, with all of the races in the galaxy, did you choose to disguise yourself as a human?" she asked aloud, not yet aware of Visage's ability to read thoughts.

"My parents are both human. Why shouldn't I look like them?" Visage defiantly crossed his arms.

Azala was taken aback. *Humans had a demon child? That doesn't make any sense. Unless…* "Kid, what kind of demon *are* you!" Her tone was more demanding than she had intended.

"The good kind." *Apparently, I'm a Silvarian.*

Of course, Azala heard what he was loudly thinking. "But they all died in the war of the gods! You can't possibly be a Silvarian because they're extin—" The Twillan reacted instantly, quickly covering her mouth with both red-tinted hands.

Visage calmed down a bit. "Yeah, I know; that's what Riza and Vira said. I don't think they mentioned anything about a war though."

Azala quickly spun her chair and went back to her book. "Just forget what I said."

Visage shrugged and went back to inspecting his new outfit. Picking up the pants first, he looked them over. They were a glossy black and felt like a mix of denim and silk. They had the normal two front and back pockets, but there were also two large pockets on the sides, extending from the mid thighs to the knees. Visage noticed that the inside of the pants had the same rainbow color as Lord Nos's cloak. Wow, they feel as good as they look! But they surely are roomy—almost too roomy! I'm glad they come with a belt. The belt was black, but on the inside, it had the same rainbow color as the inside of the pants—especially when the light shone on it. It was also studded. The clasp and buckle were thick and looked strong, but they felt light when Visage threaded the belt through his pants' belt loops. The last items on his bed were a black shirt and an extra blanket. Once he realized that the item was actually a cloak of his very own, he totally ignored the shirt and donned the cloak. He twirled and twirled around, causing the cloak to flap about and make swooshing noises. It also shimmered! I wonder why it shimmers like that, Visage mused.

"It's because it's a mithril weave." The sound of Azala's voice interrupted the boy's dance.

"Mithril, what's mithril?"

Azala chuckled."Mithril is a very rare ore that the Dwarves on Forr'Nadoon mine. The workers then turn it into a thread that is transported to Devros where the Night Elves weave it into cloth," she explained.

"It sounds like a lot of work goes into these clothes. Does that mean they're really expensive?" Visage asked, hugging his new cloak tightly about him and worrying that Lord Nos or someone else might want it back.

Azala smiled despite herself. "Visage, you don't have to worry about anyone taking your clothes from you. You see, there are other ways of making mithril cloth besides the more... traditional way." Visage remained skeptical and continued to clutch his new garment.

Azala ignored the boy and arose in order to start her stretching routine. First, she got up on her tiptoes. Then she interlocked her slender red fingers and stretched her arms out and over her head. The sleeves of her cloak fell down past her elbows and revealed her well-toned arms. After a few more minutes of stretching, she passed by her smaller companion, gave his hooded head a few quick pats before she headed into the refresher.

Visage was surprised to see bright white light emanating from the room without the door having closed behind Azala. Without pursuing the thought, he folded up the unused shirt. He then noticed, out of the corner of his eye, a strange looking object. *What is that?* He picked up the small metal device and walked over to his own black-leather chair. He threw his small form into the oversized seat, all the while holding fast to the device by clutching it between his index finger and thumb. The metal thing looked like a headphone, but Visage only had the one piece.

Still, it had a clip that looked like it went over the ear and another piece that fit inside the ear canal. Visage gently tugged at the clip part of the device. The clip bent as if it were on a rotating hinge. *So, it can be used in either ear?* Visage wondered. He opted to put the clip over his right ear.

"That's your armored mask, and, yes, it's designed to be used in either ear; just put it on and press the button twice," Azala instructed from the refresher.

"And if you ever need to use the refresher, you can—just not while I'm... occupying it. Got it!"

"I got it!" Visage blurted, without hesitation.

"I'm going to be getting into the rinser, so the Zor'nok will be free if you need to use it!" Azala said. Then the sound of running water was heard.

Visage was now confused. *What's a Zor'nok? What's a rinser?* As soon as the thoughts had gone through his head, he heard a squeaking noise come from the refresher. Azala had almost fallen while bursting out with laughter over Visage's naïve musings. She was still laughing when she emerged from the 'refresher,' as she called it.

Visage was sitting in his chair and using his right foot to push off the floor in order to make the chair spin in a counterclockwise motion. Then, stomping his left foot to make him stop, he'd kick off again, putting him and the chair into a clockwise spin. Feeling a little embarrassed, he thought, *Lord Nos told me I had a lot to learn, but Azala thinks I'm stupid, I just know it.* In order to hide the deep-purple blush on his cheeks, he pulled the hood of his cloak as far down over his face as he could.

"I don't think you're stupid, Visage. You're not used to all of the new changes yet. Remember, it's still only your first deronn," Azala said, taking off her damp robe and allowing it to fall into a heap on the floor. Visage halted his spinning and sat straight up, throwing off his hood. Azala, who was rummaging through some things on the other side of the bed, was standing stark naked before him.

Azala is the same color as Riza and Ali'stia—well... except for their pretty tattoos, Visage thought while he glanced at his roommate from beneath his hood. *She looks a few years older than me.*

She was well muscled, especially in the upper thigh and legs. Her arms weren't bulging, but they also had noticeable muscle. Her stomach was lean, and her chest was well developed, considering her youth. Her head was bald; her ears were actually two stumpy bone-white cones, and she had twin tails that hung from either side of her skull and narrowed to points in the center of her back. Though she barely had eyebrows, she did have eyelashes that stood out in the forefront of those blood red and amber-colored eyes. Once she noticed she was being stared at, she stared right back.

"What's the matter? Never seen a naked Twillan before?" A small smirk appeared on Azala's dark gray—almost black-colored—lips.

Visage was about to say something until he noticed something else about Azala; there were several noticeable black and dark-purple spots on her skin. One spot was long and started just below her left breast, angling down to her lower right side. There was another on her right thigh, two on her left arm, and one on her right shoulder. As soon as he realized what the spots were, Visage arose from his chair. His thoughts became clouded with anger and his eyes narrowed to slits as they turned from their normal sapphire blue to an icy blue.

Small angry white-and-blue hued flames erupted from his body. Azala was overwhelmed with shock at his sudden transformation. Visage's normally soft voice took on a chilling tone, and he clenched his fists. "Who did that to you!"

Azala didn't speak. She could no longer read Visage's mind, since anger had overshadowed all of his thoughts. At first, she didn't understand the question. *Who did what to me?* After looking at her bruises, she understood.

"Oh, no, no, no—you don't understand. I got these in a sparring match with my master this menronn," Azala explained.

Visage went silent. *Master?... Sparring match?... Lord Nos?* It took him a dironn for things to click, but then he calmed down.

Azala breathed a sigh of relief when she could see that Visage's flames were dying and his eyes were changing back to their bright sapphire color. She also could tell that the entire incident had taken a toll on her new roommate. He was obviously very weak.

At least Lord Nos was right about these clothes—they are fireproof, the young Silvarian thought before collapsing onto his bed. *Why would Lord Nos beat on his own apprentice in a sparring match?* His mind was full of questions, but after having such an unwelcomed outburst, all he could do was crawl up onto his bed. He managed to crawl just far enough so his feet weren't dangling off the end and then fell off into a dreamless sleep.

Azala stood, as though frozen. The air in the room was charged with Visage's now dissipating power. *When he manages to control his indren'freth and the power of the Verse, he'll be a force to be reckoned with,* Azala thought while turning and slumping onto her bed. While she lay there, she put her arms up, using the left to cover her eyes and her right hand to play with one of her twills–most of which were splayed out behind her on the bed. *At least he's better than my last roommate was.*

After the last of Visage's indren'freth faded, the mechanical being, which had been standing in the corner, activated. Its two red-glowing eyes snapped on as its human-like head turned about and took in its surroundings. Its sensor locked onto the unfamiliar being who was lying on the bed farthest from it. Its gloss-black arms and fingers made whirring sounds when they moved. Taking several steps, the being halted in front of Azala and waited.

"I see you have a new roommate, Mistress," the mechanical being said aloud. Even though there were no signs of a mouth, nose, or even lips, it still was able to speak. Sensors and the voice box, which were built into its throat, allowed the robot to audibly communicate.

Azala groaned, and then responded to her T.A.D. (Tactical Assault Doll), One-Dash-Seven. "So, you're done recharging then, Onsev?"

"Yes, Mistress, my capacitors are all back to full strength. But you still haven't answered my question," the mechanized being flatly stated.

"Yes, yes, he's my new roommate, but he's nothing like the last one. You should introduce yourself when he wakes up," Azala muttered before she sat back and up and rubbed the bruises on her side. The rinser had helped with the swelling, but her bruises still ached.

Though Onsev was better able to scan Azala's bruises, now that she was unclothed, he made no comment. He proceeded to activate a green gem, which was located on his left hand and which produced a glimmering green mist. Out of the mist, a bundle of fresh clothing materialized. "Here, Mistress—fresh garments for you." Onsev offered Azala the clothing, which was draped over his two metal arms.

Azala scowled slightly while she looked at the clothes and then at her T.A.D. "More gifts from mi'thia, no doubt," Azala quipped as she reluctantly accepted the offered clothing.

The mechanical doll stood motionless before Azala pushed him out of the way, walked over to her discarded robe, and put it back on. Then, after returning to her chair, she sat down at her desk and started peering over the tome that lay open in front of her.

"Mistress, you should wear more than just your robe," One-Dash-Seven said, laying the clothing on her bed. "You are no longer the only organic being in the room."

Lifting her cloak-covered head from her book, Azala turned her chair and faced Onsev. She then glanced over at the sleeping mass on the other bed and smiled. "Onsev, you worry too much; the kid is safe.

He's a demon, and you know how they are. He's nothing like our previous guest. Besides, these bruises still hurt like frak, and putting those tight-fitting things on would only make them hurt even worse," Azala explained before turning back to her desk and book.

Onsev processed this information. Once again, his head turned to the sleeping form on the other bed, his glowing-red eyes now doing a full scan of the other organic. "Scan complete. Species: demon. Race: unknown. Blood type: unknown. Seven-point Vorihelcom seal detected on upper back. indren'freth level: currently thirty-five hundred krenns. Status: sleeping. Threat level: unknown." The doll paused, turning his head back to Azala. "Mistress, I do not have any information on this organic other than that he came from the forbidden planet." Onsev watched his mistress slowly sit up in her chair. Because her back was turned and her head was covered by a large hood, he couldn't see just how big her Zah'harrim-tainted eyes had gotten. After a full dironn passed, Azala finally found her voice. She spoke softly.

"The forbidden planet—you mean *that* forbidden planet?" Her mouth turned into a scathing sneer while she spoke.

Onsev knowledgeably replied, "Yes, Earth is the only forbidden planet in the Empire, Mistress."

"Fraking god killers; I can't believe I'm rooming with a fraking pathetic god killer!" Azala was tempted to take out her blade and put the sleeping being out of his misery. The only thing stopping her was her own curiosity. After her anger subsided, she asked Onsev a simple question. "Why is he here?"

Onsev accessed all the information he had concerning the sleeping boy on the bed. "The Council, including your master, felt it best to bring the boy here for several reasons. First, he's a demon. If the Earthlings found out that there was a demon born among them, the Council feared that they would treat him the same way they treated their own God. Secondly, nobeing on the planet could teach him how to control his power. Bringing him here was the only option, and, apparently, he's the fiancé of both Lady Riza and Lady Vira." Onsev then paused. "I just found his race; he's a Silvarian—though the records in my data banks say that Silvarians are extinct."

Azala's red-and-amber eyes darted about. *So, it's true then; he is a Silvarian. But why was he born on Earth, of all the planets in Eendril's great universe? Its inhabitants willfully killed our own God!* Azala folded her arms over her open book and laid her cheek upon them. She started drumming the pages with her fingers. This was disturbing news, and it took some time for Azala to process it. "Onsev, I think Eendril has a very strange sense of humor!"

Onsev dutifully responded. "I don't think I have the right programming to question your deity's sense of humor, Mistress."

Azala rolled her eyes and walked over to her roommate's bed. He was sleeping. *I didn't realize how small he is.* "Onsev, do you know his age?"

"Yes, Mistress, he is seven Earth years old."

"So how old does that make him in our time?"

"He's two full onns and several rinonns old," Onsev said after performing some quick calculations.

Still very much a child. For a while, Azala was pensive, but she soon returned to her chair and resumed reading. However, it wasn't long before her stomach began to make growling noises.

Onsev heard the growling and could sense his mistress's next objective. The moment she got up, he offered her fresh clothing.

"Ugh, fine, gimme the fraking things." *I'm definitely not going to the mess hall with just my robe on. I might run into him.*

Onsev's response seemed to mimic the thoughts of his master: "I'm glad to see you're dressing before leaving, Mistress. You wouldn't want to be wearing just your robe if you met *him* in your travels."

Azala had put on the top and was pulling on her pants. "Onsev, I swear you're reading my mind." She winced. The tight-fitting clothing was clinging to her form and making several of her bruises ache. After putting her robe back on, she reached out her right hand, levitated two cylindrical metal tubes to her open hand, and grasped both. The one that she put on her right side made a ca-thunk when it latched itself to one of the metal studs on her belt. Grabbing the other with her left hand, she put that one on her left side and snapped it into place against the opposite stud. Finally, she brought her hood over her head and headed for the door.

"Mistress, if you're taking your blood sorjins, shouldn't you be taking your mask?" Onsev asked. Azala stopped in her tracks and nodded. While Onsev headed to retrieve her earpiece, the Twillan became aware of her bare feet and wiggled several of her toes. *I can't believe I almost left without my boots!* Once she managed to drag the boots out from under her bed, she slid them on with ease. Their soft inner cushions enveloped her red feet. In the meantime, Onsev had located her earpiece and now dropped the device into her open palm. Azala brought it up to her left ear cone and snapped it on. She had to press the button twice, which caused the liquid metal concoction to creep out and cover her face before flowing down both of her twills and solidifying. The only things those were visible though the slits in the mask were her two, glowing, red eyes. Now that she was finally ready, she gave her T.A.D. a slight wave and exited. Before the door closed, the light from the hallway briefly brightened the interior of the room and caused the sleeping form to make a slight groan.

9

Lord Baltrix's Reprimand

"Wait! Hold the lift!" Azala could see a cloaked young man running toward the open doors, so she pressed the hold button on the console. "Thanks, Azala," the young man managed to say in a metalicky, muffled-sounding voice. While grinning slightly under her mask, Azala took her finger off the hold button, causing the doors to close and the lift to start its descent.

"So, did you all hear about the Earthling?" one of the cloaked beings in the back corner asked, starting a conversation.

"I know, right!" the being right behind Azala scathed.

"I wonder what an Earthling is like?" the being to their left added.

"Probably just some form of slimy grotesque monster," another being muttered with a disgusted snort.

Azala tried to hide her thoughts, but that last hypothesis caused her to drop her guard and laugh. *He's just a human kid—not even three onns old. He's a bit naïve, but has a sense of justice that's well beyond that of a being his age.*

"How do you know about the Earthling, Azala?" the being in the corner asked. Everybeing was eagerly awaiting Azala's answer while at the same time attempting to pierce through the back of her twills with their eyes.

"I know because he's my roommate." Azala's answer caught the beings off guard, and they threw a thousand questions, both verbal and telepathic, her way. *Shut up! I don't know anything! If you want to know about him, ask Riza or Master Nosfaren!* Azala's thoughts were so loud that they caused every occupant to fall silent, at least for a moment.

"Um, Azala?" the being in the left rear corner meekly ventured. Azala rolled her eyes.

"Yes! What!" the Twillan sharply retorted.

"Well, I just want to know whether he really is a Silvarian or not."

Unsure how to answer, Azala hastily threw up a mental barrier in order to keep the others from reading her thoughts. *Do I tell them the truth or just a half-truth? Master didn't tell me what to do. What should I do? Well, I guess I'd better go with the truth.*

"Yes, he's a Silvarian." She braced for excited reactions, but most of the beings responded with a mere "Oh."

No wonder they brought him here; those id'rth Earthlings would have probably killed him too. Azala didn't know who had had the thought, but everybeing in the lift seemed to agree. Mask-covered heads were bobbing when the doors re-opened.

Azala left the lift first and headed to the mess hall; several other beings followed. The other beings were talking among themselves. Most of their conversation was about the newest arrival.

"Hmm, gunrek denonn, Azala. I hear you have a new roommate." Another dark-clad figure emerged from the mess hall; his arms were crossed and he was leaning slightly to the left. The whole troop came to a halt at the deceit-laden greeting. All talk, spoken and unspoken, ceased. Azala's hands went to her blood sorjins, and her fingers wrapped themselves tightly around the weapons that draped from her sides. She was a bit smaller than the being facing her, but this draw back was more than offset by her strength and ferocity.

"Zor'ret, since you crawled out of a hole, I suggest you scurry back to it." Azala was shocked to find that she had a supporter. She whipped her head around in an attempt to locate her unknown ally, since it had originated from one of the beings behind her. An intense anger emanated from the other being. The one who muttered the insult stepped forward and took a stance at the head of the group. Zor'ret merely scoffed at the supposed threat.

"Moonreth, right? Why such hostility? I've done nothing to you," Zor'ret sneered. "And Azala, I was only thinking about what I'd like to do with you," he sarcastically remarked.

"Fraking perverted glort! Kick his crath, Moonreth!" one from the rear of the group yelled. Moonreth was going for his own blood sorjin, but before he managed to withdraw and ignite the blade, another voice bellowed, "What's going on here!" Lord Baltrix was marching down the hallway with his cloak dancing behind him.

Moonreth instantly took his hand off his sorjin, turned his back to the wall, and clasped his hands behind him; all of the others did the same—except Zor'ret.

Baltrix marched past the four stunned ar'teths and stood right in front of Zor'ret. Baltrix glared down at the troublemaker and willed him into submission. Zor'ret dropped to his knees under Baltrix's imposing death filled gaze. "Zor'ret, the Council has decided to expel you from the Zaharaj!" Baltrix's pronouncement was overheard by several more beings who were emerging from the mess hall.

A sense of shock washed over the crowd like a tidal wave, enveloped every onlooker. Even some of the beings in the mess hall overheard and were stunned by what they had just sensed.

"You can't do this to me, Baltrix! My master is on the Council!" Zor'ret cried with such superfluous indignation that it was pitiful.

Not anymore! Lady Dreth has been demoted and is now under watch for her recent actions; there's an ongoing investigation into her former apprentice's death! Baltrix's thoughts were so loud that they were sensed by nearly everybeing in the temple. *As for you, Zor'ret Cerventet, for what you thought about doing to Lord Nosfaren's apprentice and for what you tried to do to Garner's apprentice, you're done here!* Baltrix's thoughts were now akin to a raging inferno.

Everybeing cheered or breathed a sigh of relief. They all thought that the matter had ended—that Zor'ret was done for and would be escorted to the upper level of the temple where he'd have his indren'freth and Zah'harrim permanently sealed. Then he'd be sent back home. Azala and Moonreth were elated at the thought and watched, almost gleefully, as Zor'ret's head and shoulders slumped forward. However—Zor'ret wasn't quite done.

When Lord Baltrix reached for his shoulders, in order to put him back on his feet, his rage and hate erupted, and he let out a primal roar! Zor'ret's hand flashed to his belt and yanked off his blood sorjin—but he was too late.

Baltrix had been in motion since the very onset of his scream. The faster and far more experienced warrior had already grabbed his own blood sorjin. The sorjin came on with a snap hiss, its bright-red blade glowing angrily. With his weapon in a reverse grip and its blade fully extended, Baltrix twirled so rapidly that his entire form was blurred.

The mouths of the beings in the crowd were agape as they gawked at the unfolding spectacle. The sorjin's blade left an impressive, though grotesque, red-trailing arc in its wake. Having completed the task at hand, Baltrix ended up about a foot behind Zor'ret. At that point, he brought his hand across in front of him, shut off his sorjin, and snapped the weapon back onto his belt. Only a few beings in the crowd could hear him whisper, "Such a waste."

The growing group of onlookers gaped at the very calm Lord and then at Zor'ret, who was frozen in a standing position. His spirit was gone. Even the two formerly glowing eye slits in his mask had become charcoal black. In slow motion, his head started to slide off his neck, which had visible burn marks from Lord Baltrix's blood sorjin. The head fell to the floor with a sickening thud before the rest of the body slumped forward and followed.

Zor'ret's hand was still gripping his blood sorjin when the weapon suddenly jerked. Then, as though yanked by some unseen force, it flew into Lord Baltrix's outstretched hand. Baltrix stared at the weapon before glancing at the fallen form that lay behind him. After turning around and stepping over the fallen head, he made his way over to Moonreth and presented him with Zor'ret's blood sorjin. "Give this to your sri'na when you see her," was all he said before heading back to the lifts.

Good riddance!

Pathetic!

Fraking slith freak got what he deserved!

He was no better than the Skathic! The thoughts were deafening!

"I can't believe we were the same race," Azala managed to say. Right after she uttered the last word, a pair of cleaning dolls passed her. Their mission—to gather up what was left of Zor'ret.

"Remind me not to drath off Lord Baltrix . . . ever!" Moonreth exclaimed, squeezing the blood sorjin in his hand and turning his head to the left in order to follow Lord Baltrix's exit.

The T.A.Ds, whose gears and motors in their joints were slightly whirring, were also making their exit, One carried the lifeless body and the other held Zor'ret's disembodied head. Two red twills became visible as they fell and swayed from side to side in time with the mechanical doll's footfalls.

***

Most beings had gone back to what they were doing before the incident. The five that came off the lift went into the mess hall together. Moonreth snapped his newly acquired blood sorjin onto a free stud on his belt. "My sri'na will be grateful for this." By the time he made it into the line for the food, he was relatively beaming. This has been a good deronn. The smiling Twillan in front of him telepathically agreed.

A storm of thought enveloped the mess hall. Some beings were thinking about Zor'ret's short lived fight with Lord Baltrix, some about Lady Dreth's demotion, and some about a newly arrived Silvarian demon from the forbidden planet called Earth.

10

Meddling Parents

Azala stood in front of the door to her room. When she was in the mess hall, she had removed her cloak and taken off her mask. She didn't bother putting either of the articles back on.

After pressing her hand to her chest and taking a deep calming breath Azala stepped forward. The door slid open and she walked in. When she found that her new roommate was still asleep, she was both thankful and disappointed. *I honestly don't know what to make of you yet,* she thought before slumping down into her chair. "Ow, those damned things hurt." With all of the excitement, she hadn't had time to notice the pain from her bruises, but now that things had settled down, the pain was now front and center.

"Welcome back, Mistress, I hope your meal was enjoyable." The black bipedal doll had activated as soon as Azala had entered the room and was now standing over the back of Azala's chair.

"Yes, it was enjoyable. Thank you, Onsev," she said while attempting to get into a more comfortable position.

"Your parents would like you to contact them. Shall I open a channel for you?" Onsev offered.

The Twillan rolled her eyes. "Fine, Onsev." *Why are they calling me—just when I need to get some sleep?* Azala turned her chair around to face her mechanical doll, who was now holding out his right hand. A glowing, light-green-colored gem was in center of his palm. As if by magick, two miniature Twillans formed and appeared to be standing in his hand.

"Go'trell, Mi'thia, Dar'nra," Azala said to the two mini beings.

"Go'trell to you, Azala. I assume you received our care package?" the tiny, holographic, female Twillan asked.

"Yes, Mi'thia, I did." Azala put her elbow onto the armrest of her chair and rested her chin onto her palm. She quickly thanked Eendril that her parents weren't adept Verse users and couldn't read her mind.

"We heard you have a new roommate; is that true?" her mini dar'nra asked.

When Mi'thia and Dar'nra leave, I'll have to give Onsev a talking-to about the dissemination of information, especially when it comes to Visage. She replied to her dar'nra's question. "Yes... it is," she hesitatingly replied.

"Oh, male or female?" the woman asked.

"He's a male. Why do you ask?"

"He isn't like your last one, is he?" her dar'nra piped up, putting his tiny hands to his sides and trying to look intimidating.

He's so cute when he does that. Azala had to stifle her snickers so her parents wouldn't hear. "No! He's nothing like that blortworm Zor'ret."

"That's good. So, what's he like?"

Azala hesitated. "Well, he's human—nothing but a child, really." She answered with the truth, just not the full truth.

"So, is he cute?" The question brought Azala right up out of her chair while her face turned a brighter shade of red. "Zella!" Azala cried, she couldn't believe her mi'thia would ask such a thing. This caused the mini Twillan woman to laugh, so her husband jabbed her side lightly with an elbow. "Oh please, Namren, admit it; you're just as curious as I am."

Namren smirked. "True, but I don't go around embarrassing our young Zaharaj ar'teth like that."

"Thanks, dar'nra... I think?" Azala half-heartedly responded after rolling her eyes. She then plopped back down in her chair, planted her face in her hands and groaned.

"Are you all right, Azala?" Namren asked, obviously concerned.

"Yeah, I'm fine. I have some bruising from this menronn's training session. Frak, does Master know how to fight!" Her parents balked at this.

"Watch that language, young lady!" Zella scolded, but Azala only ignored her reprimand.

"So can we meet your new roommate? What's his name? Will he be joining you when you go on vacation? He can come here, if he's nice." Namren's questions were incessant.

Why did I know they were going to do this to me! Azala, though ticked off, respectfully answered Namren's questions. "No, he's sleeping. His name is Visage, and I don't think my master will let him go anywhere anytime soon."

Namren briefly mulled over Azala's answers. "Visage? That's an interesting name," Namren said. "'The one who hides in shadow'—the name suits a Zaharaj."

"So what's his krenn level?" Zella asked.

Onsev flatly answered, "Thirty-five hundred." Both Twillans gasped at the number.

Namren's eyes widened in wonder. "Didn't you say, he's asleep, Azala?"

"Yes, Dar'nra."

"Sounds to me like he's a *demon*... Are you *sure* he's a human?"

"If I tell you, will you keep it a secret?"

"Of course we will!" Namren exclaimed, speaking for both himself and Zella.

Azala glanced at Onsev and hesitatingly asked, "Onsev, is this a secure channel?"

"Yes, Mistress, it is." Now the Twillans' curiosity was peaked.

Azala's voice was stern. "Mi'thia, dar'nra, Visage is a Silvarian, and he's from Earth." The Twillans' mouths hung open. They were so shocked that they couldn't speak for a whole dironn.

Once Namren had regained his composure, he jokingly offered, "At least we know that our God's sense of humor hasn't changed."

"Honestly, why was he on that miserable little mud ball. I still remember when the humans on that planet killed one of Eendril's favored kids. Eendril was so drathed off; it seems as though our galaxy has never been the same," Zella added.

Azala was rather surprised at the way her parents took the news. After all, they were both trustworthy. They were the owners of the Timarian Conglomerate, the largest privately owned corporation in the galaxy. *I guess keeping Visage's identity a secret won't be too hard for them,* she thought.

"So does His Imperial Majesty know?" Namren asked, catching the young Twillan off guard.

"Know what?" Azala attempted to act confused.

"What do you mean, 'know what?' About the Silvarian of course!" Zella's twills started wildly dancing. She was obviously perturbed.

"I honestly don't know."

Zella and Namren exchanged glances. Though Zella had calmed down a bit, Azala could sense that she remained extremely troubled. "Does your Council wish to keep the Emperor in the dark?"

"I'm only an apprentice. I don't know what the Council will do. I do know that Visage's identity can't stay a secret forever. Practically every being on the planet is a citizen of the Empire. Perhaps the Emperor will be informed when Visage is ready."

"Ready? Ready for what?" Zella curiously asked.

"I mean... fully trained," Azala dryly explained.

"Oh," Namren and Zella said in unison. The pair appeared accepting of the answer. Using a much lighter tone, Zella added, "Have a good rest my de'tari. May Eendril keep you safe."

"Come back home for a visit when you get the time," Namren added with a grin.

Azala smiled at her two holographic parents. "Don't worry, I will." With that, the transmission ended, leaving Azala alone with Onsev and a sleeping Silvarian. Once again, she returned to the open book on her desk and began to read. Onsev walked back to his corner and shut down. Visage was hoping he had successfully hidden his thoughts from the Twillan. He ripped off the irritating earpiece, shoved the metal thing into his pocket, and drifted off to sleep.

11

Classroom Catastrophe

Visage slowly rolled onto his back, sat up, and stretched his arms. He then gave such a mighty yawn that he nearly dislocated his jaw. "Ow, that hurt!" He smacked his lips and rubbed the right side of his face before surveying the dimly lit room. The first thing he noticed was that Azala was no longer at her desk; she was asleep in her own bed, the velvet-and-black covers rising and falling ever so slightly with her every breath. The metal man stood stationary in the far corner, dutifully standing guard over his master.

At least my back isn't burning like it was when I first got my seal. Now it just feels warm. Visage rubbed the area of the seal slightly with his right hand, making sure it wouldn't sting or burn if pressed. He smiled at his conclusion—it didn't even sting after a forceful push. After sitting on the edge of the bed for a few moments, he stood up and stretched again, this time getting on his tiptoes. Azala had mentioned that his clothing included a pair of boots, so he looked under the bed.

"Wow! There they are!" The boy quickly slipped them on and jumped a few times. They felt as though his feet were totally enveloped by a cool gel. It was like walking on a soft pillow—or maybe even a cloud. With his new footwear on, as well as the pants and cloak he had put on the night before, Visage headed off into the hallway. However, before

56

heading down the hall, he dug the earpiece out of his pocket and put it into his ear. He had to press it twice to activate it. Inside his ear, a tiny tendril, with a microscopic needle protruding from its tip, approached his fleshy skin. The needle jabbed into the soft flesh, causing him to yelp. He was about to rip the earpiece off and throw it, but the pain lasted only for an instant. Then he could hear a feminine voice.

"Blood sample analyzed. Operator: Visage; Blood type: unknown; Race: Silvarian; Language: common tongue—translations now available."

Once the voice stopped, Visage felt a cool liquid come out of the earpiece and start to creep across his face. He was frightened when it covered his nose and eyes before solidifying. He could now see several charts, with lines underneath, in the top right and left hand corners of his view. He gasped when he realized what lay before him.

"Cool! This thing's got a heads-up display (HUD)!" The boy's mind wandered back to the time when one of the fighter pilots in his father's carrier group had shown him his helmet and the inside of an F-fourteen fighter. Refocusing on the present, Visage noticed that every time he moved or turned his head, the HUD moved along with it. "Wow!" He spread out his arms and ran down the empty hallway, spewing metallic-sounding engine noises as he headed toward the main hall and the lifts. "Shooooom!" Unfortunately, the fake fighter came to a screeching halt; he bumped into something, or, more appropriately, some being. The large form (appearing to be a male) nearly fell forward when the disguised Silvarian ran into the back of him. Visage, however, wasn't quite as graceful as the taller being, because he fell backwards and landed unceremoniously on his butt. "Ow," was all he could say. In response to the mishap, the dark-clad male turned around and intently stared down at him. "Control, I think I have a problem," Visage squeaked while looking up at the much taller being.

"Who are you?" the being asked in a very rough voice.

"I... I'm Visage. I'm s-s-sorry," he stammered. He hunched his back in an effort to make himself appear as small as he felt.

The large being pondered the encounter for a moment before

pounding his left fist into the open palm of his right hand. "Ah, yes, the new demon kid Lord Nosfaren picked up from that pathetic little planet." Though the man sounded quite gruff, he was kind enough to assist the child. Visage poked his head out from under his cloak and hesitantly reached out for the man's giant gloved hand. The hand clasped around his own, and, with a forceful yank from the stranger, the boy was back on his feet.

"I don't think you should be playing starship in the hallways, Visage; you could hurt yourself," the man offered while at the same time assessing the boy for injuries. Once the scan was complete and everything appeared to be in the right place, he smiled with satisfaction. Unfortunately, Visage couldn't see the man's smile because his face was hidden behind his mask.

"Looks like you're in one piece." While introducing himself, Lord Niells thumped his chest.

Visage thought before answering. "Are you on the Council with Lord Nos and the others?"

Niells gave a hearty laugh. "No, I'm not, nor do I wish to be."

"Why's that?" Visage's curiosity was peaked.

"Too much responsibility, not to mention the logistical nightmare," Niells quipped before he headed for the lifts, motioning for Visage to follow.

"Where are we going?" Visage asked as he watched Lord Niells press several buttons on the keypad.

"I'm taking you to the room where the ar'teths have their lessons."

"Ar'teth? What is an ar'teth?"

Niells grinned. "Lord Nos is right; you really do belong here."

"Why's that?"

"I think it best that I leave the explanations to Lord Baltrix," Niells replied.

The lift stopped and Niells gently pushed Visage out the doors. "Head down that hall and take the third door on the right. May the Verse guide you to your destiny, Visage," Niells said. The doors then closed and left the young boy alone. Turning to the hallway, Visage headed off to meet Lord Baltrix. The doors were spaced rather far apart in this particular hallway, so it took several dironns to get to the third set.

***

The double doors in front of Visage were quite ornate and crowned with symbols. Luckily, the HUD in his new mask easily translated the symbols into English. "Lecture Hall Three" is what they read. With a tentative step forward, Visage swallowed the lump that was starting to form in his throat, grabbed the handle on one of the doors, and pushed. Once he entered, he found that the room was, like most of those in the temple, dimly lit, even though the high ceiling was filled with several rows of red and purple lights. On the lowest level, there was a small table, behind which Visage could make out the form of a being sitting in a chair. A few feet in front of the table were rows of desks, which had the same cushiony chairs as the ones in his room. There were five rows, which were divided by two rows of stairs. After Visage entered the lecture hall proper, the figure in the chair took notice.

"Good menronn, ar'teth Visage. I'm surprised to see you up this early. Class doesn't officially start for another minronn and a half."

Visage recognized the voice. "Lord Baltrix, Lord Niells told me that you could answer my questions."

Baltrix arose from his chair and utilized the Verse to pick up the child, bringing him over to sit atop the table next to him. After sitting back down, he pulled his chair over to the boy with the inquisitive mind. "So, what are these questions you wish to ask?" Baltrix leaned back into his chair and pulled off his hood, revealing his full face.

Visage noticed that Baltrix was an older human male who looked to be in his late thirties to early forties. His hair was disheveled and dark, but the lighting made it hard to determine its shade. A well-groomed mustache sat atop his lip. His nose was midsized—not very pronounced—and he had the same type of eyes as Azala. His pupils were deep black and surrounded by gold or amber irises. The irises ended abruptly, only to be overtaken by blood-red sclera. Baltrix was tickled by Visage's acute interest in his facial features.

"Well, Lord Baltrix," Visage started, "what exactly does ar'teth mean?"

"In the common tongue, it translates into learner or student." With that answer, the floodgates opened. Visage was thinking faster than he could speak.

"What does this 'Verse,' which every being keeps talking about, mean? What does mi'thia mean? What is a Vorihelcom seal? Why do I need one? Why does everyone hate Earth?"

"Whoa, whoa, whoa; calm down kid! Keep it to one thought at a time," Baltrix admonished. Visage closed his eyes and took a deep breath, let it out slowly, and focused on the man in front of him.

"Where to begin. Ah... so you know there are gods and there are demons, right?" Visage nodded. "So, let me say this: not all demons are evil, and not all gods are good. Let me explain." Visage nodded again. Baltrix knew he couldn't waste any time, or he could be facing another barrage of questions, so he quickly elaborated. "Our God is good. In fact, I think He's even more than that. I mean, you've met several Meserino demons as well as Vira, who's a Veserino. So, do you think they are good?"

Visage beamed! "Yep!"

"Good, because they are, and that is why our God, well, I guess you could say adopted them after the war."

"War, what war?" Visage tilted his head and crossed his arms trying to remember anything he'd heard about a war.

"I'm speaking about the god war."

Visage snapped to attention. "The gods were at war!"

"Like I said, not all gods are good. Only one God was truly evil—Skath. He is the one who killed your true dar'nra, or father and, indirectly, your entire race."

"But... but... why!"

"Because Skath wanted to become king of the gods, and His ambition got Him killed. However, many goodly gods, demons, and angels lost their lives because of Him. This is why you are so important; you're the last of your kind." Visage remained silent but attentive. "You see,

God ilonied, or loved those who fought for Him, so he adopted every being who lent Him aid. Vira and Riza fought alongside Him, too."

"Really!"

"Really. But the problem was that you were only a spirit child of God at that point—you didn't have a body, so God gave you to your parents on Earth. Why? We don't know; some assume it's because of His sense of humor, but honestly, you'd have to ask Him."

"So the evil God Skath is gone, and Riza and Vira fought against him?"

"Yes, they did... but no, Skath isn't truly gone; He still has many followers and we are helping defend our galaxy against them." Baltrix let out a sigh while he reflected on past battles with Skath's worshippers.

"But why doesn't God destroy them? Why do you have to fight them?" Visage sorrowfully asked.

"The answer is simple. It's because God gives us freedom of choice."

"Choice?"

"Yes, choice. You see, we are given free will—the will to choose our path in this life—and God Himself guarantees that. He cannot, or should I say will not, ever take that away; otherwise, He wouldn't be a just God."

"But I thought that God is sometimes vengeful and destroys bad people—like the Pharaoh in Egypt when he wouldn't let his people go," Visage knowledgeably stated.

Baltrix nodded. "Yes, God does sometimes smite the wicked, but that's not always about vengeance—it's about justice."

Visage was now thoroughly confused. "I don't understand."

"Here—take off your mask. I need to look into your memories for a dironn," Baltrix said, thinking of an idea that might help simplify the concept he was trying to convey. Visage obeyed, pressing the button on his earpiece. His mask retracted so the two beings could now see eye-to-eye. "This might feel funny," Baltrix said before peering into Visage's mind and looking for things to which he could relate. Fortunately, since Visage was very young and had few memories to sort through, he was quickly able to find just the thing. "Your dar'nra is in the Navy, right?" Baltrix questioned the seven-year-old.

"Yeah, he makes the world safe by killing the bad guys."

"So, he fights for vengeance then?"

Visage scrunched up his face. "No, he fights for justice."

"Are you sure about that? Didn't he go and kill the guys who invaded Kuwait?"

"Yeah, but the people who invaded were bad!"

"But your dad and his friends did go and kill them for invading, right?"

"Well, yes."

"Then they took vengeance on them for invading another country."

"No, the Navy fights for justice, not vengeance," Visage argued.

"You have to look at it from the Iraqis' perspective. They invaded Kuwait. Kuwait then asked for someone to avenge them, did they not?"

"I thought that was justice. The Iraqis did something bad by invading Kuwait, and Dad went over there to bring justice, didn't he?" Visage was more confused than ever.

"See, that is exactly my point: Justice and vengeance are almost the same thing, and in some cases they are interchangeable," Baltrix said. "Here's another example: When you saw Azala's bruised body, you got angry, right?"

"Yes, I wanted to hurt the one who hurt her."

"So you wanted to take revenge on Lord Nos—for hurting his apprentice?"

"No... Well, yes... I don't know! I just didn't like seeing her hurt. But I didn't know that Lord Nos was the one who hurt her."

"So, Visage, vengeance and justice are complicated. You see it as justice where another could just as easily see it as revenge. The thing is, Lord Nos hurt Azala because he cares about her."

Visage pondered for a moment before answering. "I don't understand!"

"If Lord Nos didn't let Azala get bruised up and beaten, she might not have learned how to properly defend herself from an opponent who doesn't want to hurt her—but to kill her. What then?"

"So you're saying that by suffering the aches and pains now, Azala may be able to save her own life in the future?"

"Yes, Visage! That's what God does. He wants us to live, but if we aren't prepared to fight then all we'll do is die, and, trust me, He doesn't want that. We do have to face our fates eventually, just not to the degree that our God did." Baltrix snickered at an old memory. "But, if we live good lives and look to God for help, we can live with Him eternally. Now, let me see. Maybe this will help you to understand. Can you tell me what it is that most beings are truly afraid of?"

"I don't know. Death?" Visage guessed.

Baltrix shook his head. "No. It's having their hearts and minds become naked."

"Back on Earth I was almost always naked," Visage mumbled while folding his arms. "I burned pretty much everything I wore."

Baltrix laughed. "No, Visage, I'm not speaking about being physically naked. I'm talking about having naked thoughts and feelings and making them bare for all to see."

"You mean like how you can see my thoughts and read them? What's so bad about that?" Visage wondered aloud.

"Most beings don't like having their minds read. They think their thoughts are private, but with the power of the Verse, we can read their thoughts. And guess what—we've discovered that some beings look nice and clean on the outside, but they are completely black on the inside."

"What is the Verse?" Visage asked.

"The Verse is one of the powers the gods use. It's broken up into two parts: the Zah'harrim and the Jah'harrim—dark and light. The Verse is like the yin and yang from your planet. Darkness and light balance each other—they are inseparably connected." Baltrix smiled, closed his eyes, and recalled several more old memories before continuing. "As Verse users, we basically invade beings' minds and make them bare before us. Then, with either justice or vengeance,"— He shrugged. —"we strike them down."

"That sounds, I don't know, evil."

"It *is* called the Zah'harrim for a reason."

"Zah'harrim? I know you mentioned that before, but what exactly does that mean?"

"It translates to dark power or dark energy. And every being in this temple is trained to use the Zah'harrim."

"So everyone here is a bad guy!"

Baltrix roared with laughter. It took a while for him to calm down enough to answer. "That's not always true. Tell me. How do you feel around Riza and the other demons?"

"They feel kinda creepy... but warm at the same time."

"That's because, even though we are attuned more to the Zah'harrim form of the Verse, we still have good hearts and minds, and we try to keep ourselves that way so we don't become like Skath or his followers. We use the Zah'harrim as our offensive power and the Jah'harrim, or light power, for defense."

"Doesn't God prevent us from learning this dark power?"

"No—that is where freedom of choice comes in. God doesn't prevent any being from doing anything. It's up to each of us to keep our hearts in the right and we, well, turn out like this." Baltrix gestured to himself.

"So, the Zah'har... err... dark power... isn't bad?"

Baltrix thought a moment. "Yes it is, and no it isn't."

Wrinkles appeared on Visage's brow. *I guess I'll never get it.*

Lord Baltrix struggled with how to convey the concept of the two powers to the young Silvarian. "As I've said, not all gods are good; even gods themselves cast shadows. Besides, if darkness didn't exist at all then there would be no light. So, because we use both sides of the Verse, we become balanced. However, as I mentioned, the darkness can taint us if we're not careful. Fortunately, we've found ways to prevent it from consuming us: we tame it, control it, and force it into submitting to our will." Baltrix wasn't sure if Visage fully understood, so he leaned forward and peered again into the child's mind. He was hoping to find something else that might help him understand. He sighed with relief when he found the something he was looking for. *Is that what the Earthlings think of me?* Baltrix laughed aloud while Visage looked on.

"What's so funny?"

"You seem to have read something about a man named Dracula, yes?"

What does an old fairy tale have to do with this dark power? Visage wondered. "Yeah so, he was a character from Bram Stoker's book. Why?"

Now the fun begins! Baltrix thought. "Many onns ago, Lord Nos visited Earth. He was trying to locate an ancient Zaharaj vessel that had crashed somewhere on the planet."

Visage was excited. "Lord Nos was on Earth! Why didn't he tell me?"

"Probably because the Earthlings didn't like him very much."

Visage's face indicated understanding, and his smile vanished. "Most people called me a freak or monster whenever I left the house. Only my family and the Navy guys really liked me." Visage started to swing his legs, which were dangling over the edge of the table.

"Most people did the same thing to Lord Nos; there were some who even tried to kill him." At first Visage looked glum, but then his brow again furrowed.

"But Lord Nos seems so friendly. Why would anyone want to kill him!" Visage protested, his head snapping back up and his sapphire eyes widening.

As to the 'friendly' part, Lord Baltrix nodded in agreement. However, his demeanor then took on an ominous appearance, and he started drumming his fingers against each other in rapid succession. "Not everyone tried to kill him; there were some humans who took him in while he looked for the lost ship. He even took a curious young man on as his apprentice."

"He did? I guess I can believe that; after all, he did pick *me* up." Visage paused. "Wait. Isn't Azala Lord Baltrix's apprentice?"

Baltrix rolled his eyes. "Yes, she is his current apprentice. Lord Nos has had many apprentices over the onns, or, in your Earthling form of time, years. Eventually, even you will have a master of your own. You can't learn everything through study alone. You also need experience, and you get that by going out into the galaxy accompanied by a master."

Visage nodded. "I guess that makes sense."

"As I was saying," Baltrix continued, "when Lord Nos went to Earth the first time, he took on an apprentice. That's when the rumors started."

"Are you talking about that Dracula guy? But he's only a myth." Visage was now acting a bit defiant.

Baltrix laughed. "Dracula is no myth... And that's not even his real name. Lord Nos's apprentice was a Romanian prince by the name of Vlad."

"Wait! You mean Vlad Tepes... as in Vlad the Impaler. But he died a long time ago... didn't he?"

"I should hope not, because I'm Vlad." As soon as Baltrix's uttered those words, Visage's face went pale.

"So you made a deal with the devil and became an immortal, blood-sucking vampire!" Visage exclaimed, pointing an accusing finger at Baltrix.

Baltrix couldn't stand it anymore. He started laughing so hard that he nearly fell out of his chair. He had to compose himself before he could respond to Visage's accusation.

"Sorry, sorry, Visage, but that's way too ludicrous. I never made any deal with the devil. I did have my blood awakened by Lord Nos, who isn't a devil but a Meserino demon. That is why I am able to use the power of the Verse, and I even have a fairly high level of indren'freth, if I do say so myself."

"Indren'freth? What's that? I heard that word mentioned last night when Azala was talking with some people."

"Indren'freth is Marcisian; in the common tongue it's called the Inner Fire. It's our second power. In all, we know about three different forms of power: the Inner Fire, the Verse—both the Zah'harrim and Jah'harrim—and the Arcane or magicks. There are more forms of the Arcane than even I can count," Baltrix offered, giving Visage a wink.

"Are there only three powers? There should be more, shouldn't there?" While Visage crossed his arms and was pondering these questions, he started to close his eyes, but Lord Baltrix wasn't about to let his mind settle—at least not yet.

"We think we know of a fourth power, but we don't know how it works. So, if you want to know more about that one, you'll have to ask Eendril," Baltrix offered with a mischievous wink.

Visage emphatically shook his head. "No, thank you! I already have enough to learn, just with the first three."

"So true. Now, to answer your previous question, I'm not the blood-sucking immortal being whom the Earthlings believed me to be. Honestly, how does blood manipulation turn into blood sucking?"

"Blood manipulation?" Visage was not grasping the concept.

"Yes—blood is very powerful when it's awake. It's what gives us the ability to use the power of the Verse as well as to manifest our own indren'freth. Since you're a demon, you probably manifested yours at birth," Baltrix explained.

"Wait, was my indren'freth the reason I burst into flames and burned my clothes all the time?"

"Yes. You're very much a living weapon. That's why Lord Nos brought you here—so you could learn how to control your own power. You could have ripped Earth to shreds. That's why Riza and Vira put that Vorihelcom seal on your back. I swear, sometimes you demons are more dangerous than Eendril himself."

"We are?" Visage asked with an incredulous tone.

"Oh, don't worry about it. You have an eternity to learn how to control that outrageous strength of yours. Until then, that seal needs to stay put. I would hate to have to move to a new galaxy, which might be necessary if you ever lose control."

"But I don't want to destroy the galaxy!" Visage cried.

"Of course you don't, my young friend, so, again, that's why you're here—so you can learn self-control." Baltrix then used his Verse power to pull Visage's hood over his head and down over his face.

"Hey! What's the big idea!"

Baltrix stifled a laugh before getting up, stretching, and rolling his chair back behind the table. He then lifted Visage off the table and sat him down onto the floor. Visage pulled his hood back off and peered up at the taller being, who was still slightly smirking.

Stupid Vlad. Wait until I learn how to do that.

"You have a long way to go, kid! Now go find a seat; class will be starting soon."

Visage was mumbling incoherently while walking over to the first set of stairs in the amphitheater. After making his way up to the third row of desks, he plopped himself down into the large comfortable chair and pulled himself up to the long semi-circular desk. He then folded his arms on the desktop, rested his chin on them, and thought about all of the new stuff Lord Baltrix had shared. Lord Nos went to Earth a long time ago and brought back his apprentice, Lord Baltrix, who is actually the Earthling, Vlad Tepes. Nos then awakened Lord Baltrix's blood somehow so that he could use his powers. Wait. Lord Nosfaren— as in Nosferatu? Visage giggled a bit at the thought. But Lord Baltrix doesn't drink blood—he manipulates blood. I wonder if I can do that. I've never tried blood manipulation before.

"It's much easier than you think, Visage!" Lord Baltrix blurted, startling Visage from his thoughts.

I hate it when people do that!

"Then stop thinking so loudly!" Baltrix retorted.

But how!

"Ow! Calm down, Visage. There's no need to shout!" After recovering from the psychic shouts, Baltrix answered Visage's telepathic question. "I'll just have to teach you." Visage was so happy that he jumped from his seat and gave a hearty cheer. "You didn't let me finish. I meant to say,"— Baltrix raised his hand to keep Visage quiet. —"I'll teach you *after* class!" Baltrix blurted before Visage could make any further psychic outbursts.

"Okay, Lord Baltrix. I'll try to be a little more patient. I want to hurry up and learn how to not think so... loudly?" Visage gave a half-hearted smile, rubbed the back of his head, and slowly sank back into his chair.

Once Baltrix and Visage finished their conversation, the door of the amphitheater opened and another cloaked being entered the room. A pair of red-and-gold glowing eyes fixed upon Visage, who tried to become as small as possible under the new being's scrutinizing gaze.

"Good menronn, Moonreth. You're up a bit early," Baltrix uttered without even looking up from the book that he was reading.

"Good menronn to you, Lord Baltrix. I see we have a new being in class." Moonreth pulled off his hood and pressed the button on his earpiece, causing his mask to retract and reveal his face. Visage thought Moonreth looked a few years older than he did, since the newly arrived being was taller. He had light gray skin, elongated ears, cool white hair, and dark gray lips, which were spread into a slight grin. His eyes had remained fixed on the other sentient being in the room. "So, who's the new kid with the loud thoughts?"

Baltrix flatly answered. "His name is Visage."

Moonreth's eyes opened a bit wider. "Oh! The Silvarian Earthling!" In his excited state, Moonreth went airborne; his feet left the ground, and he flew over to the aisle where Visage was seated, landing right next to the young demon's desk. Putting his hand to his chin, he studied the newcomer more intently, leaning in and getting a little too close for Visage's comfort.

"Sorry about that," Moonreth said sheepishly, his hand moving from his chin to the top of his head before sliding down his messy white hair. "It's just that you look more like a human than a Silvarian."

That's because Riza and Vira put some sort of seal on me—

Moonreth interrupted Visage's train of thought. "You mean a Vorihelcom seal! Really!" He was now looking at Visage with even more excitement!

"Yes, one of those." It really hurt! Visage grasped his back and winced when he remember the pain.

"I'm Moonreth, by the way; I'm a Night Elf from Devros." When he offered Visage a gloved hand the boy hesitantly offered his own, and both parties gave each other a firm handshake. He then turned to Lord Baltrix. "Lord Baltrix, thank you for what you did last trell." He followed up with a slight bow,

Moonreth's thoughtful comment caused the older man to sit up, place his book down on the small desk next to his lectern and turn his chair to face the speaker. "That *kid* had it coming. I'm more worried about the effect he had on your sri'na. How is she doing?"

"You should ask her yourself, Master Baltrix." Moonreth nodded toward the door where another being could be seen peering into the room.

Lord Baltrix spoke first. "I'm happy to see you up and about, ar'teth Le'Shara," he said before offering the shy child a warm smile.

Visage wondered why the new being was hiding behind the doorway and not entering the room. Finally, Moonreth spoke. "Come on, sri'na, aren't you going to thank Lord Baltrix?" Le'Shara hesitated before giving the door a push and entering the dimly lit classroom. After pulling off her hood, she pressed the side of her mask, revealing the face of a female Night Elf.

Visage couldn't take his eyes off Le'Shara. She shook her head and spilled her white tresses out from under her cloak. Her skin was pure white. Her long ears stuck out the side of her head passed her shoulders, and her face was similar to that of Moonreth's. After grabbing the mess of matted hair and flinging it behind her, she surveyed the room with her bright ruby red eyes, which finally settled on the red-and-gold orbs of Lord Baltrix. Looking even more nervous, she clutched her left arm with her right hand and shifted her eyes to the floor. "Thank you," she managed to say in a small, squeaky, barely audible voice; her eyes remained focused on the floor.

What's this about? Why is she acting like that? Did something happen between Lord Baltrix and the albino girl? Visage wondered. All eyes then focused on him. Le'Shara herself abruptly turned her head to face the one who had telepathically transmitted the loud thoughts.

Moonreth's eyes narrowed a bit at Visage's thoughts, but he relaxed almost instantly. "So many questions, eh, Visage?" He followed up by giving the Silvarian a light punch in the arm.

"I'm sorry. I don't know how to think quietly yet," Visage uttered, turning from Moonreth to Baltrix. Baltrix was obviously attempting to stifle a laugh.

Moonreth had a big grin on his face, sensing Visage's embarrassment. After wrapping his arm around his new friend, he offered a compassionate response. "Don't worry about it; we were all like that when we first got here." Baltrix coughed into his fist in order to garner every being's attention, causing Moonreth to release Visage, walk over to the desk across the aisle, pull out the chair, and take a seat. Le'Shara walked up the stairs, stopping to glance at Visage before making her way to take the seat next to Moonreth. She and her ber'nan then took out cylindrical objects and placed them on top of their desks.

"Visage, you seem to have many questions, and I just might have the answers." Baltrix glanced at the two Night Elves before continuing. "You met Lady Dreth, did you not?" Visage was unsure what Lady Dreth had to do with the two Night Elves, but he nodded, nonetheless. "It seems her former apprentice liked to play nasty mind games with the young Night Elf, Le'Shara." Baltrix gestured to the younger Night Elf, who seemed to be shivering, though it wasn't at all cold. Moonreth put his arm over his sri'na's shoulder, providing her some needed support. Baltrix made his hands into fists. "This injustice didn't sit well with her ber'nan—or with any of her friends. So last trell, Moonreth and several others confronted Zor'ret. They were about to exchange blows when I intervened."

"Did you punish Zor'ret, Lord Baltrix? He won't be able to hurt anyone else, will he?" Visage asked in a much lower tone than his usual one.

Baltrix then received a short vision of Visage's future. *So he's going to be an avenger or a dispenser of justice. Either way, he'll be a powerful defender of the galaxy.* Baltrix smiled widely before returning to reality. "I'm sorry, Visage, I was lost in thought. And the answer is no, Zor'ret can't hurt any being ever again."

"Why's that?"

"Because Lord Baltrix killed him, that's why!" Moonreth blurted, hugging Le'Shara a bit more tightly.

"Lord Baltrix, did you really kill Zorret!" Visage's anger turned into worry.

Baltrix sighed. "Yes I did, though I didn't plan on killing him. Last trell his master, Lady Dreth, was kicked off the Council, and her apprentice was also expelled." Baltrix paused for a moment. "Let's just say, he didn't take it well."

"In other words, he attacked you," Visage stated. *From what I've heard, this Zor'ret guy was a bully. Back on Earth, I knew several people who were like that, but I never killed them. I only scared them. That was one of the reasons Oma had to home school me.*

"Trust me, Visage, Zor'ret was much more than what you call a 'bully.'" Moonreth looked again to his younger sibling before continuing. "After what he tried to do to Azala and what he was doing to my sri'na, Zor'ret got what he deserved!"

Visage thought for a moment, looking from Lord Baltrix back to Moonreth. "What *did* Zor'ret do to Azala—and Le'Shara?"

All three beings in the room peered at the Silvarian. Emotions were mixed. Baltrix looked pained, Moonreth shot up from his chair. His heart was pounding and his muscles became tense. As for Le'Shara, she looked like she was about to cry. Moonreth was about to say something, but Le'Shara grabbed his arm and stopped him short. Surprising both Moonreth and Baltrix, she got up, walked around her ber'nan, and stood beside Visage's desk. The look in her ruby red eyes betrayed her; Visage knew instantly that she had been tormented.

"Visage, you know Azala? How do you know her?" Le'Shara asked. Moonreth now looked worriedly at his sri'na, and Visage knew there was telepathic communication going on between the two siblings.

"Yes, I know her; she's Lord Nos's apprentice, and I'm her roommate," Visage replied. *I wonder why the elf girl asked about her.*

Le'Shara stood and studied Visage for a few moments before answering. "Did... did she say anything about him?" She spoke so softly that Visage could barely hear her.

"No, not really." *That Zor'ret guy must have done something horrible* to this albino girl. That's probably why everyone is acting so strangely. Thankfully Lord Baltrix took care of him!

Since Visage was still unable to control his thoughts, every being was able to hear them, even the beings who had just entered the room. For the most part, the newcomers seemed to have ignored the conversation. They pulled off their hoods, removed their masks, and plopped down into their seats. However, a blue-skinned Twillan, who apparently knew of Le'Shara's recent encounters with Zor'ret, walked by and gently squeezed the Night Elf's shoulder before heading over to a seat in the same aisle in which she and Moonreth were sitting.

With a lot of support from her friends, Le'Shara drummed up the courage to continue her narrative. "Zor'ret—He... he kept telling me I was ugly and defective and that he would be the only one who would ever want me." After she spoke these words, Visage noticed that Moonreth was sitting at his desk with his head low, his hand so tightly clenched that it was turning white.

How could Zor'ret say something like that to such a pretty elf girl? Visage's thoughts caught every being off guard. Le'Shara was now looking down, in embarrassment instead of shame. Moonreth, who had unclenched his fist, was now wide-eyed. Even Baltrix had stopped reading his book and turned around in his chair so he could face the group.

"Y... Y... You think I'm... pretty?" Le'Shara stammered. It was a good thing Moonreth wasn't drinking anything at that moment, since his mouth hung so agape that his lower jaw almost hit his desk.

At first, Visage was dumbfounded—not sure how to react. He still wasn't used to having his thoughts read, but finally composed himself enough to respond to Le'Shara's question. "It's the truth. You are pretty. I mean, you're the first Night Elf girl I've met, but Zor'ret thought you were ugly because you're an albino? That's so wrong!" Moonreth was totally taken aback, and Le'Shara was in shock. Baltrix, on the other hand, seemed to be amused.

The Twillan glanced at Le'Shara before getting up from his seat. His skin was blue instead of red-colored like Azala's skin. His eyes, not yet tainted by Zah'harrim, were a deep cyan. Like Azala, he had bone-white cones for ears and the usual twin tails protruding from the back of his head. At this time, his two tails were mostly hidden by his cloak. Though it seemed he would normally be quite handsome—especially with his dark-blue lips—his brow was furrowed. "Slith, kid! What's an albino!" he demanded, staring passed Le'Shara and directly at Visage. The disturbance caused Le'Shara to snap out of her shock and peer at Visage. Even Moonreth seemed to be listening more intently.

Moonreth clasped his hands and closed his eyes. "I would also like to ask the same thing that Cormack did..." he unclasped his hands and glared at Visage.

Visage wasn't enjoying all of the attention and spoke without thinking. "I don't know what the big deal is. On Earth, when I was first born, everyone thought I was some kind of albino. My skin was white, too."

Moonreth tilted his head and scowled a bit. "So, an albino is a being born with white skin?"

The blue-skinned Twillan, Cormack couldn't contain himself. "That means that every Marcisian could be considered an albino then!"

Visage corrected Cormack. "No, it's more complicated than just having white skin. Most albinos have red eyes that are very weak—or sometimes even totally useless."

Le'Shara spoke up, only this time her tone appeared to be... stronger. "Yes. I was born with weak eyesight, but, with only a minor procedure, the surgeons were able to fix it."

"So, my sri'na is what Earthlings call an albino?" Moonreth asked.

Lord Baltrix couldn't help himself. He had to enter the conversation. "But Visage, can you further elaborate on what you mean by the term 'albino'?"

What does sri'na mean? Visage shook his head. "As far as albinism goes, it's a genetic disorder in which there is an absence of pigment in the skin. There are a bunch of scientific words involved, which I didn't really understand."

Cormack the blue-skinned Twillan, again piped up. "So Le'Shara has white skin and red eyes because of some genetic disorder and not a curse?"

Visage chuckled. "No, albinos aren't cursed. The white skin is simply a genetic flaw." He looked compassionately at Le'Shara. "Did someone actually tell you that you were cursed?"

Le'Shara peered at the floor, shifted her feet, and slowly nodded. Moonreth jumped up, ran past his Twillan friend making Cormack's cyan eyes get rather wide when Moonreth almost pushed him over, before he put his arms around his sri'na, and spun her around. He caught her so off guard that, if he hadn't released her immediately, they both would have fallen down the stairs. Even while he was helping Le'Shara regain her balance, he was talking excitedly. "Isn't that great sri'na—you're not cursed! And, if your white skin is from some genetic disorder, I'm sure the Marcisians, or Skelaxians can find a way to fix it! Wait until we tell Mi'thia and Dar'nra! You can become a priestess— just like you've always dreamed!"

Cormack was slightly upset at Moonreth, but he smiled nonetheless, folded his arms, and nodded.

Le'Shara's tears were flowing freely. Never before had anyone, other than her family, shown her such compassion. After leaving Devros and becoming a Zaharaj ar'teth—like her older ber'nan—she had made several new friends, and they accepted her, cursed white skin and all. But now, thanks to none other than a demon boy from Earth, her entire universe was about to change. *I'm not cursed. I'm not ugly. I'm a Night Elf, and now I have a brighter future than even I could have imagined!* Moonreth, along with every being in the room, felt something new emanating from the white-skinned Night Elf.

"I told you there wasn't anything wrong with you, ar'teth Le'Shara," Lord Baltrix interjected. He then followed up with a nod towards Visage. "Well done, ar'teth Visage."

"But I didn't really do anything," Visage closed his eyes and smiled at Le'Shara, Cormack and Moonreth.

"What do you mean you didn't do anything! Do you have any idea what my sri'na went through when she was back at home? Even her name is translated as 'the cursed' in the common tongue! But, thanks to you, we know that all Le'Shara has is a genetic deficiency which can be easily remedied!" Moonreth exclaimed, slapping both palms down on Visage's desk. His eyes were burning brightly he was so ecstatic.

"What the frak is going on here!" another red-skinned Twillan demanded. He had entered the room after throwing the doors wide open with a telekinetic blast. He then threw off his hood with such gusto that he almost ripped his mask off, since it hadn't finished retreating back into the earpiece or, in his case, cone piece. "I could feel the excitement from the lifts! What on Zharaj did I miss!" he demanded.

To Visage, this Twillan looked older; he was taller than most every being in the room except for Lord Baltrix. When he whipped his head around to survey the room with his wild-appearing Zah'harrim-tinted eyes, his long twills flopped about erratically. Even Visage could tell that he was peering into the mind of every being and assessing his or her thoughts. Ultimately, his eyes narrowed and fell upon the being who had caused the commotion. "You!" He abruptly pointed at Visage, who was trying hard to avoid eye contact. "You're that Silvarian betrak, aren't you!" the red-skinned Twillan demandingly yelled.

"Ranic, calm down." Another human had entered the room and removed his hood and mask. His short blond hair was striking, since it clashed with practically everything else in the room. His eyes, like those of Cormack, the blue-skinned Twillan, had yet to be tainted; they were sapphire-blue, like Visage's own. This being, apparently the voice of reason for the pair, seemed to have a genuinely pious attitude. He had a look of disgust due to his friend's sudden outburst.

Baltrix was highly annoyed. *Great, the trio of trouble—(Ranic, Moonreth, and Envine). I've asked the Council to break them up—to send them to different temples or different classes. I have no idea why Lord Nos has refused my request every damned time!* He put his hand to his face and slowly shook his bowed head.

Baltrix's thought permeated the room. Moonreth grunted, Le'Shara giggled, and the two arrivals pouted. "We aren't that bad, Visage," Moonreth whispered to the Silvarian.

"Come on, Master, I told you the Silvarian would make things more interesting!" Ranic whined. "I already missed out on something fun, didn't I?" he asked his still disgruntled-looking master.

I wouldn't say fun so much as... informative. Visage was now fully aware that every being could read his mind. Most beings mumbled and nodded their heads in agreement.

Ranic ignored Visage's thought and continued with his own. "So, Moonreth, what did I miss?" Moonreth reached his desk, having followed Le'Shara, who had entered the aisle first. He had just placed his hand on his chair when he felt Ranic's telepathic question; he hesitated before taking his seat. "Well, apparently my sri'na isn't cursed. She merely has a minor genetic issue. The Earthlings call beings afflicted with the disorder 'albinos.' "

"So your sri'na isn't cursed? What a total letdown!" Ranic blurted.

Cormack shook his head in slight disdain while he made his way up the aisle, he sat behind his two friends Moonreth and Le'Shara.

"And why, Ranic, is Le'Shara not being cursed 'a total letdown'?" Envine was growing even more disgusted by his friend's callous remark. His eyes were focused on Ranic, as though they were trying to bore a hole through the Twillan's thick red skull.

Ranic was too busy peering at the newest member of the class. With a big toothy grin, he walked around Visage's chair and sat in the one next to him. After removing the metal cylinder from his belt, he put it on top of the desk in the cutout where it was supposed to go. He crossed his booted feet and leaned back in his chair. Crossing his arms, Ranic gave a sideways glance at Visage and gave him a wink. *Lord Baltrix, please save me!* Visage mentally pleaded, but Baltrix was in deep thought.

I remember a time when the whole hall was full of new learners, but now it seems as though the Ja'Shari are getting every new Verse user in the galaxy. Only the Twillans and Night Elves lean more towards the Zah'harrim side of things than to the Jah'harrim. Baltrix was still drathed off at the Ja'Shari for essentially forcing the Council to sign, what he thought, was a very bad agreement. *Who cares if a being is more attuned to the Zah'harrim form of the Verse than the Jah; we teach everybeing how to use both forms here, including how to use one's own indren'freth! Thanks to that treaty, our numbers continue to dwindle while the Ja'shari's grow by the deronn.*

Lord Baltrix was startled out of his thoughts by Visage's psychic plea. He had warned his apprentice not to mess with the young demon from Earth. However, since there were very few ar'teths in the lecture hall these deronns, seats were not assigned. Baltrix surveyed the ar'teths until his eyes fell on his apprentice. Ranic had put his blood sorjin on top of his desk alongside his feet. He was leaning back in his chair with one arm on the rest and the other draped over the young Visage. Visage was trying to take the Twillan's intrusive behavior in stride, but the look on his face betrayed him. Baltrix knew his apprentice was trying to be friendly, but the way he was doing it had historically turned most beings off. Ranic had very few true friends, and the ones he did have got used to, or completely ignored, his overly affectionate nature.

"Apprentice, would you mind removing your arm from Visage's being?" Though Ranic didn't look too pleased, he begrudgingly obeyed. Visage managed to breathe a sigh of relief just in time for a chime to sound.

✳✳✳

"Let's get started, class." Baltrix surveyed the room and took a mental head count. *Everybeing's here with the exception of Azala, Dermanda, and Vok'et. I think Azala just got back from her mission with Lord Nos, and Dermanda and Vok'et are still out on missions with their masters. So, it appears that every being's accounted for.* However, before Baltrix could start his lecture, he had to deal with the proverbial glort in the room. "Visage, would you come down here please." Though Visage was hesitant, he arose. While exiting the aisle, he turned and noticed that Ranic was smiling widely and giving him a thumbs up. He was not pleased with Ranic's overly friendly approach; it sent a shiver down his spine. The discomfort caused him to walk down the stairs a little more briskly than normal. Once he reached the bottom, Lord Baltrix gestured for him to stand next to him and turn towards the audience. Visage complied, though he was nervous. Twenty or so beings now had their eyes focused on him. While varying Night Elves, Twillans, and several humans impatiently waited, the instructor fleetingly considered the enormity of the room. *So many empty seats.* However, he soon returned to the moment and broke the silence.

"Ar'teths, this is Visage. If you haven't heard from your masters, he's a Silvarian demon from Earth." Murmuring immediately commenced amongst the ar'teths. Baltrix then turned to the obviously nervous Visage and prodded, "So, go ahead and introduce yourself, Visage."

Back on Earth, Visage had spent little time in a school setting, so he was unfamiliar and a bit overwhelmed by this opportunity to speak to the class. Ranic was the ar'teth who finally broke the tension. "What's Earth like?" he offered with a wink.

"Um... it's kinda like here, only bluer and greener," Visage answered, grateful to the Twillan for the assist.

A human in the far corner raised his hand. "Yes, Nate?" Baltrix responded.

"What do you mean by bluer and greener?"

"Um... well... on Earth blue is the color of several large bodies of water that surround our land masses. We call these bodies of water oceans. And millions of green trees are grouped together into what we call forests. If you are looking down at Earth from space, the oceans and forests cause Earth to look like a blue and green planet," Visage offered.

"Is it like Devros then?" Moonreth asked.

Visage shrugged. "I don't know; I've never been to Devros."

"I'm sorry class, but you should only ask questions Visage can answer. I looked into his mind, and he can only answer basic questions about Earth. So, please don't ask him anything about his planet as compared to your own," Baltrix admonished. The beings in the room exuded a collective sigh.

"Is it hot?" Ranic asked. Visage jumped.

"I'm sorry, Ranic, you caught me by surprise." Several ar'teths giggled at his unexpected response to Ranic's rather simple question.

Ranic persisted. "Is... Earth... hot?" he asked more slowly.

Visage thought about the question for a while before answering. "Only sometimes and in some places."

"I don't understand!" Nate called out from the back.

Visage was getting frustrated when an idea hit him. Turning to Baltrix, he asked a single question. "Lord Baltrix, I think this would go faster if I just thought about everything I know about Earth. Will every being be able to hear what I think?" Baltrix was smiling widely. "Now you see one of the benefits of having loud thoughts." Visage looked confused. "The simple answer is yes," Baltrix said, trying hard not to point out Visage's obviously keen intellect.

Visage closed his eyes and opened his mind, allowing his memories to provide the class with information about his home world. He thought about Seoul, the bustling city where his mother and uncle were working and where his sisters were going to school; he thought about the flights he had taken over the forests and oceans whenever he had gone to meet his father on his destroyer; he thought about the books he had read and the knowledge they contained. He thought about the people he loved: his family and, though they were few, his friends. Visage also thought of the changing seasons: the warm sunny days of spring, the hot humid days of summer, the cool leafy autumn, and the cold white winter. *This feels good.* Then his thoughts turned darker—to the things that had transpired right before he left: burning his mother, running out into the rain-filled sky, the sorrow he felt for hurting the one he loved most, and the flames that seemed determined not to die. After a moment of sadness, his thoughts turned to the ship: meeting Lord Nosfaren, awakening to a new planet, and meeting new beings like Riza, Vira, Lord Baltrix, and Azala. Visage was truly grateful and thankful. He now felt something powerful, strong, and true. *I found hope!* When he opened his eyes, all eyes were upon him, but something had changed—every being was visibly crying. Even Lord Baltrix was affected by the visions he had witnessed.

"Thank you, Visage. That was quite enlightening." Baltrix then looked out at the class. "Unless there are any more questions..." With no questions forthcoming, he gestured for Visage to return to his seat.

Once back at his seat, Visage wondered if he should relocate, since there didn't seem to be assigned seating. *Oh, come on, I'm not that bad.* Ranic's thought entered his mind.Ranic still had his feet on his desk, a grin on his face, his arms crossed, and one eye fixed on Visage.

Were you actually crying? Visage telepathically asked when he noticed a tear-stained streak on Ranic's cheek.

"No, no, I just got something in my eye is all." Visage stifled a laugh, pulled out his chair, and sat next to the older red-skinned Twillan. "Just because we look evil doesn't mean we're past feeling. And you, my friend, have very powerful emotions. But you must be wary about opening up to everybeing. Not every Zaharaj is what you would call 'good,'" Ranic offered. After receiving the advice, the Twillan's new Silvarian friend relaxed back into his chair.

Visage didn't really know how to react to Ranic's comment. "But everybeing I've met is really nice."

Lord Baltrix then entered the psychic conversation. "You're right, Visage—so far."

"Why'd you do that, Master? I could have explained it to him!" Ranic retorted. A private telepathic debate then ensued between master and apprentice, after which Baltrix directly addressed Visage.

"My apprentice did make a good point." Baltrix then turned to the rest of the beings in the room. "This goes for all of you; you must be wary of the darkness, for there are some—not many mind you—who are dangerously close to becoming a Fallen."

"Lord Baltrix, what's a Fallen?" Visage piped up.

"Would anybeing like to answer?" Baltrix asked his ar'teths.

Moonreth stood up. "A Fallen is a being who has been fully corrupted by the Zah'harrim. Fallen are easy to spot because the gods placed a curse on them so we can tell that they've become our enemies." He then turned to Visage. "Thanks to the Earthling, I can now prove that Le'Shara hasn't been cursed!" Moonreth gave Visage a slight bow before sitting back down.

"Very good, Moonreth. Does anybeing else have anything to add?" Baltrix again scanned the ar'teths. Another student rose up. She was a demon girl, though disguised as a human. Her dark hair was enveloped by the hood of her cloak. Her eyes were tainted, and she had a mischievous smirk, which was normal for her. "The Fallen are known for their white skin and milky-white eyes; their blood becomes just as black as their hearts; they are mostly unfeeling. The only emotions they seem to possess are jealousy and hatred for everybeing who isn't like them. Once turned, they try to kill anybeing in the vicinity." The human girl looked around the room. "My dar'nra told me that they are really hard to kill." Now she was smiling evilly as she thought further about what her dar'nra had said. "So, be very cautious while playing with the Zah'harrim children!" She then turned around and sat down.

"Thank you, Arisha, for that stirring commentary. I'm sure Lord Nosfaren would no doubt have approved," Lord Baltrix sarcastically noted after rolling his eyes.

"No problem, Lord Baltrix!" Arisha replied without missing a beat, completely ignoring his blatant sarcasm.

Visage turned to Ranic. "Is Arisha Lord Nos's daughter?"

"Yeah, she is," Ranic responded, though he didn't sound too pleased. "She's also the reason why we get into trouble all the time." He put his arms on his desk and rested his chin on the tops of his crossed fingers. "Leave it to a demon to cause problems." At that, he peered at the demoness with disgust.

"But I'm a demon!" Visage hurtfully objected. For a moment, he reminisced about all of the problems he had caused for his own family back on Earth.

Ranic chuckled at Visage's outburst. Leaning back in his chair, he relaxed a bit. "Yeah, but you didn't purposely cause problems. But that one there—she's always out to cause trouble!" With a disgusted look on his face, Ranic nodded his head in Arisha's direction. The quick motion caused his twills to dance a bit.

Visage thought for a moment about Ranic's comments. "So you don't like her, Ranic?" The question hung in the air. Arisha's head turned to the right; apparently, she had overheard the conversation.

Ranic sighed. "Let's just say I don't like hanging out with her."

Visage noticed that Arisha's head was bobbing—from hearty laughter. *I think she's probably like my older noona.* He didn't mean to think so loudly, but every being in the room heard the thought.

Ranic eyed the demon next to him. "Are you talking about one of the twins?"

Visage jumped a bit at the question. *Oh, right—mind readers.* Several ar'teths laughed. "No Ranic,"— Visage slowly shook his head. —"Sara, and Anna are relatively laid back. The person I was thinking of is actually my imo, or aunt, but she's only a few years older than us, so she's more like a sister than an imo."

"So, does this 'sister' or sri'na of yours have a name?"

Oh, that's what sri'na means. "Yeah, she does. Her name is Jun." Visage shivered a bit when he thought about his imo.

Baltrix peered at Visage and at his apprentice. "There will be no private conversations going on during class time," he warned.

Two heads snapped to attention. "Yes, Lord Baltrix," the pair said in unison.

"I'm sorry—it's my fault," Visage offered while he rubbed the back of his head. He quickly glanced at the back of Arisha's head before turning back to Baltrix. "It's just that Arisha reminds me of Jun, and I kinda dragged Ranic into my thought process." Arisha was laughing with gusto at Visage's comment. Visage mused: *That's what I'm talking about!* Ranic jabbed him with his elbow, trying to get his new friend to silence his mind.

Lord Baltrix focused on Visage. "Your comparisons might be accurate, but please keep your mind focused on the here and now."

"Yes, Lord Baltrix," Visage said, looking abashed and slumping into his chair. He was about to pull his hood over his head when Ranic grabbed his wrist to stop him.

"We don't wear our hoods, masks, or blood sorjins while in class," Ranic whispered. He then released Visage's wrist from his grip.

"Oh, sorry. I didn't know... Wait—what's a blood sorjin?"

"Now, that's more like it!" Lord Baltrix enthusiastically welcomed the query and smiled widely. "So, who would like to answer Visage's question?"

Arisha's hand shot up. "Oh, me! Can I tell the loudmouth?" A series of groans came from many of the others in the class. Moonreth put his hand to his face, sliding it down to cover his mouth in order to stifle a grunt. His sri'na had put her head on her desk and was groaning in complaint.

Moonreth couldn't take it; he shot up from his desk and raised his hand. "Master Baltrix, it would be better if I explained blood sorjins to Visage!" He eyed Arisha and immediately headed to the center of the lecture hall where Lord Baltrix was standing.

"I'm sorry, Moonreth, but Arisha volunteered first," Baltrix informed the Night Elf. Moonreth looked dejected; he halted and slowly turned around before heading back up the steps to retake his seat.

"Nice try, Moonreth," Cormack quipped as his friend's ears drooped, and he plopped himself back into his chair.

Arisha, on the other hand, grabbed her blood sorjin. *Perhaps next time, elf boy.* She smirked after she sent her telepathic message to the NightElf and took her spot on the floor.

Moonreth gritted his teeth, and his ears perked up at Arisha's insult. Le'Shara sat back up and put a hand on her ber'nan's shoulder. "Let it go, Moonreth."— Le'Shara glanced at the impertinent demoness. —"she only wants to show off to Visage."

"Yeah, sorry sri. It's just that she draths me off to no end," he whispered.

"I know what you mean," Le'Shara quietly replied, taking a quick glance over at Visage. The young demon was now preoccupied; he was busy staring at the show-off demoness.

Arisha ignored all of the comments and complaints coming from her fellow ar'teths. After putting her blood sorjin back on her belt, she grabbed her cloak with both hands, ripped it off, and sent it fluttering into the air. Though she was in motion, the cloak seemed to hang in the air for a moment before fluttering about and making its slow descent. She activated the ovular green gem on her gloved right hand, and, before it could land, the cloak was surrounded by a glowing light-green mist; it then vanished into a spray of the same light-green-colored sparkles. Arisha wrapped up the drama by giving her classmates a grand bow, causing her long black hair to fall forward and touch the floor. "Thank you, thank you!" she blurted out. She then stood erect, flipped her hair behind her back with her left hand, and flashed a wide smile at Visage.

Ranic grunted and mumbled, "Fraking showoff," under his breath, barely loud enough for Visage to hear.

Visage responded to Ranic's comment with his own thought: *you're right. Jun was bad, but this Arisha girl is way worse!* At first, everybeing looked shocked at Visage's very loud thought but soon erupted into laughter. Even Baltrix was snickering. Arisha turned bright red, stomped her foot in protest, and held her arms to her sides. Completely embarrassed, she looked down and stared at the floor.

"Visage, nice!" Ranic cried, giving the Silvarian a slap on the back.

"You! Visage! Apologize!" Arisha yelled, silencing the laughter. Her eyes were wild, her face was flushed, and she was waging an accusing finger at the rude being.

Moonreth got up from his seat. "You can't make him apologize for thinking!" he retorted. "You're the one showing off, not Visage. You're just drathed off because he called you out on it! You can't demand an apology when he doesn't know how to hide his thoughts. Besides, everybeing here was probably thinking the same thing!" A cloud of tension hung in the air. Arisha balked, lowered her arm, and stood in silence.

After several moments passed, Visage couldn't take it anymore. Ranic looked on in amusement. His small eyebrow rose, and a puzzled expression appeared on his face. *What's he up to now?*

All eyes were on the young demon when he slowly walked down the steps and headed over to Arisha; she was standing like a statue, apparently unable to move. Lord Baltrix didn't interfere. He merely stood behind beside his lectern in silent observation. Like the rest of the class, he was wondering what Visage was up to.

They are so much alike; it's kind of scary. I sure hope this works as well with Arisha as it did for Jun whenever she gets this way. Visage was now only a few feet from the young demoness.

Arisha remained frozen—embarrassed and hurt by the thoughts and comments from her fellow Zaharaj. Her actions weren't completely her fault; she had always been compared to her older siblings. "Why can't you be more like your ber'nan or sri'na," her mi'thia would always ask; she absolutely hated being compared to her siblings! Lost in her own thoughts, she didn't even notice that Visage, who had started the whole incident, was standing in front of her.

Visage breathed in deeply and out slowly before quickly closing the gap and wrapping his arms around the now-stunned demoness. He wished she were a bit shorter so he could whisper into her ear that it was all right and that he was sorry.

Arisha snapped out of her funk. "What the frak!" she exclaimed when she realized that Visage was embracing her. Her eyes went wide!

Visage muttered an apology. "I'm sorry…"

A million things ran through Arisha's mind. *Why you little—I should kill you! How dare you hug me while I'm like this! I hate you! I wish my dar'nra never brought you here!*

Visage was at a loss. All he could think of doing was to finish his attempted apology. "I'm sorry, Arisha." Arisha actually heard the second apology and abruptly shoved the small being away.

"You're sorry! You're sorry! That's all you have to say after embarrassing me like that!" she yelled while tears streamed down her cheeks.

Visage, who had landed on the floor, slowly sat up. Believing that Arisha hadn't meant any of what she had screamed, he took the verbal abuse in stride. *Arisha is exactly like Jun—maybe they were twins, and, for some reason, God had to separate them.*

Though she was livid inside, Arisha managed to speak, "Lord Baltrix, can you have Moonreth give the demonstration? I'd like to return to my seat." Arisha focused her eyes downward, not making eye contact with anybeing in the room.

"You may, if Moonreth would still like to take your place. How about it, Moonreth?" Baltrix looked towards Moonreth, who appeared to be in a state of shock. The Night Elf was finding it hard to process what he had witnessed—and what Baltrix was asking of him. However, he finally managed a humble response. "I would be honored, Master Baltrix," He then headed down the stairs to take the place of the distraught demoness.

Arisha started heading back to her seat, still not making eye contact with anybeing. She retrieved her cloak from her gem, right after it solidified from the glowing green mist, she grabbed it and forcefully threw it around her body. She was grumbling something about the rule relating to not wearing hoods in class. She continued to quietly mutter a garbled mess of curses. Having walked around the first row of desks, she whipped her blood sorjin from her belt and slammed down on top of the desk. The weapon landed with a loud clang. The disgraced demoness then grabbed her chair, pulled it out, and threw her whole body into it in an attempt to disappear into the black-colored, leather, bucket seat.

Moonreth had stopped in front of where Visage had fallen and bent over to offer him a hand to get him back to his feet. The boy gladly took him up on the offer, and, with little effort, the Night Elf had him standing. Both beings glanced over at the broken demoness. *It didn't work like it did with Jun.* Visage let out a sigh of frustration before heading back to his seat.

Having watched the entire ordeal unfold, Baltrix mused, *She's the second demoness he's embarrassed. Hmm, like mi'thia like de'tari.*

"I've never seen Arisha that shaken up before," Ranic commented to Visage while the boy was taking his seat. The young demon's head hung so low that he was able to rest it on his desk, over his crossed arms. Thanks to Ranic's words, he now felt more miserable than ever. "Hey, Visage, you'd better pay attention. Moonreth's about to answer your question," Ranic, poked his glum friend. Though his thoughts were elsewhere, Visage sat up and made a halfhearted attempt at listening to Moonreth's presentation.

"Most of you know, a blood sorjin is a weapon that is used by Verse users. However, this wasn't always so." Moonreth looked around the room, making sure that the others were paying attention. He was pleased to see that even Visage, in his disheartened state, appeared to be attentively watching him. *He must be feeling badly for what he did to Arisha, though it was mostly her fault for showing off like that.*

Lord Baltrix sent out a silent, targeted warning. *Don't let what happened distract you, my ar'teth.*

Moonreth nodded. "Yes. I'm sorry, Master." He quickly refocused on his demonstration and explanation.

"Blood sorjins didn't become mainstream weapons in the Zaharaj until about two hundred onns ago when our galaxy was invaded by a remnant of the worshippers of Skath. It was after that battle that our ancestors seriously began to work on a way to counter the dark sorjins designed by the Verse-using Skathic. That is when Lord Drogoth came up with the idea of using crystallized blood to build an energy weapon. The first blood sorjins didn't work as hoped, but over several onns, and with the help of the Meserino demons, today's sorjins were developed." Moonreth smiled wide when he pulled his own blood sorjin off his belt.

"Um, Moonreth, how do you make blood crystallize?" Visage asked the Night Elf.

Moonreth's smile faded fast when he noticed that Arisha no longer seemed to be interested in the topic at hand. She still had her head down, averting her eyes and blocking her thoughts. *I can't think about her right now.* Moonreth was about to proceed when—

"Can I show him?" Ranic sprung up from his seat, startling every being, especially Visage. When he started mentally pleading with his friend, Moonreth reluctantly nodded and honored his request. The Night Elf placed his blood sorjin back on his belt and slowly made his way back to his seat next to his sri'na.

Ranic wasted no time grabbing his blood sorjin from his desk and quickly heading to the front of the class to stand next to Moonreth. Moonreth shook his head but followed up with a pat on his friend's shoulder. "Good luck," he whispered before he walked past Ranic and returned to his seat.

Ranic held out his hand, which was clutching his silver-and-black cylinder. After pressing the button on the hilt, the blood red blade came to life with a snap hiss. Ranic grinned widely when he noticed Visage's facial expression. *Ohhh!* the young child thought while Ranic started twirling the white-and-red blade. A streak of red trailed behind the blade in its wake. After doing several quick flourishes and two horizontal cross slashes, Ranic held the blade perfectly still.

"This, is a blood sorjin. It is not just a weapon—it's a companion." Ranic then pressed the button twice to shut off the blade, causing it to retreat into the hilt with the emitter still glowing red in the dim lighting. He then tossed the weapon into the air where it spun end-over-end for several feet before plummeting downward. However, using the power of the Verse, Ranic was able to halt it and suspend it vertically at the level of his chest. He then closed his eyes, and the cylinder burst into pieces. The metallic outer shell blossomed out like a flower, and the curved metal pieces, consisting of the weapon's outer shell covers, were held in place, revealing the weapon's inner workings.

A brightly glowing red marble, the very heart of the blade, lifted up and out of the sorjin's central chamber before levitating to Ranic's eye level. When he opened his eyes, the light from the gem reflected in his red-and-gold orbs. In order to inspect the jewel, he reached out slowly, grasped it between his thumb and forefinger, and brought it more closely to his eyes. For a time, he seemed mesmerized by the gem's beauty, but he finally spoke.

"Blood gems are the very core, or heart of our weapons. They contain the blood of the sorjins' owners—however that's a story for another time." He held out the orb, slowly moving his hand in a wide arch so it could be clearly seen by every being in the room. "Blood is the essence of mortal life. It flows through us and sustains our bodies. Some Marcisian scientists have stated that our blood and blood are vessels are our internal tree of life. They have also indicated that our beating heart is like a spring that constantly nourishes our tree. When our blood is crystallized, it becomes like our heart, only it feeds the wires and circuitry of the blood sorjin, creating an energy blade that can cut our enemies and save our lives. And, because it's part of us, we can focus our Verse powers through the blade, creating devastating techniques."

Ranic's lecture was now finished, so he proceeded to restore his sorjin to its previous state. The blood gem left his hand and returned to its central position in the skeletal-like circuitry. Then the pieces of the outer shell returned to their place, clicking when they covered the inner parts and hid the red-glowing gem—along with the rest of the more sensitive guts—behind the safety of the re-formed metal case. With the sorjin restored, Ranic reached out and grabbed hold of the vertically positioned hilt, tossed it lightly into the air, and quickly rescued it from its short fall. He then, unobtrusively returned to his desk and placed the weapon back into its previously assigned slot on the desk. Now that he was again sitting with his feet up, he appeared to be content.

"Thank you, Moonreth and Ranic, for your explanations. Visage, if you have any more questions, please ask Ranic, Moonreth, or Azala after class." Lord Baltrix eyed Ranic and gave a slight nod to Moonreth.

But… I have so many questions, Visage mentally whined.

"Yes, ar'teth Visage. It's gratifying to have an ar'teth who has such a thirst for knowledge. However, we can't keep using class time for common-knowledge questions. You'll have plenty of time to get your questions answered, but you will do better if you are taught one step at a time. After all, this is only your first deronn or, as they say on your planet, 'first day,' here."

Visage caved, giving Baltrix a half-hearted smile and slumping back into his chair, his small frame disappearing into the soft leather cushions.

"So, we'll continue where we left off yederonn," Baltrix began. Once he activated the green gem on his right-gloved hand, the ovular gem emitted a soft green glow from which several transparent charts materialized. The entire room darkened. The dim red overhead lamps shut off only to be replaced by a bright and well-defined image of the galaxy. Solar systems and nebulas spun around a giant black hole. Five distinct arms—consisting of stars, asteroids, and varying nebulas—spun counterclockwise around the massive black anomaly at the galaxy's central apex. The display was enormous, nearly filling the room. The stars shone so brightly that even the planets and their orbiting moons could easily be seen. And, along with this enormous display, a smaller image of the same galaxy was projected on the top of each desk. Visage was so amazed by the technology that he couldn't decide whether to watch the overhead presentation or to focus on the one on his desk.

"As you all know, the Marcisian Empire makes up about seventy-five percent of the Firaxian Galaxy," Baltrix stated while pressing the glowing emblem on his own green-and-transparent display. The ar'teths could now visualize the large portion of the galaxy that was covered in light blue, marking the Empire's territory. "And, even though Zharaj is within the Empire's borders, we are not considered to be a part of it," Baltrix added.

"Yes, Master, but most of us are from Imperial planets, and I've heard that the Empire has been sending delegates to negotiate for Zharaj to be brought under its jurisdiction," Ranic stated with more than a hint of concern.

"Is that true, Lord Baltrix?" one of the other human males asked from the back.

Lord Baltrix sighed. "Unfortunately, that is true." Baltrix looked agitated while he spoke. "We are going to be receiving another envoy from the Empire next mcronn." The room now erupted with chatter.

Ranic scoffed. "What's the big deal? Most everybeing knows that the Zah will be taken over by the Empire—it's only a matter of time. The odds of a takeover are even greater now that those goody, goody Ja'Shari have opened their academy on Firax."Moonreth folded his arms defiantly. "I heard that the Ja'Shari were given Firax by the Emperor himself!"

Visage leaned over to Ranic. "Do you not like these... Ja'Shari?" he whispered.

Ranic shrugged, "It's not so much a matter of like as it is a matter of angst."

"I don't understand..."

Baltrix couldn't help but overhear the conversation. "I wouldn't say angst, exactly, my apprentice."

"Oh, really. Then what would you call it, Master!" Ranic blurted.

"You know, Ranic, the Ja'Shari are not our enemies," Moonreth interjected, attempting to calm his friend.

Ranic grunted. "They're not our friends, either, Moonreth." Ranic mumbled so quietly that only Visage heard his gripe.

Baltrix re-joined the conversation. "No, but they are our rivals, Moonreth. After all, both the Zaharaj and the Ja'Shari are vying for the same Verse users, and since more beings feel attuned more to the Jah than the Zah, the Ja'Shari are getting the majority of them. This is why our own numbers are thinning." Baltrix looked at the mostly empty room with frustration and disgust.

"But my master told me that there were over a million Zaharaj! Isn't that a lot!" Nate yelled out from the back.

Visage gasped when the Twillan next to him started mumbling incoherently.

"Considering the size of our galaxy, not to mention the Skath worshippers who are still lurking about the universe, no, Nate, we don't have all that many. To be exact, there are one point four million beings in the Zaharaj. Does any being know how many Verse users there are in the Ja'Shari?" Baltrix scanned the room and noted that the one being who probably knew the answer was sitting silently with her head down. *That's odd. Arisha normally would have blurted out the answer.* Since no being was responding, he answered his own question. "The Ja'Shari have three point one million beings in their ranks."

"But that's more than twice what we've got!" Nate exclaimed.

Baltrix stretched out his arms to accentuate his point. "Hence all of the empty seats! Unfortunately, it's like this in all of our temples. I remember a time when all of our lecture halls were full. This... this is disheartening and aggravating!" Baltrix lowered his hands; his eyes followed. While standing under the spinning galaxy, the dark lord seemed smaller than usual to his ar'teths.

"So, Master, what changed?" Ranic queried. He started playing with his left twill, twirling the tip of his lengthy head tail around his index finger. He was concerned about is master's state of mind.

Baltrix's eyes immediately shot up. "What changed?" he said to himself more than to his audience. *What changed? The fraking Ja'Shari are what changed!* he telepathically shouted. His breaths were shallow; he inhaled and exhaled in rapid succession. Baltrix had lost his cool in front of his class, but he couldn't help it—he wanted his ar'teths to know the truth. "We were forced into an id'rthic deal with the Ja'Shari! And it was none other than my fellow Councilors who signed it! I was one of only two who protested! But Lord Nosfaren refused to listen to reason and signed the fraking—"

"Master, please calm down!" Ranic pleaded.

Baltrix looked as though he was about to attack his apprentice for his outburst, but after looking around the room at the faces of his terrified ar'teths, he closed his eyes and settled down. His anger slowly ebbed.

"I apologize for my outburst." Baltrix then bowed to his class. "But it wasn't a fair deal," he said, rising back up with a scowl.

Boy, that scowl makes him look just like the monster from Bram Stoker's book, Visage mused.

"What deal was it that the Council agreed to?" Moonreth timidly asked, still looking terrified. He wasn't sure if he was adding fuel to the fire or, in this case, inferno.

Baltrix clenched his fists; his eyes narrowed, and his scowl became a full sneer. "It was called the Treaty of Firax, and in it was an edict stating that all beings attuned more to the Jah would be taken and trained by the Ja'Shari and all beings attuned more to the Zah would come to the Zaharaj." Baltrix spoke softly, but his tone was so scathing that his class thought his very words would kill any being who got too close.

"That's not fair!" Visage rose from his seat. "I know I'm new here, but you said that most beings were attuned to the light form of the Verse. With the deal the Council made, of course the Zaharaj numbers would decrease! My om..." Visage shook his head. "I mean my mother, she works for my uncle, and she's always talking about bad business deals, and that sounds like a bad one to me!" He rubbed the top of his head before sinking back into his seat.

"I agree, Visage, it was a bad deal!" Baltrix spat. He remained silent for several moments before calming down enough to continue. "I'm sorry class, my passion and anger seem to have driven away my will to teach, and with the tension I have caused, I sense you are in no mood to learn so... class dismissed." With that said, Baltrix turned off the glowing gem and the holo image of the galaxy quickly vanished.

While watching his master exit the room, Ranic picked his blood sorjin up from his desk and snapped it to his belt. "He knows you're right, Visage. We did get the slith end of the stick, but it was either sign the treaty or go to war."

Visage peered up at the Twillan in disbelief. "Would it really have come to that?"

Ranic shrugged. "That's what has my master so aggravated—we honestly didn't know."

"You didn't know?" Visage looked pained when several emotions hit him all at once. "But I thought the Council was powerful?"

"Oh, it is; it's just that the members all had different visions of the future. Several saw the 'war' outcome if they didn't sign the treaty while others foresaw the Zaharaj being wiped out by an unknown force if they didn't sign. So, of the thirteen members on the Council, only two voted against it." Ranic patted Visage on his shoulder and headed for the stairs.

"So, Council members believed there was about an eighty-five percent chance of war if they didn't vote to ratify the treaty?" Visage asked while he stood up.

Ranic halted halfway down the steps and quickly turned his head, sending his twills flailing out widely before landing and draping down his right side. "Good observation, Visage, and yes, that is why, as my master said, we were forced into it." Ranic turned his head and started playing with one of his twills. "The cost would have been too great." After finishing his sobering thought, he continued his trek towards the door.

Visage was about to say something else when he was startled by Arisha. Since Arisha was standing several steps below him, he was able to look her in the eyes. "Visage, I challenge you to a dual in the pit." She spoke slowly. Her eyes were ablaze, and an evil smirk adorned her normally pretty face.

The room went silent. Ranic bumped into the door. Fortunately, he was hardheaded, so the door probably felt more pain than he did! He then did a double take when he thought he misheard something in his audio cones. Moonreth, Le'Shara, Envine, and Cormack were all in a state of shock. "You can't do that, Arisha!" Cormack, the blue-skinned Twillan blurted. "He hasn't been here for a full deronn yet. He can't fight; he doesn't know how!"

Arisha turned on her toes and faced the Twillan, who was standing on the floor of the hall proper and looking up at the imposing demoness. "Cormack, shut the frak up! I wasn't talking to you!" She then turned back to face the much younger demon. "I'll teach you not to humiliate me in front of the class, pathetic Earth child." The look of disgust on her face made Visage wince.

"But I didn't do anything!" Visage protested while his arms reached for the ceiling in exasperation.

"You didn't do anything! You did something all right! You thought things about me and then went and hugged me! I hate you, so now we fight!" Arisha countered.

The frustrated Silvarian was fed up. "Fine, I'll fight you!"

Arisha smiled gleefully. *Now I get to pummel this pathetic Earthling into paste in front of all of the Zaharaj!*

I have a bad feeling about this, Ranic, Le'Shara, Moonreth, and Cormack simultaneously thought.

A large group of ar'teths headed for the lifts. Arisha was at the head of the gathering; Visage walked behind her. Moonreth and Ranic were flanking their friend while Le'Shara and her friend Cormack followed several steps behind. *I feel sorry for him,* Moonreth thought.

I know what you mean, Ranic responded, glancing at the glum-looking Silvarian who was standing between them.

Do you think we can talk our way out of this one? Moonreth added, looking from the Silvarian to his friend.

Ranic shrugged; "I seriously doubt it. This *is* Arisha, after all."

The group arrived at the lifts and Arisha stepped in. "Ugh!" she moaned in disgust when Visage followed her, taking up residence in the far-right corner of the lift. Moonreth and the others climbed in. Then the doors closed. Arisha pressed the keypad, sending the lift down into the very bowels of the temple—into the ancient caverns of the planet itself.

"I'm usually excited about going into the pit," Envine commented while he eyed the being in the corner, "but not this time. I hope you won't die, kid. Arisha isn't one to hold back." He clearly recalled his matches with Arisha, the memories of which sent a chill down his spine.

12

Duels are the Pits

The lift stopped, the doors opened, and all of the occupants exited. The ar'teths were now far below the bottom levels of the temple. The place was known as the pit. It was essentially a large ancient cavern, which had been hollowed out by ancient miners. Visage was the last to leave the lift. The other beings spread out and headed for several different sets of stairs that were carved out of the rocks. The stairs led up to an observation deck. The young demon walked alone down a short and narrow passageway. Before him lay a grand stadium or coliseum. His sapphire-colored eyes went wide when he noticed that the sets of stairs not only led to an upper deck but also to multiple rows of benches, which, like the stairs, were carved out of stone. *This looks just like the coliseum in ancient Greece where all those gruesome events took place. I remember the book that oma had that described everything that went on in that place.* Once Visage was done musing, he stared up and beheld an amazing sight: red lighting intermingled with stalactites. The combination yielded a totally unexpected and spectacular display. This display was in stark contrast to the stadium's walls, floor, and seating, which were all constructed from the same cool black stone that had been used to construct the entrance to the temple. The onyx-colored stonework was intricately carved out of the cavern itself. The dim-red lighting reflected off the stone, creating a fantastic, though eerie, ambiance.

***

Arisha flashed a malicious smile before taking center stage in the large rectangular field. She then pointed an accusing finger at Visage and yelled at the top of her lungs, "Hey, Earth boy—we're here to fight not take in the scenery! Get over here so I can shove your punishment down your throat!"

***

The whole temple was in an uproar over the news of the impending fight between the demons. As soon as Lord Baltrix learned about it, he stormed over to the lifts. His goal: to get to the pit and stop the fight. *Of all the fracking, imbecilic, reckless—*His thoughts were interrupted by a loud cough from behind. After snapping his body around, he realized that not only was Lord Nos there, but Lady Vira and Lady Riza were directly behind him.

"I heard my de'tari is causing havoc again." Nos sounded irked but not necessarily surprised.

Baltrix rolled his eyes. *That's the understatement of the onn.* Riza and Vira snickered in agreement.

The four beings exited their lift while several others exited the four adjacent ones. Lord Nos had been hoping to stop the fight before it started, but, with his de'tari involved, he didn't know how he could pull that off, especially considering the size of crowd. And more and more observers were arriving all the time.

By the time the group reached the field, the fight had not yet commenced. Arisha was continuing to have a conniption fit, and Visage was wandering around the grand coliseum, still attempting to take in its full scope. The longer the boy wandered around, the more intense Arisha's ire became. The young Silvarian obviously didn't seem to care, even when more and more black-cloaked beings took their seats around the circular stone-carved structure. *It's a good thing my wife isn't here to see this,* Lord Nos thought as he watched his frustrated de'tari trying unsuccessfully to get Visage's attention.

"Hey! Visage! Get over here and face me!" Arisha screamed. However, Visage was too busy surveying the training weapons, which were resting in a rack on the wall, to pay any attention to the crazed girl's rants.

Riza startled Arisha. She had made her way up behind the girl and nonchalantly commented, "I guess he's not too worried about your challenge, Arisha." Arisha froze for a moment before slowly turning around. Two pair of bright red eyes met, but the older and wiser demoness easily stared the girl down. She then turned to Visage, who was continuing to inspect the training equipment, and shouted, "Visage! Get your twin-tailed crath over here!"

Visage jumped several feet back from the rack on the wall. "I... I didn't touch anything. I didn't mean to..." After waving his hands emphatically to stave off any forthcoming accusations, he turned around. "Riza?" was all he could squeak out when he noticed the tall demoness. She was leaning on her left leg with her arms crossing just below her massive chest. A disappointed look adorned her fine-featured face. Her right foot was in constant motion, and her bare foot was slapping against the cool, smooth surface of the coliseum floor.

In a literal flash, Riza's body evolved into a blur of motion. She flew over to the smaller demon and grabbed the two front folds of his cloak, just under his neck. After squeezing the two halves together, she picked up the boy and elevated him to her eye level. His feet dangled about helplessly while the demoness stared at him, her pupils nothing more than slits. Despite being in such a precarious position, Visage was able to muse, *She definitely looks demonic all right.*

Riza simply ignored Visage's insolent thought and demanded, "Visage, what did you do to cause this!"

At first, Visage averted Riza's gaze. He then began taking short glances at the ominous-looking demoness and apologetically replied, "I honestly don't know." No sooner had he uttered the words than his mind was flooded with scenes from the lecture hall. Everybeing in the place was able to see his thoughts—and hear them.

Riza's eyes widened. She considered hitting the boy but instead let go of his cloak. Though he landed hard on the floor, he managed to keep his balance. Riza's face contorted only briefly before she burst out laughing. "That's what this is about... Seriously!" she exclaimed. She looked over her shoulder at Arisha and laughed even more heartily.

Arisha was not taking Riza's outburst well at all. Her anger flared, and she pointed towards the smaller demon. "Stop laughing Riza! That fiancé of yours already agreed to this duel, so you can't interfere!"

Riza straightened, slowly turned to face the angry girl, and quickly retorted. "Oh? You think so?" She reached down, took Visage by the arm, and dragged him over to the center of the arena. *Don't test my patience child; there is much I can do. First, I can level the playing field.* After letting go of Visage's arm and standing between the two combatants, Riza held out her right hand. "Now, Arisha, give me your blood sorjin." Her voice was cold and commanding.

Arisha peered at Riza's open hand and huffed before begrudgingly taking off her weapon and slapping it into the demoness's palm. "Here!" she spat.

Riza ignored Arisha's snide attitude and continued with her instructions. "Now, both of you remove your boots and cloaks. Visage obliged, immediately removing his footwear and taking off his cloak, though saddened by its pending confiscation. He was so attached to the cloak that he draped it across his arms for a moment before offering it to Riza. Realizing that Visage was on the verge of tears, Riza gave him a reassuring grin. *Don't worry; you'll get it back after the fight is over.* Her encouraging thought brought a smile back to the young demon's face.

Arisha was more defiant as she whipped off her boots and brought them up to her right hand—the one that had the glove with the green gem in it. The ovular emerald started glowing, and her boots turned into a light green mist, quickly vanishing into the gem. She then whipped off her cloak and the same thing happened; it also disappeared into the emerald-colored mist.

Riza was satisfied and looked to Visage, whose myriad of questions were already being broadcast to the group. She spoke. "Save your questions for later, Visage! Concentrate on the duel! Now, here are the rules. First, there won't be any use of weapons; secondly, if you're sent out of the field, you've lost and the match is over; thirdly, if one of the beings loses consciousness, it's also over; fourthly, in this match, Verse powers are restricted." Riza paused to glare at Arisha. "In addition, if you douse them, we'll know," she warned.

Arisha mentally whined, *Yeah, yeah, whatever.*

Riza continued. "The fifth and final rule is—don't break anything that's outside the designated area." She then headed off the field of battle.

Visage estimated the battleground to be about the size of two American football fields. It was square and its edges were marked by a series of double-layered glyphs. The walls of the stone bleachers were several feet from the corners of the arena. If one had an aerial view, the field would look like a square that sat inside a large bowl; again, it was very much like the ancient coliseum of Rome.

Riza was now standing just outside the first layer of glyphs. Using her indren'freth, she rose from the ground and flew into the air to a spot where all of the gathered beings could see her. Spinning around slowly and prepared to present the speech that was customarily used in these types of duels. After reaching for her gem, she pulled an earpiece out from the green mist, positioned the device into her pointy right ear, and then spoke. "Lords and ladies of the Zaharaj, this deronn two ar'teths have decided to settle their dispute with a duel. They are Arisha from Zharaj and Visage from Earth. This match will be held in a rocky environment." When Riza raised her hand, the glyphs around the battle area started to glow purple. "Aaand, begin!" She lowered her hand in a frontal chop, and the match commenced.

***

The ground rumbled beneath Visage's feet as the smooth black stone was replaced by something with a much rougher texture. The whole floor seemed to rise several feet. Pillars of stone then erupted from the now turbulent rock-filled area. Visage had to dodge to the right when one of the pillars rose up where he had just been standing. Immediately thereafter, he had to contort his body in order to avoid being slammed by yet another smaller pillar. Forced to get into a low crouch, the young demon didn't stand again until the rumbling had ceased, and the floor had become solid and stable. Unfortunately, by the time he was able to focus on the task-at-hand, Arisha was nowhere to be seen. "Ah, there she is." He finally spotted his quarry. She was flying over a stone pillar, which was several yards away and over to his left. The fact that Visage could barely keep up with her movements could have proved to be disastrous. However, just in nick of time, he detected the young demoness's charge. Arisha was already in motion. She let out a blood-curdling scream before leading with her right knee. Visage threw his hands up in order to protect his face from the expected blow—a cross block—but the blow never materialized. Instead, Arisha was now on the ground. In a flash, she covered the remaining distance. Visage's response was too slow. He had no time to mount a defense before Arisha carried out her plan. She had delved flat onto the floor, pivoted on her hands, and sent both of her legs into a full circle. Her first leg swept Visage off his feet; the second came at him, hitting him in the center of his chest. The blow sent the boy flying, his body smashing hard against one of the stone pillars. The force of impact was so massive that he created an indent in the side of the solid pillar. His whole body jerked violently, after which his small form hit the ground and lay completely still.

"Well, that was... anticlimactic." Lord Baltrix was atop the highest tier of the stone balconies. Leaning on the metal railing, he could see Visage's lifeless appearing body lying prone on the ground.

"I wouldn't count him out just yet," Lord Nosfaren replied to his former apprentice and friend. He was smiling widely under his mask. His two red orbs burned brightly for an instant when he looked over at Baltrix. "After all, Lord Baltrix, you know what he is."

I know he's a Silvarian, but he has that seal on his back now, and your de'tari just knocked him out. Baltrix's silent statement caused Nos's eyes to roll.

"You forget who his *real* dar'nra is, my young friend."

Baltrix balked, and his eyes now focused more intently on the seemingly unconscious Visage. "Arnen?"

Lord Nos laughed. "Arnen indeed! My de'tari has no idea what she'sjust awakened." Lord Nos's thoughts drifted out into the crowd.

"Is it over? Already?" Moonreth asked nobeing in particular. His mouth then hung agape, along with the mouths of all those who were observing.

"Is he dead?" Le'Shara asked, turning to her ber'nan, who was still staring in disbelief.

"Arisha! That fraking bakrath! She doesn't pull any punches, even for a newbie!" Ranic cried. "I just knew she was going to do this!" Ranic was pulling on both his twills—an indication of how upset he was after having witnessed his new friend get the slith beaten out of him.

"I don't think that was enough to kill a demon, nor do I think that this contest is at all over, as you all seem to believe." Envine shared his insight, then crossed his legs, put his left elbow to his knee, and rested his chin on the palm of his hand. He then started drumming his chin with his fingers. Without realizing it, he mimicked Lord Nos's sentiment: *I don't think Arisha has any idea what she just did.*

Right after the Therosian's telepathic message permeated the group, Visage's prone body began to stir. The expressions on the four friends' faces ran the gamut from worry to hope to wide smiles when the Silvarian slowly got back to his feet. Arisha couldn't believe what she was seeing. Not only was Visage not out cold, but he was back on his feet and seemed to be smiling! His countenance had changed completely. The smirk that had previously been on his face had disappeared and was replaced by disturbing cackling. "Oh, this is great! I've never felt pain like this before! I feel so alive!" Visage's body then burst into blue-and-black flames. The seal on his back glowed brightly, and the first ring of runes turned from a soft blue to a dark purple. Visage's body slowly returned to its demon form. His fangs, claws, and talons all grew back.

Behind him, two black tails with fiery-purple ends erupted from the top of his pants' waistline. His skin turned to a shade of the midnight sky, and the normal blue designs and splotches that adorned his body were now a sickening shade of purple. The young demon's once sapphire-blue-colored orbs opened and now revealed much colder, ice blue ones. His pupils were again slit, and both were focused on his opponent.

Arisha began sweating and her mind began racing. She remembered having heard about this "technique" from her parents. However, her thoughts were quickly cut off. Like an angry meteor, the blue-and-black creature charged her. In an attempt to avoid the terrifying attack, the demoness flew backward. However, since she had had no time to assess her surroundings, she flew right into one of the stone pillars. Luckily, she had her wits about her enough to jump, thus just avoiding Visage's flame-covered fist. Unfortunately, Visage's fist did not miss the pillar, which buckled under the impact of the blow. Shards of stone, like mini comets, shot out and either collided with other stone pillars or hit the invisible shield produced by the glyphs that were surrounding the arena. Wherever the projectiles landed, a splash of purple energy could be seen at the point of impact, causing the barrier to take on a purplish hue. With its structural integrity now compromised, the pillar started toppling. The pillar made many great cracking and groaning sounds when it collided with the defensive barrier. The whole shield rippled in a flash of bright purple as waves of energy bounced around the shield's full perimeter, the top of the shield being just below the stalactite ceiling. The mass of shield energy and the debris of rock and settling dust obscured observers', as well as Visage's own, vision.

The blinding screen of dust gave Arisha, who was now standing on top of one of the smaller pillars, an opportunity to break the first ring of her own Vorihelcom seal. She closed her eyes and began her chant. "May my demon's blood awake! First seal break!" Within a moment, her form began its transformation. Two bat-like wings emerged from the two holes that were cut out of the back of her shirt. A long, slender, red-and-black tail swished around behind her, and her skin changed from cream colored to red; the red was randomly adorned with black patterns and designs. Her hands and feet now ended with razor-like claws and talons, and fangs grew and lengthened inside her mouth. Her demon eyes changed from the normal amber-and-red tint to a deep red, and her pupils became slit. Once the dust finally settled and the shield had again become invisible, two demons prepared to reignite their battle.

Arisha's demon eyes focused on the still fire-engulfed Silvarian. *I don't know if even this will be enough to take him down.* Before Arisha had time to unwrap and open her wings, the Silvarian was upon her and grabbed her by her tail.

"Just where do you think you're going?" the ice-cold voice asked in response to Arisha's yelp.

This is crazy! What kind of monster are you? How do you know that technique? Are you trying to kill me! Arisha's mind was racing with thoughts when, in a single motion, Visage yanked her tail and sent her flying. This time she was the one who made a crater, only this crater was in the stone surface below the pillar under which she had just been standing. She tried to stand but couldn't; Visage was standing on top of her. Three of the talons on his toes were pushed up against her neck. Though he wasn't pressing down hard enough to draw blood, Arisha could definitely feel their dangerous tips against her skin. *I'm sorry. I'm sorry,* she mentally pleaded. While she looked up at the black-and-blue inferno, she could barely make out the demon child's cold-blue eyes.

"Oh, now you're sorry," Visage sneered. "Aren't you the one who wanted this duel? I wasn't trying to purposely hurt you, and then you went and did this to me!" Visage hesitated a few moments before removing his talons from his opponent's neck.

13

Cloak of Darkness

Lord Baltrix and Lord Nos were astonished by the ferocity of the battle. Though Arisha had made a desperate attempt to win by breaking her own seal, she was outmatched by the younger Silvarian. "That was unexpected," Baltrix said aloud.

Nos assertively shook his head. "No, my apprentice, it wasn't."

Baltrix went wide-eyed and his mouth opened, but he wasn't able to speak. *I wonder what he meant by that?*

Nos gestured towards the Silvarian. "He's using the Cloak of Darkness; this fight was over the moment he transformed."

Cloak of Darkness—I've never heard of that technique, Baltrix thought.

"Not many beings know about it, because it's a skill that only a high-level demon can master," Nos responded.

"High level? Are you talking about the greater demon races?" Baltrix asked.

"Well, technically, all three greater demon races can use it, but only those of noble heritage can wield it like he can," Nos explained, nodding his head slightly towards Visage.

"Nobility? I know Arnen was the Silvarian king, but is it true that Visage is his dar'tari?"

"Indeed he is, my apprentice," Nos solemnly proclaimed.

Baltrix took note of his friend's demeanor. "Why so down, Master?"

"Arnen gave us the Cloak of Darkness and Orran as his legacy. It's just sad that he's gone and that Orran is forced to walk down this path. Now, I believe you asked me about the technique. It's created by using the Zah'harrim and then combining and mixing it with one's own indren'freth. Since this planet is permeated with Zah power, it's very easy for those who know about the technique to use it. It seems our Silvarian friend figured it out all by himself. The thing is, it's a nearly unbreakable defense: It repels all attacks, except for those from God Slayers or Soul Eaters. That's why I said that my de'tari lost this match the moment Visage used that technique."

Baltrix focused on the Silvarian child. "Do you pity him, Master?"

Nos thought a moment before answering. "Yes, Baltrix, I do pity him. I don't know—has any being told you about the God Wars or War of the Gods?"

"Not really, Master. Why? Are they really that important?"

"That depends on your point of view. To some, they matter a lot; others could care less. To me, that time was very dark. I'll never forget it!"

There's something very wrong here. I can feel it. Baltrix's thoughts betrayed him.

"Very wrong indeed," Nos replied. Baltrix could tell that his friend was carrying a heavy burden and waited patiently for him to open up. His patience paid off.

"A long time ago, the gods were at war. Skath, a greater God of Darkness, found a way to kill a soul. His new discovery armed him with power beyond even his wildest dreams. He approached the Meserino demons and asked them to join him in overthrowing the Gods of Light. The Meserino king refused, but his rejection did not deter Skath. The God of Darkness found a willing ally—one of the larger Meserino clans."

Baltrix's curiosity got the better of him. "Which clan joined him, Master?"

"The Ze'therac clan."

When the pair of Lords saw Visage remove his foot from Arisha's neck, their conversation temporarily ceased. Lord Nos let out a deep sigh of relief.

"Master, I think I read somewhere that the Meserino clan that joined Skath was wiped out after ferociously fighting with the Silvarians. Is that true?" Baltrix ventured to ask.

"For the most part, yes, that is accurate. The Silvarians had joined The Gods of Light and defended their home from Skath's forces and his demon allies. In the end, Arnen was the only Silvarian left. He set out to confront the Dark God in his own universe, fighting him three times to a draw."

"Wow, a Greater Demon fought a Grand God to a draw—that's impressive!" Lord Baltrix touted.

Nos again nodded towards the Silvarian and responded to Baltrix's comment. "Arnen was able to confront and hold his own against Skath because he used the same technique that Visage had used against Arisha."

Baltrix also gazed at Visage. "You mean he used the Cloak of Darkness!"

"Yes, but in the end Arnen himself was killed. I told him not to go back. I tried to convince him that Skath was a problem for the gods, not for us!" Nosfaren was reliving the pain from his past. He clutched the metal rail so hard that he left his handprints.

Lord Baltrix put his hand on his friend's shoulder in an attempt to calm him down. "I'm sorry, Vlad," Nos offered. Baltrix was surprised that Nos had addressed him by his real name, but smiled, nonetheless, and continued to listen. "Of all the races, only the Greater Demons had power on par with the Grand Gods. Arnen and his Silvarians—despite their power—did the bidding of the gods. Gods create, but they also need beings who can destroy, at times. I don't remember how or why the demons became equal to the gods, but they did. The Vorihelcom vanished, and the Meserino demons became lazy; they didn't get involved in the flow of the universe. They cared neither about the gods nor about their creations. The Silvarians became the living wrecking balls of the universe. They received orders from the gods, and, like obedient dogs, they carried them out."

Baltrix was shocked at Nosfaren's assertion. "The Silvarians were destroyers!"

"Well—yes. Gods created planets, solar systems, and galaxies, but they needed beings who would be willing and able to destroy the creations they no longer used or needed, so the Silvarians took the job, as distasteful as it was," Nos explained.

Baltrix looked downcast. "I had no idea."

"Most beings don't. The truth was covered up and forgotten when Arnen was killed. That was a long time ago, but I... I still remember. I was there, and I will never forget the gods and demons who died trying to protect our very existence." By this time, Nos was on the verge of tears. When he looked at Baltrix the man could see how wet the mighty Meserino's eyes were.

"Lord Nos, how can a soul be killed?" Baltrix asked, not sure if he really wanted to know the answer.

Before responding, Nos peered over at the battle scene once more, just to make sure his de'tari was alright. He used the sleeve of his cloak to dry his eyes. Once assured that the battle appeared to be over, he continued. "That information is extremely sensitive and should not be uttered, Lord Baltrix. Nevertheless, I trust you to keep this conversation to yourself. Do you agree to do that?"

"Of course, Lord Nos, you can trust me. I will never reveal a confidence."

"Alright, Baltrix I'll tell you, but first, do you know how a soul is made?"

"No, I do not." Baltrix was intently listening to his former master.

"Before we are even considered souls, we are born of the very universe itself. We are nothing more than globs of energy that are self-aware, intelligent, and endlessly seeking for further knowledge, life, and purpose. In that state, we are taken by either gods or demons and our energy becomes a soul, through spiritual birth. After some time, we gain physical bodies, born to physical beings. When this happens, most beings become mortal, whereas demons are born into immortality. The common thread we all share is that, in our pre-soul life, we are nothing more than energy, and that energy, though it cannot be destroyed, can be eaten."

"Wait, Master, what do you mean by 'eaten'?" Baltrix asked, interrupting his friend's thoughts.

"I was just coming to that. Be patient," Nos admonished. Baltrix silenced his mind at Nos's stern command. "Energy—even the energy of one's being or soul—can be devoured by a weapon—a weapon that the Dark God Skath designed and created. God killers are no ordinary blades. No. These blades have a piece of their own creator's soul embedded within them. The soul is then bathed in the creator's physical essence, or commonly referred to as blood, the blade is essentially quenched by the life supplying liquid, after having absorbed it into itself. Once forged, these God killers can then eat another being's life energy. The enemy's soul then becomes a part of the soul of the weapon, providing it with the energy it needs in order to grow and strengthen."

Baltrix went wide-eyed. "Wow, that's a lot to take in."

"Yes, I believe that is enough for any being to take in, Baltrix." Nos proceeded to seal up his old memories. Once this feat was accomplished, he returned to his normally cheerful self. "That was the past, and now we look to the future. Unfortunately, Arnen is gone, but Visage is here—though I do wonder why Eendril has decided now, of all times, to grant the child a physical body? Perhaps we will learn in time, or perhaps old Eendril will keep the secret forever."

Nos was finished instructing and musing and again turned his attention to the battle. He peered at the Silvarian and realized that, for some strange reason, Visage's presence was providing him with a renewed sense of hope. After giving his former apprentice a slap on the back, he made a surprising statement. "You know, Baltrix, even though I'm already immortal, at least you have the opportunity to gain eternal life."

Baltrix was stunned by Nos's pronouncement and took a moment to recover. "Wait! I thought immortality *was* eternal life."

Nos chuckled "No, my friend, they are completely different."

"How so?"

Nos's answer was not delivered in his normally reasonable fashion. Rather, it could be classified as a downright curt response. "Are you serious! You are from the same planet where God's first son was born, are you not!"

Baltrix thought back to his time on Earth when he was known as Vlad the Impaler, a dark prince who fought the Turkish army, laying it to waste. He now reached to his neck and, from under his shirt, pulled out one of the few keepsakes he had brought from his home world. Hanging from his silver necklace was his most prized possession—a cross, which had been crafted out of pure silver. He remembered his old faith, never having lost hope in the God who had shed His own blood on his behalf. *I've tried my entire life to make up for all the terrible things I did back—*

Nos interrupted. "I see you're still wearing that cross around your neck."

Baltrix diplomatically replied to Nos's somewhat snide remark. "Yes, and I always will be wearing it. Now, can you explain something to me? Just what is the difference between immortality and eternal life?"

This time, Nos outright laughed at his friend's question. "You carry your God's death device, call yourself by His name, consider yourself to be one of His disciples, and you really don't know the answer to that question?"

Baltrix was perplexed, angry, and curious all at the same time. Nos, himself, was astonished at his friend's response, made very apparent by the look on Baltrix's face. "To be blunt, that God of yours granted all mortal beings immortality when he died on the cross—as signified by the one you're wearing. Why do you carry such a trinket, anyway? I don't wear a scythe around my neck to remember my dar'nra." Lord Nos rubbed the underside of his chin a few times before continuing. "As for eternal life, only the beings who, as you say, 'endure to the end', gain eternal life. I thought all you Earthlings knew this. I mean, didn't He teach you beings anything while He was still in the mortal realm?"

Baltrix shook his head. "Actually, some of what He taught was lost after the deaths of his first disciples. This is the first time I've heard anybeing teach about the difference between immortality and eternal life. I'm surprised that a demon would even know about it!"

"Oh, please, I've been alive for ages, Baltrix. And that God of yours adopted us Meserino demons after the war, so of course we know what his favorite kids are up to..." Nosfaren shrugged. "At least most of the time," he said dismissively while rubbing the back of his hood-covered head.

"So, if you're as powerful as the gods, why don't you do what they do?" Baltrix asked, a bit taken aback by Nos's sudden outburst of laughter.

"Not a chance! Like I've said, we Meserino demons are lazy. Do you have any idea what looking after a universe would entail? The logistics alone would be a complete nightmare, not to mention looking after all of those untold trillions of kids! My wife and I only have four, and even they're a handful." Nos then turned back to the field. "Speaking of kids, I wonder what happened to my own little troublemaker?"

Baltrix stared at his friend for a while. *Wow! Being a god sounds like a lot more trouble than it's worth. At least I won't have to deal with any of that until I die, and, with this awakened blood of mine, that won't be for another hundred onns or so. Until then, I'll teach as many Zaharaj children as I can. I hope that my teachings will help keep them safe from the remnant of Skath's forces. I don't understand why Eendril can't just wipe them out of the universe.*

Nos was quick to respond. "The short answer is, He wants to keep us focused and humble."

Baltrix smiled at the thought. "Always vigilant, Master?"

"Absolutely, my friend! It's a big galaxy and an even bigger universe, and the least we can do is keep these kids of His safe. And, speaking of humble, it looks like my de'tari has finally learned a valuable lesson." *I'm glad I brought that Silvarian kid here,* Nos thought before he nodded his head approvingly.

14

Forfeit?

Visage lifted his talons from Arisha's neck, while the black-and-blue flames danced around him, his eyes were focused on the stunned demoness. Arisha had barely moved since her violent landing. However, she finally turned her head to face Riza when the elder demoness began to announce the winner of the duel. "The duel has been decided. Visage is the winner." Several beings in the crowd cheered while others murmured among themselves.

The stone pillars started to vanish, and the ground once again shook while the mess of stone began to sink and disappear. Coincidentally, the glyphs, which made up the barrier around the perimeter, stopped glowing, and the rough stone floor beneath the demons' feet suddenly returned to its smooth, cool, marble-like surface.

Riza walked over to the two demons. Arisha was still stunned and lying face up on the floor. "I'm impressed, Visage! I never would have expected one so young to be able to utilize the Cloak of Darkness!" the older demoness offered with a wink.

Arisha then did a forward handspring and was back on her feet. "I protest! He cheated!" she shrieked, causing Riza to flinch and raise an eyebrow at the younger Meserino.

"Oh really, how so?"

The protester floundered, trying to find the right words. She finally belted out, "He broke the rules!"

"And which rules did he break?" Riza's attitude was very cocky; she knew she was getting under Arisha's skin. While hiding behind an innocent smile, she was actually laughing quite hysterical on the inside.

"He used the Cloak of Darkness; that has to be breaking the rules!" Arisha blurted.

Riza shook her head. "Sorry, Arisha, but the Cloak of Darkness is not considered a weapon, and besides, even though it's an advanced technique, its use is not exactly rare among us demons. By the way, Visage, good job on discovering it on your own. It usually takes most demons several onns of study to learn and then another fifty onns to master!"

"Thanks, Riza… I think." Visage slumped with a frown. "But this Cloak of Darkness, as you call it, doesn't make me feel very good while I'm using it," Visage looked up at Riza when he replied. His voice wasn't as cold as it had been during the match, but it was still a bit edgy. After bringing them up to his chest, he realized that his hands were still emitting blue-and-black flames. By repeatedly clenching and unclenching his fists and concentrating intently, he was able to extinguish the flames. Though he felt as though he should be feeling elated about his win.

I thought I was through with turning into a fireball stuff. Wasn't that the main reason why I was brought to this planet—so I wouldn't destroy Earth by using this power? I hate the feeling I get when I use it!

"What do you expect when you gather Zah'harrim around you and then absorb it into yourself—sunshine and rainbows?" Riza sarcastically asked.

The now black-and-purple-skinned Silvarian shrugged. "So, just how long is this darkness going to last?" he questioned, while he used his hand to make a sweeping gesture towards his new, unpleasant-looking body.

"You violently broke your Vorihelcom seal and were in Zah form for about half a minronn. So, you should expect to be in this form for at least a full deronn—maybe two," Riza offered, though even she wasn't really sure herself.

"I still say he cheated!" Arisha screamed while pointing an accusing finger at the now confused looking Silvarian.

"No, he didn't!" Riza shot back, causing Arisha to cower slightly when the aggravated demoness unfurled her wings from her frame and swished her tail around behind her. "Listen, Arisha! The moment he used his Cloak of Darkness, there was no hope of you winning this fight." Riza raised her hand to silence Arisha's outburst. "Ep, ep, ep... I don't care who your parents are; there was no way you could have won—at least not without a God Slayer—and those are illegal in any matches!"

Arisha was fed up. After uttering, "Ugh!"—the only thing she could muster up at this point—she threw her hands in the air before she stormed off.

Visage ran after her, grabbed her arm, and spun her around to face him. "I am really sorry! I didn't mean for this to happen... and... and... I forfeit!" Everybeing was caught off-guard by what Visage blurted!

Arisha stood, dumbfounded. Visage released her arm, twiddled his thumbs, shuffled his feet, and stared at the floor of the pit.

Riza demeanor quickly transformed from one of shock to one of amusement. *That's twice in a deronn that he's surprised me! I guess Vira and I are making progress!*

Widespread murmuring could be heard from the crowd. However, Arisha continued to remain silent. Her face took on a deep red hue, and, for a time, she appeared to be deep in thought. Finally, her face returned to its normal shade, and she patted the top of the smaller demon's head. Visage was taken aback by her kind gesture. Though his eyes were still icy blue, their usual softness had started to return.

"Ya know, kid, you're a real pain in my crath," Arisha sneered, "but I kinda like ya." Shockingly, she removed her hand from her rival's head and extended it towards him. He quickly accepted, and the two demons clasped each other's wrists.

Visage was a bit tentative. "So, does this mean we're... friends?" He was hopeful—until Arisha vigorously shook her head.

"Nope. Rivals!" When the audience heard Arisha's proclamation, everybeing in the coliseum started clapping and cheering. Visage was embarrassed. His hand fell to his side, and Arisha withdrew hers as well. The demoness then retrieved her blood sorjin and cloak from her gem, snapped her sorjin to one of the studs on the left side of her belt, and threw on her cloak. The cloak fluttered about her while she changed back into her human form and headed for the lifts. After she exited the pit, she smiled widely, noting that the audience was continuing to cheer about the birth of the newest pair of rivals.

Riza was beaming. She retrieved Visage's cloak from her own gem and threw the mithril robe around the small, dumbfounded demon, who barely managed to get his hands inside the sleeves of the beloved mithril weave garment.

After a while Visage shook his head and found his voice, "Um, Riza?"

The boy was quite surprised at the sweet nature of the demoness's reply. "Yes? What is it, Visage?"

"What just happened?"

"Something we've all been waiting for," Riza spoke softly, her words confounding Visage more than ever. Riza was then approached by Vira.

"Rivals huh... That's interesting," Vira commented while standing beside her friend before peering down at the smaller demon in front of them.

"Absolutely!" Riza cheered.

I think that's the first time I've seen Lord Nos's de'tari that shaken! Vira thought with a bemused smirk on her face.

He is quite the fun little demon, isn't he? Riza thought back. Vira responded with a hearty nod.

The three demons were soon left alone in the coliseum. Everybeing else had retreated to the lifts and headed back up to the temple proper. Visage trained his eyes on the demonesses. They were standing over him, looking first at him and then at each other. *They're having a psychic meeting about me, no doubt.* The demonesses followed up with a round of laughter. Visage rolled his eyes. *I thought so,* he moaned to himself.

"How did you know?" Vira innocently asked.

Visage shrugged. "I may be young, but I'm not stupid," he retorted.

"You're right, Visage, we were talking about you. And, since Lord Baltrix hasn't been in the mood to train you on how to quiet your mind, we've decided to... take his place," Riza said. The short pause that ensued spoke for itself, especially since the two demonesses were now strangely eying the boy, causing him to feel awkward and uncomfortable.

I have a bad feeling about this.

"Oh, come on!" Vira cried. Her tail stuck straight up in the air, and her wings shot up and out as well. "Do not put me in the same category as her!" she exclaimed, pointing an accusing finger at the Meserino standing to her right.

"What do you mean by that?" Riza turned to eye her friend, putting her left hand to her waist and leaning on her right leg while at the same time swaying her tail in annoyance.

What is going on? What are they talkingabout now? Visage wondered.

Vira lowered her tail and wings, wrapped them around her body like a cloak, and started to explain. "Visage, do you remember what Lord Nos said yederonn—about us being your fiancées?"

Visage tried to remember. "I don't think so; what does that even mean?"

Riza spoke up. "It means we're betrothed," she eyed him with a smirk and a wink.

"Ugh! I don't know what that means either!" Visage's frustration had now reached the boiling point; he threw his arms up into the air.

Vira walked over, clutched the young demon's raised arms, and lowered them. She then put her hand on his left cheek and brushed some of his black hair out of his face. After cupping his chin, she gently raised it so she could look into his eyes. "It means we are promised to each other and are going to be married." The child's eyes went wide, and his mouth hung open.

Fiancé? Betrothed? Married? I'm going to marry Lady Vira! Visage's dark-purple lips turned up, and sheer joy washed over him. He was so overcome with emotion that he nearly fell over.

Vira reached out and had to grab hold of his arms in order to keep him upright. "Not just me, but Riza too!" she added.

Visage was confused! *I'm going to marry Lady Vira and Lady Riza? I thought I could only marry one person... err... demon.*

Vira quickly corrected Visage's erroneous thought. "Oh, no, you're thinking about your planet's restrictions. Out here in the galaxy, you have to think more... broadly."

"So, I can marry more than one person, or being? Isn't that wrong?"

Vira smirked and straightened, while Riza walked over and stood next to the pair. Closing her eyes, Riza thought for a moment. Then she and Vira silently conversed before looking down at Visage.

"I'm not sure if you're old enough to hear this, but we"—Vira glanced over at her friend—"decided we should tell you anyway." Though he was again feeling uncomfortable, Visage decided he'd better listen to what the demonesses had to say.

Vira knelt down and took the lead. "Visage, has anyone told you about Skath yet?" He nodded in confirmation. "Oh, good." Vira seemed a bit relieved. *At least I don't have to start from the very beginning.* "So, you know that the Dark God, Skath, had worshippers who attacked our galaxy many onns ago—"

Visage interrupted her. "Just what is an onn, Lady Vira?"

Vira blinked. *Baltrix must be sleeping on the job if he didn't tell him about the Marcisian standard of time.* "On Earth, you go by days and years?"

"Uh, yes."

"Well, out here a day, or what we call a deronn, is about three times longer than the one you're used to back on Earth."

Visage understood. "So, a deronn is seventy-two Earth hours?"

"It's a little less than that, but you're close enough."

Riza stepped in to take over for Vira. "I know you're curious, Visage. Even though we are immortal, and time doesn't really matter that much to us, all of the planets your friends are from go by the Marcisian Empire's standard of time. In order for you to understand the time units, I will give you the names as we use them in what we call 'Imperial Standard Time', followed by the timeframe that they cover on earth: dironn (three minutes), minronn (two point four hours), deronn (seventy two hours), mcronn (one week and six days), rinonn (two point five months), and onn (two point nine years). I saved the best for last: eon (basically forever). Over forty-seven million planets use these same units! In other words, they are the galaxy's universal language of time. Now, mind you, the equivalent measures from our times to Earth times are all approximations—just so you know."

"I guess time moves faster in the Empire."

"No, it actually moves more slowly," Vira corrected.

"Slowly? How can it move more slowly if a deronn is a seventy-two-hour day?"

"It's because of Earth's relationship with the rest of the galaxy. Our planet, Zharaj, is closer to the galaxy's center than Earth." *How can I explain this to him so he can understand?* Riza closed her eyes and thought deeply.

Vira now re-entered the conversation in an attempt to help Riza out. "Visage, did Lord Baltrix show you a map of the galaxy in class?"

"Yeah, he did! It was awesome!" Visage said excitedly, remembering the spinning cluster of stars that nearly filled the lecture hall.

Vira smirked. "Did you notice that the galaxy has several different layers?"

Visage thought a moment. "I guess so."

"Well, just like your planet has differing time zones, so does our galaxy. And the further away a planet is from the center of the galaxy, the greater the time gap. So, even though a deronn is seventy-two of your hours, because of Earth's distance from the center of the galaxy, a deronn here would still be only one day there." Vira watched while Visage's ice-blue eyes darted about, his mind trying to wrestle with the whole concept.

Visage scowled. "Does that mean time moves faster the closer one gets to the center of the galaxy?"

Wow, he does learn fast, Vira thought. "Exactly! You've got it!"

"So, I guess I can understand the time thing, but what really has me worried is that marriage thing."

The demonesses exchanged worried glances. "Does he really need to know?" Vira whispered to her friend.

Riza quietly responded, "I think it would be for the best. He is Arnen's dar'tari, after all, and he'll find out the truth eventually." The smile on Riza's face was now turning into a serious frown. "Lord Nosfaren told me that several women already have their eyes on him. And the knowledge of a live Silvarian has been spreading planet wide. Lord Nos and the Council can't protect him forever." The demoness brought her hand to her face and rested her chin on her palm. She started drumming her cheek in annoyance. "But, he's so young! I mean, I know he's my fiancé, but still..." Now Vira was making a similar face as the one on the Meserino.

Visage was acutely aware of the change in the facial expressions and body language of the older demonesses. "Is there something wrong?" he asked the pair.

He sure is *sharp,* Riza thought while she mentally prepared for what was probably going to be a very difficult discussion.

Vira put her hand on Visage's shoulder and took a deep breath. "Listen, Orran..."— She was surprised when the young demon shook a bit when she uttered his name. His mouth opened widely for only a moment. He then stood and silently waited. —"this is going to be hard for you to understand right now, but you..."— Vira looked to Riza who gave a sharp nod for her to continue. —"you need to know that, because you are a Silvarian demon, there will be women who will... offer themselves to you." That opened the floodgates.

What? Why? Offer themselves—as in sex or that kind of thing! But I'm just a kid! My oma said I wouldn't have to worry about that until I was much older! Visage had started to hyperventilate, so Vira had to shake him to rescue him from his panic-stricken thoughts.

"Orran, first, I'm rather shocked that you know anything about such things, and secondly, it's really not that surprising, knowing what you are," Vira calmly told him.

Visage averted his gaze away from Vira and peered at the ground. "I read one of my uncle's biology books last year. That's when I started asking my oma a bunch of questions. She didn't like having to explain sex to a six-year-old, but she said I wouldn't have to worry about any of that till I got a lot older." The boy now looked back up at Vira. "What did you mean that it would make sense if I knew what I was? Is it because I'm a demon?"

Riza grinned and muttered under her breath, "Sharp indeed."

Vira ignored Riza's interjection and slowly nodded. "It's not so much that you're a demon—but that you're a *Silvarian* demon." She removed her hand from Visage's shoulder and continued. "Let me explain. Most beings in the universe are born into mortality, whereas demons are born into immortality. However, Silvarians are special. The Silvarians had worked so hard for them that the gods wanted to give them a special blessing. Therefore, from that time forward, any de'tari of Eendril who was born into mortality and who married a Silvarian would automatically inherit his immortality. This provided an easy way for a mortal woman to escape the clutches of death. Orran, you, as the sole-surviving Silvarian, must understand that you are in danger, no matter where you are, from women who have less than good intentions. That's why the Council decided to give you a new name."

"Oh, so that's why my name had to be changed." Visage was pensive.

Riza and Vira nodded. "That's also why Vira and I are here. We have to protect you from beings like Chirras who will try to use you for their own gain," Riza told him before she got to one knee to give him a hug.

Use me for what I am? Visage's memories flipped like pages as they dove into the recesses of his mind. He could vividly remember all of the kids gawking at him on the playground and saying horrible and hurtful things:

"What are you supposed to be?"

"Look at those; he has tails!"

"Are you some kind of dog boy?"

"Dog boy! Dog boy!"

As if those hateful words hadn't given him enough torment, one day several bullies called him even worse names. *"He's a monster! Monster!"*

Riza, having heard every one of Visage's unspoken thoughts, suddenly pushed him to arm's length and clutched his shoulders. "Never say that again!" Visage didn't even flinch. His mind was still wrestling with the memories. His normally ice-blue-colored eyes were now devoid of light; darkness overshadowed them and they took on the color of a deep spectral abyss.

Right after Visage's memories had entered her mind, Vira's face contorted and her own dark-blue eyes erupted—ethereal flames began dancing within them. Her teeth and fists were clenched so tightly that blue liquid started to spill out of her gums and run down the left side of her mouth. If she were not wearing her Mithril bracers, she would have punched holes into her own palms with her clawed fingers. *Such ignorance!* The demoness's mental shout reverberated, startling the beings who were on the first few levels of the temple.

It's not ignorance, it's fear. Earthlings hate anything they don't understand. Even that young God was killed because they feared him. And He had been sent there to save them!

Riza's thoughts triggered Visage's memories from a sacred book and briefly replaced the drumbeat of tormenting voices. *God, Oma, Dad, Uncle John, Sara, Anna, family*—the boy's thoughts turned to all of the ones he loved. Vira and Riza relaxed a bit; they could literally tell when the boy's mind emerged from the darkness. The light in his eyes returned. He spoke in a near whisper. "Do you know our God?" The abrupt question threw both demonesses off balance.

Vira unclenched her fists and rubbed the blue liquid from her chin and cheek with the back of her gloved hand, leaving a blue smear on the glove's black leathery surface. Riza gently put her hand on Visage's cheek. "Not personally, no," she said—now using a warm though more distant and sentimental-sounding tone. "But we do know *of* Him."

Vira took over for Riza, whose emotions were starting to get the best of her. "When your God took us in, we briefly met. But that was before the Earth was even created. The war with Skath had just ended, so the Grand God Eendril invited all of his allies—those who fought for Him—to a grand gathering."

Visage was in shock! "You met Him and His Father's name is Eendril?"

Riza and Vira shared a glance, smiled at Visage, and nodded. "Em," they both said in unison.

Riza frowned a moment later. "No, we didn't meet Eendril's son at the time. The war took its toll on the gods as well as the demons. Many universes were left without a deity to oversee them and provide them support. We, as Meserino and"—Riza nodded to Vira—"Veserino representatives were invited to attend the gathering to see which god or gods would take stewardship over the various universes of the many who had perished."

"So all of the demons didn't go to the gathering? Didn't they all fight for the gods?" Visage was overcome with sorrow when Riza slowly shook her head.

"No, not all of us—" Vira was interrupted by a silencing glance from Riza.

"Orran, there is something more that we have to tell you about the Silvarians," Riza offered. "Did Lord Baltrix tell you about the Meserino clan that fought for Skath?" Orran shook his head. "I thought not. When Skath started his war, he asked my dar'nra or, in your Earthly language, 'father', to fight for him. My dar'nra promptly refused."

"So your fath... dar'nra... was the king of the Meserino demons? He turned down Skath? Didn't that make Skath mad?"

Riza chuckled. Vira shrugged a bit and then continued. "For sure, but he didn't exactly leave empty handed."

"Oh," was all Visage managed to say at this point; he was too upset to offer any further input.

"It was much more than, 'oh', Visage. An entire Meserino clan joined Skath. This rift, as it was called, would inevitably lead our entire race to get involved in the war—a war that would erase entire worlds, galaxies, and universes—including many of their mortal beings, gods, and demons—from existence." Feelings of past anger welled up from within, choking away Riza's speech.

"It was the greatest tragedy ever known. I have been told that time heals all wounds, but when reality itself was what was wounded..." Vira shook her head. She was overwhelmed.

Visage could easily feel the distress both demonesses were suffering. All he could think of was to tell them, "I'm so sorry. If it hurts to talk or think about the past, then don't. Your past doesn't have anything to do with me, anyway."

It has everything to do with you! Riza and Vira both psychically exclaimed, nearly knocking Visage over. Their thoughts hit the boy like a tidal wave.

Riza got back to her feet and stood tall, her tail lashing about behind her. "Orran, you are the very last of the Silvarian race, thanks to the Meserino traitors who joined Skath. My dar'nra himself took the blame for the slaughter! He took my ber'nan and me along with him to hunt down the rest of the fracking Ze'therac clan. I am the one who erased that pathetic ingrate Crazec from existence! My dar'nra set out on his own to face Skath. That's why my ber'nan is now the one sitting on the throne! That scum-sucking blortworm, Skath, took my dar'nra— the same as he did yours!"

This revelation from Riza hit Visage harder than the demon's previous telepathic outburst! He lost his balance and his legs buckled. The fight with Arisha, the Cloak of Darkness technique, and all of the anger and sorrow that had exuded from the demonesses had sapped his strength. His next realization was of his face reflecting back at him from the floor. Acting swiftly, Riza managed to reach out and break his fall. For a brief instant, his head rested against her toned stomach, then slid down until his face was on her lap. Once his strength began to return, he was able to turn over and look into Riza's eyes, which were now moist with tears. *And the people back home think that demons are nothing more than the hell spawn of The Evil One. It's so sad that they don't know them like I do.* His thoughts abated and he sat up, only to discover that Riza had even more to say.

"Orran,"—Riza's voice became no more than a whisper—"your dar'nra cared about you so much. I wish you could have seen his face when he told my dar'nra about your birth." At this point, she was no longer able to speak and her tears fell freely. The warm drops emitted small rings of bright-red energy when they splattered against Orran's forehead. "That was when my dar'nra, our king, made the decision that we should marry." She was once again silent and more tears flowed, her face appearing pained—so full of sorrow, anger, and guilt. However, somehow, she managed to go on. "Arnen knew that if Skath found out about you, he would do everything in his power to end your existence." Riza started squeezing Visage tightly, leaning down so her face was inches from his own. "Arnen died to protect you, and his sacrifice led to Skath's eventual defeat."

Vira came over and sat down next to the pair. "We still don't know which god it was who brought Skath down, but it was your dar'nra who opened our eyes. Because of him, we joined our sorjins with the Gods of Light—Frezeth, Indren, Eendril, Elindil, Elderin and many others. Arnen is the one who brought us all together, and it was your adoptive father, Eendril, who took all of us in, making us part of his family. So, Orran, we all owe you a debt we could never hope to repay." By now, Vira was fighting back her own tears.

"You don't owe me anything. I'm happy I got this chance to know—both of you. If anyone owes a debt, I do. Nobeing here seems to care about what I am, and they treat me like everybeing else. I have found something here that I never could have found back on Earth." Visage beamed. "I found the place I truly belong!"

Vira, whose tears were now flowing freely, joined Riza. The two sat for a long time, letting go of years of pent-up anger and sorrow it was replaced with hope and joy. Visage was happy to see the two demonesses were coming to terms with their past and moving toward a much brighter future.

While the trio sat in the arena of the pit, their powerful emotions sent massive waves of energy up and out. The beings in the lower levels of the temple were overcome by this unprecedented energy flow.

Though the wave of energy had lost much of its power by the time it reached the levels above, every being was affected to some degree by the strong ripple of Verse power that permeated the sacred structure.

15

A Mess in the Hall

Half a minronn had passed since the match in the pit, and several friends were now sitting together at a table in the mess hall. They were excitedly talking about the fight they had witnessed.

"That was incredible!" Ranic ecstatically blurted.

"Ranic, would you please calm down; you don't have to shout about it. We were all there." Envine leaned on his left palm, propped his elbow on the table, and, with only one eye open, gave his friend a warning glare.

Despite Envine's admonition, Ranic continued to rant. "Did you see what Visage did? He used the Cloak of Darkness! I mean, not even Arisha knows that technique! He's gotta be some kind of genius!" Ranic stood up and slammed both palms down hard on the table, startling Le'Shara and Cormack.

Though Moonreth appeared to be oblivious to Ranic's overenthusiastic rant, Envine seemed swayed. *I guess it is amazing that the kid could even use the Cloak of Darkness without any training,* he telepathically mused.

"I iIonied the look on Arisha's face when he used it! Moonreth finally blurted. It was about time somebeing took her down a notch!" After several heads nodded in agreement, Moonreth noticed that Le'Shara had been silent the whole time. "What's the matter, Le'Shara? Why so quiet?"

"Yeah,"— Cormack chimed in, —"you haven't said anything since we watched the fight."

Le'Shara wasn't at all thrilled by the sudden attention. Her face became flushed, but she managed a light shrug and a weak smile. "It's just not fair." She spoke so softly that her four friends could barely hear her over the din in the mess hall.

Moonreth sighed. "Alright, sri'na, what's going on?" he asked, gently setting down his drink.

Le'Shara was now fully embarrassed and drew her hood up over her head; it almost fully covered her face. Her quiet voice then emanated from beneath its folds. "I wanted to be his rival," she muttered.

Ranic sat down hard, and his mouth hung agape. Cormack's eyes went wide, and his face revealed a similar expression of shock. Envine, on the other hand, had folded his arms and was nodding approvingly. Moonreth's lengthy ears were raised up as far as they could go. If he hadn't set his glass down, he would have spilled it, since his hands both went limp when he heard Le'Shara's surprising confession.

Le'Shara couldn't help but notice the overwhelming silence. *I knew I shouldn't have said that. I'm such an id'rth!* Her thoughts betrayed her. Now all of her friends knew her previously closely guarded aspiration.

Moonreth shook his head and was about to say something, but Ranic spoke first. "You're not an id'rth, Le'Shara. You were..." He tilted his head and tapped his cheek in thought. "Ah, you were a little late to the game."

Envine chimed in. "I don't think you would have liked being Visage's rival anyway."

"You'd make a much better friend than rival, Le'Shara. You need to be patient; you'll find a suitable rival,"— Cormack added, attempting to be supportive. —"eventually." he muttered under his breath.

The albino Night Elf meagerly nodded. "I guess you're right."

Ranic was again on his feet. "Speaking of rivals, I heard that Lord Baltrix killed that pathetic crath Zor'ret yederonn and gave you his blood sorjin! Is that true, Le'Shara!" Ranic excitedly asked, eager to know if what his master had told him was correct. His outburst, though surprising, was quite typical.

Moonreth and Cormack groaned. Did you have to mention that *fraking glort* while we're eating? Moonreth asked before he eyed his friend and shoved his tray away. Ranic merely gave a shrug of indifference.

Cormack slightly scowled. "Ranic, this is not really the appropriate time or place to be discussing that betrak."

Le'Shara looked down as if deep in thought. After pulling her hood back off, she lifted her head" a grand smile adorned her face. Her white ears were extended all the way up and out when she took the blood sorjin in question from her belt and lifted it out from under the table to show it to the excited Twillan.

The glass of water Cormack had been twirling slipped from his fingers. It was about to fall and spill its entire contents all over the table when Moonreth caught it using telekinesis. Envine wasn't sure what impressed him more, Le'Shara's sudden change from being down in the dumps or Moonreth's Verse use in averting what could have been a soggy mess.

Despite the distraction from Cormack, Le'Shara continued to show off her new the blood sorjin. Ranic, who had been eyeing it, now began to stroke his chin in contemplation with his fingers. Lowering his hand rather abruptly, his face contorted. "Frak me! I should have been there! So, Le'Shara, did Baltrix totally kick Zor'ret's crath or what!"

Le'Shara enthusiastically nodded while she clutched the blood sorjin a bit tighter. "He sure did! He was amazing!" Then she frowned a bit. "I'm sorry you weren't there to see it, Ranic," she apologetically offered.

Ranic gave Le'Shara a dismissive wave. "Ah, it's all right, I can just peek into your ber'nan's mind and see what went down."

"Hey, hold on! Who said you could go poking around in my head, Ranic!" Moonreth protested.

Ranic's response was obviously sarcastic. "Uh... your sri'na." He gestured to the young woman sitting next to the now disturbed-looking Night Elf.

Why do I put up with this guy? Moonreth silently muttered to himself.

"I was there too!" Envine piped up. "I wouldn't mind showing you what happened, Ranic!"

Moonreth sighed heavily in relief, causing Le'Shara to giggle. He was surprised by his sri'na's response. "I can't remember the last time I've seen you this happy, little sri'na."

Le'Shara held her new weapon to her chest. It's because of you, Moonreth. She glanced around the table. Actually, it was because of all of you. You all stood beside me when everybeing thought I was cursed. But none of you cared about that; you still befriended me. The Night Elf's thoughts then drifted to the new ar'teth—the one who told her that her looks were nothing more than a genetic flaw and not some curse the Goddess had placed upon her.

Ranic was pleased by Le'Shara's new outlook and was about to say something but was suddenly overcome by very powerful thoughts and emotions. He had to cling to his stool in order to prevent falling to the floor. He peered around the mess hall in an attempt to ascertain whether he was the only being who had had the disconcerting experience. He noticed that the sudden psychic wave had completely overtaken Le'Shara; she was leaning on Moonreth for support. Cormack and Envine weren't faring much better. They had both put their hands on the table and were gritting their teeth.

"What the frak was that!" A voice Ranic recognized as Nate's emanated from the back of the mess hall.

Moonreth, who wasn't nearly as affected by the wave as most, managed a reply. "That was Visage, and, if I were to hazard a guess, Lady Riza and Lady Vira, too!"

"Ugh, can't they feel a bit more quietly!" another being shouted from several tables over.

Um—aren't you forgetting—they're demons! Ranic wasn't sure who was thinking so loudly, but he couldn't help but agree.

"Oh, yeah!" the being from the distant table shouted back. "I get it."

Ranic, now stabilized on his stool, mused, *I wonder what's going on down there in the pit. I wish I could see what those three demons are doing to cause such a commotion.*

16

Bound and Chained

It was dark and cold. Visage groaned, slowly opened his eyes, and double blinked. In order to make sure they weren't playing tricks on him; he rubbed his ice-blue orbs. The arena was gone, Vira and Riza were gone, and panic gripped the demon's entire being. His heart was beating so loudly that he could actually hear it.

Visage got to his feet. "Wow! It doesn't even feel like I'm standing. Okay, I guess I must be in space... somewhere... but how did I get here, and where did Riza and Vira go? Am I alone?" After making a three-hundred-and-sixty-degree inspection, the boy determined that he was indeed alone. All he could see was the vastness of space. Stars and nebulas of reds, whites, and greens filled his vision. Even further out into the distance, he could vaguely see several swirling galaxies; one was the same size as the one in the display Lord Baltrix had shown him in the lecture hall. *Am I dreaming?* he wondered, all the while standing in what seemed to be the heart of the universe. He was in awe when a cluster of comets streaked passed, he put out his hand to see if he could catch one of the golf-ball-sized cosmic missiles. Surprisingly, it passed harmlessly through his hand, leaving nothing more than a warm sensation in his palm. *That's amazing and strange!* After touching his face with his hand and clenching his fist a few times, the frightened child uttered, "Am I dead?" Immediately, an eerie sounding laugh emanated from the area of space off to his right, though he couldn't be one hundred percent sure of that, since the place was totally skewing his sense of direction.

"I should hope not, demon child."

At first, the ominous-sounding voice caused Visage to cringe. However, despite its dark nature, the recipient managed to find something hopeful: *at least I'm not alone.* "So, I'm not dead?" Visage ventured to ask.

"Far from it. But, just out of curiosity, how did you get here?" was the response.

Instead of answering, Visage started heading toward, what he thought was the direction of the unseen being. The resultant laughter (from the unseen being) caused the universe itself to shudder.

Visage ignored the being's laughter and responded to the question. "I don't know. I was with Vira and Riza on Zharaj; then I think I passed out or fell asleep?" He frowned a bit.

"Ah, yes, Riza. Are you one of that Meserino Demoness's pathetic minions? Did she send you here to mock me?"

Visage halted, tilted his head to the side, folded his arms, and boisterously responded to what the being had just imparted. "No! Of course not! Wait! How do you know Riza!"

"Almost *every* god knows King Zereck's de'tari!" the being demeaningly shot back.

Visage was in a state of shock. His arms dropped to his sides, and he again headed out in the direction of the voice. *Who is this... this... being?* "Are... are you... God?" Though he had stuttered, he was amazed that he even got the words out!

"Yes, but not the one you're thinking of," was the answer. For a moment, the young demon's eyes darted about and viewed the universe in its splendor. He then refocused on the message from the unseen being. "So you're really a... god?"

"Yes, though I was unsure if anybeing even remembered me; I've been imprisoned for a very long time."

"What do you mean by that?"

"Why don't you come here and see for yourself." Instantly, a red-glowing road appeared under Visage's feet. As requested, the child hesitantly set off down the road that seemed to be fazing in and out of reality.

Visage wasn't sure how long he had walked, but the red road finally vanished and a circular staircase ascended before him. The way the staircase was set up reminded Visage of a large cone. It was rather wide at the base and became increasingly narrow with every ascending step. Sitting on the narrow top tier of the staircase was some sort of being who was, quite literally, bound by heavy chains; the chains encircled his entire body. Ironically, several paper-like talismans, which were supposed to ward off evil spirits, were fastened on the outside of the being's chains. The only thing Visage could clearly see of the being was a single blood-red eye, which was now staring directly down at him! He could feel his very soul being measured and weighed. He was unable to move; his body was frozen in place under the gaze of the chained up being. As soon as his limbs were again able to function, he covered his ears and made a valiant attempt to block out the being's earth-shattering laughter, but to no avail.

"He failed! I can't believe he failed! How do you like that, Skath! A Silvarian still lives! Arnen's dar'tari still lives!"

The power exuding from this god was overwhelming; despite the chains that were holding him bound. His energy flow forced Visage to his knees and so astounded him that he could not speak. Finally, the boy managed a mere whisper, but the god was able to hear the utterance: "you're a Dark God, aren't you?"

"Yes, I am Chaos, youngest dar'tari of the Dark God Skath!"

Visage's heart sank. "You're the son of Skath! Why aren't you gone? Didn't the Gods of Light destroy all of yo—?"

The irritating laughter returned, cutting Visage off. "No! I rebelled after my ingrate dar'nra erased the Silvarian demons from existence! He punished me by binding me in these chains and leaving me here to rot! I hate my dar'nra! He dragged his own family into a pointless war with the Gods of Light!"

Visage balked. "The Gods of Light and the Gods of Darkness are related?"

"Of course! My uch'nra, Eendril, is the one who adopted you, did he not?"

"Our God's name is Eendril, and he's your uncle!" Visage's tails were now swishing wildly about. "How can that be!"

"Yes, Eendril is my uch'nra, and He was more of a dar'nra to us than Skath ever was!"

After hearing Chaos's pronouncement, Visage decided to climb the steps. He couldn't tell if he was being brave, or foolish, but he was sure of one thing—Chaos was telling him the truth. If he stood on the side of the Silvarians, he must be a friend. With each upward step, Chaos's power became increasingly apparent. When Visage finally made his way to the top of the platform and stood in the presence of the Dark God, an overwhelming sense of pity and iloni washed over him.

Chaos was chained in a kneeling position. His arms were spread out widely and chained to a metal pole or rod. The chains themselves were black; each link had purple or orange glowing runes etched into its surface. Underneath the chains, Chaos seemed to be wearing a full body cast, which was thick and black. The black color of the cast was in stark contrast to the purple, orange glow emitting from the links and there was a dark red glow emitting from his one visible very sinister looking eye.

"My, you are a curious one, my young Silvarian friend," Chaos quipped while Visage walked around to inspect this being.

"I am a Silvarian, or at least so I'm told, and my name is Visage, but I'm not your friend," the demon told the bound god. Visage spoke with a degree of defiance while his ice-blue eyes peered directly into the Dark God's blood-red one.

"Well, Visage, I would iloni for you to stick around and chat, but, as you can see, I'm a bit tied up at the moment," Chaos chortled. "So, it's time for you to wake up!"

17

❧

The Chaos Prophecy

Riza stared down at Visage and sounded panicked. "Visage, Visage, wake up already!"

In a flash, Visage's ice-blue-colored eyes shot open and he bolted upright, surprising the demoness, they both banged their heads together bringing on a bad headache. "Ugh, that wasn't a good idea." Without allowing time enough to fully regain his senses. "That was... different," he weakly offered.

Riza was rubbing her forehead where she and Visage's had collided. Vira immediately became worried. Vira was the first to speak due to Riza was still a bit busy rubbing her head. "What are you talking about, Visage? What was different?"

"I dreamed I met a god—a Dark God. It was weird; he was all chained up."

The demonesses exchanged glances, which were laden with disbelief. "Was his name Chaos by any chance?" Riza almost whispered after she lowered her hand.

Visage stopped rubbing his head in order to focus on Riza's question. "Yeah. How did you know that?"

A hastily opened but short-lived telepathic conference immediately took place. Vira then spoke softly—in hushed reverence. "There is an

136

ancient prophecy. When Chaos rebelled against his dar'nra, Skath had him bound up and chained. Chaos was forced to helplessly look on while the betrak slew his family."

"He killed his own son's family!" Visage hunched over, putting his hands to his knees. "What kind of dar'nra would *do* that!"

"Skath was no dar'nra to any of his children. Most of them saw their uch'nra as their dar'nra, for he was more of a dar'nra to them than Skath ever was." Though Riza was speaking quietly, there was an edge to her voice—an edge that couldn't belie the anger that still dwelt within her heart.

Visage closed his eyes. *He pretty much told me the same thing.* The two demonesses ignored the boy's thoughts and continued their explanation.

"Chaos, despite his parentage, was a friend to us demons." Riza was suddenly more cheerful. "And if you, Visage, are the one who will fulfill the prophecy, then we will help you in any way we can!"

"I agree. We owe Chaos much for what he did for us," Vira added.

"Wait! What prophecy!" Visage was taken so off guard that he stepped back—fast. He lost his balance and fell down, landing on his butt with his legs splayed out in front of him. He decided to make the best of the situation and sat cross-legged in front of the demonesses.

"The prophecy states that 'In time a demon born will undo the chains of a Dark God's scorn.' " Riza was the one who began reciting the ancient prophecy, but Vira couldn't resist and took over the second verse of the prophecy.

"'No more than a child who could see, and, with compassion in his eyes, would set him free.'"

Right after Vira left off, Riza resumed. " 'Chaos now bound no more, will start to heal the wounds from the Grand God's war.' "

Then the duo spoke in unison. " 'With light and darkness in balance again, no more to be broken, when the great healing begins!' "

Visage sat in awe; his mouth hung open after the power of the demonesses' words faded. "And you think that prophecy is about... me!"

The demonesses glanced at each other, then at Visage. After nodding, they said in unison, "Yes, indeed!"

Visage sighed, flopped onto his back, and looked up at the red lighting and stalactite sealing far above. He was overcome by the weight of the demonesses' pronouncement. *I've only been here a... what was it called, again... a deronn? And I'm supposed to free Chaos from his imprisonment!*

You're the one who had the vision, Orran, so Eendril has apparently chosen you for this mission. Riza telepathically told her irritated fiancé.

Riza, please get out of my head. It's kind of weird—and annoying. His thoughts were met with laughter.

"That's actually the main reason why we stayed down here in the first place—to help you quiet your thoughts so you won't... share them with everybeing," Vira reminded him.

Visage sat back up. "Fine. So when do we start?"

Riza and Vira, now sitting at Visage's level, quickly arose. "Right now!" The two Demonesses chimed in unison.

"Visage, don't get up; stay just as you are," Riza told him.

"Okay, Riza..." He replied. *Can I at least sit up,* he thought to himself.

"Of course," Riza responded. Visage then adjusted his position so he was sitting cross-legged. Vira sat down behind him. Getting as close as she could and pressing up against his back, she put her hands over his shoulders and clasped them together near his stomach. Visage could feel the demoness's breath on the back of his neck while she spoke into his ear. "The trick is to imagine a barrier in your mind."

Visage closed his eyes and frowned. "Um, Vira, do you have to be this close to me?" he whimpered.

"It's not really necessary, but it does help. You see, Riza is going to try to break your barrier I'm here to help you stabilize and maintain that barrier. With my mind this close to yours, it's much easier to not only get us in sync, but also to establish a mental link," she explained.

"There's an even better way to do it, but we figured you probably wouldn't like it," Riza offered.

Visage was afraid to ask, but his mind did so anyway. *What's the better way?*

"It's when two beings' minds become one through membrane-to-membrane contact," Vira told him, tickling his ear when she spoke.

Visage was confused. "What does that mean?"

"It's what you call a 'kiss' back on Earth," Riza chimed. She followed up with a wink.

Visage blushed, but he wasn't sure if it was because of Vira pressing against his back and breathing into his ear or because of what Riza had just said. Either way, he was completely flustered. *Why do I get the feeling you're going to be doing this a lot?*

"Remember, we *are* going to be married," Riza stated flatly before closing her eyes. Visage's ability to muse was suddenly curtailed when Riza let loose a torrent of psychic waves. Visage clenched his teeth and tried to imagine a barrier around his mind—one that would be strong enough to block the intrusion.

"Come on, Visage, concentrate. Think of the psychic waves as though they were a physical attack," Vira encouraged.

Physical—physical—I know! Visage then imagined being inside a vault, protected by three feet of steel on all sides.

"Very good!" Vira cheered.

Good, yes, but not good enough. Riza was not about to give up. She started battering the vault, gradually tearing away the mentally constructed walls. Visage could see cracks starting to form inside the shell. Soon Riza would be able to attack him directly. Right when the vault was about to rip apart, he countered by setting up layers upon layers of shields made of pure energy. "Now you're getting it," Vira proudly sheered, since she was the one who had given him the idea.

Right after the vault vanished, Riza attacked the first shield with everything she had. *You're not holding back, are you, Riza?* Visage mentally whined.

I don't believe in doing things half-crathed, the demoness replied after the last psychic wave nearly destroyed the first layer of shielding. Vira then stepped in and offered Visage some crucial information: *the shields can also be fused together, making them twice as strong.* Visage wasted no time utilizing the advice. He fused the first two shields together, then added the third and fourth. Soon all of the shields were fused, creating an energy barrier as thick as the vault walls themselves. However, Visage didn't halt. Knowing Riza's determination, he immediately started creating even more back-up shields.

Though Riza had successfully broken through his outer vault shielding, she now deduced that her young protégé had the power to ward off any potential thought-spying intruder and therefore ceased her attack.

"Visage, that's enough; you can stop now." Vira couldn't help but give the boy alight, pride-filled squeeze.

"Aren't you the quick little ar'teth," Riza added with a thumbs up and a wink.

Quickly brushing off the compliment, Visage humbly offered, "But Vira was coaching me the whole time. Thank you, Vira. You're amazing!"

For a few moments, Riza was feeling a little hurt by Visage's words of gratitude to Vira, but she quickly regained her pride-filled attitude towards Visage's accomplishment. "Now, Visage, you know how to defend against mental attacks."

"Yes, but you also need to be able to use what we taught you to hide your thoughts," Vira said, resting her chin on top of the boy's messy black hair.

"I think I get it. I can use the same barrier principal to hide my thoughts from others!"

"Are you sure this is your first time doing this?" Riza playfully asked.

"I think so," Visage replied. He really wanted to rub the top of his head but couldn't because Vira's chin was still resting on it. However, he did give the demoness a toothy grin.

"Don't bare your fangs at me, Orran!" Riza exclaimed. Her whole demeanor suddenly changed! Now, she looked—almost ferocious!

"What did I do? I don't understand... Why are you angry with me? I was trying to be nice." Visage was feeling confused and a bit hurt.

Riza then cursed herself. *Frak, of course he wouldn't get it. After all, he was raised by humans.* "I'm sorry, Visage."

Vira held Visage tightly. "When a demon bares their fangs at another demon, it's, well, like a major insult, and it can even be considered a challenge to fight," she explained.

"But... but... I didn't know. Back home it's more like a goofy gesture of affection. It's not like I want to bite your head off or anything!" The young demon had struggled to find the right words to explain himself.

Riza balked. "Wait..." She held the bridge of her nose. "You mean to tell me that, on Earth, showing your fangs to a being is considered a sign of affection?" She spoke a bit faster than normal.

"Yes, that's right." Visage gave them a halfhearted shrug because he didn't want to disturb Vira, who was still leaning herself against his back.

Riza swiftly turned her back on them. Her tail started to vigorously sway, and she began debating with herself. *Bearing one's fangs is a direct insult to Demons. But on Earth, it's a sign of affection? No. It's tradition going back eons that one must not break.* She then vigorously shook her head, causing her hair to flutter about wildly. *Wait, when did it become a tradition that showing one's fangs is considered an act of aggression?* She folded her arms under her chest and tried to remember.

"Uh, Vira, has she always been like this?"

"No, it's only when she's around a certain demon that she shows this part of herself." Vira smiled, and then glanced up at her distraught friend.

So it's my fault that she's like this? Visage was quite taken aback by the thought. "And Vira, just how long are you going to hug me?"

"Yes!... And for as long as you let me. Why? Am I disturbing you?" Vira didn't want to let on that she was really enjoying herself. *It's been eons since I've been this close to him,* she thought, being careful to shield them from her pouting Silvarian.

"I wouldn't say disturbing. In fact, it feels like you've been this close to me before. I just can't remember when." The young demon's new black skin did not betray the fact that his face had gotten a bit flushed.

"Yes, I was." Vira's tone was nostalgic.

Visage opened his eyes, now curious about the demoness's response. So much so that all he could muster up was, "Really?"

"Really. It was a very long time ago. When you were a newly-born soul; Riza and I carried you to Eendril—" She fell silent.

"That's it! That's why you and Riza seem so familiar!" Visage paused while determining how to express his current thoughts. "I don't know if you'll believe me, but I remember you! I remember you too, Riza!"

Riza turned and peered at Visage when she heard her name. "I don't think that's possible... Is it?" She was doubtful.

Visage thought for another moment. "It's not that I remember you, but rather that I remember your hearts." Vira now had a puzzled expression on her face. Riza folded her arms under her chest and raised an eyebrow.

"Our... hearts?"

Gah! I just can't say it right! How can I put this? After letting out a heavy sigh, Visage tried again. "It's like this. Whenever I'm around you, I feel a sense of familiarity. And Vira," he said while Vira was holding him so close to her body that he could hear and feel her heartbeat, "I remember a feeling from that time long ago. You know how close we are? It's like how children know their mothers, err... mi'thias. That's the feeling I get when you're this close to me. And, with you so close to me right now, I can even feel your heartbeat, It's... comforting."

Suddenly, Vira withdrew her embrace. She got up and shoved Visage hard at Riza, who rescued him when he fell forward. Riza eyed Vira, who was now looking at the floor. Her black and dark blue hued hair was hanging over her face, completely hiding it behind the thick curtain.

"What was *that* for!" Visage demanded. Riza had let go so he could turn around to face the disturbed demoness.

"Orran has it right; what's wrong, Vira!" Riza was frustrated that she couldn't read her friend's mind anymore.

Vira stood silent for a moment before she slowly turned around. After she started heading for the lifts, she turned her head over her right shoulder. "I'm sorry; I can't be around you right now." Then she took off, leaving the two demons standing there, dumbfounded.

"What was that about?" Visage was hoping that Riza would be able to shed some light on Vira's rather odd behavior.

Riza was quite surprised at her friend, she smiled with both intrigue and amusement. "Don't worry about it," she told him.

Visage was confused. He didn't know why Vira's entire demeanor had changed so suddenly, but when he tried to come up with an answer it only further confused him. After glancing from Riza toward the direction the Veserino Demoness vanished a few times he gave up. *I don't understand them,* he thought, having put up a mental barrier so Riza couldn't listen in.

"It seems I have you all to myself," Riza eyed Visage with a wry smirk.

Visage closed his eyes. *This isn't so good.* As young as he was, he could usually tell things about the beings he met. To him, Riza seemed to have a personality like that of Arisha and of his older sri'na Jun, whereas Vira was like his sri'nas Sara and Anna. He wasn't too happy about being alone with the Meserino demoness without Vira and her tempered attitude there to help keep Riza in check. His fears were realized when Riza knelt down and looked him in the eyes.

"Visage, shall we do something fun together, now that Vira's gone?" The very tone Riza used made the young demon want to bolt for the lifts. Unfortunately, Riza grabbed onto his shoulder right when he was about to make his escape. Visage slowly turned his head towards the demoness, a sense of dread washed over him. Riza's menacing grin caused him to swallow hard. *Oh, this can only mean one thing—I'm in trouble!*

"What's the matter Visage?" Riza gave him a wry grin and her eyes narrowed a bit before she licked her lips. "Don't you want to hang out with your fiancée?"

Vira... Nosfaren... Anybeing... Please save me! Visage's mental cries went unheard.

Riza had placed a barrier around them. Riza tilted her head and flashed him another wry smile. "Oh, come on, it's not like I'm going to hurt you..."— She averted her eyes and coughed a bit, causing several sirens in Visage's head to go off. —"much." She muttered under her breath.

"I think I need to go now!"

"I don't think so!" Riza grabbed his shoulder again when he tried to flee.

Visage was furious. He grabbed Riza by the wrist, threw her hand off from him, but before she could react, he jumped back several feet. Visage landed hard. His talons scraped across the black stone floor, sending sparks flying after they dug in and left several long scrape marks in their wake. After grinding to a halt, he faced Riza, who was now appearing quite shocked by his actions; his tails were swishing angrily behind him while he took in her full measure.

"Now that's the proper way a demon should act!" Riza cheered and gave him a brief applause. I'm happy to see that your time on Earth hasn't fully erased your Demonic heritage," Riza coyly stated.

Visage was angry and then confused about Riza's little performance. *She did that on purpose. She was trying to make me angry... But why?* Standing straight, he watched her movements and body language. The way she acted was strange. *She's nothing like Jun or Arisha. She's more like... Oma!* His eyes went wide, and he slapped his face after realizing he'd fallen right into her trap.

Riza laughed heartily before retorting, "So, I'm like your mi'thia, eh?" she asked before she started walking towards the child with a coy smile again donning her face. "I don't know if I should be flattered, or insulted?"

Visage's mind was racing. *Can she still read my mind, even with my mental barrier in place? No, that's not really the problem. It's the way she's acting—definitely like a tactician—purposely getting under my skin, to purposely make me angry—flaunting that coy smile and cocky attitude. Maybe she is like Arisha and Jun, but... I don't know.* He shook his head, trying to clear it. *Either way... she's dangerous.*

Oh, you have no idea. Riza's thought broke through Visage's mental barrier. *Listen, Orran, you're a demon; that means you should learn how to act like one... And I'm the one who's going to teach you.*

Visage threw both hands up. "Oh, that's just great!" *What does she mean by that? Should I be happy—or worried?*

Riza tapped her chin in thought. "I think both!" She smirked and shrugged.

That doesn't help... I give up. "Fine. You win."

"Orran, I'm your wife. So I *always* win." Visage was totally caught off guard with that one! His jaw nearly hit the floor.

Wait! What? When did we get married? Are we married? Oma told me I was way too young. Did I miss something?

While Visage was distracted by his thoughts, Riza walked over to where the dumbfounded boy was standing. "That's it,"— She grabbed the folds of his cloak and lifted him off the floor. —"you're coming with me!" She placed Visage down, but held him with her left hand and waved her free hand. She started to chant in the same strange language she had used while imbedding the Vorihelcom seal into his back. After she finished a small ripple of energy washed over them and a portal opened. The spinning kaleidoscope of white, red, and pink patterns appeared. Before he could react, Riza casually tossed Visage into the multi-colored mess. Visage didn't have time to think. All he knew was that the whirling rainbow-colored patterns were making him feel dizzy and warm all over. He traveled, or more appropriately pulled thru a pastel-colored tunnel.

***

The trip thru the swirling tunnel was short. The pit of the temple, stalactite ceiling and all, had vanished and was replaced by a red sky. Visage's dizziness and disorientation were now overshadowed by the fact that he was free falling from the sky, and the ground was fast approaching! *I'd better right myself—fast!* Visage thought before he managed to right himself while he tapped into his indren'freth.

Though Visage's indren'freth was not as powerful as the Cloak of Darkness, it did allow him to halt his rapid descent. With the emergency averted, he stood in the air, folded his arms in indignation and frowned. After breathing a heavy sigh he opened his eyes back up to take in his new surroundings.

Am I on a different planet? Visage thought.

Below him, he noted that the grass on the planet appeared to be either black or very dark green. While doing a three sixty, he saw some mountains and in another direction a castle. *Wait! What! A castle!* He started rubbing his eyes to make sure he wasn't hallucinating, but he wasn't; the castle was still there.

The castle looked like something out of the Middle Ages, having all of the normal castle-like trimmings. Parapets, turrets, and great spiny towers jutted up from what appeared to be a great wall; the wall encircled the large central structure. *Definitely looks like something out of Bram Stoker's book—like a place where Vlad would have lived.*

He was intrigued by the red sky, he narrowed his eyes while he scanned it, he was grateful to see that the portal Riza had conjured up was still open. Amazingly, at that very moment, Riza flew through the portal headfirst and caused the messy-looking puddle-like opening to close up behind her. She didn't have to use her indren'freth to fly; instead, her bat-like wings unfolded allowing her to float down to meet Visage.

"Nice, Orran. It seems you figured out how to control your indren'freth," Riza told him while she flapped her wings and flew down to greet her protégé.

With his concentration now broken, Visage peered up at the demoness and gave a pouty reply. "I wouldn't have had to use it if you hadn't thrown me through that portal of yours!" He cried while throwing his hands into the air. "And where in the galaxy are we, anyway?" He was annoyed—and excited.

Riza closed her eyes and scratched her cheek. "Actually, this planet isn't even a part of the Firaxian Galaxy, Orran; this is our planet, in our galaxy, in our universe." She smiled widely, even showing her fangs! "Welcome to Demeros, the home world of the Meserino demons!" She then made a grand gesture by stretching out both arms, which caused her to look more angelic than demonic.

Visage spun around so his head was pointing downward, his dark hair dangling obscuring his face from view. After crossing his legs and arms, he closed his eyes. *Oh, this is just great! I'm on the Meserino home world, and I suppose that castle belongs to whom, the demon king?*

Riza interrupted Visage's thoughts yet again. "How did you know that?" she asked. Perplexed, she even started rubbing the top of her head.

Visage nearly fell out of the air; he gasped in shock. His eyes shot open before he righted himself and flew up to look Riza in the face. "I was joking!" he exclaimed before he stared, pointing at the castle in the distance. "You mean to tell me that the Meserino Demon King really does live there?"

Riza nodded. "Yes, Orran, I brought you here to meet him. Just don't be too disappointed when you do." After making this rather intriguing pronouncement, she started an angled descent downward towards the castle in the distance.

What did she mean by that? Visage wondered before flying after the Demoness.

In flight, Riza was doing barrel rolls, tight angular turns, and several other over-the-top maneuvers. Visage rolled his eyes. *Now she's really showing off,* he thought. After Riza performed a rather overzealous summersault and came close to colliding with him, Riza got a piece of his mind. "Hey! Watch it!" he shouted, but the demoness simply ignored him, continuing her aerial performance.

The when the two demons closed in on the castle. Riza suddenly halted in midair and angling herself into a steep dive. Visage gasped when he realized that she was mere feet from hitting the ground. Abruptly, she reversed her momentum by angling her wings in order to create drag, causing her whole body to jerk backward. Visage winced a bit while attentively observing her skillfully executed her frightening maneuvers. After she managed to right herself, Riza threw both feet forward, simultaneously throwing her shoulders back before bending her left wing a bit. These adjustments threw her into a violent spin. Her feet hit the ground and her talons dug in, kicking up grass and dirt as the spin continued. Because of the cloud of dust that now covered her landing area, Visage lost sight of her, and his heart began to race. Leaving his mid-air perch, he dove into the cloud of debris.

"Riza! Riza! Where are you?" Since he couldn't immediately locate the demoness, he panicked and started running around aimlessly. Tears were forming in his eyes, but he wasn't sure if they were from his panic or from the dust. Finally, after what seemed like eons, Visage managed to make out Riza's faint laugh; it was coming from the left, so he quickly headed in that direction. After exiting the dust cloud, he could clearly see Riza. She was standing there, shaking off the dust, and continuing to laugh. At first, the young demon was disturbed by Riza's taunting attitude.

"That's not very funny!" Visage shouted, but after shaking his worry and fear away he raced over to hug her. He had to stand on his toes in order to give her a big hug around her waist. The good feeling didn't last long though, since he followed the hug up with a few harsh words. "Riza, don't do that to me again! I thought you were hurt when I couldn't find you in that cloud of dust!"

He was worried? About me? It took a while for the demoness to understand Visage's cutting remark, but his concern finally registered. She put her hand on top of his head and was about to thank him when she was rudely interrupted.

"Don't waste your tears on a demon like her, kid." The male voice grated on Riza as she and Visage turned their heads to get a look at the being who was approaching. Visage let go of Riza right when a male Meserino reached her side. After folding his wings into a makeshift cloak, the Meserino peered down at Visage. Being even taller than Riza, he towered over the boy. He wasn't wearing any shirt, but Visage noted that his pants were very similar to the ones the Zaharaj wore—black and shimmery with pockets on the sides. The only real difference was that his pants ended right below his knees. His eyes, though blood red, were bright. His hair was anthracite black with two red streaks that ran down the right and left sides. He also had intricately designed black tattoos that adorned his body, they were fashioned into that same thorny pattern that all Meserinos seemed to share. He was rather intimidating, but by no means threatening, since he greeted them with a smile.

"Na'tagall, Uch'nra Zed. What business brings you here?" Riza sarcastically asked while at the same time brushing the leftover dust from her body. Zed didn't even react; his eyes were fixed on the smaller being beside her.

"By the Verse, a live Silvarian demon—and here I thought those fraking traitors obliterated them all!" Zed dropped to a knee in order to get a better look at the strange-looking being before him. *He has a rather interesting skin color and biree pattern. I thought all Silvarians had white skin with azure biree, but this one has black skin and dark purple biree.* "Tell me, my young friend, are you *really* a Silvarian? Do you have some sort of skin disorder? Or, perhaps you're some form of hybrid?"

Riza jumped in. "Yes, Zed, he's a Silvarian and no, he doesn't have a skin disorder. He just used the Cloak of Darkness, so that's why his coloring is off. Now, if you'll excuse us, we're here to see my dead beat ber'nan. Come on, Visage, let's go." She abruptly grabbed Visage by the hand and they headed for the castle.

Cloak of Darkness, eh? Such a high-level skill for one so young. After contemplating for a moment, Zed decided to tag along. *This ought to be interesting.*

***

Right when Riza and Visage arrived at the entrance, the castle gates opened. The doors were as grand as the doors on the Zharaj temple, though these doors were dark green instead of burgundy. There didn't seem to be any portcullis, but, since all demons had the ability to fly, it was kind of a moot point. When the duo got closer to the magnificent structure, Visage noticed that the walls were made of that same black smooth stone as the walls of their own temple. "Riza, was this castle made in the image of the Zaharaj Temple?"

Riza chuckled at the question. Riza thought back through Zharaj's history. "Mmm, more like the other way around. Those who first taught the Zah'harrim form of the Verse to the Zaharaj were none other than

the Meserino demons. That's why Zaharaj temples resemble our castles."
After passing under the large opening to the castle, Riza stood in front
of Visage and held out her hands in a wide gesture. "Our 'castle', as
you call it, has a grand outer wall. The main castle is surrounded by
seven different townships . . . or districts." For a moment, the demoness
glanced behind her, then paused and frowned before adding, "The seven
districts are run by the seven Meserino clans."

Zed caught up with them and was now eager to participate in Riza's
history lesson. He stepped right up to Visage. "But one was"—

Riza ran over, forcefully covered Zed's mouth, and violently shook
her head. "He doesn't need to know that!" Visage was puzzled when the
two demons turned their backs to him and started whispering. When
they finally turned around, they both wore obviously forced smiles.

*That's actually pretty cool—what Riza said about the castle layout. But
I wonder what has them so upset,* Visage mused. *I guess if I need to know,
they'll tell me later.* Brushing aside all thoughts of Zed and Riza's brief
exchange, he refocused on the castle. He had to crane his neck, but he
finally succeeded in getting a better view of the parapets and battle-
ments that ran along the top of the wall.

While her fiancé was busy with his investigation, Riza finished her
"discussion" with Zed. *I'm glad V didn't try to break down my barrier. He
didn't need to hear that disagreeable little chat. Now what on Zharaj did he
mean by 'cool'. I don't think he was talking about the coolness of the moribite.
So, what did he mean?*

As usual, Zed came up from behind the pair and interjected, "What
do you mean by that, my small Silvarian friend?"

Visage stopped and did a one eighty. "What do I mean by what?"

"You said our castle is cool. Do you mean the moribite is cool?"

"No, I mean cool as in 'that's cool'. Ugh. It's a slang term from Earth!"
he exclaimed.

"Slang?" Zed folded his arms, closed his eyes and frowned a bit.
"Earth?"

"You mean to say you don't know any slang terms, even though you speak English... ah, sorry,"— Visage rubbed the back of his head in abashed shame. —"common tongue?"

Zed appeared puzzled, and Riza offered only a shrug, so Visage continued. "Seriously! The Navy guys use slang terms all the time . . . along with lots of other more colorful language." He blushed at several memories of his exchanges with Kevin and Andrew who were two of the most fowl mouthed individuals in the Navy.

By this time, Riza, having lost all interest in the conversation, made no comment. She simply continued to walk toward the main castle. Visage ran to catch up with the demoness, but Zed remained bewildered and scratched the top of his head. *Slang... cool... Earth—Hmm... interesting.* An evil smile crept onto his face. *I might just have to visit this... Earth,* he thought before he resumed his trek after the pair. The Silvarian had given him much to consider.

***

The interior of the castle was as majestic as the interior of the temple on Zharaj. Not only were the structures made out of moribite, but the roads were as well. Visage noticed that the stone works weren't mortared together but rather fused or welded. Every building they passed was apparently constructed to be structurally sound as well as aesthetically pleasing. Every weld was fashioned in a manner that would adorn its wall with elaborate designs and shapes, turning every wall into a masterpiece. However, the whole place, though eye appealing, felt empty. Despite the fact that the buildings had windows, their interiors were dark.

The trio wandered around a while before finally arriving at what appeared to be the town square. A grand fountain, made up of statues of three Meserino demons wielding weapons of one kind or another, was the central feature. When they got closer, Visage could see that, despite its grandeur, the fountain was dry. The shops that lined the square were as empty as the houses were. The whole place was lifeless—a true ghost town.

Neither Riza nor Zed had spoken a word since they entered the town. Visage also remained silent while obediently following the pair. When the trio skirted around the right side of the fountain, the young demon could see that the faces of the statues had been battered leaving them so disfigured nobeing could tell who they once were. The spectacle made Visage shiver. He was about to ask Riza why the three Demons were disfigured, but she gave him such a disdainful glare that his words died in his throat.

The group passed another empty street and ran into another wall. This wall was much smaller than the first and had arched entry ways placed every hundred feet or so. After stepping through one of the archways, Visage felt a tingling sensation throughout his entire body. "Did we just pass through a barrier of some kind?"

"Wow, you have keen intuition!" Zed blurted. Visage was startled by the outburst, since he wasn't aware that Zed had caught up with them he was much too preoccupied looking at the sights in the ghost town.

"No time for idle chatter,"— Riza muttered with a slight sigh. —"my ber'nan knows we're here, and he isn't the most patient being in the cosmos" She slumped a bit and sighed again before she quickened her pace.

Finally, the trio reached the castle steps and proceeded to enter the majestic structure. Visage couldn't help but notice that the castle's interior, like its exterior, was very similar to that found in the Zaharaj temple. The only major difference was the existence of a set of curved stairwells, both leading to a second floor balcony-like area. From this area, one could hang onto an ornately crafted railing and partake of the grandeur of the castle entryway below.

Riza headed for the stairwell on the left, so Visage and Zed followed her. After reaching the upper level, they all turned and headed down the long connecting hallway. The hallway was "guarded" on both sides by a row of empty sets of armor. The armor was similar in appearance to that worn by the knights of old. Windows, which were lining the lefthand wall, were letting in the red-tinted sunlight, which caused the shadows of the armor to appear large and ominous. The suits all held finely crafted blades in their left hands. In their right hands, they carried kite shields, which had coats of arms engraved onto their faces. Every suit looked as though it were ready to attack, putting Visage on edge. At the far end of the hallway was another set of ornate doors, which started to open when the trio approached. Visage was relieved that the group's trek had finally ended.

***

The enormous room was breathtaking. Its moribite walls were stained in reds and purples instead of the normal black color. Two columns of pillars stood along the far walls. The pillars had been cut to resemble leafy vines, which appeared to vanish into the ceiling. The polished floor resembled the vastness of space. Visage couldn't help but remember his vision of Chaos—the one where he had seen the swirling galaxies, stars, nebulas, and even comets. Riza disrupted Visage's thoughts and beckoned him to follow. Though he was standing at the entrance, awestruck, he complied.

Zed had also halted right outside the entrance of the throne room. He grunted and his face contorted when he noticed that that demon king had other company. "I'm sorry, but I will have to take my leave." He gave Visage and Riza a slight bow before heading down the hallway on the left.

What's wrong with him? Visage thought. Riza sighed and shook her head when her uch'nra turned the corner and disappeared. After climbing a small set of steps, the pair was shocked to find a male Meserino demon literally hanging off from his large throne. The demon's right leg was draped off the right-side armrest; his left foot was on the floor, bouncing impatiently on its heel. He held his head up by leaning his cheek on his fist while his elbow was propped up on the left armrest. He was busy playing with the ring that was at end of a chain that was hanging around his neck. He only had one eye open. Visage couldn't decide if he was annoyed, apathetic, or both.

The being seemed to be halfheartedly speaking to another being who was standing in front of the throne. "Well, look what the Arc Dragon dragged in," the first demon said, completely ignoring the other demon who was now patiently standing at his side.

Riza folded her arms under her chest and glared at her ber'nan. "Na'tagall, ber'nan. I see you're taking your duties very seriously—as usual," she sarcastically remarked before rolling her eyes. Turning her head to the other being, she smiled and offered, "Hi, Hal. Is my ber'nan bothering you again?" The angelic being turned to face the demoness. "Not exactly, Princess Riza. I'm here at the request of Eendril,"— The Archangel folded his arms across his armored chest and frowned. —"but King Zareth doesn't seem to care." He nodded towards the lay-about on the throne. Visage finally realized who the being was: Halifel, one of Eendril's Archangels. The boy was amazed by Halifel's brilliantly glowing, golden-colored eyes.

Halifel was wearing his usual long white robes, which revealed only his bare hands and feet. His chest was covered by a golden breastplate. Around his waist was a white leathery-looking belt, and hanging off from it was a superbly ornate sorjin. His right hand was resting upon the white leather wrapped hilt and golden pommel. His long white hair was tied up into a tight ponytail, and it was emitting a brilliant white-colored glow. Hal smiled in amusement when he noticed the small being gawking at him. "And who is this young demon with you, Princess?" His eyes went from the child to Riza.

"Oh come on, Hal, you know him—he's Arnen's kid."

Halifel appeared delighted when he recalled the memory of meeting Orran in the pre-mortal life. Even Zareth seemed to perk up upon hearing Arnen's name.

"Orran, is that really you!" Halifel exclaimed. "I see you have a phys-ical body now! I guess Father thought your time had come!" He smiled in pure delight.

"Wait! You know me?" Visage was dumbfounded. "And why do I vaguely remember you?" He shook his head before narrowing his eyes at the beaming Archangel.

"Let's just say, we were together a lot while you were still in heaven,"— Halifel chuckled at the shocked look on Visage's face. —"while you were waiting for your mortal birth. You probably remember me from back then."

Visage was more confused than ever and his expression proved it.

"Don't worry about it," Halifel said, giving him a dismissive wave. He followed up with a wink.

Riza had been looking around while the other two were conversing. "Um... Hal, where are Mikey and Gabe? I always thought the three of you came as a set."

Halifel balked at this.

"I really can't say." Halifel's face went from cheerful to grave. "The only thing I can tell you is that they are on an important mission for Father."

Riza's disappointment was apparent; she slouched a bit. "Well that sucks," She sighed in disappointment before she straightened. "So what about you, Hal, is yours an important mission?"

"I wouldn't say important." Halifel rubbed the back of his head in a bit of shame. "It was something I volunteered to do."

Riza gave the Archangel an incredulous look, before she glanced at her grinning ber'nan, and then back at Hal.

"You mean you volunteered to see my ber'nan! Hal, I'm surprised at you." Riza pressed her hand to her face and slowly started shaking her head. "Actually, I'm more than surprised; I'm disappointed in you. And here I thought you were one of the smart ones."

Halifel laughed. Zareth scowled before he chimed in, "Hey!" but, he quickly fell silent after he thought better of even trying to protest.

Halifel turned towards the Meserino king and gave him a bow. "Now that I have concluded my business, I must take my leave." In an instant, the archangel started glowing, six pure white feathery wings with golden tips shot out from his back. When he waved his hand, a portal opened to his left. He smiled at Riza, nodded to Visage, and stepped through the swirling techno-colored opening. Then he was gone.

"I thought he'd never leave," Zareth grumbled. Once the remaining traces of Halifel's indren'freth had dissipated, several Meserino demons entered the room. Immediately thereafter, another Meserino woman made an abrupt entrance. To Visage, it seemed as though she had walked through the wall behind the throne. The woman, who was sporting a smug look, leaned against the royal throne and started to toy with the top of Zareth's head which made his scowl return, only tenfold. Riza snickered because of how annoyed her ber'nan was at their mi'thia's playful teasing.

Visage ignored what the demoness was doing. He was too fixed on her facial features. *Wow, she looks a lot like Riza!* "Riza? Is she your oma… I mean mi'thia?" he whispered. The woman stared down at the young demon below and chuckled.

"Yes, Orran. I'm Rashia, the wife of this good-for-nothing." She nodded and toyed with Zareth's hair and head with a bit more fervor.

Zareth was so annoyed that his temple was noticeably throbbing in irritation. Riza snickered behind her fist to try to hide it, but she only served to irritate her already irritated ber'nan even more.

I'm not sure I get this. She's Riza's oma, but she's Zareth's wife? Riza called Zareth her ber'nan. How does that work! Visage closed his eyes and folded his arms before he levitated off the floor to sit cross-legged in the air. He was trying to hide his thoughts, but every demon in the room was laughing—except for Zareth who's irked face turned into a bemused smirk.

"Orran, you have to understand our Meserino culture." Riza told him while she continued to snicker a bit. "When the head of the family dies, the wife is given to the successor," She raised her index finger while she stated matter-of-factly.

"Wait!" Visage held out his hand to stop her while rubbing the bridge of his nose in disbelief and a bit of disgust. "Riza, do you mean to tell me that your ber'nan is married to your mi'thia!"

Before any demon could answer, a much younger Meserino ran into the room, nearly colliding with Rashia's leg as he exclaimed, "Wow, is that a Silvarian demon next to big sri?" After hopping down the steps, the younger demon made a beeline to Visage and started inspecting him. Visage guessed that this Meserino was about his age.

The demon boy's eyes were deep red in color and sparkled with youthful enthusiasm. His hair was shoulder length—a combination of black and red. He was only wearing a pair of mithril weave style long shorts with the big cargo pockets, leaving his entire upper body exposed, though it was partially concealed by his wings, which were draped about his body in typical Meserino demon fashion. Visage had to take a step back when the boy had literally gotten right into his face.

Why is your skin black? Why do you have dark-purple biree? Why don't you look like the other Silvarians in my book? Can you turn into your other forms? Where did you come from? Are there other Silvarians here with you? Can I play with your tails? The child pounded Visage with a slew of telepathic questions. Visage was deciding whether to throttle him, or run away until Riza came to the rescue.

"Z! Silence!" The demoness's scream echoed throughout the room. It was so loud and harsh that all of the onlookers covered their ears and winced.

"But, but, sri"— The boy had started to complain about Riza's edict, but was abruptly silenced by another female Meserino who had entered the room. This demoness appeared to be decidedly perturbed and briskly made her way over to the boy. She harshly grabbed him by the shoulder, quickly turned, and marched back the way she came, dragging the disgruntled child along behind her. "Prince Zerak, your lessons are not over, and you are disturbing the king's guests." As she walked away with the prince, he held out his arms and reached out to Riza and Visage. He continued to protest, intermittently uttering something about the Silvarian's tails bringing good luck.

After Zerak and his attendant exited, the room became so silent that even the sighs of relief, exuded by the two Meserino guards, could easily be heard. *Zerak is a handful,* thought the male who was standing on the left hand side of the throne. *You have no idea,* thought the female guard who was standing to the right of the throne.

Rashia made her way down from the throne's stage. Bending over, she grabbed Visage by the hems of his cloak and lifted him up. *So, she is Riza's mi'thia after all,* Visage thought when the demoness brought him to her eye level. No demon knew exactly what Rashia's intentions were

—not even Riza. However, all agreed they were probably sinister in nature, since she was peering at Visage with an obvious look of disdain.

Zareth didn't offer to assist in the slightest, despite Visage's tele-pathic pleas. *I'm sorry, Orran, but when Rashia gets like this, all we can do is watch.* The Meserino Demon King let out a disconcerted yawn before he continued to play with his ring.

Rashia's eyes narrowed and started glowing with intense hatred. She brought the Silvarian in close. Visage had no time to react before their lips abruptly met, and he became encompassed by darkness. Past memories replayed in his mind but quickly dissipated, having been fully replaced by Rashia's presence. He was kneeling on the visually disturb-ing floor that looked like an endless abyss, with his palms down, and he was panting heavily. Rashia stood before him. "What's going on!" Visage blurted. The expression on the imposing-looking demoness's face was causing him to become irate.

"We are currently inside the void… Orran." Rashia's nonchalant atti-tude was not helping. Visage stood up slowly; he was now quite queasy. "I've temporarily connected our minds so that I can have a…" she paused a moment to think. "heart to heart conversation with you…" she smiled, but it was a very sinister smile. "Without any outside interference."

Visage's eyes widened in fear and wonder. *So that's why you brought me here!* The young demon's thoughts, though infused with anger, didn't seem to faze Rashia at all.

"Foolish child!" Rashia's intense disdain for him reignited. "You don't understand us! You don't even understand yourself! Now, ask me again why I've brought you here inside my head."

Visage wasn't stupid—naïve perhaps—but not stupid. He took a slow deep breath and stood tall. *Your Majesty, what is it that you want to show me?* Rashia was a bit taken aback by Visage's sudden change of attitude.

"Pretty quick on the uptake, Your Majesty," Rashia mockingly retorted, before following up with an even more mocking bow. Rashia noted Visage's obvious confusion and realized that she needed to help the young demon understand what had just transpired. "You are the son of Arnen, King of the Silvarian demons, are you not? Does this not make you his successor? Are you not now the Silvarian King?" Visage's eyes darted about as he tried to comprehend the queen's words. *She must be crazy! I don't know anything about being a king! Until recently, I thought I was just a strange-looking human.*

"That is why I needed to talk to you—privately," Rashia pronounced. She crossed her arms under her chest, mimicking one of Riza's mannerisms.

"Your Majesty, do you know why you're the last of your kind?" The question ripped Visage from all other thoughts. He nodded. "Yes. Skath killed them"— Rashia erupted in laughter, cutting him off. After quickly calming down and dropping her hands to her sides, her whole demeanor changed once again. She became intimidating. Not only did the slits in her eyes almost disappear, but she also started to make guttural growling noises.

"Oh, he did more than simply kill them! Skath erased them from existence!" Rashia howled. "The gods and the demons had lived in harmony for untold ages. Then Skath came along and changed everything! Before him, everybeing knew what to do and for what reason. We, the Meserino demons, stayed out of every other god or demon's business. Though it doesn't fit the humans' narrative about us, we only wished to be left alone. Thanks to that Dark God, we were dragged into that war of his! He started it all. Do you want to know how?" Rashia knelt down, her face mere inches from Visage's own. Her countenance displayed a range of emotions: anger, sadness, pity. All Visage could do was quickly shake his head, though he continued to keep his eyes on Rashia.

"He started it with his weapon! He forged a blade that can devour souls! These soul slaying weapons can steal the energy! Even from immortal beings! The sick thing is that, in order to try out his new weapon, he used it on his own family!" After Rashia finished speaking, the void, which she and Visage had been in, suddenly vanished.

The black void was replaced with the image of a giant tanned skinned man with blood red hair and burning red eyes wielding an oversized sorjin and, in a mad frenzy, he was cutting down everybeing in his path—most of whom looked to be women. Visage was nauseous from the gory scene. He felt even worse when he saw how gleefully the man committed these heinous acts. He was laughing while cutting down being after being; his laughter, that mad laughter never ceased!

Tears streamed from Visage's eyes. "No more!" He could barely whisper. "I don't want to see anymore!" He closed his eyes, yet the image remained. Then he was back inside the void. His vision was blurred behind his tears, but he could see Rashia standing several feet away with her back turned. She had her hands clasped tight behind her back, her right hand clutching her left wrist. Her tail swayed about before she slowly turned her head back towards the awe and fear struck demon. Her voice was like the edge of a well-sharpened blade.

"Did you see?" Visage couldn't even respond. "Did you see?" Rashia asked, her voice now an octave higher. Visage still couldn't manage a response. When the demoness vanished and reappeared in front of Visage before she grabbed him and held him up by his neck, her eyes were a an intensely glowing crimson color! "Did you see!" She screamed right into Visage's face. He nodded.

"Y... y... yes... I... s... s... saw," was all Visage was able to stammer in answer. Rashia withdrew her hand and dropped him back onto the visually disturbing floor.

"Now you understand."

Visage was still in a shock-like state when Rashia abruptly released him from her kiss. The vision vanished, and the pair was once again standing in the throne room.

***

Though Visage had not yet recovered from the horrors he had witnessed, Rashia picked him up and threw him across the room! His body twisted in mid-air before he landed hard and skidded across the floor. He had to dig in with his talons in order to stop. Though he was in shock from what Rashia had done. he was finding it hard to fully stand up, his jaw dropped when he saw that the scrapes on the floor had magically disappeared! However, his state of awe was short lived.

With his eyes bulging and his body trembling, he lashed out at Rashia. "Why did you do that to me! Why did you show me that... that... madness! What's wrong with you! And what did I do to bring on that kind of venomous rage!"

Riza and the other demons in the room were so horrified by what Rashia had done that they were unable to move. Rashia, on the other hand, responded to Visage's tirade by chanting in the demon tongue. The eyes of the onlookers all widened while they took in the ghastly spectacle that was unfolding before them.

The next thing Visage realized was that Rashia had a terrifyingly wicked-looking rapier in her hand and was now charging him! He closed his eyes and awaited the inevitable outcome. When he was not immediately slashed to pieces, he thought, *"Why am I still alive?"* At that instant, there was an ear-piercing metallic-sounding clang! Visage gasped! Zareth was standing over him, wielding a large strange-looking sorjin that was eerily reminiscent of the one that Skath had used. He had used his blade to stop Rashia's rapier from piercing Visage's heart. Riza, who was standing several feet behind Rashia, was now holding a giant scythe! The two blades the main one was longer than her arm and the shorter one was half her arm's length. The two evil blades were an abyss black that changed to an ugly crimson-colored where the bevel of the blade started. The juncture with the two blades and spike at the top attached to the shaft was longer than her arm. The shaft of her menacing weapon was an even deeper black than the two blades were and it looked to be even taller than its wielder. At the base of Riza's scythe, a great black chain with glowing red runes on each link with a wicked studded cone attached to the end of the chain. The nasty looking chain was wrapped around Rashia's midsection.

The wrapped-up demoness grunted in annoyance when the chain wrapped around her. "What do you think you're doing!" Rashia narrowed her eyes at Riza, before she slowly turned her head to focus on her impertinent de'tari.

"That's my line, mi'thia!" Riza shot back. Rashia's right eye twitched a bit at Riza's statement. She then the older demoness focused on Zareth.

"You don't understand what you are doing, do you!" The edge in his mi'thia's voice made Zareth wince a bit, but he wasn't about to back down.

"Yes, mi'thia, I do." Zareth wasn't very pleased at all that he had to fight his wife. "I'm saving Orran from you!"

Zareth and Riza were aghast when Rashia responded with a shrill laugh!

"No, I'm saving you from him!" she shouted while her eyes shot from Zareth back to Visage.

Zareth was stunned but managed to throw off his shaken state. He peered at Visage, before he refocused on Rashia. *What do you mean by that, mi'thia!* Telepathy did have its uses, Zareth was trying not to add to Visage's trauma.

If you must know, Rashia telepathically retorted, *I saw what that demon boy becomes!*

Your clairvoyance may be helpful at times,—Zareth scowled. —*but, more than anybeing in the universe, you should know that the future is uncertain and changeable!* he shot back.

*Perhaps...*Rashia countered with a sneer of her own.*Or, perhaps I'm preventing a being even worse than Skath from coming into existence!*

Riza's face contorted in outrage. *He isn't anything like Skath!*

Not yet he isn't... But in the future—

Riza yanked hard on the scythe, hauling her mi'thia away from her ber'nan and Visage. "He's my fiancé, and I won't allow you to devour him!" She spun her scythe overhead, twirling it in a wide arc. When she did so, she jerked back on the lower end of the shaft, causing the chain to tighten. Rashia having been restricted by the chain, Riza jerked hard on her scythe, sending the demoness into the air. Her body careened back down and landed violently against the floor. Zareth joined the fight, positioning his taloned foot over Rashia's right wrist and pinning it to the floor. Riza followed suit by putting her foot on the chain that was wrapped around Rashia's waist. She then pinned down her left hand, preventing her from retaliating. The siblings finished the job by crossing their blades right above Rashia's neck.

So, the children will kill their own mi'thia... How ironic! By the time Rashia's thoughts struck the duo, Visage was on the move. His eyes glowed icy-blue and blue-and-black flames erupted from his body. With lightning speed, he flipped in the air, twirling as he went and catching both demons off guard. While he spun down between them, he kicked out hard with both of his legs, knocking both Riza and Zareth off from their felled foe. The pair were in shock and unable to move. Visage, on the other hand, had landed and was straddling Rashia. He was hidden behind the fires of his Cloak of Darkness, the flames causing the cloak to wildly dance about his body. Nonetheless, from his vantage point he was able to peer down into the eyes of the one who had sought to erase him from existence.

Does he think he can kill her with that technique? Zareth's thoughts only served to anger the child when he unabashedly glared at the demon.

Children should never injure their parents! Visage's thoughts caused the two siblings to balk. "I don't know what caused you to attack me, but, whatever it was, I'm sorry." The young demon's calm, cool voice caused the demoness to shiver. At this point, Visage got off from Rashia, stood to her left side, and offered her a fire-engulfed hand.

"What makes you think I won't attack you again?" Rashia asked before she glanced over at her fallen rapier.

"I know you won't—because we're family." The jaws of the other demons hit the floor right after the words escaped Visage's lips. He then continued, "Besides, you planned all this. And you never really wanted to hurt me, though this kind of test is rather demonic—if you ask me."

Rashia rolled her eyes. "Was I that obvious? Perhaps I'm getting old," she said, taking the boy's offered hand and allowing him to assist her to her feet.

"Or, perhaps you shouldn't have shown me what's in your heart while we were inside your head," Visage countered.

Rashia looked abashed while she rubbed the back of her head and sheepishly grinned. "I'll try to remember that next time." After turning her back towards Visage, Rashia stretched out her hand, and her rapier flew into it; she gripped the handle tightly.

Riza and Zareth had prepped for another bout with their mi'thia. Zareth had put his right foot forward and was clutching his giant sorjin with both hands. The chain that was lying loose on the floor had magically wrapped around the shaft of Riza's scythe. After swinging the blade out, in order to have it face backwards, she had tucked the shaft under her right armpit and gripped the middle of the shaft with her left hand. However, her fingers, having not yet gripped the lower end, now relaxed. Having heard the rivals' conversation, she realized that Rashia no longer posed a threat.

Rashia returned her rapier to the source from whence it came, and it subsequently vanished into a spray of red sparks and black mist. Before she started walking away, she fluttered her fingers at Orran and said, "I've finished what I set out to do, so I'll see you around, King Orran."

Monsters, devils, demons—agma... oni... yokai—what does it matter. We're none of those things. I am what I am, and we are what we are.... so long as we still feel. After clenching his fists, Visage's flames dissipated. "Rashia, I am no king, and my name is not Orran. It's Visage. I am an ar'teth of the Zaharaj. And I'm nothing like Skath!" Riza and Zareth were dumbfounded by the boy's thoughts and words. They both stood with their mouths agape.

Rashia's eyes went wide, and she slowly turned her head, the child's pronouncement having taken her by surprise. *I think this is the first time I've been this soundly defeated. Eendril might actually know what He's doing.*"Visage, tell that self-righteous Nosfaren to stop by and see us once in a while." With that said, she strode up to the throne, walked past it, and disappeared into the wall. Visage let out a huge sigh of relief, fell onto his back, and gave Riza and Zareth, who had raced to his side, a big toothy grin.

Zareth responded with a smirk. "If I didn't know any better, I'd say you were challenging me to a duel, but right now, frak it!" He returned the smile down at the fallen, but beaming Silvarian.

"When did that even become a thing?" Riza asked now that things had settled down.

Zareth thought a moment. "I have no idea, but it's a rather dumb-crathed rule if you ask me." Riza nodded in agreement and proceeded to swing her scythe in a wide arch. After she did so, it disintegrated into a spray of sparks and red mist. Zareth twirled his great sorjin over his head before it disappeared in the same fashion. Riza then bent down and helped Visage up.

"I've been wondering why your coloring was off, "Visage," Zareth commented while he looked the boy over. "But I think I've figured it out. Using that Cloak of Darkness technique has really messed you up, hasn't it?" he asked while making his way back up the few steps to before throwing himself back into his grand throne. Zareth used his arm to cover his eyes and let out a long sigh of relief.

Visage and Riza sat down on the top step of the throne's raised platform. Visage splayed his legs out in front of him and leaned back on the palms of his hands. Riza crossed her legs and put her hands under her head as she lay on her back. "I think it makes him look like a bad crath," she told her ber'nan, who was again lazing about on his oversized throne.

"*Hmm... I guess,*" Zareth offered—not caring one way or another.

"Oh well, it's not like it's permanent, anyway," Visage offered before refocusing on a different topic. "Your Majesty, can I ask you something?"

Zareth chuckled at the formality. "Visage, you don't have to call me that. Zareth is fine. After all, you *are* family." Zareth took a quick glance at his sri'na. She didn't seem fazed by his comment, much to his disappointment. "By all means, ask away." He gestured for Visage to ask his question.

Visage took a moment to think a bit. *He acts as if that whole incident never happened.*

Riza laughed. She stared up at her ber'nan before turning to Visage. "I told you, Visage, we are known as the laziest demons in existence." She leaned on her right side and propped up her head with her right hand in order to get a better look at her fiancé. One of his tails was wagging slightly. It was as though it was teasing her, so she grabbed it, causing the child to jump up in surprise. Riza looked rather shocked when the purple-tipped tail was suddenly yanked away from her. The tail felt like silk strands tickling her palm when it slid though her clenched fist. *I didn't think I grabbed it* that *hard,* she thought as she watched Visage clutch his tail in his hands and hug it close to him. She could see that the Silvarian was looking troubled. *Is he blushing?* She couldn't be sure because of his currently black-colored skin.

"Why'd you do that, Riza!"

Riza was so shocked by Visage's reaction that she couldn't respond, so Zareth jumped in. "Sri'na, didn't you know that Silvarian tails are rather—sensitive?"

"No... I didn't." She turned to Visage. "I'm so sorry, Visage; it was an honest mistake. It's just that those tails of yours are so fraking cute." Feeling badly about his reaction, Visage sat back down next to the contrite demoness.

"No, Riza. You... startled me is all. I don't mind if you pet them." He spoke softly. Riza looked like she had just won one of Earth's big lotto games. This time she handled his tail a bit more gently. Visage arched his back, looking though he was going to stand up, but he didn't move. Riza started stroking his bushy tail, and he let out a rather cute, "ep," when she did so. All of a sudden, he got the strangest look on his face. He laid flat on his back, and his purple tongue hung out of his mouth. Riza squealed "Really!" and quickly let go of his tail. She turned and glared at her ber'nan. *You said their tails were sensitive, but you didn't tell me you meant* that *kind of sensitive!* Zareth responded with a chuckle.

Visage was still feeling the effects of the tail petting. "Why'd you stop? That felt really good."

"You're too young to be feeling *that* kind of good." Riza cried with a mix of shame, intrigue, and irritation. "Has anybeing *else* ever touched your tails like that before?"

"Not really." Visage shrugged. "When I went to school, some of the kids yanked on them because they didn't think they were real. Now that really hurt." Remembering the pain, he held the tails close. When he noticed that Riza was frowning, he immediately shook his head and gave her a grin. "Don't worry, Riza, everything worked out. My mi'thia took me out of school the next day. She didn't like the way the kids... treated me. Oh, and when I was little, my sri'nas liked to brush my tails. They were so happy whenever I allowed them to stroke them..." he blushed at the memory, but then he vigorously shook his head. "I think my family likes them the same way you do."

Riza raised a quizzical eyebrow. "What do you mean by that?" Her curiosity was now piqued.

Visage started playing with his tails and appeared embarrassed. "You said they were 'cute.' "

"They're not cute! They're a demon's most prized feature!" Zareth exclaimed, surprising every demon in the room, especially his two guards. His demeanor quickly changed, and his voice lowered. "Visage, you shouldn't let anybeing touch your tails... except for Vira and my sri'na that is." He wiggled his eyebrows at him.

"King Zareth,"— Visage muttered in embarrassment. —"am I really married to your sri'na?" Visage felt really embarrassed after asking, so he tried to hide his face behind one of his tails.

Zareth closed his eyes and had a half grin on his face. "Hmm," he muttered. "all I know is that our dar'nra's determined that you should be together, though I don't know why Riza agreed to the proposal. It baffles me that she's waited for you all these eons," Zareth sarcastically offered while eyeing his stunned sri'na.

Riza wasn't too thrilled with her ber'nan's pronouncement. "Did you really have to tell him that!"

"Come on sri,"— Zareth shot back with a smirk. —"you should know by now that I will tease you whenever I get the chance."

Riza chose not to get into a debate with her ber'nan over the issue. Instead, she got up and stretched. "I'm still angry at mi'thia's behavior. I wonder what she needed to show Visage that was so important?"

"I was wondering the same thing." Zareth's one open eye focused on the still blushing Silvarian. "Visage, what did my mi'th... I mean wife... show you?"

Visage suddenly clutched his tails again, only this time he clutched them even more tightly. "She showed me what Skath did... At least I think it was Skath." He was so emotionally traumatized that he buried his face into his tails and fell silent.

"Skath is the being who changed everything!" Zareth angrily growled. "That sorjin he built makes even immortal beings have to fear for their lives!"

"Not only our lives, but our very existence." Riza sat and hugged her knees. "If it weren't for him, the Ze'therac clan wouldn't have ever betrayed us like that. And dar'nra would still be alive!"

"Yeah,"— Zareth frowned and nodded. —"and I wouldn't have to be tied to this fraking throne!"

Visage raised his head out from under his tails. "Is that the clan that... killed mine?" he almost inaudibly asked.

Riza nodded. "Yes, V. It was the Ze'therac clan who killed the Silvarians."

"My sri'na brought you thru their village," Zareth added. "Didn't she?" He glanced at his frowning sri'na who reluctantly nodded.

"You mean that empty ghost town?" Visage cried in shock. "*That* was where the Ze'therac clan lived? Why isn't anybeing living there, now?"

"It's there as a silent reminder that even *we* can be led astray by false gods offering false promises." Zareth paused. "It's true. We could re-occupy it. But those who do so would just be haunted by the memories of the ones who are gone."

"Visage, you really shouldn't worry about such things. After all, Skath is gone now, so all we need to do is focus on the future." Riza put her legs down, leaned over, and gave her fiancé a reassuring hug.

"Were they all killed? I mean... did any of the Ze'therac clan survive?" Visage whispered.

After bringing the boy back to arm's length, Riza shook her head. "No, Visage, they were not all killed; there is still one Ze'therac left." The demoness' shoulders slumped and her head bowed. "Lord Nosfaren... is a Ze'therac."

Visage's eyes widened in astonishment. "Lord Nosfaren is a Ze'therac!" He shook his head in disbelief "But... he's so cheery. I mean... wasn't he angry, or sad about the loss of his clan?" Visage directed his question to Zareth who shrugged in reply.

"No, he was the clan's only voice of reason." Riza answered for her ber'nan.

Zareth frowned before he picked up where she left off. "Nos... he tried to convince his parents not to join Skath—so they exiled him. It's ironic, because that's what saved his life. And Visage, just so you know, no Meserino demon harbors any ill will towards him. In fact, we've been trying to convince him to return home. But he's so fraking stubborn!"

Riza rolled her eyes. "No, that's not it; he's simply become too attached to the mortals who befriended him"—She shrugged and sighed —"not to mention that crathing id'rth who chased after him when he left."

"Aren't they the ones who started that cult—?"

Zareth was interrupted by his sri'na, who was really drathed off. "It's not a cult, big ber'nan... It's an organization!"

"Either way, I'm surprised that he lets you stay in that little temple of his. After all, sri, you're the one who killed his dar'nra during the war." Zareth smirked while he watched Visage's face contort in fear and confusion.

Riza got up, turned on the balls of her feet, and raised her toes so her talons wouldn't scratch up the floor. She got right into her ber'nan's face and glared daggers at him, "There you go again! You didn't have to tell him that!"

Though Visage's mouth hung agape, Zareth, on the other hand, appeared amused. "Whoa, whoa, whoa! Calm down there killer! I was only telling him the truth."

Riza scowled. "The truth hurts ya know, you slime covered blort-worm!" she humphed before whipping her head around. "Come on, Vis-age, I think it's time we left His Majesty to his devices," she sarcastically blurted before grabbing the boy by the shoulder and helping him to his feet. Visage did not protest. Riza proceeded to wave her hand and open the swirling portal of pastels. She pushed Visage through the portal, but then she turned to Zareth, pulled the lid of her eye down and blew him a raspberry. Riza also flipped him off for good measure, right before she jumped through the portal herself.

Just how childish can one get? Zareth thought while he watched the portal vanish with a slight pop.

18

What Was Lost Can't Be Found

The Firaxian Galaxy—a giant spinning wheel in the infinite cosmos of space—is populated by countless numbers of beings inhabiting worlds that are capable of supporting life. Unfortunately, the majority of the worlds are unable to do so. Yenos Three is one of those worlds. It's a giant ball of desert sand that circles a fading star. Raging storms tear across its surface unabated. Only fools would attempt to land there, much less try to live there. However, the Zaharaj were no ordinary beings.

***

Two black-cloaked figures walked through hurricane-force winds though, to them the winds were like a mere spring breeze. Their raspy breaths went unheard as they trudged, surrounded by sand and noxious gases, towards their destination. Thankfully, their mask filtration systems were well designed. While the pair moved along, they could see weather-beaten rocks sticking up from the nearby dunes. The rocks became more and more plentiful as the duo drew closer and closer to what appeared to be the remnants of an ancient temple. The only thing the pair knew about the temple was that the ones who built it were Zah'harrim users from eons past.

The smaller of the two Zaharaj walked over to one of the larger stones. Simply by placing his gloved hand against the stone it caused pieces of it to fall and meld, before fully vanishing into the red-colored sand.

Master, are you sure *this is the last planet Jetec visited before his disappearance?* He telepathically asked the older being, who had stopped. Forscythe was intently surveying the area in a desperate attempt to locate their destination.

Yes, Vok'et, it is, Forscythe replied before he waved to his apprentice in order to get his attention. Vok'et's vision was so obscured by the sandstorm that Forscythe also had to resort to telepathy. *Vok'et! Over here! I think we're very near the temple entrance!* The apprentice turned and trudged over to where his master was standing. The arm of his cloak flapped about wildly in the wind forcing him to hold up his arm in an attempt to deflect the buffeting sand.

Once Vok'et reached him, Forscythe pointed to something to their right. *Come, apprentice, if we hurry we can be out of this crathing weather in less than two dironns.*

Vok'et didn't look at all confident. Fortunately, his mask hid his face. It wasn't that he didn't get along with the older Zebrecian, but he was well aware that Forscythe had a tendency to misread his sensors; he had gotten them lost on several occasions.

Master, are you sure this the right direction? Forscythe, who was already on the move, stopped again, this time to reassure his apprentice. *Don't worry, I checked twice to make sure I got the right coordinates. Then I had Bee Three download them into my mask and U-gem. There is no way I will allow us to get lost on this planet.*

Vok'et smiled. *Well then, what are we waiting for, we have an ancient temple to find!* Forscythe led on despite the seemingly worsening storm. The wind whipped at the pair's cloaks, and the sand made its way into their boots, grating uncomfortably on their feet.

Forscythe halted and looked around. "Frak!" He cursed, but the howling wind drowned out his expletive. "I'm sure this is it, but I don't see anything remotely resembling a temple." He muttered to himself. Bringing his left glove close to his face, Forscythe activated his U-gem. Since the sand was now ankle-deep, the screen was mostly obscured. However, he was still able to glean that they were, in fact, in the right place. "Oh, this is just frakingtastic! Now what are we supposed to do!"

In the meantime, Vok'et had continued to search. He could see, though barely, that there were several rows of stones in front of him, so he headed off to investigate. Right after Vok'et neared the stones, the sand shifted under his feet, and he fell into a previously unforeseen opening.

Vok'et, where are you! Where did you go! Forscythe's telepathic messages were filled with panicked concern.

*I'm over here, Master. I think I found the temple! Just watch your—*Forscythe's tumbling and rolling body came through the completely obscured entrance, appearing like a ball of cloth and sand. *Never mind.*

Once Forscythe stood, sand cascaded off his body. "You could have warned me about the drop," he admonished his apprentice.

"I tried, Master!" Vok'et snapped. "It all happened too fast!"

Once composed, the pair emptied their boots and proceeded to focus on the dark empty maw and what little remained of the temple's entrance. They both observed that the opening through which they had fallen was probably once a staircase. Fortunately, whoever designed the place made sure the entranceway was at least covered.

The companions were out of the storm, but the darkness before them was neither comforting nor welcoming. The noises produced by the hole when the wind whipped through the entranceway caused the place to seem as though it were a living creature that was screaming in pain and giving off its final cries before death. *Master, are you sure this is—*Vok'et's thought was cut off when Forscythe shot his arm straight in front of him. He turned his head, causing one of the red-glowing eyes of his mask to be slightly visible.

"Apprentice, this is a dark place—it feels like Zharaj, but it's giving off even more Zah energy than our planet."

Forscythe's assessment only added to Vok'et's already heightened apprehension. When his master took out his blood sorjin and ignited it, bathing the surrounding area with its crimson glow, he swallowed hard. The place had been eerie enough as it was, but the red light from Forscythe's blood sorjin made the place downright foreboding.

Forscythe was now heading into the darkness. The glow of his sorjin caused great shadows to form while he moved along. Vok'et, on the other hand, was standing fast, unable to get his feet to cooperate. His attempt at stopping Forscythe from trekking ahead was unsuccessful. After accessing his own blood sorjin and igniting it, he mustered up the courage to take the first step. "Master, wait for me!" he cried before finally making his way into the structure.

The place was massive on the inside. It seemed quite familiar to the duo, especially the way the entrance hall was set up. It reminded both beings of their own temple on Zharaj. The only real difference was that it didn't have an upper balcony like the one in their temple's entrance hall, and the rows of pillars weren't nearly as ornate as the ones to which they were accustomed. The pillars stretched from floor to ceiling, but the way they were situated caused the room to be divided into four equal parts. They were also crumbling from age as well as from wind, which had whipped through the place for eons. Small and medium-sized chunks of the smooth-looking obelisks had fallen away and were sitting under, or very near, the pillars. The pillars themselves cast monstrous shadows when Vok'et and Forscythe passed between them and bathed both in the glow of their weapons.

Where's he heading now? Vok'et noticed that his master had stopped, taken notice of something to his right, and headed off in that direction. "Did you see something, Master? Vok'et knew something was wrong when Forscythe didn't answer. *I wonder what he's found...*

***

The Verse is a very powerful ally and useful tool. The gods can use it to create galaxies, planets, and life. Verse-using beings in the Firaxian Galaxy can only use a meager fraction of what a god can use. The Zaharaj train in both the Zah'harrim and Jah'harrim forms of the Verse. However, using the Zah'harrim form has consequences. If a being's heart and mind aren't strong enough, he or she will succumb to its dark influence, becoming nothing more than an animal. Beings who can master its use are rare. Forscythe is one of those beings.

***

This place is steeped in Zah power, even more than in Jah. So why would Lady Dreth and Jetec come here? Even the greatest among us would easily become a Fallen if they stayed here too long. Forscythe's mind was wandering, while at the same time, he was being led on, but by what, or whom, he wasn't sure. *Dear God, please let us get out of here safely. Please give us the strength to withstand the great darkness that we now face. Please help us find out what has become of Jetec and why Chirras is acting so strangely.*

"Master, do you even know where we're going?"

Vok'et's question snapped Forscythe back to reality. Though Forscythe was the Master, he was relieved that his apprentice was with him. He stopped, peered at his young charge, and responded, "Honestly, I have no idea."

Vok'et shook his head and let out a frustrated grunt. "I'm sorry, Master, but that isn't very reassuring."

Forscythe was neither hurt nor fazed by his apprentice's observation. "I did send out several scouting dolls before we entered, apprentice, if that makes you feel any better."

Vok'et stood still for a moment. *At least Master isn't a complete id'rth.* Feeling a little encouraged, he switched his blood sorjin to his left hand. Using the Jah'harrim, he activated his U-gem and made a holo image of the ruin's interior, which had been mapped out by four of the small scouting dolls. Based on the dolls' input, the main area appeared to be fashioned in the shape of a square box. Extending out from the box-like room were several hallways, each with rooms lining their sides. "Well, Master, at least you can't get lost in this place," Vok'et joked after he saw the two large blips representing his master and him in their current location. Apparently, they were halfway down one of the hallways, which was branching out from the right side of the room. What was puzzling was the big gap that was located in the center of the structure.

The dolls had completed the mapping of the smaller rooms and had now converged on one spot in another more distant hallway. Something was preventing them from scanning the blank area—but what? "It seems to me that our little metal friends have hit a snag," Forscythe said after he observed his apprentice's holo map. "Perhaps that area is where we will find our answers."

Vok'et balked. "Are you sure, Master?" He was disappointed that Forscythe blithely dismissed his question before trudging ahead to see what was in his reconnaissance dolls' way. Before obediently following, he mused, *I hate it when he does that.*

***

While the duo made their way to the dolls' location, they noticed that the walls had drastically changed. They were still crumbling and cracking but had gone from a sandblasted tan color to a dark, menacing, black, or deep rust-colored red. Vok'et couldn't be sure about the color since the glow of his sorjin was making everything look red. He was curious, so he stopped and ran his hand along the wall. After doing so, he was surprised to find a new smudge on his glove. Once analysis of the smudge was complete, the HUD in his mask informed him that whatever the dusty black stuff was, it was originally organic. *Some form of corrosion? Or mold perhaps? I'm surprised that anything can survive in this environment.* Using telekinesis, he let go of his sorjin's hilt, causing it to float in place while he rubbed his gloved hands together in an attempt to get rid of the organic matter. His attempt was successful. With the sorjin back in hand, he looked around in order to relocate Forscythe. "Oh great, what's wrong now?" he muttered; Forscythe was standing motionless and staring at the floor.

***

Now that the wind had died down, Vok'et's footfalls sounded like crunching noises as he walked along the crumbling sand-strewn floor.

The sounds were beginning to grate on his nerves. By the time he reached his master, Forscythe was down on one knee.

Though Vok'et's uch'nra wasn't the best master in the Zaharaj, he was far from the worst. He didn't like putting his young apprentice in danger. However, based on what he had just discovered, he was afraid that Vok'et and he were now in a very grave situation. While he scanned his disturbing find, the red eyes on his mask glowed in the infrared spectrum. "Scan complete. Analysis: blood; Zebrecian male; identity confirmed. Sample is a genetic match to Zaharaj apprentice, Jetec." The voice in his right ear caused Forscythe to cringe.

Vok'et was now standing right behind Forscythe. "What's wrong, Master?" Forscythe ignored his inquiry while he rubbed the small drop of blood with his index finger. It was dry, which wasn't surprising considering the planet's environment and the amount of time that had passed since Jetec's disappearance. What had been surprising was Chirras's attitude regarding his disappearance. She appeared to be curiously apathetic when the Council questioned her about it upon her return. *Just how did she manage to return alone? Why would she leave her injured apprentice behind?* With these thoughts in mind, Forscythe turned to Vok'et.

"I'm sorry to tell you this, my apprentice, but it seems your ber'nan has been injured." Vok'et grimaced at the news.

"Well, what are we waiting for, Master! We have to find him... now!"

"Calm down, Vok'et, I only found a drop of his blood. He could have cut himself on something while he was exploring this place; you know how he is." Vok'et took a deep breath and let it out slowly in order to steady his senses and reign in his emotions. *That's true; Jetec used to forget everything else whenever he was overly excited.* He smiled as further memories of his ber'nan enter his mind. *I remember the time when he was so engrossed in reading that old history book that he forgot to eat!* Vok'et stared down at the small drop of blood. *I hope Master is right.*

Forscythe was now on his feet "I share your concern for Jetec, Vok'et, but with the amount of Zah Verse power this place emits, you must keep your emotions under control. If you can't do that, I suggest you go back to the entrance and wait for me there." Forscythe's voice was calm, yet commanding.

Vok'et's head drooped and he slowly nodded. "Yes, Master." His response had a distinctly despondent tone. Forscythe loved his sri'na's dar'tari, and, though he was trying hard not to show it, even he was beginning to feel that something dreadful might have happened to Jetec. "Well, my apprentice, there is no time like the present."

Master and apprentice headed down the far hallway, fear gripped their hearts. With each step, they encountered more and more splatters of blood—Jetec's blood. Fear turned to panic after the realization hit— Jetec is, or was severely injured. The blood spots had gotten considerably larger and more clustered. About a quarter of the way down the hallway, the pattern changed. Two smear lines could plainly be seen in the sand ahead. "He was being dragged!" the pair shouted in unison.

"Master, we have to save him!"

Forscythe's mind was racing. *Who would attack such a powerful Verse user... and why? And where the frak was Chirras while all of this was happening!* He mentally shouted. His heart was simultaneously beating faster and louder. Now he had more questions than answers.

After giving each other a sharp nod, the pair took off fast, kicking up sand and dust behind them while they raced to where the reconnaissance dolls were still milling about. They landed in front of a giant door, which had been magnetically sealed. Here, they could see that the baseball-sized mechanical dolls were utilizing their small sensor arrays as well as several tentacle-like scanners. All four of them were bobbing about the door, assessing how best to enter.

"Alright, that's enough. You can shut down now," Forscythe commanded. Immediately, all of the scanners retreated into the dolls' spherical bodies, and the dolls proceeded to start falling to the ground. Forscythe acted fast, using his telekinetic ability to snatch them out of the air. After all were rescued, he deposited them into the U-Gem in his left glove. Right after they vanished into the green mist, they were replaced—via the same mist—by four larger black balls.

"Do you think the tactical assault dolls are going to be necessary, Master?" *Well, that sure was a rhetorical question.*

Forscythe peered down at the bloody drag marks, which had disappeared under the giant daunting-looking door. Then he gave a directive. "Vok'et, if you have any of your own T.A.Ds with you, now would be a good time to use them." Vok'et immediately took three more black spheres from his own utility gem. On command, the seven mechanical dolls came to life, turning into giant, lanky-looking, metal men. They were covered in black Marcisian-alloy plating. Their eyes, which were embedded into their smooth metallic faces, glowed red. Their lengthy metallic fingers ended in sharp claws, and two barrels popped out from the tops of their forearms.

Forscythe's four T.A.Ds had an added layer of mithril plating on their chests, causing them to be a bit more bulky-looking than Vok'et's three more-streamlined versions. Not only did they have extra armor, but they were also carrying very large plasma rifles. They swung them about, before clasping them in both hands. The seven tall T.A.Ds then turned to the two mortal beings, awaiting their respective master's orders.

"Greetings, my metal friends," Forscythe began. "We are in need of your assistance. For, you see, on the other side of this door is an unknown enemy, and we may need you if they are still in there." Forscythe knelt down and motioned for the T.A.Ds to look. Seven metal heads bent over, and seven sets of red-glowing eyes scanned the blood on the floor.

"Scan complete. DNA: matching Zebrecian male, Zaharaj apprentice, Jetec. Status: unknown. Reported missing by his master, Lady Dreth, one mcronn and two deronns ago," the T.A.D on the far left announced after analyzing the blood.

"Master Vok'et, has Master Jetec ceased functioning?" His T.A.D's question shocked Vok'et. He gazed down at the trail of blood, his hope waned. He shook his head before downheartedly replying, "I honestly don't know, Four-Ten." Vok'et steeled his resolve. "But we can at least bring his killer to justice!" The T.A.D. on the far end then spoke.

"So, this is a search and destroy mission, not a search and retrieve mission, Master?"

"We don't know yet, Twotripen." Forscythe looked up. "Just be ready for anything." He took a long glance at the other T.A.Ds. "That goes for all of you." Each of the metal men responded with a sharp nod.

"Are you ready for this, my apprentice?"

"As ready as I'll ever be, Master."

With their conversation ended, Forscythe and Vok'et stood at opposite ends of the circular door. The door had a magnetic locking mechanism that sealed the two half-moon-shapes together. Vok'et knelt down, plunging his blood sorjin into the bottom of the door on the left side; his master mirrored him on the bottom right. The metal liquefied while they forced their red blades around the edge of the doorway. Because of the great size of the door, the two had to levitate in order to finish their cuts. At the top of the door, their blades met and squealed angrily after they were withdrawn.

After the two beings landed back on the floor, the pair gave each other a quick nod. Vok'et then spun around, extending his left leg high and out and kicking violently at the door. Forscythe gathered indren'freth energy into his right fist and let loose a great blast at the door at the same time his apprentice's kick landed. The door flew into the room, spinning end-over-end and landing several yards away.

"We're going in!" Vok'et loudly announced before he lowered his leg, readjusted his stance, and grabbed the hilt of his sorjin with both hands. All of the T.A.Ds rushed passed the two Zah'harrim wielders and entered the room first. Their weapons were at the ready. Their red eyes scanned for hostiles as well as for the missing apprentice. The group created a semicircle in the middle of the large room. The four armored beings made up the center of the perimeter while Vok'et's two mechanical dolls took up the ends. Vok'et's third doll broke away from the group. He raised his arm and made a fist, then brought the arm down with a fluid motion, giving the two sentient beings the all clear signal.

The room resembled that of the Council Room in the Zaharaj's main temple. Immediately as they entered, Forscythe and Vok'et noticed that there were several ancient decaying thrones facing the center of the room, though most of the thrones were now nothing more than piles of dust. Vok'et moved around to the left side of the room and Forscythe moved to the right. Neither of them could make out much of anything, though they bathed the area in the red glow of their weapons. The floor looked as though it had had some kind of intricate design carved into it, but the design was so withered by time that it was indecipherable.

"This place is... beyond evil," Forscythe whispered.

"Well, it does permeate with the Zah energy, Master," Vok'et replied, though Forscythe was already out of hearing range.

Forscythe had been following the trail of blood and drag marks, at least until now. The trail suddenly vanished behind the wall at the back of the room! The man's curiosity was now beyond piqued. *Why did they drag him around the edge of the room instead of straight through the center?* Holding up his blood sorjin, he noticed that the wall where the trail ended was in a direct line with the former entrance. *That's strange. This place is in ruins, but the door looks rather new. These thrones... thirteen.... no, twelve...*He trailed off, his thoughts returning to the trail of blood. *Why did they drag him around the thrones? What's so special about them? And what's behind this wall?* After leaning in to inspect the wall more closely, Forscythe, though hesitant, touched it. Thoughts of death, destruction, and an insatiable hunger hit him so strongly that he literally fell backwards, landing hard and almost dropping his blood sorjin. Vok'et was immediately at his side.

"Master, are you all right?"

It took him a few moments, before Forscythe responded. "Yes... Yes, Vok'et, I'm all right." However, right after his apprentice helped him back onto his feet, he mumbled incoherently, grabbed Vok'et, and pushed him back toward the entrance.

"That's it, Master! What's wrong!"

"We have to leave—NOW!"

"But what about my ber'nan?"

"He's dead! And we'll be joining him if we don't get out of this place,

FAST!" Forscythe hardly ever raised his voice, so his obvious panic caught Vok'et off guard.

Forscythe, who was determined to get his nephew safely back to Zharaj, let out a powerful wave of telekinetic energy. The wave was *so* powerful that it cleared the thick levels of dust off from the walls and ceiling. Vok'et's arms fell limply at his sides, and his sorjin slipped from his grasp. When its hilt hit the floor, the clanging sound seemed to be more deafening than the sound the door had made after Vok'et and Forscythe had sent it flying. With the dust cleared, Vok'et's jaw fell open, and his Zah'harrim-tainted eyes went wide behind his mask; he was in complete shock. He fell to his knees and gazed at the now-revealed massive work of art that was before him. It depicted a giant man who was wielding a truly demonic sorjin. The man's great cape was fluttering behind him, exposing his well-chiseled chest. His face sported a mocking sneer as two squinting and very dark red glowing eyes looked down upon the duo. Even as aged and crumbling as the mural was, those eyes seemed to Vok'et to be peering into his very soul, trying to rip it out and feed it to his evil blade. Tears welled up in his eyes. "Impossible! Impossible! Skath! This is a temple for Skath!" he blurted, still kneeling and gaping up at the likeness of the Dark God.

Forscythe merely stood by and watched his apprentice sink into despair. He glanced back at the mural before hastening over to him, putting away his blood sorjin, and hugging him as closely as he could. There they sat, the older uch'nra holding his young sri'na's dar'tari in his strong arms. Darkness, which was now descending, seemed to be mocking the pair.

"You won't leave here alive, little Zah... And that God of yours can't save you now."

Forscythe and Vok'et heard Skath's rant and immediately responded. After arising and assisting Vok'et to his feet, Forscythe ordered, "Come, apprentice, we've got to get out of here!" Vok'et nodded and the pair took off, lighting their way after they both reignited their weapons. The T.A.Ds followed after their masters re-entered the hallway, banked right, and headed back the way they had come. The entire group stopped short at the intersection with the next hallway. There, they could hear rumbling sounds—as well as the sound of stone scraping against stone—emanating from the horrid room they had just exited. After these sounds waned, they were replaced by the sound of slow stocky-sounding footfalls and metal dragging across stone. Chills shot down the spines of both mortal beings; they gave each other a quick glance and again took off.

This time Forscythe and Vok'et flew down the hallway (with their T.A.Ds attempting to keep pace) while the overwhelming darkness—full of fear, rage, and insatiable appetite—gave them chase. Right after they entered the grand entrance hall the wind started howling, drowning out most sound, the two T.A.Ds guarding the mortals' flanks turned and fired their weapons. The powerful balls of super-heated energy zoomed through the two Fallen that were in the front of the pack; their upper bodies blew apart from the blasts while their lower halves slumped to the floor. Two more of the glowing energy-laden orbs were sent toward the pale white creatures who were in a frenzy to reach them.

Though one would think their small size would inhibit the orbs' effectiveness, this was not at all the case. The first blast hit another one of the pale creatures right in the midsection, ripping its body into three pieces; the torso and the head shot into the air, and the lower half of the body violently smashed into the floor. A spray of black ichor splashed onto the walls. In the meantime, the second ball of energy violently collided against the ceiling. The weathered stone slabs came crashing down, crushing the next three lines of Fallen and blocking the path of the ones in the rear.

With the ceiling now collapsed, the nine escapees thought they were in the clear—until they heard the dragging of metal on stone—close behind them. Two hallways joined, and now there was a hoard of Fallen nipping at their heels. The two Zah could see the exit, but the Fallen were rapidly closing in, despite the onslaught of fire that they were receiving from the T.A.Ds. The beings in the rear didn't even slow down when the ones in the lead were blown apart by the T.A.Ds' laser and plasma blasts.

Forscythe flew up the sand-covered steps. In several quick motions, he shut off his bloodsorjin, snapped it back onto his belt, and retrieved his starship from his U-Gem. The ship materialized in a display of green mist and high-speed sand. Forscythe was up the boarding ramp before it even had the chance to fully lower. He got to the cockpit in record time, jumped into the pilot's seat, and hit the antigravity thrusters and shields in quick succession. Vok'et was next up the ramp. His T.A.Ds were following, continuing to fire into the lines of Fallen, which were now bottlenecked at the temple's entrance.

Vok'et, who had reached the top of the ramp, quickly noticed that one of his master's dolls was about to be overrun. Without a second thought, he ran back down the ramp. His hands and arms were charged with lightning. Before the leading Fallen, with its black, three-pronged spear, got close enough to stab at the poor mechanical being, Vok'et unleashed a torrent of hot white-and-blue lightning bolts. The bolts sent all of the Fallen, which were starting to climb up out of the temple, back down into the bowels of the ancient structure. The creatures tumbled over each other, fully incapacitated by the storm of lightening which coursed through their bodies.

Vok'et lowered his hands while turning to the T.A.D. "MOVE!" he yelled, unsure if the doll could hear over the gusting wind and flying sand. Fortunately, the T.A.D did hear, and the two ran, both making it safely to the ship. The doll made it up the ramp first, but when he turned around, he saw that Vok'et had a Fallen right behind him! Immediately, he brought his rifle to bear on the creature, but the sand and wind were messing with his optic sensors. Vok'et jumped, landing on the edge of the ramp. He barely turned, but the Fallen was on top of him, its wicked spear aimed directly at his heart. He stretched out his hand and caught the creature in an invincible vice-like grip, causing the spear to drop within a hair's breadth of his chest. The Fallen's bald-head, milky-white pupils, and black sclera erased any sense of what or who it may once have been. Vok'et was starting to lose his grip on the attacker while it struggled against him. His strength finally giving out, he fell, giving the being—or creature—an opening to finish him off, bare handed. However, at that very moment, a ball of plasma hit the creature in the head and exploded, causing a spray of black blood and white chunks to rain all over Vok'et's cloak and mask. A metal hand then reached down, grabbed the back of the cloak, and dragged the slightly shaken Zebrecian into the ship.

The ramp retracted, the door sealed over, and the ship began to move. Vok'et, though breathing heavily, managed to get up from the cool metal floor and make his way to the cockpit. One of the T.A.Ds was operating the chin gun and pounding the Fallen with massive plasma blasts. At this point, the creatures were growling angrily at the ship from their vantage point just outside the temple's entrance.

Right after Vok'et landed in the copilot's seat, Forscythe's commanding voice yelled out an order. "Apprentice, target the entrance and fire a thermite missile down their fraking throats!"

His breathing now normalized, Vok'et smirked under his mask and shouted back, "Aye, aye, Master!" He gleefully pressed several buttons in order to prep the missile and then launched the deadly projectile.

Once the ship stabilized, Forscythe yanked hard on the stick, sending the vessel through the sandstorm, through the cover of dark clouds, and into the upper atmosphere. He then turned the ship over onto its back, enabling the occupants to watch the impact of their little package.

The missile trajectory took it right down into the entrance of the temple, where it rammed through the army of Fallen before slamming into the far wall of the entrance hall. The space actually collapsed upon itself, creating a micro black hole for a moment before the thermite kicked in and violently exploded. Everything within a two-hundred-mile radius was instantly vaporized. Even the storm that had been raging couldn't withstand the overwhelming explosive power delivered by the thermite warhead.

The two Zah watched the devastation from the safety of their ship. Vok'et shot out of his chair and gave a hearty a cheer. "That's for Jetec, you scum-sucking Skathic slith!"

Forscythe wasn't as joyous as his apprentice was, but, when the light from the explosion began to fade, a satisfied grin gradually spread across his face. "That's one less temple to the Fallen's God that we have to worry about." However, his brief moment of pleasure was replaced by worry and urgency when reality began to set in. *The temple was a problem, yes, but now we have an even bigger problem. The Zaharaj have been infiltrated. We must warn the Council.*"Apprentice, set a course for Zharaj; take us home."

Vok'et gave a salute and spouted, "Aye, aye, Uch'nra!"

Before turning and leaving the cockpit, Forscythe grinned a bit at Vok'et's antics. However, while heading towards the communications section, his expression hardened—like moribite. He was planning to inform Lord Nosfaren and the others of his discovery and knew the Dark Lord was not going to be happy. *And so, the witch-hunt begins.*

19

⚜

A Traitor in the Midst

The temple on Zharaj was bustling while trell was closing in. The asteroids, which hovered near the planet, were growing darker when the sunlight waned and was posing increased danger for the last returning starships. In another minronn, the majestic doors of the temple would be closed, and the cold chill of the trell air would be blocked. The lingering masters, knights, and ar'teths were going about their various duties, preparing for the close of yet another deronn.

From the window of his office far above the temple entrance, Lord Nosfaren could gaze out and watch the beings scurrying about like insects. The hood of his cloak was pulled down, revealing his dark hair and ponytail. The ponytail draped over top of the hood and ended up in the center of his back where his hands were clasped tightly together. He slowly rotated his head to the left, unnerved by what Lord Forscythe had just related. "Could you repeat that again, Lord Forscythe?" His voice was soft, low, and chilling.

The foot-tall holo image of Lord Forscythe came out of a projector, which was embedded into the top of Lord Nosfaren's bulky looking desk. "I think we have been infiltrated, Lord Nosfaren," the image of Forscythe again announced.

"This news is disconcerting... but not entirely unexpected." Lord

187

Nosfaren moved from his post at the window and slumped down in his chair after using telekinesis to pull it out from under his desk. "Are you sure the Skath temple has been destroyed?" he anxiously queried.

Lord Forscythe chuckled. "I'm quite sure, Lord Nos, unless the Fallen have found a way to survive the impact of a thermite missile cramming up their craths!"

Lord Nos remained tranquil at the man's remark. "And what of Jetec—did you find him?" Forscythe's mood became somber, when he shook his head.

"No, we didn't; the only thing we found was a trail of his blood. We were unable to recover his remains. I think his body may have been used by the Skath worshipers in one of their sacrificial rituals... But I can't be one hundred percent certain." Nos discerned that Forscythe had an even greater burden on his shoulders. "I don't know what I'm supposed to tell my sri'na when I see her." Forscythe's holo image slumped forward after he spoke.

"Perhaps I can assist you with that, Lord Forscythe. I know someone who can give you answers for your sri'na's questions." Nos's face contorted in anger. *I'm going to have a little chat with Chirras—and soon!* His anger clouded his thoughts.

"No, Lord Nosfaren! You can't let Chirras know about any of this! We don't even know for sure if she's involved!"

Nos slammed his hands down on the top of his desk. "Explain!"

Forscythe folded his arms and thought a moment before speaking. "We have an opportunity here..."

Nos raised an eyebrow, his curiosity now piqued. "What are you thinking?"

"Lord Nos, Lady D... I mean Chirras... doesn't know that you've sent anybeing to investigate her apprentice's disappearance, right?" Forscythe sounded hopeful.

"No. Why?" Nosfaren raised a suspicious eyebrow. "Where are you going with this, Forscythe?"

After digesting Nos's response, the small image of Lord Forscythe smashed his right fist into his open left palm. He was beaming behind his mask. "With your permission, Lord Nosfaren, I have a plan!"

Though rarely blindsided, Forscythe caught Lord Nos completely off guard. Nos spun around in his chair and mentally pondered the situation at hand. *Plan! What plan! Just what is he up to?* He sighed. *Caution and patience are valuable allies.* He turned his chair around and faced the waiting Lord. "All right, Forscythe, let's hear this plan of yours," he offered, leaning back in his chair. *This had better be good.*

"Not over the holo network. I'll tell you and the Council when I arrive."

"This had better not be some mess of slith you're giving me. Because I have half-a-mind to storm into that traitor's room, take her into custody, and rip all of her crathing secrets from her pretty little Skath-worshipping head!" Lord Nos arose; he wanted to make sure that Forscythe got the point.

Forscythe wasn't fazed in the least by Nos's outburst. "I assure you— this plan will work." He was calm and resolute.

Nos retook his seat. "Fine, I will assemble the Council when you return, and you can tell us this plan of yours." Though he had tried hard not to sound drathed off, he knew he had failed.

Forscythe didn't even care. He was more than elated to be allowed the honor of speaking to the Council. "I'll be there in less than a minronn!"

"You'd better be—" Nos was cut off midsentence as Forscythe's holo image gave a slight bow and the transmission ended. Nosfaren rubbed his temples. *I can't wait to hear this.*

"He does have a point you know." Ali'stia was leaning against the edge of the desk. Her legs were crossed and her hair was fluttering about when she tilted her head back and to the left so she could get a better look at her husband. "You're not actually interested in Forscythe's yet-to-be-explained plan... are you?" Nos was quite shocked at his wife's comment. He leaned back in his chair, awkwardly placed his booted feet up on his desk. He crossed his legs and arms before sinking into deep thought.

"Now, my pathia, don't pout," Ali'stia taunted, giving her husband a seductive grin.

"I'm not pouting... I'm worried! And you should be too! Come on, Ali'stia, we might have at least one Skath worshipper in our midst, and who knows how many more!" His eyes were burning while he spoke. He closed them and attempted to sort out his feelings.

"That's precisely why I think Forscythe has the right idea!" The demoness turned around, pressed the knuckles of her left hand down onto the desk, and gestured with her right hand. "I know you don't like it any more than I do, but we have to feign ignorance—especially in front of Chirras. If Forscythe's plan is what I think it is... then, we should be able to flush out every last one of those Skathic-sucking slime that's infiltrated our Order!" She leaned over in order to get closer to her husband's face so she could fully take in his reaction.

Nos sighed. "That's not what has me worried."

Ali'stia stood erect and folded her arms under her chest. "Oh. So just what is worrying you?" she sarcastically spat. Nos was oblivious to the sarcasm and continued with his train of thought.

"I'm worried that the risk will outweigh the reward. Plus, we don't even know if she really is a Skath Worshipper."

Nos's comment admittedly shook Ali'stia. *I hate to admit it, but he could be right. I only hope Lord Forscythe's plan is solid.* She turned and sat on the edge of her husband's desk with her tail hanging to her right. *The more I think about it, the more I believe Nos's fears may have merit. I hope the Council listens to Lord Forscythe's full plan before they make any rash decisions. But, if my husband is right, we'll simply have to deal with Chirras in the usual way.* She was about to smile evilly at that thought when her husband interrupted her.

"On another note, has anybeing told you about what happened in the pit this menronn?" he asked with a playful smile creeping across his face.

Ali'stia shook her head in response. But she also wanted to clear the rather nasty thoughts she had had concerning the former council member. "I don't think so. Why?" Putting her hand to her face, she groaned. "No! Wait! Don't tell me. Did the trio-of-trouble do something id'rthic again?"

"Surprisingly, no." Nos started chuckling, trying to make his wife guess. *I'm surprised she hasn't heard yet; everybeing's been talking about it.* Nos enjoyed letting Ali'stia's anticipation build before finally blurting out the news. "Our de'tari has finally gotten herself a rival!"

Ali'stia was dumbstruck; her arms dropped to her sides, and her mouth and eyes opened widely. "Really! Who! Who's her rival! Come on iloni, tell me!" She was literally giddy with excitement.

"Visage—" It was all Nos could say before his wife let loose with a bunch of questions: "When did this happen? How did they meet? Does she know he's a Silvarian? He's only been here a deronn! How did they become rivals?" She leaned in so far that she fell onto her husband, who wrapped his arms around her to save her from hitting the floor. He then brought her in close for an eager kiss.

Right after the couple's lips touched, Ali'stia was greeted with Nos's memories of what had occurred in the pit that menronn. It was as though she were standing right next to her husband and Lord Baltrix, watching her de'tari fight. Thinking her de'tari had won the match, Ali'stia was shocked when Visage was enveloped by the Cloak of Darkness. With lightning speed, the demon was on top of Arisha, his talons digging into her neck. Then, in a matter of moments, he was off her and helping her up! *Riza called the match!* Ali'stia was completely blown away when, Arisha was walking away, Visage forfeited! All she could do was smile widely as she watched the pair give each other the arm clasp of friendship and rivalry.

Nosfaren ended their kiss. Ali'stia crawled off the desk and curled up on her husband's lap. Wrapping her arms around his neck, she hugged him and rested her head on his shoulder. "This is soooo exciting! I mean, who would have thought that our little Silvarian could use such an advanced technique at his age! And the way he forfeited... I mean... who does that!"

"Certainly not you," Nos facetiously quipped.

"And what pre-tell do you mean by that, iloni? Ali'stia removed her hands from their position around Nos's neck, to playfully push on his chest, and peer into his eyes.

Nos glanced away. "Oh, nothing," he offered, feigning ignorance. For a moment, he thought Ali'stia was going to hit him, but instead, she put her hands back around his neck and snuggled even more closely. "Why you..."

Lord Nos grinned. "If only moments like this could last forever."

"Not with Skath worshippers still infesting our galaxy, my iloni."

Nos nodded in agreement. "I agree. Unfortunately, peace is indeed fleeting." The entire Code of the Zaharaj—thinking back to the time when he first helped the mortals establish their organization—now entered his mind.

Peace is fleeting, so I thirst for knowledge.

Through knowledge, I gain power;

Through power, I gain strength;

Through strength, I learn wisdom;

With wisdom, I become enlightened;

Through enlightenment, I will become one with the universe!

Such an easy code to learn— yet so hard to live and even more so to master.

"Ali'stia?"

"Hmm?" his wife replied.

"Am I naïve?"

Confused by her husband's question, Ali'stia perked up. "No, Nos, you're not naïve; there are just too many beings who don't fully understand the Zaharaj. I mean, we are the only other group that uses the Zah'harrim besides the Verse-wielding Skath Worshippers. But we are nothing like them. Even the Zah'harrim can be used to heal, just as the Jah'harrim can be used to kill. I've heard several Zah say there's no difference between Zah and Jah; it all depends on the being who's using it. For instance, look at your apprentice—Vlad! Didn't you say that the people back on Earth treated him the same way they treated you—like some kind of monster? And just think about how many innocent lives he's saved since then. The Zah'harrim didn't corrupt him—it only made him stronger, since he's always trying to make up for what he did back on Earth. Don't you think it's because of your influence that he's found redemption?" Ali'stia was very serious as she looked into Nosfaren's eyes. "Aren't you still trying to find the same? Iloni, you know you have done nothing but try to redeem yourself, even though no one blames you for what your family did. In fact, I know that Riza has asked you to return to Demeros many times. Yet you choose to stay here among the mortals. Why?" Ali'stia had finally done it. She had asked her best friend in all of existence why he chose to stay on Zharaj and why he continues to punish himself. On the verge of tears, Ali'stia noticed a great brightness in Nos's eyes—brightness like that of an undying flame. *How could I have missed this all this time?* she wondered.

Nosfaren peered at his wife. He brought his hand up and brushed some stray hair out of her eyes. Then he smiled. "Ali'stia, that's just it. I'm not punishing myself. I've come to iloni all of the Zaharaj. I don't feel guilty at all! In fact, I'm very grateful that thanks to my dar'nra I was exiled to the mortal plane all those eons ago. If it weren't for him, I would never have met Vlad—or the other founding members of our Order. I don't owe any being, except Eendril. He adopted me despite the fact that I'm a member of the Ze'therac clan. So, the only thing I can do to repay Him for His kindness is to watch over His kids in this galaxy and make sure those Skath remnants can't hurt them."

Now Ali'stia understood. *My husband is not some self-righteous martyr. He's a protector! I think I'm the biggest id'rth in the galaxy. How could I have missed this. I can't believe that he actually ilonis these mortal beings! I've heard that iloni is blind, but this is ridiculous!*

"Really, Ali'stia! After all this time, you weren't aware of how much I care about the Zaharaj?"

"No, I only kept thinking you wanted to make up for your family's involvement in the war. Instead, you've become some sort of a guardian angel!"

"I wouldn't go so far as to say that. I am still a demon, after all." Nosfaren let out a sigh. "But, I suppose I can't keep avoiding His Majesty's summons forever."

Ali'stia was totally caught off guard. "Really! You mean we're going back to Demeros!"

Nos put his finger to his wife's lips in order to squelch her anticipatory excitement. "Only to visit. I still have a lot to do here, iloni, and I don't really care for that lazy crath who is currently on the throne." Even the thought of him caused Nos to cringe. Ali'stia looked a bit disappointed.

I suppose, at least it's a start, she thought.

"As much as I'd iloni to just laze about with you, Ali'stia, Lord Forscythe is going to be arriving soon, and we have to prepare to hear that plan of his." Ali'stia was reluctant to get up, but she gradually removed herself from her husband's lap and headed for the door.

Right before the last trickles of light were fading thru the asteroid laden sky, Nos stretched a bit and turned his attention to the scene that was unfolding outside his window. At that exact moment, Lord Forscythe's starship came barreling through the asteroid belt, heading directly for the landing area. "And, there he is!"

Ali'stia turned to the window and then to Nos. His comment was quite anticlimactic: "at least he's punctual." She then turned back to the door and exited.

"I'm not looking forward to this," Nos muttered before he glanced from the window to the now closed door. Reluctantly, his hand went to the U-gem on his right wrist. After typing on the green-glowing and transparent display, he turned off the gem, walked out the door, and headed for the Council chambers. *I have a feeling this is going to be a very long denonn.* Entering the central area where the lifts were located, he was happy to see his wife waiting for him in front of an open lift. They both entered, and Ali'stia pressed the console to send the lift to the floor where the twelve council members were scheduled to convene.

20

Random Encounter

Visage cringed when Riza pushed him through the portal. He stumbled forward but managed to save himself from falling by flailing his arms in a reverse circle. After righting himself, he realized he was back in the coliseum. Once again, he was bathed in the dim-red overhead lighting emanating from the lamps that were hidden among the stalactites. Several strands of his black flowing hair were partially blocking his vision. However, he was still able to make out the icicle-like formations that were hanging menacingly, far above his head. *Why did Rashia even think I'd become like Skath! Why did she even show that stuff to me?* For what seemed like eons, thoughts of Skath carrying out his brutal killing spree played repeatedly in Visage's mind. He started shaking his head vigorously in an attempt to force the images away. He regained control of his tumultuous emotions right in time to see Riza flying through the portal.

"Damn that insufferable ber'nan of mine!" Riza muttered when the portal closed behind her. After plunking her hands down onto her sides, she noticed Visage, who appeared to be in a daze. "Visage? Visage?" With no acknowledgement forthcoming, she clenched her fists. "Orran!" Nobeing could ignore Riza when she was irritated especially not Visage. After getting the young demon's attention, the disgruntled demoness curtly blurted. "Now that I have your attention, what in the verse is bothering you!"

Visage shook his head. "Nothing—just a bit disoriented with all of this... portal travel," he responded.

Why is he lying to me? She shrugged. *Oh well, he'll tell me the truth eventually. He did have a private psychic conversation with my mi'thia, and she can emotionally damage an Archangel if she wanted to! I'll have to tell Vira and the Council to keep a close eye on him for a while, just in case.* She was about to say something, but the gem on her hand started chiming and glowing. *A Council summons—well isn't that convenient.* "Sorry Visage, but I have to leave you."

"Uh, yeah, Riza," Visage mumbled, lowering his head. "Thank you for everything."

The demoness walked passed him and headed for the exit. "Oh, before I forget, I have something for you."

"Really? What is it?" His step was now quite perky. He was anxious to see what Riza's gift could be.

Though he seemed cheerful enough, Riza noticed a distinct change in his eyes. They seemed more distant—like he had just lost something. She could only guess what had happened when Rashia had kissed him.

"Close your eyes and hold out your hands," Riza requested. The young demon was a bit skeptical about the request but complied. Riza waved her hand in front of his face several times, making doubly sure those eyes of his were closed. Then she activated her U-gem. The gem glowed soft green as a black orb, a little smaller than a basketball, formed in her hand. She then carefully placed it into Visage's waiting palms.

The abrupt weight change in his hands caught Visage off guard. His eyes shot open, and he nearly dropped the precious gift. The orb was very smooth. The outer layer was quite cold, but warmed up quickly.

Riza smiled widely. "I hope you enjoy this little gift. The woman I received it from doesn't hand these things out to just anybeing." Visage was about to ask Riza what she meant, but she took off. She reached the lift in record time, pressed the button, and was gone.

***

Now that Riza was gone, a dazed Visage stood alone in the coliseum. *Now that Riza and Vira are gone, I may as well head for the lifts.* He clung possessively to his new treasure while walking to the tunnel entrance where the carved-out hallway began. After reaching the lifts, he carefully maneuvered his hand so he could hang onto the ball while pushing the button to summon the lift. The third set of doors to his right opened. When he stepped in, he realized that he had left his earpiece in his pocket, and, with both of his hands occupied, he couldn't reach into the pocket to retrieve it. Since he couldn't decipher the characters on the console, he shifted the weight of the ball and used his elbow to press two random characters on the keypad. *I hope I can find somebeing who knows his way around this place.* With this thought in mind, the doors closed and the lift began its ascent.

When the doors of the lift opened, Visage stepped out, still holding fast to his orb. He peered down the hallway to his left, but wasn't sure if he was even on the right floor. Everything looked the same. After a minor silent debate, he started walking, hoping to see something that was even remotely familiar. Fortune was with him; a human woman was coming towards him from the opposite direction. The woman's long brown hair swayed a bit with each step. When she got closer, Visage couldn't help but notice that she was wearing a rather clingy and revealing shimmery-black nightgown. She was also carrying a small rectangular box, which was tucked tightly under her left arm.

"My, my, who do we have here?" she asked when she was only a few steps away. Visage didn't like the way she was staring at him, though she did have a somewhat familiar presence. He brought his black ball closer. "Well, well, if it isn't the Silvarian betrak who got me removed from the Council." The woman's voice was harsh and demeaning.

"Lady Dreth, is that you!"

The woman shook her head and laughed. "Nope. It's only Chirras now, no thanks to you!"

Visage didn't know what to make of this, he closed his eyes and frowned. *Ali'stia had told me that it wasn't my fault. She said specifically that*

Lady Dreth herself had made some rather poor decisions, which had caused her to be removed from the Council. What do I do now? All I wanted to know was whether I'm on the right floor. But, of all the beings in this huge temple, I just had to run into the one who hates me.

Chirras erupted with laughter. "Oh, come on now, I was only teasing you, Orran..." She seemed puzzled. "It is Orran, isn't it?"

Visage thought a moment. *At least, thanks to Vira and Riza, she apparently can't read my mind. Nor can I read hers—at least not very easily.* He slowly began to shake his head. "No. Lord Nos said I should go by 'Visage' now."

"The one who hides in shadows. Lord Nos *would* give such a name to a Silvarian. I mean, we wouldn't want your secret to get out, now would we?" she mocked, her voice reverting back to its more grating and vindictive tone.

Ugh! Why me? Why her! Visage clutched his ball more tightly. Riza's gift was the only thing helping him remain calm while Chirras continued to eye him even more intensely than before. Those frighteningly dark blood-red irises of hers were darker than any he'd previously encountered. *She's giving me the creeps!*

After a lengthy pause, Chirras let out a hearty sigh. "I guess I should be thanking you, Visage."

Visage was taken aback by Chirras's sudden change in attitude. "Really?" He was not buying it. *There is something... off about this woman. I wish Lord Nos or Lord Baltrix or anybeing else was here with me!*

"Thanks to you, I got kicked off the Council, and Lord Baltrix killed my apprentice, yederonn. Now I have lots of free time on my hands. As a matter of fact, I was just heading out to deliver Jetec's blood sorjin to his parents." Chirras motioned towards the rectangular box she was holding under her arm.

"Jetec?"

"He was my former apprentice—the one before Zor'ret. He disappeared on Yenos Three. The only thing I found was his blood sorjin."

"What happened to him?"

"The Council asked me that, too. I'll tell you what I told them... I don't know!" Chirras seemed to be genuinely angry at losing her former apprentice which shocked him. "All I know is that we found a very old star map and holo log on a previous mission. Yenos Three was a planet that was mentioned more than a few times, so we decided to investigate. The only thing we found were the ruins of an ancient temple of some kind. Or at least we thought it was a temple." Chirras shook her head and frowned. "Anyway, when I was trying to set a marker in place, Jetec took off on me and vanished." She peered at the box containing Jetec's sorjin. "I actually tripped over his blood sorjin in the sand, but couldn't find him anywhere." She seemed heartbroken when she took the box out from under her arm and pressed it to her chest.

How could Lord Nos and the Council think she had something to do with Jetec's disappearance? It's obvious that she has feelings for him. "You loved him didn't you?" Visage asked, startling Chirras. He was surprised when she started laughing.

"Love? Isn't that common tongue for iloni?" She was a little perplexed by the question. "Yes, I guess I did iloni Jetec, after a fashion." Her eyes went back to the box. "I ilonied how powerful he was. That was why I proposed to him."

She proposed to her own apprentice just because he was powerful! Visage gaped at the woman.

"His whole family has been part of the Zaharaj for seven generations, but Jetec—he was something special. Very few Verse users are born with the kind of power he had." Chirras's mood suddenly turned sullen. "I only wish I knew who took him from me!" Her face contorted in anger. "Then the Council dumped that arrogant Zor'ret on me. Thank the Verse Baltrix took care of that pathetic glort, I couldn't stand him it's no wonder why Le'Shara and Azala..." She pressed her hand to her rather abundant chest in order to calm herself. "Sorry, Visage, for dragging you into my problems."

Visage shrugged. "I don't mind." *What did Zor'ret do,* he wondered behind his mental barrier.

"Hmm. I sense that you're also dealing with something; I've told you about me, now it's your turn. What is it that seems to be eating at you?"

The irritating way Chirras spoke made Visage quiver. It was hard to tell if she was honestly interested or only goading him into sharing information. *I hope she can't read my mind,* he thought while he started rotating his precious ball in his hands. With his decision made, he looked into Chirras's eyes, took a deep breath, and proceeded to tell her everything that had happened to him.

"And then Riza brought me to Demeros where I met Rashia who told me I might become something even worse than Skath! Then she threw me across the room then Riza and Zoric stopped her from attacking me... and—"

"Whoa, slow down kid. Are you telling me that you met Rashia, the Meserino demon queen, and she told you that you are going to become worse than Skath... as in the Dark God who declared war on practically everybeing in existence!" she belted out, excitedly attempting to obtain confirmation of Visage's story.

Visage was caught off guard by Chirras's interruption. "Well, yeah, something like that... I guess." He closed his eyes and tried to remember exactly what the Meserino queen had said.

"Now that is a very interesting piece of news!" Chirras's voice had become much colder. *So, even the legendary demoness fears this Silvarian child. Perhaps the war with Skath was nothing more than a prelude to an even greater war in the future.* She couldn't help but smile at the thought.

Visage didn't like the way Chirras was smiling. "What is your deal, anyway?"

Chirras's pupils became dots at the question. After they returned to their normal size, she began to cackle. "My deal is that I thirst for power!" She pointed her finger at Visage. "And from what you just told me, you might become the next Skath!"

Visage narrowed his eyes at her. "You sound like a Skath worshipper!" He knowingly accused her just to see how she would react.

Chirras cackled again before harshly responding. "No, I don't worship fools. I do have respect for Skath's tenacity and power. I mean, He made every god in existence feel true fear, for the first time ever, when He built that sorjin of His!" She readjusted the box, putting it under her other arm. "For a time, He had all of existence within in His dark grasp. The heavens themselves shook under His might. He had such power that He and His followers gained victory after victory over Eendril and the other gods' overwhelming forces, which included the demons,"— She snickered but it made Visage nervously swallow. —"not even the combined forces from all around the Universe stood a chance against Him." She sighed in lament. "Well, I guess you know how Skath's little war with the gods turned out,"— Chirras sneered —"so I won't bore you with those details. Then, after the war ended, our God came up with a plan—supposedly offering us, His spirit children, a choice. Of course, some id'rth had to stick his fraking self into the execution of the plan"—

"Wait, are you referring to the being who the people back home call 'The Devil'?"

"You got it." Chirras snapped her fingers and pointed at him with a freaky smile on her face.

What does The Devil have to do with Skath? Visage's musings were interrupted as Chirras continued her walk through the past.

"You see, during Skath's war with the gods, 'The Devil' (Satan—also one of God's spirit children) began to lust after Skath's power. So, when God offered His spirit children a chance to go down to a new planet and have the right to choose their own paths in life, The being you know as the devil, or Lucifer was all in. He offered to go down and, basically, force them to follow God's laws, and, if He were successful in doing so, He wanted all of the glory and subsequent power for Him-self. When God didn't accept His offer, He became so enraged that He started *another* war with God and those of His spirit children— one third of them—who were faithful to Him. Naturally, Lucifer and his followers lost the war and were exiled from Heaven before they received a mortal body." Chirras put her hand to her face and groaned. "At least I wasn't such a colossal id'rth that I got myself tossed out, along with that pathetic blortworm Satan and those losers who chose to follow him. I was obedient enough that I (half-heartedly) fought on God's side during the war," she seethed through clenched teeth. Of course, God Himself did not fight. However, the Archangels, Halifel, Michael, Gabriel, as well as millions of other faithful spirit children, were under big ber'nan Jehovah's command."

Visage gasped. "And you actually remember everything from when you were still just a spirit, before you became mortal!"

"No, I don't remember *everything*... only bits and pieces... And that's after heavy meditation," Chirras explained. "Besides, that guy and all of his fraking friends were tossed out and imprisoned on that little planet where you're from... if I'm not mistaken. He just didn't have enough patience."

What does that mean? "What do you mean by that?" Visage whimpered while the woman's evil-appearing eyes peered into his.

"I mean, if he had not brought on the war, he would have made it to Earth and gotten his physical body." She groaned in aggravation. "But, because he rebelled, he'll have to spend eternity without a body."

It took some courage, but Visage finally asked his most provocative question: "Do you worship God at all? After all, He *is* the Father of your spirit."

Chirras went wide-eyed and laughed. "Pshaw... No, I don't. There is only one thing I worship... and that's power!" She walked over to the cowering Silvarian, bent low, and stared directly into his eyes. "Power of the Verse, power of the indren'freth, power of the ancient magicks— these are what we were searching for before God took us from our path and turned us into..."— She stood back a bit, straightened up, and gestured to herself. —"this!"

Visage was at a loss for words. *This woman is both crazy and dangerous. She may even be more dangerous than an actual Skath Worshipper!* After these thoughts crossed his mind, he was grateful to Riza and Vira for teaching him how to shield his mind by using the protective barriers. *If she'd heard what I was thinking, I'd probably be dead by now.* He shuddered at the thought.

Chirras started heading for the lifts and beckoned Visage to follow. He took a quick glance at his ball and begrudgingly complied. She was still the only being he'd encountered, and she knew her way around the temple a lot better than he did.

"You know it's a lie, right?" she asked when she looked over her shoulder at the confused and frightened child.

"What's a lie, Chirras?"

"Eendril's whole freedom of choice thing."

Visage stopped in his tracks. "I don't understand."

"Listen to me, Visage. Do you remember what you were before you were even a spirit?" He shook his head. "And I don't, either. All I know is that we were self-aware intelligent globs of energy. In that form, we searched for knowledge... and power." Chirras's pause and her emphasis on power made Visage's right eye twitch a bit. She continued. "My problem with this is that I was born a woman... yes?"

"Um... yes, you're a woman. So?" Visage was hoping she was eventually going to make some sort of point.

"But, did I choose to be born as a woman!" she exclaimed, raising her hand to accentuate her point.

Visage really didn't get it. "How do you choose to be anything?" "That's exactly my point! When we were just masses of energy, did we choose to become a spirit or did God make that decision for us? Then did we choose what gender we were going to be? Or was that also decided by God? And if we didn't choose, just how much freedom of choice did we really have?" she ranted.

Visage was completely floored. "That's true! If we all start out as beings of pure energy, who decides if we should become a spirit or not? Do we make the decision ourselves, or does God decide that for us?"

"I can see that even you understand." Chirras flashed a conniving smile. "I mean, just how vindictive is God—or whatever deity created you Silvarians had to be?"

"What do you mean by *that!*" Though the insinuation was repulsive, Visage's curiosity was heightened.

Chirras's eyes narrowed and she glared at the young demon. "Well, you're probably not aware of the fact that Silvarians were an entirely male species."

Visage shook his head a bit. "I don't—"

"Oh, come on! How do you think the Veserino demons came into existence?" Chirras's arm shot forth, waving outward in a grand gesture. "Since there were no female Silvarians, the race—your race—was doomed. From their very beginning, they were destined for extinction. So, they had two choices: They could live until their race died out, or they could breed with the other two greater demon races." Chirras paused just long enough to flash Visage an evil grin before continuing. "But, with their looks, they of course attracted the Meserino women!" Chirras blurted, following up with a chuckle. "What I'm saying is that the Veserino demons are, in fact, Silvarian-Meserino hybrids! So, your race didn't become extinct wholly because of Skath's War. A big contributing factor was that whoever created them created them in a way that they couldn't reproduce without the help of the other two demon races!"

Visage almost dropped his ball; he felt angry and betrayed. "Who... Who would do something like that? And why?"

Chirras noticed that the child was now distraught, so she turned her back to him, smiled widely, and twisted the proverbial knife. "I don't know kid... nor do I really care!"

Visage was pained. *Why would anybeing make a race that could not self-propagate?* He peered up at the older woman; her hair bobbed about and her hips swayed rather seductively as she walked. That gown, or whatever that thing was that passed for clothing, wasn't helping matters. Visage gritted his teeth. *I can't stand this woman! I wish Vira or Riza were here with me.* He clung to the black orb, which by now was quite warm.

The pair had now reached the lifts, and Chirras pressed the button to summon a ride. She gestured for Visage to enter, holding the door open for him by leaning on it in a way that made him both abashed and livid. *I know Riza warned me about beings like this, but this Chirras woman gives me the creeps!* His eyes grew colder looking while he gave her a sideways glance. *That lust for power will be your undoing you vindictive bitch!* He wanted to scream the sentiment aloud but bit down on his tongue, hoping his glare would give her the hint.

Chirras paid the other passenger no mind and merely pressed the console button. The doors slid closed and ushered the lift into an ascent. Visage was relieved when the doors opened; he noticed the familiar hallway lined with windows on the right and a row of numbered doors on the left.

"Here's your floor, ar'teth Visage," Chirras said after the boy stepped off the lift. Visage hurriedly walked away, but then heard Chirras's voice. Despite himself, he turned to see what she wanted.

"By the way, Visage, I like the new look!" Chirras shouted, wearing that hateful-looking smile of hers. Visage did the polite thing and responded with a half-hearted nod before heading off to his room. He sighed in relief when the shrill chuckling noise faded right after the lift doors closed.

***

Visage was still shaken by the time he reached the fifth door in the hallway. The door automatically opened upon his approach. The dim-red lighting seemed much brighter than usual, now that trell was settling in. The asteroid field was also looking a bit more ominous. The asteroids looked like black holes outlined by starlight.

Once the door closed and Visage was fully in his room, he headed directly to his bed and gingerly laid down his precious ball. *It almost seems alive.* Once satisfied that the ball was in no danger of rolling off the bed, he stood back up and sighed deeply. After retracting his talons and wiggling his toes, he could feel the softness and coolness of the dark carpet under his feet. "Oh that's just great," he griped. "Riza forgot to give back my boots after the match with Arisha."

"I was really shocked when you won that match. Why did you forfeit, anyway?" Azala's voice made the still-on-edge Silvarian jump.

"Azala, don't scare me like that!" Visage pressed his hand to his chest while he gasped for breath. "I've already had enough disturbing encounters for one day... I mean deronn."

Azala leaned back in her chair and spun it around in order to face the rather grumpy Silvarian. At first, she wasn't going to ask him about his 'disturbing encounters,' but she couldn't help herself. "And just who managed to disturb a Silvarian demon?"

Now that his breathing and heart rate had settled down a bit, Visage sat on the edge of his bed and opened up to Azala. "First, Vira and Riza told me some... interesting things. Then, after Vira left us, Riza brought me to Demeros where I met her ber'nan, Zareth, and her mi'thia, Rashia. Rashia told me more things, which I really wish she hadn't. Then, when we got back, Riza had to go to some Council meeting and that's when I ran into that... that Chirras woman!" Visage folded his arms in disgust after spitting out her name.

Azala bolted off her chair and shoved her face as close as her roommate would allow, much to his chagrin. He was disturbed by her abrupt close personal contact. Azala was usually very calm and cool, but now her eyes were narrowed to slits and her pupils had become nothing more than the size of pinheads. She spoke softly. "Visage, what happened? What did she say to you?" Visage gritted his teeth. His fangs burrowed into his gums and were about to draw blood when Azala put her hand on his shoulder. "You don't have to talk. Just think." Then she pressed her lips to his.

***

The young demon appeared in the same black void into which Rashia had brought him. However, this time he was accompanied by Azala. "Well, Visage, aren't you going to show me, or do I have to sift through *all* of your memories?" Azala demanded. She emphasized her angst by putting her hands on her hips and tapping her foot on the absent floor. Visage was going to ask her how her foot was actually making sound whenever it slapped against nothing but thought the better of it. He showed his roommate by visualizing what had transpired when first encountered Chirras.

It was less traumatic for Visage to be see a replay of his horrible experience with Chirras while Azala was at his side. The replay started at the point when he got into the lift, pressed two random keys, and waited for the doors to open. He watched himself look perplexed after he got off the elevator and headed down the hallway, only to meet Chirras coming from the opposite direction. Azala's face scrunched up when she noticed what the woman was wearing. "Fraking show off!" She giggled a bit at Visage's facial expression but soon fell silent; she was eager to watch the exchange. Visage was trembling while he watched, for the second time, himself having his earth-shattering conversation with Chirras. Azala grabbed his left hand with her right and squeezed it tightly. Then the trellmare was over, and they were back in the void.

***

"I'm so sorry she did that to you, Visage," Azala offered before they returned to their room. Though Azala had broken away from him, she still had a fiery look in her eyes. "Visage, you need to show this to the Council! Come on, let's get going!" She was quick to grab his hand and drag him toward the door.

"Why? No! Hold on Azala!" Visage wrestled his hand from his roommate's grasp. "What's going on! Why the urgency!"

Azala put her hands on his shoulders. "Because your memories are damning evidence! Your memories, Visage, are the proof we need in order to convict that crathing bakrath of being a Skath Worshipper!"

"But Azala, Chirras isn't a Skath Worshipper!" Visage countered.

"You're right! She's something far worse—she's a fracking Deser'rec!" Azala retorted.

Visage lowered his head. "I don't know what that means."

Azala threw up her hands and rolled her eyes. "It means she wants to replace Skath with either herself or some other powerful being! And the way she was eying you, I'd say it's a good chance it's the latter."

"No way! I'm nothing like Skath... I don't want anything to do with him!" He started marching in circles and erratically waving his arms.

"That's why we need to get to the Council, NOW!" Azala screamed, grabbing his hand once again. This time, he made no move to resist. The pair was out the door and at the lifts in no time. As soon as the doors opened, they were inside and on their way to the Council room.

21

Conspiring Councilors

Riza got off the lift and entered the Council Room's waiting area; her pupils constricted from the much brighter light. The two ornately decorated double doors were just to her right, the lifts being on either side of the Council Room's entrance. The demoness was not too pleased that she was forced to leave the young Silvarian in the pit.

Duty calls. Nos's reason for summoning us had better be important. I don't like leaving Visage unattended. Putting her hand to her face, Riza shrugged off her worries in order to concentrate on the present and managed to muster up a smile before heading over to her fellow councilors.

Vira, Baltrix, Glavian, and Serishin were mingling about in the front foyer of the Council chambers. The counselors greeted her with varying degrees of smiles and appearances of worry. All had removed their masks, since masks weren't allowed inside the holy chamber. They also had removed their boots out of respect for the room, their positions, and each other.

The lift, located on the left hand side of the Council Room doors, now opened and out walked Lord Nosfaren, Ali'stia, Michael, Fenrir, and Zoric. Lord Nos took in all those who were present. "I see that every being's here except for Sharas and Barren."

"Yes, Lord Nosfaren," Glavian, a human male, said. He scowled a bit before he rubbed his messy-and-matted dirty-blond hair. "I think I speak for most of us when I ask—just what is so important that you had to summon us like this?" Glavian was rather brash, but several other councilors nodded, or flashed expectant looks at Lord Nos.

Nos sighed. "All I can tell you right now is that it's very important!" He was trying hard not to blurt out what he knew before the full contingent of members was present. Luckily, the wait was short. When the doors opened, Lord Barren, Lady Sharas, Forscythe, and Vok'et all exited the lift.

"Now that we're all here, let's see what the future has in store for us!" Nos exclaimed, grabbing onto the two handles of the Council Room doors and opening them widely.

Inside the chamber, a large chandelier was hanging from the ceiling and bathing the whole room in yellow-tinted light. Thirteen chairs greeted the group. They were made from obsidian and adorned with red-velvet cushions and high backs. The heads of various animals were carved into their legs and armrests. The chairs all faced inward towards the mural of the galaxy, which was carved into the floor. The stars stood out against the deep abyss-like color of the central circle. A plush, purple-colored carpet was carefully laid out just behind the chairs; the chairs formed a crescent-moon shape along the room's edge. There were giant, triangular, transparisteel windows on the far wall, giving those who stood in the center of the room a grand view of the asteroid-filled sky. Nos and the others entered the room in silent reverence, barely making a sound as their bare feet hit the cool moribite floor. Every council member took his or her seat and waited anxiously for the meeting to commence.

Lord Nosfaren took the central seat; his wife sat in the one to his left. Riza took the seat to his right, and Vira sat next to her. The Zebrecian female, Serishin, and the human male, Fenrir, then sat down next to Vira. The seat next to Fenrir was empty, and Michael filled in the last seat on the left hand side of the room. Zoric, the red-skinned Twillan male, took the seat next to Ali'stia, laying both of his twills over his left shoulder before sitting down. Glavian, also a human male, sat next to

Zoric. Lord Baltrix, Lord Barren (a human male), and Lady Sharas (the only human female) rounded out the right hand side of the room.

Forscythe and Vok'et were waiting outside the entrance, allowing time for all of the council members to take their seats. Lord Nosfaren then announced them. "Lords and Ladies of the Council, I give you Lord Forscythe and his apprentice, Vok'et. They have something urgent to tell us." After his proclamation, he beckoned the pair to enter. As soon as Forscythe and Vok'et stepped through the opening, the doors closed, and twelve sets of eyes trained on them.

Lord Forscythe stood in the center of the circle and bowed politely. When he arose, he swallowed hard. "My fellow Zaharaj," he began, "my apprentice and I just came from Yenos Three." His pronouncement caused several of the councilors to gasp. Lord Baltrix and Glavian leaned over to each other and started whispering, giving Forscythe time to take a deep breath and let it out. After the Council fell silent again, he continued. "Vok'et and I were sent to Yenos Three to investigate the disappearance of my nephew, Jetec." Forscythe clenched his fists before calming down a bit. "I can't really explain in words what we found so we"—he gestured to Vok'et—"would like to show you." Both closed their eyes. The entire Council followed suit. When the members opened their eyes, they were all inside Forscythe's conscience. Forscythe's recent memories overtook the void changing it to Yenos Three's harsh environment.

The councilors looked on while Forscythe and Vok'et battled the wind and sand. They even chuckled a bit when Forscythe tumbled into the hole that Vok'et had uncovered. However, they quickly re-focused as they watched and felt the pair become unnerved when they discovered the trail of Jetec's blood. Their breaths quickened upon the discovery of the drag marks. Even Nosfaren grew cold when they summoned their T.A.Ds and cut open the door. All felt the fear and despair as they watched Forscythe and Vok'et enter a room that was eerily similar to their own Council chambers. Fourteen hearts sank when they saw the duo's discovery of the crumbling mural. The Dark God seemed to peer down at His audience when His evil hate-filled eyes met with their own. Then the chase—two Zaharaj trying to escape from a hoard of Fallen. The councilmen and women watched the T.A.Ds fire devastating plasma bolts and laser blasts into the hoard of undead, blowing several of them into pieces and bringing a ceiling down on the rest. Every councilor breathed a sigh of relief when Forscythe and Vok'et made it out of the perilous situation and into the safety of their ship. However, the horrifying scenes were not yet over for the onlookers. They had yet to see the Fallen's spear come within inches of Vok'et's heart and were elated when, at the last critical moment, one of the T.A.Ds saved him. The detonation of the thermite missile along with Forscythe and Vok'et's safe escape from Yenos Three brought a heart-felt cheer from every councilor.

After Forscythe opened his eyes and the vision faded, all of the councilors re-appeared in their designated chairs inside the Council Room. In no time, the chatter began.

"Chirras is a Skath Worshipper and a traitor and should be dealt with promptly!" Lord Fenrir boldly stated, pounding his fist on the armrest of his chair.

Barren slightly nodded. "I feel the same, Lord Fenrir, but we don't have enough proof that Chirras was actually involved," he said while he tried to calm his fellow council member.

Baltrix sighed. "I have to agree with Lord Barren's assessment. There just isn't enough evidence to prove that Chirras is a Skath Worshipper." He nodded to Barren and scowled at Fenrir.

"We can prove that she was there and that she was the only one to return," Sharas protested.

"But we don't know if the Fallen found him first while Chirras was setting up the transponder," Zoric objected, "or if she was actually involved with his apparent murder."

Vira spoke up. "This is all conjecture. There is no way of knowing for certain unless Chirras lets us see what happened, and, with the way she is, I doubt she would let us look inside her memories." The Veserino put her right elbow onto the armrest of her chair and leaned her cheek onto her fist. The whole situation was disheartening.

"That's why"—Michael spoke with malice—"we rip them from her Skath-worshipping crath!" he exclaimed. Many of the council members were obviously disgusted at what he had just proposed.

Lord Nos frowned. "You know very well that we don't do that, Lord Michael. Using such a Zah technique would make us no better than our enemies." *I will let it go this time, but next time think before you speak, Lord Nos silently warned the overly ambitious man.* At that, Michael started sulking and fell silent.

Forscythe listened to the Council debate the issue for several dironns before clearing his throat and speaking up. "Lords and ladies, I actually have a plan." His words brought an abrupt halt to all conversation.

Lord Nos groaned. Ali'stia responded by giving her husband the evil eye. *Let's just hear him out, iloni,* she silently urged.

"Fine, Lord Forscythe, let's hear this… *plan* of yours," Lord Nos stated dryly, rolling his eyes.

Forscythe smiled broadly, seemingly not having noticed the obvious sarcasm in Nos's voice. "You all understand that we don't know for sure if Chirras is indeed a Skath Worshipper, right?" The council members all nodded or muttered their agreement.

"So, what if we set a trap for her?" This idea got the immediate attention of his audience.

"What kind of trap, Lord Forscythe?" Sharas asked with an obviously skeptical tone.

"Well, think about it. What do all Skath worshippers seek—more than anything?" Forscythe knew he was posing a rhetorical question, but he had to get his point across.

"Power. Why?" Zoric questioned.

"Isn't that obvious?" Fenrir sarcastically added.

"So, what if we find a way to bait Chirras, as well as those like her, with something that no Skath Worshipper could possibly resist?" Forscythe's tone was dripping with smugness.

"And just what might that be, Lord Forscythe?" This time Riza was asking the question. Nobeing could determine if she was being sarcastic, or overly concerned.

Riza's question embarrassed Forscythe a bit. "Yeah, that's actually the part I have yet to figure out," he meekly replied while rubbing the back of his head.

Lord Nos now chimed in. "What you're saying, Lord Forscythe, is that we need to offer something so powerful that any Skath worshipper would do anything to get his or her hands on it, but you haven't figured out what that 'something' might be?"

Lord Forscythe nodded in continued embarrassment. "I know it sounds foolish, but I'm sure it would work if we just had the right bait."

"I don't disagree with Lord Nosfaren," Baltrix rested his chin on his clenched hands before he leaned forward. "The question is, what kind of bait can we use to set this trap?"

"Perhaps a holo-journal of one of the older masters?" Glavian suggested.

"But everybeing in the temple has access to those," Zoric countered, causing Glavian to slump back in his chair.

"What if we were to use a powerful being as bait rather than some ancient relic or tome of knowledge?" Serishin offered.

"That might work: An offer of apprenticeship to a demon perhaps?" Glavian perked back up as he gave the councilors his new idea while at the same time eying the two demonesses, who didn't have apprentices.

"No way!" Vira exclaimed.

"Absolutely not!" Riza shouted, agreeing whole-heartedly with her friend's rapidly expressed sentiment.

"Calm down, all of you." Nos peered at the council members. "Though I hate to admit it, Forscythe's plan does have merit."

"We know that Skath worshippers, as well as Fallen, insatiably thirst for power. They become blinded to practically everything else around them," Ali'stia contributed.

"This is why, if Lord Forscythe's so called plan is going to work, we must tread lightly." Lord Nosfaren spoke both cautiously and sternly.

"What plan!" Lord Michael belted, quickly rising from his chair and putting both his arms out in an exasperated gesture. "What Lord For-scythe proposed can hardly be considered a plan!"

Lord Fenrir decided to intervene. "Lord Michael, calm the frak down. We get your point!" Fenrir's words had the desired effect. Though Lord Michael's initial response was a scowl, he followed up by going silent, plopping himself back down into his chair, and folding his arms in aggravation.

"I'm sorry, Lord Forscythe, for Lord Michael's outburst." Lord Fenrir extended an apology in Lord Michael's behalf, but the Zebrecian man did not seem at all disturbed by Lord Michael's accusations; he only stood there, appearing to be deep in thought.

"I'm sorry, Lord Fenrir, did you say something?" Lord Forscythe asked after a moment's pause.

Fenrir, who was dismayed by Lord Forscythe's apparent lack of interest in his apology, half-heartedly responded, "Never mind."

"The plan is to find somebeing who is powerful enough to entice Chirras, and any other Skath worshippers in our midst, out of hiding. Once we find out who the Skath worshippers are, we use said being to lure them into a secluded area where we can eliminate all of them in one fell swoop." Forscythe beamed. "Is that not a good plan?" he rhetorically asked his fellow councilors. Though the councilors had initially been skeptical, once Forscythe had a chance to expound on how his plan would work, he was pleasantly surprised at the body's response.

Lady Sharas leaned forward and clutched the armrest of her chair a bit more tightly. "Yes, Lord Forscythe, it is a sound plan. It's just...who do we use for bait?"

"Not just that, Lady Sharas, but what happens to the one playing the *part* of the bait during this operation?" Zoric was so concerned about the potential for harm to the individual who might be chosen to be the "bait" that he ceased playing with the end of his twill. And he was not the only being in the room who looked worried.

Lord Nosfaren was about to say something when the doors flew open and Azala barged in, dragging Visage behind her. "Master!" Azala yelled. "You have to see what Chirras just did to Visage!" the young Twillan female cried. Her outburst was quick to gain everybeing's attention. Azala took Visage's arm and twisted it slightly so he was in front of her, then gave him a hard shove.

Visage stumbled forward. He actually lost his balance, but Forscythe caught him before he fully fell. When Visage looked up, Forscythe took his hands off his shoulders and his pupils became as wide as saucers. "By the gods, it's a Silvarian!" His face scrunched up a bit. "At least I think it's a Silvarian?" The child's odd coloring had thrown him off.

Visage made no comment; he was too absorbed by the older man's features. Forscythe had dark brown or heavily tanned skin. His eyes had that usual Zah'harrim tint, but there was still a noticeable kindness about them. The man's ears were oddly shaped—they bent at nearly forty-five-degree angles and ended at sharp-looking points. In addition, and even stranger still, were the three horns and two small bumps that stuck out of his straight brown hair. To Visage, it looked as though the being was wearing a crown, since the central horn was the tallest, and the other four got smaller as they made their way around his head.

"A crown of thorns?" Visage whispered aloud, then blushed in embarrassment and averted his gaze to the floor.

The man was a bit puzzled by the child's utterance. "I'm sorry, I didn't quite understand what you said, my young Silvarian friend," Lord Forscythe commented, still unsure about the child's heritage.

Lord Nosfaren cleared his throat. Everybeing turned to him when he got their attention. "Lord Forscythe, you have just met the very last of the Silvarian race, and his name is Visage." Lord Nos stood and gestured towards the Silvarian demon.

"Oh! Wow!" Lord Fenrir exclaimed.

"Unbelievable!" Lord Glavian agreed.

"Are you sure he's a Silvarian?" Lady Sharas asked, not quite convinced.

Lord Barren piped up, "I know you weren't here for the meeting, Lady Sharas, but the child is most definitely a Silvarian."

"I think he's cute!" Lady Serishin pronounced while she placed her hand against her cheek and eyed the child.

"Don't even think about it!" Riza and Vira exclaimed rather

threateningly. Lady Serishin slumped in her seat when the two demon-esses glared at her.

"That's it!" Forscythe suddenly shouted.

"What's it, Master?" Vok'et queried, speaking for the first time since the start of the meeting. Visage looked to the smaller being. He had all of the same features as Forscythe, but looked to be about Azala's age.

"Vok'et, don't you get it? This Silvarian can be our bait!" Forscythe glanced from the Silvarian to his apprentice and back. He was simply ecstatic, believing that the gods themselves had provided him with the solution to his problem.

Forscythe thought his plan could go forward, Lady Vira and Lady Riza blasted it out of the galaxy before it could enter hyperspace. Riza shot up from her chair, her tail whipping about. Pointing a clawed finger, she screamed at Forscythe, "Not on your life!"

Vira was even more distraught. She lunged at the Zebrecian in a swift motion, clamped her hand around his neck, and hoisted him up. "I will not have Visage be a part of your Skath hunt!" Her tone was low and threatening.

Forscythe struggled against the more powerful demoness, glancing about the room and hoping that somebeing might come to his aid. He started gasping for breath when his and Vira's eyes met. The demoness's blue eyes were focused on him, her pupils were nothing more than thin black lines inside of an endless abyss. Forscythe feared they would swallow his soul if he continued to focus on them.

"Vira, that's enough! Release him!" Lord Nos commanded. Vira broke eye contact with her captive when she turned her head towards Lord Nosfaren. He did not look at all pleased. "I understand your frustration, Vira, but we really don't have many options. Now release him."

As soon as Vira loosened her grip, Lord Forscythe fell to the floor and started coughing and gasping for breath. After clicking her teeth, Vira gave the sprawled-out Lord one last glare before going back to her chair and taking her seat.

Vok'et rushed to his uch'nra's side and assisted him to his feet, though Forscythe was still coughing and rubbing his neck.

Azala couldn't help but smile; she had watched the whole thing unfold. "Your uch'nra is an id'rth, Vok'et. Doesn't he know enough not to drath off demons. It's a sure way to get yourself killed."

"Go frak yourself, Azala! Vok'et retorted. I know my uch'nra shouldn't have suggested getting the Silvarian involved—but Vira didn't need to do that to him!"

"Don't you know that Visage is the fiancé of Riza and Vira?" Lady Ali'stia accusingly asked Forscythe.

Forscythe stammered a bit, he attempted to make amends for his unwitting behavior. "I'm so sorry, Vira. You, too, Riza—I didn't know."

Visage was busy trying to sort through everything that had just transpired when Lord Nos abruptly spoke. "Alright, Azala, what's so urgent that you had to barge in here? And why in the galaxy did you bring Visage with you!"

Azala ran up to her master, placed her hand down on one of the armrests, and got right into his face. "Master, I came here to tell you about Chirras!" She then turned and urgently gestured towards Visage. "Come on, Visage, show them what happened!"

Now that he was on the spot, though, rather confused by the entire situation, Visage closed his eyes, shattered his mental barrier, and let his thoughts flow freely. All the council members, along with Forscythe, Vok'et, and Azala, were now inside the void in his head. The councilors watched. Visage who first stood alone inside the pit and then left the pit. Many even chuckled while watching him type in several random keys on the lift's keypad. Riza groaned. *Why didn't I tell him how to get back to his floor? If I had told him, he never would have run into that woman! And, on top of that, I still have his boots!*

While Riza self-reflected, the other councilors were on the edge of their seats, watching the drama unfold inside Visage's head. The group saw the lift door open and none other than Chirras heading down the hallway towards Visage! "What's she got in her arms?" Zoric asked, pointing at the black box.

"It looks like a casket for some being's blood sorjin?" Michael mused aloud.

"When she ran into me, she told me she was delivering Jetec's blood sorjin to his family," Visage offered.

"Shh!" Lord Nos and Ali'stia simultaneously hushed them all. "I want to see how this plays out!" Lord Nos frustratingly added.

"Not well," Visage muttered. Lord Nos, Lord Baltrix, and Lord Fenrir all raised an eyebrow. Visage grimaced while he and the onlookers watched the scenario unfold. However, this time he wasn't alone or just with Azala. Riza and Vira had found their way over to him and each took one of his hands and gripped it tightly. The expressions of anger displayed on the council members faces were all projected towards Chirras.

The vision abruptly ended and every being was back in the room. Michael jumped to his feet. He was fuming. "That's it, Lord Nosfaren, we have enough evidence! Now can we do something about that fraking deser'rec?"

Lord Nosfaren not only didn't say anything. The Meserino Demon was so lost in thought that he appeared to be asleep. And he wasn't the only one. Practically every other being on the Council was in the same sleep-like state.

"There is no time for meditation!" Michael shouted while he raised both hands high into the air. "We have to do something about Chirras—now!" For a moment, his roars were ignored.

Once all of the beings' eyes reopened, they simultaneously stared at Lord Forscythe. Lord Nos was the first to speak. "Lord Forscythe, we have all agreed—we will be putting your plan into motion."

Forscythe's eyes went wide, and he grinned from ear to ear. He was about to say something, but Lord Nos cut him off and continued his declaration. "We have also decided that, in order to put your proposal into effect, we are going to make you a member of this Council; you will be taking Chirras's place." The councilors could detect a bit of glee in his voice.

Bowing lowly, Lord Forscythe managed to meekly utter, "I am honored, My Lord."

Vok'et's jaw hit the floor while he watched in awe. *My uch'nra is going to be on the Council? And he's taking the place of the woman he's trying to trap! Just how ironic is that!* he thought.

"Don't get too excited, Lord Forscythe," Lord Nos cautioned after the Lord arose from his low bow and gave Nos his full attention. "You will only be on this Council if you can get our small Silvarian friend to help with this operation." Once Nos finished, all eyes turned to Visage, who was feeling lost, embarrassed, and frustrated.

"I don't like this plan…. Nor do I like getting my fiancé involved in all of this," Riza muttered under her breath. She peered at Nos with an unmistakable scowl on her face.

I agree with you, Riza. Vira also scowled at the Dark Lord.

Though Lord Nos didn't let on, even he was none too pleased with using Visage for bait. Unfortunately, nobeing in the room could come up with a viable alternative. He quickly glanced at his wife. She gave him a reassuring nod, though even she was having some misgivings about voting for Forscythe's plan. *I wonder if we'll be putting the poor child in too much danger.*

"Visage!" Lord Nos wanted to make sure he had the boy's attention. Visage's currently ice-blue eyes fixed on his own. The Lord's heart sank. Though he'd had many opportunities to look into Visage's eyes, this was the first time he noticed the hope and life that they emanated. *Eendril, I'm going to need help with this. How the boy responds will either make us or break us. I can only hope that he has as much courage as I think he does.* After succeeding in getting his thoughts back on track and swallowing the lump in his throat, Nos began. "Visage, I know that you've only been here a short time, but we need your help."

Visage cracked open his right eye and could immediately see the anxiety and displeasure that were apparent on the faces of many of the attendees. "What kind of help?" he tentatively asked the head of the Council.

It's my plan, Lord Nos; I can't put this burden on you, no matter what his answer ends up being. Forscythe had sent a silent message, but everybeing could easily sense his thoughts.

Slowly, he made his way over to Visage, got to one knee, and placed both of his hands on the boy's shoulders. "Visage, you met Chirras in the hallway, right?" Forscythe paused, and Visage responded with an affirmative nod. "Well, Chirras is a deser'rec, and we need to use you for bait so that we can capture her and all of those like her. Would you be willing to do this for us?"

Visage started tearing up, his face clouded over, and then he bowed his head. After he gritted his teeth, his head shot up. "That woman is evil! I don't want anything to do with her!" he shouted. Bringing both of his arms up, he knocked Forscythe's hands off from his shoulders, turned on the balls of his feet, and marched to the door. He was both hurt and angry. However, instead of exiting the room, he suddenly turned his head and made eye contact with Lord Nosfaren. "Is this why you brought me here—to use me as bait to lure out that manipulative bitch! Well, Lord Nos!" The Silvarian's tears were now cascading down his cheeks. The group frowned when they noticed the small ripples of purple energy that his tears made when they hit the floor. His eyes were much colder looking now—more like the color of a deep abyss than their normal blue color.

Lord Nos was unnerved by the sudden change in the child's eyes and by his words, which shocked everybeing. "No, this was not my intention, Visage," Nos whispered. He now realized that he was the cause of the Silvarian's current despair.

"This is my plan! I'm the one you should blame!" Lord Forscythe jumped to his feet and slammed his fist onto his chest. He desperately wanted Visage to understand that *he* authored the plan—not Lord Nosfaren.

"And that's what... supposed to make me feel better!" Visage yelled before he again, defiantly, made his way to the door. Once there, he turned his head slightly to his left. His face and eyes were hidden while he softly, but scathingly spoke. "Lord Nos...I want you to take me back home. I don't want anything more to do with this cult of yours!" Visage's words were like ice—cold and piercing. They hit all of the councilors like a sledgehammer it pierced all of their hearts. Nobeing was bold enough, nor coherent enough to even offer a rebuttal.

Visage grabbed the handle of the door. The burgundy door was so highly polished that he could see his reflection. He was shocked by his own appearance! Surprisingly, his greatest distress wasn't from the anger and pain reflected back from the eyes that faced face him, but rather from the sheer depth of emptiness they revealed. *Is that what I've become: a cold, angry, empty-souled being? What am I going to do? If I leave, what's going to happen to me? Will I always be like this! How will I ever look myself in a mirror again...? Or trust again! And how will anybeing ever be able to trust me!* In a state of mental and physical exhaustion, the young Silvarian wrestled with what to do. Then, almost miraculously, something Kim had told him, back when he was being bullied by the kids in school, came into his mind, and, in a flash, he was back home.

***

Kim knelt down and looked into her son's eyes. After putting her hands on his shoulders, she told him something he'd never forget. "Remember this, Orran: courage isn't just about having the physical strength to overcome; it's also about having the strength to forgive, to smile, and to walk away. But there will be times when you can't walk away—when you'll have to take a stand."

"But Oma, how will I know when to take a stand and when to walk away?"

Kim smiled at the question. "That's why God gave us a mind as well as a heart. We need both in order to make that decision. Do you understand?"

Visage half-heartedly responded, "I think so."

***

Visage's mi'thia was one of the smartest women he knew, and her words now weighed heavily upon him...but not for long. His mind again wandered, and he recalled a sentiment he had once read: *The only thing necessary for the triumph of evil is for good men to do nothing.* He knew in his heart that the sentiment was true. *But can I do it?* After grasping the door handle more forcefully, he glanced once more at his reflection. His eyes had returned to their more pleasant sapphire-blue color. Reluctantly, he released the handle and turned around, much to the dismay of some beings. His oma's words seemed to encompass his entire being. While making his way over to Lord Forscythe, he repeated them, hoping to boost up his courage.

"What is it that you keep muttering?" Azala's curiosity was piqued.

"Just words I heard and read when I was at home," the boy responded. Azala appeared satisfied with the response, but Visage proceeded to explain his utterances. " 'Courage isn't just about having the physical strength to overcome. It's also about having the strength to take a stand.' That's something my oma told me. The other saying I was muttering is about what happens when good men do nothing in the face of evil."

"Those words were spoken by very wise people, Visage. Are they the reason why you came back?" Forscythe asked, shocked by the boy's sudden change of heart. *I thought for sure he was going to leave. Is he really going to stay and help with my plan!*

Visage reluctantly nodded. "But that woman still scares me. And I'm not thrilled about being the bait for your trap!"

Baltrix arose. Standing tall, he announced, "Don't worry, ar'teth Visage, I'll be right beside you!"

Riza and Vira then stood up. "And you have us too!" they declared in unison. Visage was overcome with emotion when every council member arose and offered him the same heartfelt support.

"See, I told you! You belong here, Visage!" Ali'stia blurted. "Besides, if you left, my de'tari would lose her rival, and I've waited too long for someone like you to show up! And I really didn't relish the thought of having to drag your twin-tailed crath back here!"

"She'd totally do it, too," Azala whispered to her roommate, shielding her mouth with her hand when she did so.

Forscythe and Vok'et stifled their chuckles. "I think she'd do a lot more than that to him, Azala," Vok'et added after taking a quick glance at the demoness in question.

Azala chimed back, "You're probably right about that, Vok'et."

Lord Nos cleared his throat. "So, Visage, have you changed your mind about being our bait?" Everybeing's attention now focused on the boy's answer. Visage sighed and reluctantly nodded.

"Excellent! That will give me ample time to get everything ready within one or two onns!" Forscythe excitedly announced.

"Wait! What? One to two onns? Seriously!" Visage blurted.

"Visage, do you think we'd just throw you at that traitor without a foolproof plan?" Lord Nos asked.

"Well, yeah!" Visage threw his hands in the air. He was totally unprepared when they mentioned the timeline, but, at the same time, his antics made everybeing laugh.

"We aren't that heartless, Visage," Zoric said with a grin.

"We never do anything without a sound plan, and if we're looking to capture that fraking deser'rec and any other Skath-worshiping glorts, then you'd better believe we'll do this right!" Michael folded his arms across his chest. He was eager for a chance to lock sorjins with Chirras or with any other Skath worshipper who might be hiding in the shadows.

"Visage, I told you, we Zaharaj are family. That means we protect each other; we would never let Chirras do anything to you!" Lord Nos glanced at the two demonesses. "And I'm pretty confident that Riza and Vira would do something drastic if you were ever in any *real* danger." He gave the two women a wind and flashed them a sly grin.

The two demonesses were obviously pleased by Nos's apparent compliment. "Now then, Lord Forscythe"—Lord Nos rose from his seat and gestured for the Zebrecian to come forward—"please kneel." Forscythe wasted no time in complying with Nos's request and quickly assumed a kneeling position. Nosfaren then took his blood sorjin from his belt. After igniting it with the press of a button, the crimson blade came to life with a snap hiss. "Lord Forscythe, by the power of the Verse, and by my authority as head of the Council of the Zaharaj, I appoint you to the position of eleventh seat on this Council and bestow upon you all of the authority and responsibility that this title entails." Forscythe bowed his head and clasped his right hand over top of his left fist. "Do you accept this honor, Lord Forscythe?"

"I do, My Lord, and I promise that I will bring Chirras to justice!" He raised his head but kept his hands firmly clasped.

"Very well. Lord Forscythe, welcome to the Council of Thirteen!" After he spoke, Lord Nosfaren brought the edge of his sorjin close to Lord Forscythe's left shoulder, then lifted it over the top of his head and did the same to his right. Taking several steps backwards, he held his weapon with both hands and centered it in front of him, making sure to keep the blade vertical.

When the newly appointed council member arose, the rest of the members arose from their own seats. They grasped their own sorjins, ignited them, and held them so that the blades were vertical, the same way Lord Nosfaren held his.

"We will now close this ceremony with our oath. Lord Forscythe, would you please take your position and lead us?" Lord Nosfaren asked.

Forscythe was beaming. "I'd be honored," he replied before he walked over to his new throne. He turned on his heels, stood straight, and took out his own blood sorjin. After igniting it, he began to recite the oath. "Peace is fleeting, so I thirst for knowledge." Right after he finished the first line, Vok'et and Azala took out their sorjins. All of the council members picked up the oath where Forscythe had left off. "Through knowledge I gain power; through power I learn wisdom; through wisdom I become enlightened; through enlightenment I will become one with the universe!"

Visage stood in awe. Though he could only look on, he felt the power and conviction emitting from all those around him. The members' faces appeared stoic, though also bright, since they were bathed in the glow emitting from their blood sorjins. The weapons were emitting a mixed array of red and a more crimson-colored light. Vira's sorjin was the only exception. Since it was glowing dark blue, it really stood out.

With a chorus of hisses, all blades were shut off, and the members began stretching and mingling. Lord Nos interrupted. "I know it might be difficult, but none of you are allowed to speak about anything that transpired here tonight," he warned.

"I think that's a given, Lord Nosfaren," Lord Fenrir said with a hint of sarcasm.

"If Chirras were to find out about our plan, the outcome would be disastrous!" Lord Michael added. "Though I'd iloni to just run her through and be done with it." Several members groaned at the comment.

"We have to play nice with her...at least for a while. Vok'et, Azala, Visage—that goes for you too." Lord Zoric glared at the trio, making sure they got the message.

Azala rolled her eyes. "You don't have to worry about me. I'm usually off in the galaxy with my master. Isn't that right, *Master* Nos?" She made sure she put the emphasis on 'master' in order to get his attention.

Lord Nos appeared a bit confused. "What was that?" When he saw his apprentice glaring at him, he responded, "Oh yes, Azala, that's right."

Azala pressed her hand to her face and shook her head. After turning around, she grabbed Visage's cloak by his left shoulder and started dragging him back to their room. "Come on Visage, let's get out of here and leave the Councilors to their business."

Visage whined in complaint, not too happy that he was being hauled away. Riza waved at him, but Vira only smiled and chuckled. Nosfaren and Ali'stia were preoccupied, busy talking with Lord Forscythe, Michael, Zoric, and Fenrir. The other members of the Council were busy discussing the proposed plan and totally missed Visage's plea for help.

Azala threw both doors open while at the same time continuing to drag her rather uncooperative captive behind her. The pair was heading for the lifts when Visage noticed that Vok'et was hot on their heels.

"Azala, wait up!" Vok'et yelled.

"What is it, Vok'et? I'm kinda busy." Azala's twills flopped about when she jerked her head to the side in order to speak to the Zebrecian.

Vok'et was well aware of Visage's displeasure with his current situation. "I can see that you're busy . . ." he dryly responded before continuing, "but I think Visage can walk on his own; you don't need to drag him around like that, do you?" He shot Visage a reassuring wink.

Azala blurted back, "Oh yes I do!"

Vok'et grimaced. "And why's that?"

Though Azala paused and silently fumed about Vok'et's interference, she finally released her captive. Visage squinted at his roommate. *I wonder why she's treating me so badly. I thought Azala was a nice girl, and now I'm not so sure.*

Azala pointed at Visage and began to rationalize her behavior to the intrigued Zebrecian. "This kid ilonis to ask questions, and there are two complete knowledge junkies in that room! If he started asking anything, they'd both want to answer, and we'd be there all trell!" Azala was glaring at Vok'et with her hands firmly planted on her hips.

"Good point." Vok'et glanced at Visage who was scowling at the two older beings. "So, you're headed back to your room then?"

Azala relaxed, nodded, and put her hand on top of Visage's head just in time to prevent him from running back to the Council Room. *Not on your life!* she telepathically declared.

"Please, Azala, just a *few* questions," Visage begged.

Azala responded by pressing down on V's head and making a fist with her other hand. *Me and my big mouth.*

"Visage, you know, if you really want to get your questions answered, you should ask Envine or Cormack." Vok'et flashed a smile at the boy before cupping his hand near Visage's ear and whispering, "They're both apprentices of the master librarian and grand cataloger of the Zaharaj, so you should talk with them when you get the chance."

Visage's eyes widened, a smile spread across his face, and he vigorously nodded his head at Vok'et's suggestion. The Zebrecian stepped back and grinned. "I think he's satisfied with that, Azala."

Azala let go of Visage's head. "I guess so," she responded, though she was still skeptical.

Vok'et threw his cloak back on and shoved his hands deep into his pockets before delivering his thought to Azala. *I'm surprised you haven't offered to explain things to him. You are Lord Nosfaren's apprentice. So you know as much, if not more, than Envine, Cormack, or even I do.*

Azala shrugged. "That never even occurred to me. Anyway, we have to get back to our room. Come on, Visage. Let's head for the lifts."

"In that case, have a go'trell, and I'll see you in class tononn." Vok'et followed up with a quick wave. After receiving return waves from Azala and Visage, he stood alone in the waiting area just outside the Council chambers. Feeling relieved—and frustrated, he gazed up at the ceiling and began to contemplate what had occurred over the past few deronns. *Silvarian demon, huh. I wish my ber'nan were here to meet him. I still don't know what to tell Mi'thia when I see her.* Vok'et balked at the thought. *Can I even tell her what I found? Or do I need to wait until Uch'nra Forscythe's plan to trap Chirras is finished?* His mind was in turmoil. "I wish Forscythe could advise me on what to do, but I guess this one belongs in the hands of a higher power." Concentrating, he used his Indren'Freth to levitate. He then crossed his legs, bowed his head, and shut his eyes tightly. "Dear God, I hope You're listening, because I need answers!" After opening his mind and heart, the Verse flowed freely throughout his being.

22

The Call from Home

Azala and Visage entered their dorm room, and Visage immediately grabbed his black ball and hugged it tightly. Azala walked past him, slumped into her chair, and started spinning around. Once done, she leaned her cheek onto her fist and watched her roommate lying on his bed, clutching the black sphere to his chest. Her curiosity finally erupted. "What is that thing, anyway?"

"I have no idea. Riza gave it to me. The longer I hold it, the warmer it gets." Visage then proudly raised the ball up and began spinning it, taking great care not to drop it.

"Riza gave it to you?" Azala raised her tiny left eyebrow.

"Yes. She dropped it into my hands just before she left me alone." Again, the boy brought the ball back up to his chest, and, as expected, it immediately began to get warmer, providing comfort to its owner. *Hey, I have an idea!* Visage climbed off his bed, walked over to Azala, and said, "Here!" before he excitedly offered her the strange warm ball. Without awaiting her response, he plopped the curious object into her hands. Azala blinked in surprise and straightened up in her chair. Her face started to glow when the already warmish orb became even warmer, and she was able to experience the same level of comfort that Visage had enjoyed. However, the moment was short lived, since Visage interrupted with a question. "What is it, Azala?" Azala combed through her memories and attempted to find even a tidbit of information that related to a cool black ball that got warmer when held. Visage's smile faded when Azala informed him that she knew nothing about his precious ball. The boy slumped for a bit but quickly perked up. "That's alright, I'll ask Riza about it when I see her."

"What's wrong?" Azala asked when she saw that Visage, who had just been sounding so upbeat, now appeared dumbfounded.

"I completely forgot to ask Riza to give me back my boots!" he exclaimed while peering at his bare feet. He wiggled his taloned toes. Even though he had the talons retracted, they still stuck out a bit. "Not that I could even wear them right now."

Azala chuckled before leaning over and resting her cheek on the orb. *This warmth feels great—almost therapeutic. I wonder where Riza got this ball. What in the world is it, anyway? I don't even care...All I know is, I want one.* She would have liked to stay right there with the ball but reluctantly handed it back to Visage. "Sorry, V. I'd love to keep it, but I have to make a trip to the refresher." Once she got into the refresher, she noticed something odd. *Wait a minute! Visage hasn't used the Zor'nok —not even once!* "Must be nice not to be cursed with all of these mortal urges and bodily functions that we have to deal with," she grumbled.

✳✳✳

Visage was back on his bed, hugging his orb and feeling its warmth wash over him. After giving a sigh of contentment, he heard several strange noises, which sounded like the whirring of small gears. "What is that?" The sounds grew ever louder. Out of the corner of his eye, Visage noticed movement off to his left. The metal man, which had been stationed in the far-left corner of the room, was now just a few feet away. It was looking down at Visage and managed to scare him half-to-death before it finally spoke.

"Go'trell, Silvarian. I am T.A.D One-Dash-Seven. My mistress told me to introduce myself when I had the chance."

Visage calmed down, and his heart gradually returned to its normal pace. He took a deep breath and stammered, "H . . . h . . . hi," but the metal man continued to stare at him. "Uh, Azala?"

"Yes, Visage, what's wrong?"

"There's a big metal man staring at me," he stammered.

"Oh, right, that's just my butler. I told him to introduce himself to you when he had the chance."

Onsev immediately turned towards the refresher, jumped into the conversation, and brusquely offered a correction to Azala's characterization of his position. "Mistress Azala, I'm your bodyguard, not your butler."

"You are not my bodyguard, Onsev!" Azala yelled back loudly enough to drown out the sound of the running water from the rinser.

Now convinced that "Onsev" was not a threat, Visage breathed a sigh of relief. "So, what's a T.A.D?" he asked, peering up at the metal being with a sense of wonder.

"T.A.D is the acronym for Tactical Assault Doll," Onsev obligingly responded.

Azala said he was her butler, but he sounds more like the bodyguard type of robot to me, Visage mused. "Onsev, why does Azala need a bodyguard?"

"Ugh! Visage, he isn't my bodyguard—he's my butler!" Azala again yelled from the rinser.

"I was assigned to watch over the young mistress by Master Namren and Mistress Zella," Onsev formally explained.

Visage was now curious. "And who are they?"

"They are Mistress's mi'thia and dar'nra, though, in the common tongue, they are referred to as parents."

"So, you were a gift for Azala from her overprotective parents?" Visage asked. He was disappointed that Onsev was unable to answer the question.

"Something like that." Azala had come out of the refresher and tossed her clothes at Onsev, who caught them as she passed by and headed for her chair.

"Mistress Azala, I suggest you consider wearing clothing, since you're no longer the only organic being in the room," Onsev said in a rather metallic, almost motherly-sounding tone.

Azala rolled her eyes. "Listen, Onsev. One, Visage is nothing like Zor'ret; two, my bruises still hurt; and three, those clothes really need to be washed. So shut up, do your job, and leave me alone!"

Despite Azala's loud reprimand, Visage's attention was focused on something else. Though they didn't look as bad as they did the previous trell, Azala still had noticeably black blotches on her skin. "Azala?"

"Yes?"

"Can't you get your bruises looked at? I mean, there's a nice woman in the infirmary. I bet she could do something for them."

"No, I don't think so, Visage, but thank you for your concern." Azala then spun her chair and stared at her T.A.D, who had gone back to his corner. "See, Onsev, he's nothing like Zor'ret."

"I can see that mistress, but you should still wear something. You can catch a cold with all of that moisture clinging to you," Onsev offered. His hand proceeded to glow, and all of Azala's clothes, including her cloak, vanished into a green mist; the mist was swallowed up by the gem, and the gem stopped glowing.

"Azala, don't you have anything else to wear?" Visage was a bit shocked and embarrassed by his roommate's nakedness.

Azala spun her chair back around. "Yes, I do, but Twillan clothing is very tight and clingy, so it makes my bruises ache," she complained.

Now understanding Azala's predicament, Visage slid off his bed, set his orb gently down onto the soft mattress, and removed his cloak. Carrying the cloak over his arms, he walked over to Azala and offered it to her—though he did look a little sad. "It might be a bit small, but I agree with Onsev; you don't want to catch a cold. I felt really badly when both my sri'na and om . . . ah . . . mi'thia had colds and I couldn't do anything for them." The memory was unpleasant, but Visage quickly shrugged it off.

Azala was surprised at her roommate's offering. She knew how much he cherished his cloak. *Absolutely* nothing *like Zor'ret*, she thought before she bundled up in the offered garment.

However, Visage was not satisfied. After handing over his cloak, he walked back to his bed, picked up his ball, and brought it back to Azala. "Here, this will help keep you warm."

"That's it! What do you want? What are you after?" Azala asked, figuring there must be some kind of angle to all of Visage's caring gestures.

Visage was confused and a little hurt by Azala's unwarranted accusation. "The only thing I want is for you to not catch a cold," he replied in a hesitant low tone.

"I'm sorry, Visage; I'm not used to having a roommate who doesn't have any ulterior motives," Azala explained before graciously accepting the ball. The ball was cool at first but warmed up bit-by-bit as she again lay with both her twills draped over it. "Mmm...This feels so good."

Onsev spoke up. "Master Silvarian, Mistress's clothes will be clean in six dironns, so would you let her keep your cloak till then?"

Visage turned to face the metal doll, who was speaking from the corner. "Six dironns—is that like what, thirty minutes?"

"No, it would be over eighteen of your Earth minutes, Master Visage," Onsev instantaneously replied.

"That's not bad. I was going to let her use my cloak and ball till she went to bed," Visage responded, now glancing over at the Twillan, who was looking a bit zoned-out.

"You have no idea how good this feels. I have to ask Riza where I can get one," Azala muttered with a bit of a slur.

This caught both Visage and Onsev's attention. "Are you all right, Mistress?" Onsev walked over from the corner and stood right behind Azala's chair.

"I'm fine, Onsev. This thing is amazing." Now she had both beings rather worried.

"Mistress, I think you should give the Silvarian back his ball."

Though groggy, Azala managed to raise her head slowly. Her eyes were partly closed and appeared to be a bit more bloodshot than usual.

"Azala, are you Okay?" Visage had been lying on his bed but bolted upright when he realized that his roommate's overall condition was deteriorating.

Onsev scanned the ball in search of answers as to why his mistress was acting so strangely. "Scan complete. The ball is organic in nature. It's producing low levels of an unknown energy," Onsev informed Visage.

"What does that mean, Onsev?"

"I cannot compute, but with the state Mistress Azala is in, I'd say the ball generates something similar to high levels of ultraviolet radiation."

Azala hid her face with the ball and started chuckling. "Come on Onsev, I'm only playing with you." After wiping her face, she turned her attention to Visage. "But seriously, where did Riza get this thing?"

Visage relaxed when he realized that Azala was actually alright. However, he was a bit irritated by her deception, and his state of mind was apparent in the tone of his response. "I told you, I don't know." Azala's eyes were fixed on him. "Riza only said something about a woman giving it to her to give to me and..." Visage lowered his head, cocked it to the side, and started rubbing the back of his neck... "that she doesn't give these things out very often."

"So, some woman gave this ball to Riza and asked her to give it to you. That's strange." Azala unwrapped her twills, which had been encircling the ball, and stared at Visage's precious possession. "If it's producing a low level of unknown energy that means it must be magickal in nature." Though she was guessing, her voice had a tone of certainty. When she held out her hands and offered the ball back to Visage, he immediately got off his bed and raced over to retrieve it. "Are you sure you wouldn't like to hold onto it a bit longer?"

Azala shook her head. "Nah. I've got to get back to reading, and the ball would be too distracting."

When he accepted the ball back into his custody, Visage was grinning so widely that Azala couldn't refrain from chuckling. She followed up with a stretch, which caused her to wince. "Well, pain or not, I've got to get back to reading. And Visage..." Azala trailed off.

Visage, now back on his bed with the ball, gave his master his complete attention. "Yes, Azala?"

"Thank you for your concern."

The Silvarian gaped a bit, shook his head, and replied with gusto, "No problem, roomy!" He then lay down on his bed and clutched the orb to his chest.

***

Azala was busy reading her book when Onsev announced that her clothes were done. Visage watched him pull the cloak and other clothes out from the green mist of his gem. *Just how does that work?* he wondered as he watched Onsev lay the clothing on his master's bed.

Azala arose from her chair, disrobed, and threw the cloak at Visage. Visage became disoriented when his cloak fell over the top of his head and obscured his vision. Azala laughed while watching him struggle to hold onto his ball with one hand and get his cloak off his head with the other. He finally had to put the ball down in order to get his cloak properly situated. Once he had the garment straightened out, he got down from his bed and sauntered over to his chair.

By this time, Azala was back into her own cloak. She had the hood down and both of her lengthy twills lying over her left shoulder. After kicking off with her right foot, she spun her chair in a near three sixty in order to face Visage. Visage had pulled off his own hood, which was now giving off a sweet, unfamiliar odor—an odor which was a little too strong for his sensitive nose. The odor caused him to scrunch up his face. Not that it was an unpleasant odor—it was just very different. *Is this what she smells like? Or is it the smell of her soap?* He glanced over at the Twillan, who was eyeing him in return. *I'm so glad that Vira and Riza showed me how to shield my thoughts. I certainly don't want to offend Azala.*

Azala started laughing, having heard every word Visage had thought. However, laughing caused her to wince in pain.

I guess I didn't make my barrier strong enough...

"I'm not offended in the least, Visage." Azala muttered between chuckles. "In fact, I took your thought as a compliment! And stop making me laugh; you're making my bruises hurt!"

"Sorry; I'm still getting used to this whole mind-reading thing." He rubbed his head in embarrassment.

"Don't worry about it," Azala cheerfully responded. "You know, you are one of the strangest beings I've ever met!" Suddenly, the tone of Azala's voice lowered. "You really need to watch what you think around others, Visage...especially when Chirras is around."

"I still can't believe that the Council is going to use me as bait."

"Hey, you don't have to worry about her...yet." Azala sounded cautious but cheerful.

Visage knew that this was true, since it would take some time to firm up Lord Forscythe's plan. He was feeling relieved, though still a little worried. "Azala—" he started, but was interrupted by his roommate, who was vigorously shaking her head.

"Time is on your side, and, since you are a demon, there is very little —if anything—that Chirras can do to you. Besides, you have thirteen of the most powerful beings in the galaxy looking out for you." She averted her eyes and whispered. "You also have Vok'et...and me."

Visage instantly felt better. "Thanks, Azala!"

Azala's mood seemed to lighten after Visage expressed his gratitude. When she was about to respond, Onsev came up and again stood behind her chair. "Mistress, your parents would like you to contact them," the T.A.D announced in a rather dry manner.

Azala pressed her hand to her face and slid it down, turning it into a fist just past her chin. She looked up and mumbled. "For the iloni of God, can't they leave me alone for one trell?"

Visage responded with a whispered. "At least you know that they love you."

Azala gave the boy a quizzical look. "Love? Isn't that the word in the common tongue for iloni? Yeah, I know. It's just that they're sooo annoying."

"Mistress, your parents are waiting," Onsev said.

"Yeah, yeah, Onsev, I got it." She turned her chair to face her "butler."

Visage peered on as a small door opened up in the center of Onsev's palm, and another emerald gem rose up and glowed. Two, small, green-tinted beings appeared from the glow of the gem. They looked to be Twillans, since they both had those twin tendrils that grew out from the backs of their heads.

"Go'trell, Azala! How's our young Zaharaj doing this fine trell?" the male on the right asked.

"I'm fine, Dar'nra, other than the bruises I got from my sparring match with Master Nos yederonn."

"Oh, honey, do they still hurt? Why didn't you go see a healer? Don't the Zaharaj have one of the finest medical facilities in the galaxy?" The small female Twillan couldn't hide her concern.

"That's what I said," Visage added before quickly covering his mouth with both hands and butting out of the conversation.

Three Twillan heads turned towards the speaker. "Azala, who's that? Is that the Silvarian you told us about len'trell?" the woman asked, this time acting childishly excited. Her small form hopped up and down a few times and she clapped her hands.

Azala balked. She was not pleased by the sudden turn of events. *Well, there's no point in crying over spilled yanak,* she thought before she beckoned for Visage to get his twin-tailed butt over there so she could introduce him to her mi'thia and dar'nra. Visage was hesitant, but obeyed, slinking off from his chair and cautiously making his way over to stand next to Azala. "Mi'thia, Dar'nra, this is Visage; he's a Silvarian and my new roommate. Visage, meet the co-owners of the Tarminian Conglomerate, Zella and Namren."

"Um, are you sure he's a Silvarian?" Zella asked.

Azala's jaw dropped at Zella's question. "Yes, he is! Can't you see his tails!" she blurted. Exasperated, she reached down and grabbed the closest tail to her, causing Visage to jump. She held up the tail, enabling Onsev to scan it with his optical sensors so Zella could clearly see the results.

"Azala, please let go of my tail!" After seeing the distraught look on Visage's face, Azala immediately let go. "I'm so sorry, V, I just wanted to prove to my mi'thia that you really are a Silvarian." Visage, however, was past the forgiveness stage, already happily swishing his tails about. Once satisfied that all was well, he promptly hid them behind his cloak.

"My wife only asked because his colors look . . . well . . . off," Namren said, sounding a bit worried.

"Oh yeah. Visage here had a little fight in the pit with Arisha tendronn. He used the Cloak of Darkness and kicked her crath. It was great! Ali'stia's betrak was finally taken down a notch by none other than my Silvarian roommate!" Azala exclaimed.

Azala's pronouncement astounded both of the holo beings. They stood like statues, their mouths gaping in disbelief. Namren was the first to regain composure. "I see. I'm impressed that such a young demon knows how to use that technique."

"It was kind of an accident," Visage confessed. "I didn't like the feeling I got when I used the power." He shamefully lowered his head.

Both Azala and Zella shared a smile. "Visage, you have nothing to be ashamed of," Zella said before turning to Azala and totally changing the subject. "You're right; he's nothing like your last roommate."

"Rumor has it that Lord Baltrix killed Zor'ret. Is that true, Azala?" Namren asked, obviously eager for the answer.

"Yes, Baltrix did kill him—though he wouldn't have if that fraking id'rth hadn't gone all feral on him!" Azala beamed as she reflected on Lord Baltrix's very brief encounter with Zor'ret.

"Azala!" Zella narrowed her eyes at her de'tari, now that she had her undivided attention. "How many times have I told you not to use that kind of language!" The small holo woman put her hand on her hip and wiggled an accusing finger at her de'tari as she delivered the stern reminder. However, Azala just shrugged off her mi'thia's words.

"Language? What language?" Visage asked aloud, thoroughly confused. He looked from Zella to Azala and back several times.

Every being now turned their attention to the puzzled Silvarian whose tails were twitching beneath his cape.

"Really! Does Earth not have any curse words?" Azala brashly queried.

"Yes, we do," Visage responded. "The Navy guys, especially Roy,

Bryce, and Tony, are really foul mouthed—but they aren't bad people!" He was exasperated; he didn't know what cursing had to do with anything. But, in Azala's defense, he added, "And, I hate to admit it, but I picked up some of their vulgar phrases, and, well, they just slip out sometimes."

"Lord Nos is foul mouthed sometimes too, and his daughter Arisha is—all the time. She's got more of a mouth than I do, Mi'thia!" Azala protested. She spoke with such sarcasm that Zella was fuming.

Zella balled up her tiny fists, pursed her lips, and shouted! "Azala Sherah Temeran, if you ever sass me like that again, so help me I'll—"

"Bore me to death?" Azala countered, rolling her eyes while interrupting her mi'thia's tirade.

Zella went from being angry to being shocked. She couldn't believe that Azala had the audacity to speak to her like that. Her husband, on the other hand, completely lost it; he was laughing so hard he doubled over.

"Azala! Why you—!" Zella then turned on her husband. "And you, Namren, are supposed to be on my side!"

Visage couldn't take it. He started crying. As his tears rolled off his cheeks and landed at his feet, they splashed onto the carpet, causing wisps of energy to rise as they made contact.

Azala was visibly shaken. "Visage, what's wrong? Why are you crying?"

"I'm sorry." Visage was overwhelmed by all of the bickering. "It's just that you don't know how hard it is to see you like this," he muttered as his eyes met all of theirs. "Just before I left home, I burned my...I burned Kim...because I couldn't control my power. And, when I saw you fighting, my heart hurt, because I don't know if my parents will ever want to see me again. So please don't fight over such pointless things...because right now I'm not sure I even have a family anymore."

Every being felt ashamed that their actions had rekindled Visage's pain, but Namren was the first to speak. "Visage, yes, we fight and argue, but that doesn't mean we don't iloni each other, because we're family. And despite my de'tari's distasteful speech patterns, she will always be our de'tari and we'll always iloni her. So, I'm sure your mi'thia and dar'nra still iloni you, too. Never let doubt get the better of you." Visage gave a slight nod, which Namren acknowledged with a hearty, "Very good."

Azala leaned over in her chair and gave Visage a hug. *I had no idea he left his family like that. He burned his own mi'thia! Even though I argue with mine, I've never hurt her, not even unintentionally. It's no wonder he's acting like this!* She then wrapped her twills around the child. Now resting her chin on top of his head, she realized how much she took her own family for granted. "Are you all right now, Visage?" she whispered.

"Yeah, I think so," he muttered back.

Once satisfied with Visage's answer, Azala turned to her own parents. "I'm sorry, Mi'thia, I'll try harder not to curse."

Zella was distressed by the whole situation; she couldn't stand seeing the boy cry. She actually didn't like seeing any child cry, especially if she knew the child was really hurt; and it was obvious to all that the Silvarian had been seriously hurt.

"Azala what is going on here?" Zella painfully asked her de'tari.

Azala was pained as well. "I'm sorry, Mi'thia, but I can't tell you."

"You can't, but I can!" Visage blurted, still wiping the tears from his face.

Azala gasped! *NO, Visage, you can't tell them anything!* she telepathically shouted.

Visage faced her. "I can't tell them about the plan, but I can tell them about everything else." Azala balked; he had her there. There were actually very few things within the Zaharaj that outside beings couldn't know.

"Fine. You win. I know my parents are trustworthy, but don't say anything about Chirras or the plan."

Visage nodded, and then began the story—from the time he burned Kim up to the time when Riza gave him the black ball. The three Twillans were overwhelmed by everything, especially the part about Visage's mi'thia.

"Did the Meserino queen actually show you Skath's rampage and tell you that you were going to become something even worse!" Zella was wroth that the demoness could even think of doing that to any being, especially to a being as young as Visage.

"Don't worry, Visage. I'm sure she's wrong about you!" Namren exclaimed as he crossed his arms and huffed.

"I know. I just don't know why she would show something like that to me," he wondered aloud.

"What do you mean by that, Visage?" Azala asked.

"When we were inside her head, I was able to see into her heart. That's how I knew she wasn't really trying to kill me. I just don't know why she thought I'd become anything like Skath." The young demon shook his head in disgust as he reflected on the memory.

"Perhaps she was testing you," Namren said matter-of-factly.

"Why would she need to test me?" Visage looked suspiciously at the small holo image.

"I don't understand either, Dar'nra," Azala informed Namren as she slumped a bit in her chair.

Namren's ensuing silence put everybeing on edge. However, he soon gathered his thoughts. "I believe that Visage has some destiny that involves both the gods and the demons, and the Meserino queen wanted to know whether or not he was up for what might lie ahead. However, I also believe that the way she went about determining his readiness left much to be desired," Namren muttered—still rather drathed off that the demoness would show something like that to a mere child.

Visage thought that the Twillan was probably right about Rashia's motives. "Do you know about the prophecy concerning a Dark God named Chaos?" He posed the question to both Namren and Zella, hoping that at least one of them might know something.

Azala looked perplexed when her parents both shook their heads at the mention of Chaos's name. Zella questioned, "Where did you hear that name, Visage?"

"From Chaos himself," Visage honestly responded.

"Just who the fr . . . I mean . . . who is Chaos?" Azala asked, editing her language just in time to avert Zella's wrath.

Namren, still in a mild state of shock that Visage even knew the name, chimed in. "The Dark God Chaos—now there's a name I never thought I would hear outside of ancient records and lore." Zella then proceeded to answer Azala's question.

"Azala, Chaos is, or was, Skath's youngest son. However, he was apparently killed by Skath. He had rebelled against Skath after the Silvarian demons were wiped out by the Ze'therac clan; many of his friends were Silvarians."

"He wasn't killed!" Visage cried. "Skath imprisoned him! Riza and Vira told me there is an ancient prophecy that a demon will set him free, and they think I might be that demon!"

Zella gasped at the child's knowledge, and Namren did a double take. "How do you know this, Visage; even our own God doesn't like us knowing too much about that prophecy."

"Do you know what Visage is talking about, Dar'nra?" Azala asked.

"Yes, but it isn't what you'd call common knowledge," Namren said in a worried tone.

Zella then faced her husband. "And just how is it that you know about this...this...prophecy, iloni?"

Namren turned his gaze away from every being. "Let's just say I bought an old book from a traveling trader one deronn, and it had lots of...things in it." Namren sounded like a child who had just gotten his hand caught in a cookie jar.

Zella spoke again. "Iloni, how many times have I told you not to waste danaries on old books? You should know that most of them are fake!" she scolded.

"But this one wasn't a fake; it contained multiple gems of knowledge," Namren rebutted. "It even included the prophecy about the Dark God Chaos," he said proudly, giving Visage a wink. Before Zella could start complaining again, he continued. "Visage, tell me if you've heard something like this before. 'Soon a demon will be born who'll undo the chains of a Dark God's scorn. Just a child who can see and, with compassion in his eyes, will set him free. With Light and Dark in balance again, no more to be broken as healing begins.' " Namren finished reciting the ancient prophecy and eagerly awaited Visage's reaction.

"That's it! That's exactly what Riza and Vira told me!" The Twillan was delighted. Neither Zella nor Azala could believe what they had just heard; they were too shocked to speak.

"I knew that book wasn't a fake!" Namren announced with glee. "Visage is the demon from the prophecy! That means he's the one who will free Chaos and restore balance!" he loudly announced, nearly falling backward. "You've got to be kidding me! My de'tari is rooming with a Silvarian demon who is the legendary peacemaker—the demon who bridges the gap between gods and demons!" Namren was so excited that he actually began to hyperventilate.

"Iloni, are you all right?" Zella went to her husband's side and put her right arm around him to give him some support.

"I'm all right. I'm all right. This is just...too much to take in!" he said. It took him a few moments to catch his breath. Once recovered, he straightened up and looked very sternly at the young Silvarian. "Visage, whatever you do, don' tell any being what you just told us! Got it!" Visage nodded emphatically, affirming that he understood. Namren then turned to Azala. "Azala, that goes double for you!" His eyes narrowed a bit as he spoke.

"I promise, Dar'nra. I don't think any being would believe me anyway."

"Um...iloni, before you tell me 'I told you so,' I have to ask—just where that book is right now." Zella was worried about the outcome if the book, especially if true, was to fall into the wrong hands. Namren was embarrassed. After giving an apology to his de'tari, he quickly exited the screen.

Zella put her hand to her face for a moment and groaned. *Just as I thought, he has no idea where that book is located.* After expressing her heartfelt love to Azala, she turned to Visage. "I'm so sorry about your mi'thia, Visage; just remember that time can heal all wounds. I'm sure that, despite what you did, your mi'thia still ilonis you. And, I'm so glad I got to meet you." Zella smiled and waved as the transmission ended.

For a dironn, Visage and Azala appeared spellbound. Once Visage was able to speak, he turned to the Twillan. "You have totally awesome parents, Azala!" He was beaming!

"I know," was all Azala managed to say in response to Visage's pronouncement. She sighed, got up from her chair, and stretched. "You know, Visage, it's been a long time since I've seen my parents that excited. I bet Dar'nra is rummaging through our entire library right now, trying to find that book!"

When Visage headed to his bed, Azala came up behind him and hugged him. "Thank you, Visage, for being my friend," she whispered.

Visage stood motionless, on the verge of tears. "Azala, I'm so happy that I got to room with you. I know you care about me and will always be here for me if I need you."

After letting Visage go, Azala grabbed the hood of his cloak and playfully threw it over his head. She smiled when he turned around and gave her a goofy, fang-filled grin. The feisty Twillan couldn't help but chuckle while she headed to her bed.

"You should really get some sleep, Visage. It's getting late." Azala started taking off her cloak and skin-tight shirt, grimacing when she did so. After undressing she glanced over at her Silvarian friend, she found that he was lying face up on his over-sized bed—at least for him it was oversized. He was still wearing his cloak and pants while clinging to his magick ball. His eyes were closed, and the orb was slightly rising and falling in rhythm with his slow, shallow breaths.

I can't believe he can fall asleep so fast, especially after the deronn he just had! Azala thought. She gathered up her cloak and clothing before she handed it all to Onsev. She stifled a groan and held her bruise, before climbing into bed. Though she tried to sleep, it didn't come to her as quickly as it did to Visage.

While continuing to watch the boy's sleeping form, tears welled up in her eyes. *It doesn't seem fair that God could place such a burden on one so young, but then again . . . He did sacrifice a lot for us. I wonder if I will live long enough to see the prophecy fulfilled. Even though Twillans live longer than humans—or even Marcisians—we are all mortals. But not him.... Unlike us, he does not have to earn his immortality, since he was born as an immortal being. Perhaps when I'm dead, I'll be able to… No, I'm not even going to think about that. I still have lots of time.* Then she closed her eyes and fell asleep—all the while thanking her God for this chance meeting.

"Azala, don't you know that there are no such things as coincidences?" a small voice whispered to the sleeping Twillan. "You have a big part to play in my plan. So does the Silvarian, but first you have to grow up." Though the voice made no more sound than that of a pin hitting the floor, it had the force of a galactic storm. It was quiet, yet powerful. Even though Azala was half-asleep and unable to hear it, she was able to feel it.

23

Hidden in the Past

Visage looked around, unable to make out his surroundings. A thick heavy fog obscured his vision. He shouted desperately, but no answer came. Unsure where to go, he randomly picked a direction and started walking. However, because the fog was so overwhelming, he had to proceed with caution. He could barely see the landscape—to say nothing about his feet. Though the menacing fog briefly lifted, enabling him to move ahead more briskly, the Silvarian quickly realized that his progress was not in any way a blessing. With no warning, he was faced with such a horrific scene that all he could do was stand with his mouth agape. Before him loomed a great field, littered with what appeared to be a sea of corpses. And he was standing at the edge of the field! The corpses were literally touching his feet! Red blood was flowing from the bodies and smearing his taloned toes. The blood had turned the scattered patches of grass a bright crimson color. For a time, Visage carefully picked his way through the bodies. "What... what happened here? Does it go on forever? Will I be here forever?" Encompassed by a feeling of immense fear, he unexpectedly caught a glimmer of hope— the outline of two beings standing in the distance.

The time was early morning, and the sun's rays were barely starting to pop up behind the distant mountain range. In the new light of dawn,

Visage turned his focus back to the corpses and was able to discern that they were wearing chain-linked armor. Their helmets were tall and gave the appearance of great cones protruding from their skulls. Most of the corpses had swords or spears as well as bucklers and shields lying at their sides. The scene looked like something out of Earth's Dark Ages. Visage was continuing to move cautiously in the direction of the beings, but he ended up stumbling over one corpse and fell forward. Visage landed with his knee on one of the other fallen soldiers. He managed to utter one word: "ewe," before scrambling to his feet. After what seemed like forever, the distraught young demon worked his way over to a point where he could see that the beings were men.

Visage's eyes widened in realization. "Hey!" He shouted. "Lord Baltrix, what are you doing here!" he tried to get the man's attention, but his friend didn't respond; it was as though he couldn't hear him. "Where am I?" All the while, he was getting closer and closer to the Lord and his companion. Once close enough, he could make out that Lord Baltrix wasn't wearing his usual Zaharaj uniform. Instead, he, like the dead soldiers, had on a full suit of red and black armor, which had a great gold serpent or dragon emblazoned on the chest area. Not only was his armor different, but his eyes were as well. They were a brilliant blue and no longer had their Zah'harrim tint. He was also covered with blood, even more so than was the other being. Now that Visage could see the other being clearly, he realized that Baltrix was not talking with another man but rather with a Meserino demon.

The demon's red eyes glanced about the battlefield. He folded up his great bat-like wings, clasping them with two small claws that protruded from the central joint, so he could now wear them like a cloak. With a look of disgust on his face, he folded his wings across his chest and gritted his teeth. The latter action revealed his fangs. His skin was red with thorn-like, black biree—the strange looking tattoos that adorned every demon's body. He was wearing only a black pair of knee-length shorts, which had pockets on the sides. Visage was horrified because the Meserino was covered with the red blood of his enemies.

Visage's eyes went wide. "Lord Nosfaren ... is that you! What are *you* doing here!" he demanded, but the pair continued to ignore him. With his patience waning and the smell of blood becoming more and more nauseating, he decided to use his indren'freth to levitate closer to his friends—close enough to hear their discussion.

"Vlad, I believe that we've taught those Turks a lesson, wouldn't you say?" Lord Nosfaren asked while he surveyed the battlefield.

Vlad also looked over the horrific sea of carnage. "Yes, Lord Nosfaren, but at what cost? I lost a lot of good men this day."

"True, Vlad, but now your people will be safe—and we've prevented the Turks from invading Europe. All in all, we paid a stiff price, but I believe it was worth it."

Vlad responded with a question. "And what about you, my friend? What will you do now?"

"I'll continue to hunt for our missing ship. I still have a few sectors left to scan."

"And what of me? I have nothing left... Nor do I have a home to return to now that I've been branded 'Nosferatu' by the church." A downhearted Vlad hung his head.

"I wouldn't mind taking you with me, though I'm not sure if your God would like you consorting with demons."

Vlad's mood lightened at Nosfaren's apparent proposal. "That may be true, but I seriously doubt you even are a demon." He couldn't resist a chuckle.

Lord Nos was intrigued by Vlad's accusation. "And what makes you say that?"

"Because I don't think *any* demon has such an attitude as yours."

Nos chuckled a bit. "I'm glad you think so." However, his mood suddenly changed. He spoke softly and in a dejected tone. "Still, I'm sorry I didn't make it in time to save your wife."

Vlad shook his head. "Don't be sorry my friend, you did everything you could. And it wasn't even your fight."

"That's where you're wrong!" Lord Nos shouted. "It *became* my fight when you and your people took me in, despite who and what I am.

You all showed me great kindness. How could I not have fought along-side you?"

"Like I said, how could you possibly be a demon?"

Lord Nos let the question die. "So, Vlad, what say you? Would you like to be my apprentice?" Without hesitation, Vlad nodded his head.

"Good, then it's settled. Kneel!" Nos commanded.

Vlad got to one knee. "I'm sorry, Father; please forgive me, for I have decided to follow this demon into Hell itself if need be," he whispered. When Nos laughed, Vlad peered up and scowled at his mockery.

"I'm sorry, Vlad. It's nothing personal, but I'm afraid to say that there actually is no such place." Vlad's eyes narrowed and his brow furrowed. "Really? But the scriptures say—"

Nos raised his hand to silence his companion. "That book you follow is full of holes—many truths were removed."

Vlad didn't know what to make of Lord Nos's brash declaration. "Why would you say something like that, my friend?"

"I can't elaborate, but I would never force you to turn away from your God. After all, He *is* your creator.

"But I thought if I followed a demon that I'd damn my soul for all eternity!"

Nos pondered for a moment before bringing his hand down and resting it on Vlad's shoulder. "Listen, Vlad. I may be a demon, but it was your God who actually adopted us after the war."

Vlad's eyes went wide. "Wait. War? What war?"

Nos shook his head "I'm sorry, Vlad, but this is neither the time nor the place for such a discussion. So, do you still want to become my apprentice?"

Vlad's eyes darted about while he searched for the answer. Then he stared straight into Nos's eyes and gave him a firm nod.

"Excellent!" Nos declared. He proceeded to pull a rather wicked-looking two-handed sword out of a black mist.

Visage stared at the sword with wonder. The pommel was egg shaped and silver colored, though it was embedded with a red-glowing ruby. A silver band separated the two leathery wraps. A being would grip the hilt over the silver band. The guard was silver and crimson, and its sides housed a pair of eerie-looking red eyes with slit pupils. The eyes appeared alive, darting about for a moment before quickly snapping shut. The blade was a combination of black in the center surrounded by a deep crimson color. The crimson shade ran along both of the edges. The sword itself created a black-and-red haze, which trailed behind it every time its master made even the slightest move. Nos grasped the unfamiliar-looking weapon in one hand and began to speak. "Vlad, by the power of the Verse, I name you Baltrix and make you my apprentice in the Zaharaj." Nosfaren brought the flat of his blade down on Vlad's right shoulder before swinging the blade up over his head and down onto his left shoulder. "Now, my young Baltrix, arise! I welcome you as a fellow ber'nan of the Zaharaj!"

Vlad rose from his kneeling position. "Lord Nos, what does 'Baltrix' mean?"

For a moment, Baltrix was unsure as to whether or not Lord Nos had heard him. The demon was focused on putting his blade away. When he twirled it in his hand, it vanished, but left a lingering trail of inky-looking black and red mist when it did. "'Baltrix'? Hmm," Nos closed his eyes and smiled a rather sinister smile. "'Baltrix' is a word in the demon language. In your tongue it translates to 'the bloody trickster,'" he explained.

Vlad peered again at the sea of carnage. "Seems fitting," he replied, agreeing that his new name fit him perfectly. "So, Master Nos, what now?" he asked the demon.

"We continue our search for our elusive ship."

"Will we travel in your flying ship!" Baltrix was unable to contain his excitement.

Nos shook his head. "No, my apprentice, we will walk."

"Walk?" Baltrix was obviously disappointed. "Fine." Then he perked back up. "So, where are we going?"

Lord Nos flashed him a fang-filled smile. "I've heard some rather interesting stories about an island in the far east." Baltrix raised an eyebrow. "In the common tongue, I believe it is called 'Japan'."

"Why are we going there? And why would you have us walk?" Baltrix demanded more than asked.

"My young Baltrix, don't you know that the journey can be even more important than the destination?"

"I agree, but you still didn't tell me why we are going there," Baltrix countered. His new master started heading east towards the rising sun. After turning his head to a point where Baltrix could only see one eye, he said, "I've heard about a man who is very much like you, my apprentice."

Baltrix's curiosity got the better of him. "How so?"

"Let's just say he has a thirst for knowledge," Nos replied. However, before he could turn his head back, an excited Baltrix was ready with another question.

"Master Nosfaren, who is this man?"

Nos continued on, smiling widely. "I don't know his full name, but I do know he's part of the Oda clan." He then returned to his brisk forward pace. His newly ordained apprentice was barely able to catch up.

***

Visage looked on from his perch in the air and watched the pair disappear into the fog, which had now returned. Thankfully, it again engulfed the scene of carnage. However, this also meant that Visage could no longer see his hand in front of his face. Surprisingly, however, the fog quickly dissipated, and a paved street suddenly formed beneath the young demon's feet. Its oh-so-familiar rough texture reminded him of home. He started following the road, stopping suddenly before running into a parked car. After sidetracking the car, he found himself standing in the middle of another street. Abandoned cars were backed up in both directions; doors had been left wide open, it seemed that the occupants had apparently tried to flee. Some people had even lost purses and shoes when they fled. The skyscrapers and buildings were in total disrepair. Visage could see that most of the buildings' windows had been shattered, and the tops of several of them appeared to have been blown apart.

The young demon began to feel nauseous, and a feeling of familiarity flooded his mind. *I know this place! This is downtown Seoul! But it looks like a war zone!* His heart started racing. He levitated off the ground, searching for anyone who could give him answers. He flew down several main streets and landed right in front of the building that housed his grandparent's company, but it too looked dilapidated and abandoned. He walked up to the front entrance where the two sliding doors used to be and found that the entrance was nothing more than a mess of twisted metal and broken glass. He was about to make his way inside when he heard heavy footfalls along with the sound of something metal dragging on pavement. After turning to locate the source of the sounds, he froze in fear.

He saw what looked like people—but they were not people! Remembering a very old zombie movie, which he had watched with his sri'nas and his two older cousins, he determined that the things before him looked very zombie-like, having pale-white skin and black veins. All of their heads were bald and contained a set of milky-white eyes that had small black veins running along their outside edges. The sets of eyes were constantly open wide and appeared to bug right out of their sockets. The zombie-like creatures were naked, though they didn't appear to care while they milled about, dragging their long, black, one to four-pronged spears behind them. Visage cautiously made his way over to the creatures, but they didn't acknowledge his presence.

*What happened here? What are these things?*At that point, he noticed two females, who had more than a striking resemblance to his own mi'thia. He raced to them. *No! No! Not my oma!* he mentally pleaded after he encountered more and more of the pale white creatures, all of which looked just like Kim. Visage ran up to one of the creatures and hugged the thing about the waist, hoping for some kind of recognition. His heart sank, when the female-appearing creature didn't even slow its forward pace.

"Oma, can't you hear me?" Visage pleaded, looking up into the creature's blank face. For what seemed to be an eternity, he begged for the creature to see him, but to no avail. Finally giving up, he slumped to his knees and watched the creatures saunter off, dragging their spears behind them. Hopeless, he peered into the sky, which was no longer blue but now a sickly shade of red, and begged God for some answers. "What the frak happened here!" he desperately yelled.

"Hey kid, there's no need for that kind of language." Visage turned to see a heavenly being—who was none other than Halifel—stepping out from a pastel portal. Halifel was glowing brightly, his gold-colored eyes focusing in on the boy. After a short while, he retracted his six white and gold tipped wings into his back causing a plum of glowing white feathers to appear and then vanish in a blink.

"Halifel, what's happening! What are those creepy-looking things, and why do some of them look like Kim!" Visage ran over to the archangel, clutched his robe with both hands, and sobbed.

Halifel knelt on one knee and embraced the child, letting his light flow over him in an attempt to calm him down. When Visage stopped crying, Halifel ended their embrace, withdrew a ways, and positioned his hands on the boy's shoulders. "Visage, this is only a dream."

"It is?" Visage asked, still unsure.

Halifel nodded. "I hate to say it"—He took his right hand from Visage's shoulder and gestured to their surroundings—"but this might become Earth's future."

Visage was so devastated at Halifel's pronouncement that he nearly fell over. Fortunately, the Archangel still had his left hand firmly clasped onto the boy's shoulder. "To answer your unspoken question, Visage, Skath did this. Or at least his followers did," Halifel clarified. "And those things are called the Fallen. All beings who would not denounce their God and swear allegiance to Skath were turned into Fallen."

"So Skath turned my oma into a Fallen!"

Halifel shook his head. "No... at least not yet. This is only a glimpse of what the future could look like. Only the Marcisian Empire stands in the way of Skath's followers and Earth. But if the Empire collapses, the entire galaxy, not just Earth, will fall."

Visage's brow furrowed and he clenched his fists. "So how do we stop these... fraking things from taking over?"

"The Zaharaj will be heavily involved in destroying Skath's minions. And you, your family, and the Navy guys also, will play a key role in Father's plans. You, along with your family and other Navy guys, will help defend against the Skath worshippers and their legions of Fallen. Those who fight on the side of our Heavenly Father, after they die their souls will be immediately taken up to heaven by our Father Eendril," Halifel told him with a bright smile.

"But what if we can't stop the Fallen!" Visage cried in panic while glancing at more Fallen creatures walking down the street. "What if this horrible future actually comes true!"

"Don't worry, Visage, after mortal beings die they'll still be fine," Halifel reassuringly offered. "And even the Fallen aren't entirely without hope." Visage remained quiet while he eagerly awaited information about how he could save his oma from an unthinkable fate.

"Like I've told you, the Skath worshippers can turn an unbeliever into a Fallen. And sometimes they organize small armies made up of people like your oma, who was turned into two hundred and twelve Fallen soldiers!" Halifel flashed a smile. But this time Visage scowled up at him.

"How can you smile like that when they turned my oma into over two hundred of those—creatures!" Visage cried while throwing his arms into the air.

Halifel ignored the child's outburst. "Visage, you need to know that every soul is made of energy, and the stronger the soul, the more Fallen soldiers can be created from it. Your oma had a very strong soul; that's why she was, or could be, turned into so many Fallen. So, you should be proud of that fact!"

"What difference does it make how many Fallen can be created from her, in the end, she may even become... one of those creatures!"

Halifel sighed. "Orran I've already told you, even a Fallen isn't without hope. You see, if all of your oma's Fallen clones are destroyed, then her soul will be restored, and God will be able to take her back into His rest!" Halifel announced.

Visage breathed a sigh of relief before Halifel continued. "Only the ones who follow Skath are truly without hope. See. Look there." The Archangel pointed to a cloaked man who was walking up the street with a hoard of Fallen behind him. At first, Visage thought he was one of the Zaharaj, but his Zah'harrim-tinted eyes were devoid of all life; instead of being white, they were black. The man's pupils looked cloudy, and even the usual red veins around his eyes had become a sickening shade of black. The man looked and felt evil. His upper lip was raised, resulting in a scornful façade. Though he and his army of Fallen marched right past Halifel and Visage, they were totally oblivious to the pair's presence.

"Halifel, why don't you fight them? Why would you let them take over Earth or any other planet?" Visage whimpered. He couldn't bear the thought of Skath worshippers taking over the galaxy.

"I wish we could fight them Visage, but the gods have laws they must follow, just as we must obey God's law—or face the consequences. So, all we can do, in earthly terms, is grit our teeth and look on helplessly while our brothers and sisters are killed or turned into these abominable creatures." Halifel sounded none-too-pleased at his metaphorically tied hands. "However, that's where you come in, my demon friend. You see, your kind isn't under any such restriction; that is why you can fight those abominations on the mortal plane—and you're as powerful as most gods. So, we look to you for hope because, even though none of us like to admit it, you demons are able to save more lives than we can. And once Chaos is free, He will become an invaluable ally in this fight! So, keep your faith. Even though God can't help you physically, he can guide you spiritually! Though you are a demon, He thinks of you as His own son!" Halifel exclaimed.

"But Riza said that gods, angels, and demons all died in Skath's war!" Visage blurted in frustration and grief.

"Yes, that is true. You see, there were several gods who decided to break the law when they saw Arnen get killed by Skath. Your father—the demon king—was an inspiration to us all. Though we can't fight in the mortal realm, in the spiritual realm we'd take up arms in a heartbeat. And, even though it sometimes may seem like it, you never fight alone!" Halifel gave the Silvarian another hug. "We all love you, Orran. Never forget this!" With these final words, the archangel was enveloped by the fog.

***

Visage awoke with a start, gasping and clutching his ball, which was still giving off its comforting warmth. It almost felt like Halifel's warm embrace. "Neither Skath nor his worshippers will ever take this galaxy!" Visage adamantly declared, trying not to awaken his roommate. Azala barely stirred when he got up from his bed, put his magickal ball down, removed his cloak, and draped it over the end of his bed. *So far so good,* he thought before he went into the refresher. At first, the light disoriented him a bit, but after blinking a few times, he was able to make it over to the sink. When he reached for the faucet, it turned on by itself. *Just like home,* he thought. After testing the water and finding it to be warm, he cupped both of his hands and splashed his face. The soothing warmth of the liquid seemed to wash the memory of his trellmares away, but the calming feeling lasted for mere moments. *Now what! What is that... noise!* Since he suddenly felt as though he was being watched, he cautiously turned his head towards the source of the noise—the toilet. His eyes went wide in panicked surprise. A tentacle was sticking up out of the bowl! Though the boy was basically in shock, unable to move or speak, he was able to note that the tentacle was bent at a right angle and that it had an eyeball on it! The eyeball popped open and looked around in, what appeared to be, eager anticipation. "Okay, that's it!" Visage's tongue was loosed and he screamed bloody murder before jumping up into the corner of the room, where he pulled off a decent impression of Spiderman. His feet and hands suspended him tightly into the furthest corner of the room—as far away from the eye-balled, tentacled, toilet creature as he could get. In the meantime, the creature seemed to go into a state of shock before it seemed to sulk.

Azala was already awake when Visage went into the refresher. She had rolled over and was about to doze off again when she heard Visage let out the blood-curdling scream. She tossed off her covers and flew out of bed and ran to the refresher. "Visage! What's wrong!" After quickly assessing the boy's plight, she burst out laughing. She laughed so hard that she had to clutch her stomach. The sight of Visage, overcome with fear and suspending himself in the corner of the ceiling, was just too much to bear.

Visage turned to his roommate with a pained expression on his face. "Azala! Stop laughing! And what the frak is that thing in the toilet, anyway!" he cried while pointing at the sulking eyeball creature.

Azala could barely mutter, since she was still heartily laughing. "Visage... that's... only... the Zor'nok. You made it sad when you didn't deposit anything, and now... now you've hurt its feelings!" She burst out laughing again, sunk to her knees, and started to cry. "Oh, this hurts! Please... I can't... take it anymore!"

Visage had no idea what was funny enough to make Azala act so weird, so he gave up trying to figure it out. Instead, he stared at the tentacle. *So, that thing in the toilet is a Zor'nok? And somehow, I offended it?* Visage jumped down from his perch, making sure to avoid the Twillan, who was still in hysterics. He noticed that the Zor'nok was again possessing the look of eager anticipation.

By this point, Azala had composed herself, and Visage had generally recovered enough from the incident that he was able to help her get back on her feet. "I'm sorry Visage; I should have explained the Zor'nok to you... but this was way worth it!" she elatedly stated while wiping away her tears. "Thanks! I really needed that."

"Fine. Whatever. Glad you... had a good laugh. Now seriously what's a Zor'nok?" Visage asked, pointing at the tentacled, eyeballed thing.

"A Zor'nok is a creature that eats the waist of other organics, then secrets water and a mineral-enriched kind of mud. I mean, every Imperial home has at least one of these creatures. Though they aren't very intelligent, they do have feelings. Doesn't Earth have Zor'noks?"

Visage shook his head emphatically at her question and disgustedly responded, "No!"

"So, how do the beings on your planet take care of their waste?" The Twillan shook her head, causing her twills to flop around behind her.

"Never mind; I probably don't want to know!" She closed her eyes and stuck out her tongue as if the thought was making her sick and then continued. "Anyway, Zor'noks are like an every deronn appliance, so you'd better get used to them." Her face then scrunched up. "Speaking of the Zor'nok, I need to use it!"

But, I'm still in here! Visage mentally whined.

Yeah, so?

Ugh! I'm a guy! Aren't there any rules about men and women sharing the same bathroom and stuff? Visage kept his eyes closed and turned his back to Azala.

No. Why? Is there a problem with me being a female? Azala telepathically huffed. *If there is, then your planet is really fraked up!*

Really? I was told that it was wrong for different genders to share bathrooms, or refreshers... or whatever. Visage realized that he was grasping at straws at this point.

"Is there really that much of a gender discrepancy on Earth?" Azala was incredulous.

"I guess so, if that's what you call it. I've never thought of the way we share bathrooms as being a 'gender discrepancy'. It just seems like normal behavior to me."

Azala lowered her head and closed her eyes in thought "I guess there are times when I might be happy with the way you do things on that backward planet of yours. Like, I wasn't happy having Zor'ret as my roommate. He seriously gave me the creeps. I didn't like the way he looked at me or... treated me for that matter." She let out a sigh. "Guys like him are rare. But then I could say the same thing about Chirras; I wouldn't have liked to live with her, either," she stated. "But, from what you've said, the male beings on your planet sound as though they are a lot like Zor'ret."

"Yeah, I guess my oma..." Visage shook his head a few times before correcting himself. "I mean, mi'thia... could have thought that about me sometimes—especially when I'd leave the house naked! But I couldn't control my indren'freth or inner fire back then, so I always ended up burning everything I wore. When I was five, my parents finally gave up and only made me wear clothes whenever we had company."

"Pshaw." Azala gave him a dismissive wave. "Being naked isn't that big of a deal. I mean, just look at my race; we don't wear much because our sun is so intense. And the Skelaxians..." she sighed in exasperation. "Those insects. They never wear anything, except for maybe a lab coat. And there are lots of human planets where the people don't wear much because of their work or because of the fact that there aren't enough raw materials to fashion clothes. Earth is way behind the times if being naked is an issue. Seriously, how many beings do you know who were born wearing clothes?" Azala's voice dropped, since she believed she had made her point.

Visage's face lit up. "No one is born with clothes!"

"My point exactly! Now get those pants off and get into the rinser. I mean, I like you, Visage,"— Azala narrowed her eyes at him at took a few tentative sniffs. —"but that doesn't mean I want to smell you!" At this point, Azala made her way over to the boy, spun him around, and shoved him into the shower-like contraption.

Visage stumbled into the rinser, and the two transparent doors automatically closed. "Hey!" He was definitely annoyed.

"Throw your pants over to me, and I'll have Onsev particle wash them for you," Azala flatly responded.

Visage muttered several incomprehensible words, but he finally complied with Azala's request and threw his pants over the top of the 'rinser'.

"And Visage, it's still early, so you can take your time if you want— just not too long because I need to use the refresher!" Azala yelled from the other room.

Visage's two black-and-purple tails wagged in annoyance. "Yeah, yeah. It's not like I love to shower anyway—though showering is defi- nitely much better than having to take a bath." Memories of home now flooded his mind. He recalled the many times that his two older sib- lings dragged him into the tub with them. He thought it was because they really liked to scrub his tails, though he couldn't prove it. And his oma always liked having clean kids. So, eventually, whenever his sisters hauled him off to the bathroom, he went without a fight. *I really miss those times.* His train of thought was rudely interrupted by a soaking spray of warm water that was now shooting out from the rinser head.

Visage shook the old memories away while he looked around for some sort of soap and scrubber, or washcloth, but he couldn't see anything even remotely similar. Instead, two hoses appeared from either side of the rinser head; one foamed up his wet hair, and the other slathered his skin. After they finished their work, two more rinser heads dropped down, spun around him, and rinsed off the soap. He felt a bit tingly once the whole process was over and was more than relieved when the rinser heads shut off and recoiled back into the ceiling. Though his experience from the rinser turned out to be relatively pleasant, misery set in.

His hair was sticking to his back, and his tails were heavy, weighted down by the water. He had to wag them viciously in order to get the excess water off. After pulling the curtain of black hair away from his eyes and shaking himself off as best he could, the refresher doors opened. As soon as he stepped out, he was slammed by a blast of warm air. It didn't completely dry him off, but at least he was no longer drenched.

Azala started laughing when she saw her roommate. Visage retaliated by swinging his tails hard in her direction, hitting her with a spray of water droplets. "Visage, watch it! Some of these books are really old, and I don't want them to get wet!"

"Oh, I'm sorry, Azala. I didn't mean to damage the books—I love books!" Visage loudly lamented. However, Azala barely heard his apology; she was focused on making sure that none of the books were badly moistened, carefully inspecting each one. Fortunately, most of the spray had hit her, and only one book had been affected. With the inspection over, she now turned to the Silvarian and gave him a stern glare, ensuring that he would never pull the same stunt again.

The dark and naked Silvarian trudged over and slumped down into his chair. Azala stretched her neck, causing a loud popping sound, which made him wince. She then went into the refresher to take her own shower. "Must be nice not having any hair to worry about," Visage muttered, because his hair still clung to his body. Even his tails were now sticking to the chair. Onsev startled him out of his misery when he bent over and offered him some sort of towel. "Thank you, Onsev," he gratefully responded before getting up from his chair and drying off his body. His drying job made his tails all poufy, so now they looked as though they belonged to a raccoon instead of a demon. He smiled after he handed the towel back to the mechanical doll, who, in return, gave him back his pants and cloak. Visage hurriedly put them on, thanking Onsev again for his kindness. Onsev only nodded, and then returned to his corner.

Since his tails were still a bit moist, Visage decided not to wear his cloak, but instead wrapped it around the ball in order to prevent it from rolling off his bed. He then sauntered over to the head of the bed and grabbed his shirt, which was still folded up. He put it on, returned to his chair, and waited for Azala. Once out of the refresher, the Twillan dressed in a flash, and the roommates headed out the door to Lord Baltrix's class. Visage smiled while he reminisced about his meeting with Lord Niells. He then placed his hand in his pocket and made sure his earpiece was still there. "Azala, why weren't you in class with us veronn?" Visage asked, though he wasn't sure if he was using the right word for yesterday.

"It's because of the bruises my master gave me. We had also just gotten back from a mission, and they usually give us a deronn to re-cuperate," she explained.

That makes sense, Visage thought while he and Azala entered the lift and headed down to the lecture halls. After exiting the lift, Visage noticed that Azala was limping slightly on the leg that was the most bruised. *There has to be a way to use the Zah'harrim to heal injuries,* he thought as he watched his roommate limp along, obviously in pain. *I'll have to ask Lord Baltrix when I see him.*

***

Azala and Visage entered the third lecture hall, and, just like veronn, there sat Lord Baltrix. The Lord looked up to see who had come in. His red-and-amber colored eyes flashed brightly, and he kind of grinned. *Hmm, I wonder how many questions the Silvarian will pummel me with tendronn.* "Gunrek menronn, ar'teth Visage. Apprentice Azala, it's good to see you up and about," Lord Baltrix commented in a tone indicative of his concern. Azala flashed a halfhearted smile as she walked up the left hand side of the amphitheater. About halfway up, she claimed the first seat in the row on the right. Visage headed over to Baltrix, who was awaiting the menronn's question and answer session.

"Lord Baltrix, did you and Lord Nos successfully reach Japan?" Visage asked, obviously eager for the answer.

The question stunned Lord Baltrix! His eyes went wide, and his eyebrows went as far up as they could go. *How does he know about that!* Baltrix's mind raced back to the memories he had locked away eons ago. At first his countenance depicted shock, but then his mouth turned down into a deeply cold-looking scowl. He glared at his ar'teth. *Visage, I don't know who told you about that, but it's none of your concern!* he telepathically shouted.

Visage, undeterred by Baltrix's obvious anger, forthrightly answered the original, though silently offered, question. "I saw it in a dream last night...er... trell," he shook his head a few times. "I saw Lord Nosfaren take you on as an apprentice when he was looking for a missing Zaharaj ship. I really wanted to know if you ever found it," Visage hesitantly asked while he pressed his index fingers together.

Lord Baltrix was flabbergasted! It took a while, but he finally relaxed. "No, we didn't. And, with all the enemies we had made, it became too dangerous to continue our search."

"That's too bad," Visage replied, a bit downcast. He then perked up. "But Earth isn't like it was back then. Maybe you could get the Americans to help you look for it!" he exclaimed, full of youthful hope. However, he slouched a bit when Baltrix immediately shot down his idea.

"No, Visage, I will never go back to that planet, and I'm sure Lord Nos would say the same. You wonder why everybeing hates the Earth.

In all honesty, it's because, out of all of the planets in the galaxy, that is the only one whose inhabitants would willingly kill a god. But even worse than that, the people themselves are in a constant state of war over—everything!"

Visage could only nod in agreement. "Yeah, the Communists in the north don't like us, and the Chinese don't like us. Our only real ally is the United States, and maybe Japan?" Visage wondered aloud.

"That is why that planet will always be forbidden from becoming part of the galactic family. If its people can't even get along with each other, how can they possibly get along with the other races in the universe?"

No argument there. Even I was called 'monster' by the kids at school—just because of the way I looked, Visage thought, saddened by the memories.

"So, nothing's changed then, Visage, and that's why we brought you here." Baltrix grabbed the lip of his desk and leaned into it. "You know, you're actually a lot like me." Visage was shocked!

"Listen, we are both from Earth, though not many beings know that..." Baltrix related quietly. "and we were both thought of as monsters: you for being a demon and me for associating with one."

Visage went wide eyed in amused amazement. *He's right. We are a lot alike.*

Since neither Baltrix nor Visage wanted to continue their current conversation, which was becoming too depressing, Visage decided to ask Lord Baltrix about something else that had been bothering him. "Um... Lord Baltrix... what is that gem everybody, er... everybeing, has on their glove, and why does it glow and stuff?"

Baltrix was drawn away from his memories by Visage's new question. He shook his head and even sighed in relief when the old memories faded back into the recesses of his mind. *You know that the past can't stay buried forever, Vlad.* Baltrix was startled by the quiet whisper but chose to ignore the prompting.

"That is an excellent question!" Baltrix spoke with enthusiasm, grateful that the child had changed the subject. He then took his hands off the desk and pointed at the emerald in his right glove. "This is called a Utility Gem or U-gem for short." He then brought his hand down so Visage could get a better look at it.

"What does it do, Lord Baltrix?" Visage's eyes were wide as his usual youthful enthusiasm swelled.

Baltrix couldn't help but grin at the child's contagious eagerness for learning. *He reminds me of how I was when I first got here, but I wasn't as young or as enthusiastic,* Baltrix thought before he said aloud, "As the name implies, it's a multipurpose tool. It can be used as a communication device while simultaneously displaying an infinite amount of information on multiple screens. However, it's most commonly used as a sub-dimensional storage facility." Baltrix then touched the gem and made it glow. Several transparent screens with glowing, green-colored writing appeared inside the same glowing, green-colored box. Baltrix touched buttons on the top of the first screen as well as on a second screen that looked like a keyboard.

"Wow! That is really cool... But what's a sub... whatever... storage thingy?"

Baltrix pressed the gem, causing the screen to vanish. "It's a sub-dimensional storage facility or SSF, though some beings simply call it a 'sef.' " Baltrix paused as he put one hand on his hip and brought his other up to stroke his chin.

That has to be something he picked up from Lord Nos, Visage thought after noticing that Baltrix had mannerisms similar to those of the older demon.

Baltrix stopped rubbing his chin. "Visage, a sub-dimensional storage facility can hold anything from a pen to a battle cruiser!"

Visage's eyes went wide. "How does it do that!"

"Just think of it!" Baltrix again pointed at the gem in his glove. "It's like an infinite closet in which you can store pretty much anything— but there's a catch—it can't hold anything that's living."

"Okay, so no people or demons... but what about food... or plants? Can you keep those in it?" Visage asked excitedly.

Baltrix pondered a moment. "I don't know about food, though I do know some beings who have preservers inside their gems... But plants?"

Now Baltrix looked puzzled. "That I don't know." Looking up into the mostly empty amphitheater, he waved at Azala in an attempt to get her attention. "Hey, Azala, these sefs your company makes—can you store plants in them?"

When she realized that Baltrix's question was aimed at her, Azala looked up from the book she was reading. "Um... kind of. I know you can store things like seeds, but I wouldn't recommend storing full grown plants."

"Well, Visage, there's your answer," Baltrix said while Azala was now sporting a bit of a smile on her face, returned to her reading.

Visage was about to ask another question when the doors violently swung open, startling all of the beings in the room. Azala jumped to her feet, slammed her book closed, and grabbed both of her blood sorjins off from her desk. Baltrix had also taken his blood sorjin out and was gripping the metal hilt with both hands. Visage stood poised to use the Cloak of Darkness at the intruder but was shocked to see none other than Vok'et!

The intruder ripped his mask off and, without even allowing it to return into his earpiece, glanced around the room. Once he spied Visage, he zeroed in on him. After storming over to Visage, he ripped off his cloak and stuffed both his mask and the cloak into his U-gem. No being could believe this was the same Vok'et they had been with the previous trell.

Vok'et's anger was boiling over. There were bags under his obviously bloodshot eyes. It looked as though he hadn't slept at all. *He's going to attack Visage!* Azala and Baltrix both thought, since Vok'et was standing right in front of the boy. However, to the contrary, instead of attacking Visage, he embraced him in a big hug!

"Visage, I'm with you. I'm going to help you take that vial woman down!" he blasted through clenched teeth.

"Vok'et, what happened?" Visage asked, now that his state of shock had worn off.

Vok'et pulled away. "It would be much easier if I showed you."

Closing his eyes, he brought everybeing in the amphitheater with him into a very familiar-looking void.

Lord Baltrix, Azala, and Visage stood in a circle around Vok'et. "Lord Baltrix..." Vok'et gave the older man a stern look before he lowered his head, but lifted his eyes at him. Baltrix tilted his own head, putting his blood sorjin back on his belt and letting his hands hang loosely at his sides while he waited for Vok'et to continue.

"Yes," he replied, pushing the young Zebrecian to go on.

"Don't tell my master I showed this to you," Vok'et pleaded, biting his upper lip and causing Baltrix to raise an eyebrow.

"I know there's going to be a 'but,'" Baltrix said after accurately reading the troubled look on Vok'et's face. Vok'et closed his eyes and took a deep breath. "I need you to show this to the other Councilors." Vok'et turned his head to glance at Visage. Azala was a bit concerned by the look he had given the Silvarian.

Baltrix had also noticed the look and pondered for a moment before offering his answer. "I will, Vok'et... if I think it's important enough to share."

Vok'et thought about Baltrix's comment, and then reached a decision. "Fair enough, Lord Baltrix." Then he closed his eyes, baring his recent experience before all of the onlookers. He and the others were now in the waiting area of the Council Room. Vok'et was waiting by the lift for his master, since Lord Forscythe was busy conversing with Lord Barren. Next, Vok'et and Lord Forscythe were in the lifts together and headed for the lower levels of the temple, where their whole family lived in one of the converted caverns.

The onlookers all watched the pair leave the lift and head down a lengthy hallway; the red overhead lamps illuminated their path. The pair was talking about the meeting and about Forscythe's plan. They got to an area in the hallway that was lined with doors and headed for the fourth door on the right. After reaching their destination, they both frowned, realizing that they had company. "Chirras is dropping off Jetec's blood sorjin," Vok'et whispered to his master.

We can't let her know about the plan, so keep your thoughts shielded,

Forscythe silently warned. *It's imperative that we don't let her know that the Council sent us to Yenos Three to investigate Jetec's disappearance*, he added.

"I know, Uch'nra Forscythe," Vok'et whispered back.

The pair nodded to each other before opening the door. Forscythe was the first to walk through the door, followed closely by Vok'et. The place was like a condominium. To the right of the entrance, there was a kitchen combined with a dining room. Directly in front of the entrance was a very luxurious living room. Situated throughout the room were several couches and chairs that were covered with a foamy, plush-velvet cloth. A hallway extended off the back of the living room and along the length of the hallway were four doors. Another door could be seen at the hallway's end. Several rows of red-colored lights were embedded into the very high ceiling. The lights basked the entire apartment in a dim-red color, causing it to look quite surreal and otherworldly.

Two Zebrecian women were sitting on the living room couch. One was embracing the woman next to her and speaking softly into her ear. The other woman was clutching a blood sorjin to her chest and sobbing. Chirras was sitting in one of the large, comfortable-looking chairs across from the two Zebrecian women. A male Zebrecian, who had come out of the door at the far end of the hallway, joined the rest of the group. He looked worn out and tears were freely flowing down his cheeks. When he looked up, he was able to discern, through his tears, the identity of the pair of beings who had just entered the living room. "Go'trell Forscythe, Vok'et." He made his way over to Vok'et and hugged him. "I'm so sorry, Vok'et, but your ber'nan is gone!" He could barely speak through his sobs.

"I know, Dar'nra, I know..." Vok'et was trying hard not to break down in tears.

Forscythe walked over to his sri'na and wife. "I'm so sorry, Ni'shia." He spoke softly while getting to his knees. Ni'shia meagerly nodded, too choked up to speak. Forscythe knew that the loss of her dar'tari was overwhelming her. Zor'ret had been young for a Zebrecian, and, though he was in a much better place, Forscythe was very aware of the pain his loss was causing.

Chirras gave Forscythe a smile that made him want to rip her face off. Nevertheless, he had to keep his wits about him, as he couldn't betray the Council—or himself.

"I should have returned his blood sorjin to you sooner, Ni'shia," Chirras offered, "but I was too busy getting tossed off the Council." She then smiled—or was it a smirk? None of the watchers could tell, what they did know was that the woman was irritating.

Chirras's comments grated on Forscythe because he knew the truth about her. He had to work hard in order to control himself, but he somehow managed to smile back. "I thank you for returning Jetec's blood sorjin. I know that my sri'na really appreciates your consideration," Forscythe said, as calmly as he could.

"Don't worry about it. Thanks to the Council I have a lot of free time on my hands, especially now that Baltrix killed my apprentice." She spoke as though she were upset over Zor'ret's demise. However, Forscythe and Vok'et knew she was actually happy to be rid of him. Forscythe had to turn away so the liar wouldn't see him grit his teeth.

"I'm also so very sorry for your loss," Chirras said to Ni'shia. "Jetec was my fiancé; I only wish I could have found the one who took him from me."

Everybeing was shocked, except for Vok'et and Forscythe, at Chirras's astounding pronouncement. Vok'et and his uch'nra had to play the part, for they already knew, through Visage's memories, about Chirras's proposal to Jetec.

"You were going to marry my dar'tari!" Ni'shia was so visibly dazed that Vok'et and his dar'nra had to move over to the other end of the couch. Vok'et was disgusted by Chirras's deceit, but continued to do his best to hide his thoughts.

"Yes. Jetec was so powerful; in time he would surely have taken over Lord Nosfaren's position on the Council." Chirras smiled that evil smile of hers.

We have to agree with you on that one, Baltrix and Azala telepathically related to Visage.

What's that? Visage silently asked, not having a clue as to what they were getting at.

She definitely does have an irritating smile, the pair responded. Visage smirked in return, and the group continued to watch Vok'et's memories from the previous trell. Vok'et then skipped through some parts of the vision in order to get to the more critical parts.

"This is what I need you to see, Lord Baltrix," Vok'et eagerly related. Baltrix nodded. He already didn't like the conniving woman, but now he was starting to think that Lord Michael's plan of ripping the information from her head was actually not a bad idea.

Azala went over to stand in front of Chirras and said, "If only she were real, I'd..." She trailed off, though she *was* clutching her two blood sorjins. Her face contorted in anger. She even attempted to bore holes into Chirras with her eyes.

"She's much more powerful than you, Azala," Baltrix warned. "So please don't try anything foolish. We've just lost two students, so the Zaharaj can't afford to lose any more."

Azala spun about, walked over to Vok'et, and whispered, "If you ever need me, I'll be there in a heartbeat." She then moved over next to Baltrix, snorted, and folded her arms under her chest.

Everybeing's attention again focused on the vision when Vok'et's memories resumed. Chirras was standing—about to leave. Forscythe and Vok'et looked relieved when she headed for the door. However, she was not quite finished. Instead, she turned and again faced the group. "I iloned Jetec very much, but I've found a being who's more powerful than he ever could have become." She flashed her evil-looking smile and then made her exit.

Forscythe and Vok'et were outraged! They knew exactly whom Chirras was talking about, but all they could manage to do was stare at the door. Then Vok'et's memory faded, and the participants were back in the amphitheater.

Baltrix immediately made his way over to Vok'et. "Does she know?" he asked, anticipating the worst.

Vok'et shook his head. "Forscythe doesn't think so—though I argued with him about it most of the trell. He said there was no way she could know about the plan."

Baltrix was deep in thought when Azala interrupted. "What in the universe would cause her to be interested in Visage!" she exclaimed, gesturing to said being.

Baltrix jerked his head around in order to face the Twillan. Azala was standing beside her desk, looking defiant, and even a bit imposing, while she glared right back at him. Baltrix didn't even flinch. Instead, he began speaking in an undeniably powerful tone. "It's because he's a Silvarian."

Vok'et looked from Baltrix to Visage and back. "I don't understand; he's a normal demon. I mean, they're all powerful, right?"

"Visage is far from a normal demon."

Visage interrupted. "I am?"

Baltrix shook his head in the affirmative. "Yes, Visage, Silvarian demons are anything but normal. From what little we know, Silvarians are not as powerful as the Meserino, but they do have one quality that Chirras has apparently discovered."

"What's that?" Vok'et quizzed, though he sounded a bit skeptical.

"The ability to live forever. He is immortal."

Azala rolled her eyes, and Vok'et slapped his face with his open hand. "But all demons are immortal," he protested.

"Everybeing knows that!" Azala added with a grand roll of her eyes.

Baltrix then shook his head. "No, I mean he can grant *other-beings* immortality!"

Azala slumped back in her seat, and Vok'et's jaw fell while they both took in the new information and peered at the Silvarian. "How! How is that even possible?" Vok'et challenged; he had never heard anything like this before.

Baltrix shrugged. "I'm not sure how it works. Not many beings even know about this power, since the Silvarians were all killed during the War of the Gods—or at least everybeing thought they were. The only reason I know about it is that Lord Nosfaren told me about it a long time ago. Even I had forgotten about it till just now," Baltrix explained while he rubbed the top of his head and stared at Visage.

"If Chirras finds out about this, of course she'll be after him!" Though Vok'et was excited at the prospect of immortality, he was also terrified by the prospect of such knowledge falling into the hands of Chirras—or any being like her.

"Azala, Vok'et, and especially you, Visage, don't let anybeing know what I've just told you—got it!" The trio agreed, but the most emphatic response came from none other than Visage himself. Baltrix grinned. "Very good. And Vok'et, I will be informing the Council about what you showed me. I will be recommending full-deronn surveillance of Chirras; we can't afford to leave her to her own devices—not anymore."

Vok'et wholeheartedly agreed. "Thank you, Lord Baltrix." Visage seemed to relax a bit after Baltrix's pronouncement and proceeded to the same seat he had taken the deronn before. Vok'et stood by his desk and cleared his throat. "Um, Visage, would you mind if I sat next to you?"

Visage was quick to respond. "Nope!"

Being able to sit by Visage made Vok'et's deronn. He walked around behind the boy's seat, pulled out the one at the desk next to his, and slumped down. After taking his blood sorjin off his belt, he placed it carefully into the notch at the top of his desk. He then folded his arms on his desk and laid his head on his makeshift pillow. With his worries from last trell's encounter with Chirras subsiding, he was now feeling very tired and quickly drifted off to sleep.

Visage couldn't help but grin; Vok'et was making small eeping sounds every time he exhaled. *Ali'stia was right; I do belong here. I have more friends here than I ever had back home. Other than my family, I think I had only two real friends on Earth. But how long am I going to be away from my family? I miss Oma so much. I wonder if she's still mad at me for burning her so badly. She'll probably hate me forever. I guess all I can do is pray that she will forgive me—God knows I didn't mean to hurt her! I love her!*

24

A Demoness's Worries

Riza, I really don't like Lord Forscythe's plan." Vira lay back in the unoccupied chair in her friend's room.

"We don't have to like it; we only have to keep Visage safe from that woman until we find out how many more beings like her are among us." Riza was lying on her bed with her legs crossed and her wings folded about her. Her long, slender, red-and-black tail snaked about just to the left of her legs.

"I still don't like it," Vira repeated while heading for the door.

"Uh-huh," was Riza's nonchalant reply while she casually turned the page of her book.

Vira rolled her eyes and left the room, leaving Riza to her reading. *I have no idea what she's thinking,* she thought after the door closed behind her. *I had better go and report to Lord Nos before he starts screaming those telepathic messages at me.* The demoness's thoughts continued to race—even after she reached the lifts. *The Empire's emissary is going to be here in what, a mcronn? How is Lord Nosfaren going to explain all of this to him?* "I can see it all now.

'I'm sorry, Nar'gal, we can't join the Empire right now; we have a traitor in our midst, and we're using a Silvarian demon as bait to lure out the rest.' I swear Eendril is doing this on purpose!" the demoness yelled, startling several other cloaked beings who were also waiting for the lifts to arrive. "Anything to keep the gods entertained," she chuckled when the lift light blinked, a chime sounded, and the doors opened. She stepped in and pressed two buttons on the keypad. "Ready or not, Lord Nos, here I come." The lift ascended.

25

Key to Immortality

Chirras held the holo-journal and zapped it with small doses of lightning from the outstretched fingers of her right hand. She then started reciting the verses that were the key to opening the journal. "Peace is fleeting, so I thirst for knowledge. Through knowledge I gain power; through power I gain strength; through strength I learn wisdom; through wisdom I will become one with the universe." Right after she finished, the holo-journal began to shake. The runes and glyphs that adorned it began to glow a bright crimson color and a crimson-colored mist issued out of it. Chirras threw the journal, which stopped mid-air in the center of the room. While it remained in place, a dark-cloaked being formed out of the mist. "I am Lord Dermos, keeper of ancient records and lore. Who is it that requires information?" the smoky black specter asked. Chirras stood and stared at the ghostly figure. His body was no more than vapor and smoke, and a pair of red-glowing eyes peered at her from what should have been his armored mask. He wore the old robes of the Zaharaj—robes made long before the introduction of mithril weave. The being stood patiently awaiting the woman's questions.

"I am Chirras, formerly Lady Dreth," She pressed her hand to her chest while she introduced herself. "I want to know how I can become immortal."

The specter gave a hearty laugh. "There is only one way for a mortal to become immortal, and that is to be born into mortality, live a life of triumphs and struggles, and then die a good death. God then brings about the time of resurrection, and, eventually the final judgment. Then, and only then, can one become an immortal being. Thus it is! Thus has it always been!"

"That's not good enough! How is it that the Marcisians, Twillans, Zebrecians, and even Night Elves live so long, and we humans die so soon!" Chirras raged at the ghost. "Answer me! There must be a way to become immortal without having to suffer death!"

"You know nothing, child," the specter retorted. "The Elves, though they may seem immortal to us, can still succumb to disease and illness, and they can die if they receive a mortal wound. The Marcisians, Zebrecians, and Twillans live longer because they have trace amounts of demon genes, though the Zebrecians and Twillans have a much greater concentration. However, Marcisian scientists have found more ways of sustaining their own already lengthy lives and they've also learned how to keep their youthful appearance. They have even shared this knowledge with all of the human-inhabited planets that have joined their Empire."

"I already know all that. I just need to know about immortality!" Chirras furiously demanded.

The specter sighed. He was getting bored with the conversation. "Listen, child, only gods and greater demons are born into immortality, and even most of the gods had to suffer through mortality to get to where they are now. The demon race is the only race that is granted immortality at birth." The specter then bowed to Chirras. "With this I must leave you."

"No, wait! Are you saying that my answer lies with the demons then?" Chirras held out her hand, trying to prevent the image of Lord Dermos from disappearing.

Lord Dermos replied in a raspy voice, "I don't know," before his image faded back into the small black pyramid from whence it came.

Once the image was gone, the holo-journal stopped glowing and fell to the floor. It bounced a few times before coming to rest on one of its three sides. Chirras stomped over and scooped it up. "That was a complete waste of time!" she screeched before she threw the holo-journal onto her cluttered desk and plopped herself down into her chair.

"Ha ha." A swirling mass of black, red, and green energy taunted Chirras from inside its containment unit, which was located in the far corner of the room. "I told you we can help you if you become our goddess," the mass of energy teased.

"Not on your life! Oh, wait! That's right, you don't have one!" Chirras sneered.

"Oh, I'm so hurt," the energy mass shot back before resuming its laughter. "Why don't you just give up and take our deal?"

"No! The price of your 'deal' is too high!" She spat back at the captive mass. "I already have one mind and soul inside my body, so I have no room for either you or your friends." She spat again, totally disgusted by the thing's taunting comments. She then groaned, rubbed her temples with her index and middle fingers, and continued her rant. "And here I found an even more powerful replacement for Jetec, but I'd be long dead before I could even hope to see my plans come to fruition."

"Oh, I thought that Zor'ret was your replacement," the mass of energy cheekily replied.

"Frak no; that kid was a complete id'rth. He was so pathetic that he attacked Lord Baltrix without so much as a second thought," Chirras retorted.

"So who's this new replacement?" the energy being asked while stretching as far as it could within its containment field. Its new shape made it look like a glowing multicolored snake instead of a round, lumpy, ball-like mass.

"If you must know, he's a demon." Right after the words left Chirras's lips, the thing was again laughing, this time chaotically.

"A demon? Please! You're making me unstable!" the thing blurted out between laughs.

"You're already unstable," Chirras muttered under her breath.

After a moment's pause, the energy being asked, "So, who's the unlucky Meserino?"

"He's not a Meserino," Chirras informed the snake-like form.

"Veserino then," the thing snapped back.

"He's not a Veserino, either," Chirras quipped, grinning from ear to ear.

"Then what kind of demon is he!" her captive demanded.

"He's a Silvarian!" Chirras's face was aglow with a look of pure satisfaction. "There, take that you puny little ball of slime! Just what do you think about that!"

The thing started stretching and collapsing at such an incredible speed that Chirras thought it might break her containment unit. She was relieved when it stopped. "But they were all killed during the war!" the thing incredulously shouted.

"No, there's one left, and he's very young, which makes him very impressionable." She spoke with such a menacing tone that the snake-like blob thought she might attack it once again.

Then the blob started snickering. "If he truly is a Silvarian, then he has the answer to your immortality problem," it said, trying to goad her.

Chirras, of course, swallowed the thing's bait. "What do you mean by that?" She narrowed her eyes and glared intently at the intruder.

"I will tell you if you take our deal," the thing asked once more.

"No. If you don't tell me, I'll just kill you!" Chirras countered as she arose from her chair. She reached out with her right hand, and her blood sorjin flew from the desk right into her open palm. She gripped the hilt and pressed the button, turning on the inky-black blade with a snap hiss.

The thing laughed again. "I wonder what would happen to you if one of your fellow Zaharaj saw the color of your blade," the thing countered, egging her on. "And, by the way, this will be your four hundred and ninety eighth time that you have tried to kill me."

"Yes, but I've been holding back all those other times. Now tell me, what do you mean by 'the Silvarian has the answer to' my 'immortality problem?'" she demanded.

"I won't tell you until you accept our offer—"

Chirras cut the thing off and yelled, "Not on your life!" With that, she took her black blade and plunged it into the field, through the energy ball, and out the back of the containment field.

The thing screamed at first, but quickly erupted in laughter. "I'm made of the energy of the universe itself. Nothing you can do could hurt me!"

"Fraking unborn betrak!" Chirras cried in frustration after she withdrew her blood sorjin and shut it off. With a jerking motion, she threw the weapon back onto her desk, knocking over a pile of books when she did so.

"If you won't tell me, then I'll just have to find out on my own. After all, this place contains the largest library in the galaxy!" The thing found her pronouncement amusing.

"I'm patient, Chirras; I can wait. After all, I've already been waiting for nearly an eternity. I can wait a little longer." The thing muttered so softly that Chirras could not hear it. Luckily, it didn't have a face, so she couldn't see its wide invisible grin.

26

Back into the Void

Visage found himself amidst the cosmos once again. *Oh great, what now?*

"What the...Where am I? Visage, is that you?" Vok'et had been totally lost and was ecstatic when he saw Visage. "Where in the universe are we!" the Zebrecian exclaimed while he continued to gaze about in both awe and fear.

"Don't worry, I've been here before." Right after Visage finished speaking, the familiar red road appeared, and, without hesitation, he started walking. However, he had to stop when he noticed that Vok'et was very hesitant to follow. "I promise it's safe," Visage informed his nervous friend while he beckoned Vok'et to follow him. Though still hesitant, Vok'et complied.

***

"Well now, if it isn't the little Silvarian come to visit me once again. And look, he's brought a friend." Visage and Vok'et stood at the bottom of the platform on top of which the Dark God Chaos was bound.

"Visage, who in Eendril's name is that?" Vok'et leaned over and whispered as he looked up into the one visible eye of the Dark God.

"I'm the Dark God Chaos, Vok'et. Haven't you learned anything from your time in the Zaharaj?" he chided.

Vok'et got to his knees and started to weep. Raising his head in order to look Chaos in the eye, he quietly—almost reverently— offered, "So the time of prophecy is at hand." He then glanced over at Visage and back at Chaos. "Is Visage the chosen one who will free you?" he questioned, after a long pause.

"I believe that is an accurate assumption, my little Zebrecian friend."

Visage shrugged and closed his eyes. *Hurray for me,* he thought, completely unenthusiastic about the whole situation.

Vok'et was taken aback by Visage's attitude. "Are you serious? Do you know how long we've been waiting for the time of healing to begin?"

"Not a clue," Visage responded, honestly not caring; he simply folded his arms and glanced up at Chaos.

"But this is huge! How could you possibly not care!" Vok'et raised his arms and thought of smacking Visage, just on principle.

"Calm down, Vok'et; the Silvarian is correct—you're making this out to be bigger than it is," Chaos telepathically told the irate Zebrecian.

Vok'et calmed down and lowered his arms to his sides. "I would think, of all beings, you'd be the most happy, Lord Chaos. You're the one who's going to be set free! And how do you even know me, anyway!"

The comment amused Chaos. Vok'et went to his knees again after the Dark God's power overwhelmed him. He was surprised that Visage could even stand. *Oh yeah. Of course. He's a demon!*

"So what do you want with me this time, Chaos—and why did you drag Vok'et along with me?" Visage asked the chained-up God.

"I don't want anything. *You're the one who* came *here*; I had nothing to do with it."

"I'm the one who caused this?" Visage had to shake his head in order to refocus. "Well I'm here now, so..." He stared into the Dark God's one revealed eye... "could you answer something for me?"

Chaos thought for a moment. "Only if it's within my power to do so."

"Fair enough. I want to know why Chirras has such an interest in me. And are there any more Skath worshippers in the Zaharaj?"

Vok'et got back to his feet and looked from Visage to Chaos. He had several questions for Chaos but held them back. Chaos's eye narrowed. "I would be wary of that woman if I were you, Orran."

Vok'et was a bit shocked. *Is that Visage's real name? I wish I could ask him, but I'd probably get in trouble with both of them if I interrupted right now.*

"Why's that?" Visage asked in response to Chaos's disconcerting statement.

"Chirras has an insatiable thirst for power—"

"Yeah, I know that already!" Visage folded his arms and snorted in disgust.

"Yes, but you don't know that she's looking for a way to cheat death," Chaos rather smugly stated.

Vok'et spoke before Visage could. "That's blasphemy! Nobeing can cheat death but demons and, in some cases, gods, but every mortal will die eventually." He hung his head when thoughts of Jetec flooded his mind. His heart felt raw, consumed again by the pain from the loss of his ber'nan.

"I'm sorry for your loss, Vok'et. I watched your ber'nan suffer at the hands of Skath's followers," Chaos told him. His initial empathy, however, quickly turned to anger.

"Wait! You saw Jetec's death? So they didn't turn him into a Fallen?" Vok'et asked, full of renewed hope.

"No, but they made sure his death wasn't a clean one!" Now it was Chaos who was racked with pain; his one visible eye actually teared up.

Vok'et shook his head. "It doesn't matter, Chaos. At least now I can tell my family that Jetec is with our ancestors in heaven!" His own tears of joy now fell freely. Visage was elated for the Zebrecian. Chaos had now erased one of his biggest fears.

"You still haven't told me about Chirras, Chaos," Visage prodded before he started ascending the stairs.

"I'm sorry, Visage, but I can't tell you any more than I already have."

"But what does immortality have to do with me!" Visage demanded.

"And why does Chirras want it so badly?" Visage had reached the top tier of the platform and squatted down to look Chaos in His eye.

"I can't tell you that, Orran; you'll have to figure that out for yourself."

"Fine," Visage cried while throwing his hands in the air. "I give up." He lowered his hands and tensed up, he managed to ask one last question. He spoke slowly and quietly. "So, Chaos, how do I get these chains off from you?"

Chaos's voice lowered, and he seemed to struggle a bit before answering. "I'm sorry, Orran, but I can't tell you that either."

Visage was at a loss. "But there is a way to get rid of them, right?"

Chaos smiled a rare smile, though no being was able to see it. "Of course there is."

"So if you know there's a way to do it, why can't you tell me what it is?" Chaos blinked once in response.

"So, is it that you know how I can get these chains off, but you won't say because of some sort of restriction that Skath or some other god placed on you?" Visage asked. Chaos again blinked once.

Visage was discouraged. He sat down and laid his hands onto the cool white stone. "This is going to be a real pain in the crath, isn't it?"

"I'm sorry kid, but there are rules that even Dark Gods can't break."

"It's alright," Visage slumped and sighed. "I'll figure it out eventually...I hope." He glumly muttered to himself.

"Um, Lord Chaos, have you ever lost somebeing you ilonied?" Vok'et asked from the steps below.

Visage glanced at Vok'et, and then turned and looked painfully back at Chaos. Unfortunately, he already knew the answer. *Vok'et, you shouldn't have asked him that,* Visage thought, since he could clearly see the pain in the Dark God's one revealed eye.

"Yes, Vok'et. Before my dar'nra started that war with his ber'nans and sri'nas, he first turned on us—his own children. He got rid of any god or goddess whom he saw as a threat. I not only lost a countless number of my ber'nans and sri'nas but all but one of my wives as well!" Chaos was crying while he spoke. His tears were bright red, as though they were great drops of blood, and created ripples of red energy every time they hit the platform.

So, even gods can cry, Visage mused while he and Vok'et helplessly looked on. Suddenly, Visage remembered something Chaos had said—that one of his wives was still alive! He jumped up, stared the Dark God in the eye, and impatiently demanded to know about his wife. "Where is she, Chaos! Where's your wife!"

Visage's question rudely ripped Chaos from his deep and painful thoughts. "Where's who!"

Visage persisted. "That wife of yours! Where is she!" Visage shouted, causing the Dark God to wince a bit at his bubbly excitement.

"I don't know," Chaos confessed. "I haven't seen her in such a long time. All I can tell you is that she's Riza's cousin."

Both Vok'et and Visage were dumbfounded at this turn of events. "She's Riza's cousin?" Vok'et responded, further adding to Visage's excitement and disbelief.

"Riza's my fiancée!" Visage cried in wonder. "So I can ask her if she knows where your wife is!" Visage was now determined to reunite Chaos with his missing wife. Standing to his full height, he clenched his fist and steeled his resolve. Without a moment's hesitation, the young demon ran down the stairs and grabbed onto the sleeve of Vok'et's cloak. "Come on, Vok'et, we have an important mission, so let's go back!" Visage was trying to drag the larger boy behind him.

"But how do we get back? I don't even know how we got here!" Vok'et yelled before he ripped the sleeve of his cloak free from Visage's grasp.

Chaos started laughing at the absurdity. Both beings turned to look up at him, he said, "All you have to do is wake up!"

"Wait! You mean we're asleep?" Vok'et asked.

"Yes, and seeing that I'm still tied up, you'll need to see yourselves off, now!" In the blink of an eye, the two visitors vanished, and Chaos grinned. "It seems you really do iloni your ironies, Eendril. You choose a Silvarian to fulfill the ancient prophecy, and, to top it off, he's the fiancé of my wife's own cousin!" Chaos laughed long and loudly at the thought.

Halifel wasted no time in opening a portal so he could get back home and tell the others the wonderful news. *It seems that our little Silvarian friend is now on the path.*

***

Vok'et's eyes snapped open, his head shot up from his makeshift arm pillow, and he surveyed the amphitheater. His brief bout of confusion dissipated the minute he saw Visage. "Hurray! We're home!"

Visage pushed his chair out so hard that the back slammed into the desk behind him. After bolting out of the chair, he ran down the steps and stood in front of the bemused Lord. "Lord Baltrix! I need to see Riza!" he demanded.

"And why do you need to see her? What's with the urgency?"

"I can't explain! I just need to see her—now!"

Baltrix saw that he probably would not be able to stop the boy, even if he wanted to. After sighing and rubbing the bridge of his nose, he responded. "Very well." He glanced up at Azala, who had already gone back to reading her book.

"Azala," Baltrix muttered, startling the Twillan.

"Yes, Lord Baltrix? She closed her book and rose to her feet.

"Visage appears to have an urgent need to see Riza, and I would like you to escort him." Azala rolled her eyes, not too keen on the idea, but relented and walked down the steps to join Baltrix and Visage.

"Come on then, Visage; let's go so we can get back before class starts." Azala lost no time; she grabbed her roommate's hand and headed for the double doors.

The duo were about to exit the amphitheater when Vok'et ran down to join them. He turned to Baltrix. "I have to go too! I have to tell my family something really important!"

Though Baltrix was disappointed that he was losing all of his early-rising ar'teths, he didn't have the heart to deny Vok'et's request. *They'd better hurry. I hope they can get back fast, or the class will be so sparse that I may as well cancel for the deronn.* After checking his U-gem, he thought, *That's good. It looks like there's still plenty of time before class starts. Maybe I'll get to teach after all.* "Hold on, Vok'et, I'm going to tag along!" Baltrix's pronouncement made the Zebrecian's eyes go wide for a moment, but he reluctantly nodded his approval. The pair rushed out of the classroom, hoping to catch up to the other ar'teths. Visage and Vok'et's missions had begun.

***

Vok'et was much more chipper than he had been before seeing Chaos. Even his eyes shone brightly. Visage commented about his friend's improved state of mind and proceeded to initiate an exciting conversation about the meeting with the Dark God.

Baltrix was about to ask the duo why they were talking so eagerly about a long-dead God, but Azala beat him to the punch. "What's with all the talk about a dead God?" she asked. Her question had quite an edge to it, since she was still a bit perturbed about having to leave the classroom.

Visage and Vok'et were walking in front of Azala and Baltrix. They spun around and cried out in unison, "Chaos isn't dead, Azala!" Vok'et continued. "Yeah, he's only imprisoned, and Visage here is going to set him free!" Vok'et's pronouncement dripped with fervor while he grabbed Visage by his shoulders and rather vigorously shook him a few times.

Baltrix couldn't restrain himself from jumping into the conversation. "Let me get this straight. You're telling me that the Dark God Chaos isn't dead, as most everybeing believes, but merely imprisoned—and that Visage is going to free him!"

"Yep," Vok'et quipped without a care or even a hint of doubt. "That's exactly right. And Visage is going to see Riza because Chaos is married to her cousin!"

Azala was openly suspicious. "And just how could you possibly know that, Vok'et?"

"Because *he* told us!" Vok'et and Visage replied in unison. The two boys glanced at each other before breaking out into laughter.

Azala and Baltrix were completely baffled by the pair's revelations.

"You mean you met Chaos! Really!" Azala's eyes widened in wild excitement.

"Yeah, that's kind of my fault," Visage confessed. "I dragged Vok'et with me when I went to see Chaos, though I have no idea how I did it." He turned towards Vok'et and lowered his head. "Sorry about that, Vok'et."

Vok'et only laughed again. "Don't worry about it, Orran! It was a bit scary in the beginning, but I would iloni it if you would bring me with you again the next time you go." Visage was less than enthusiastic about Vok'et's request, since he was still rather upset with Vok'et when he used his real name. While Baltrix and Azala attempted to absorb what Visage and Vok'et had related, Visage took the opportunity to reprimand—as diplomatically as possible—his companion about using his new name rather than his original one.

What the frak just happened? Azala thought.

I have no clue, Baltrix answered, *but if it's true, that is incredible news!*

Once at the lifts, the two parties had to part ways. Azala and Visage got into the lift on the left and headed to the upper levels where Riza and several other council members had their apartments. Vok'et and Baltrix got into the lift on the right. Vok'et was eager to meet his family and give them the good news about Jetec. Azala and Baltrix had looked on with amusement when Vok'et and Visage gave each other a hug before getting into their respective lifts. "I'll see you in half a minronn, Visage," Vok'et had said. Visage had nodded in return before heading out with Azala. Azala's curiosity was peaked." She kept glancing over at the beaming Silvarian and eventually gave up. "Ugh... Would you please tell me what really happened!" she cried, with an obvious pout on her face, stared at the Silvarian.

Visage pondered for a moment. "Are you sure you really want to know?" He wasn't entirely convinced that she would even believe him.

"For the iloni of..." She trailed off before she grabbed his face and kissed him. Once they were in the void, she demanded that he should show her what had happened with him and Vok'et.

Visage was hesitant but finally conceded. "Fine," he cried in exasperation before he unfolded his most recent memory.

The doors of the lift opened right when Azala withdrew from Visage. She was essentially in shock. "That was... that was... I don't even have the words," she muttered.

"That's why I need to see Riza! I have to find Chaos's wife!"

Azala shook her head in agreement, causing her twills to sway back and forth in the process. "You're right. If the time of healing is truly upon us, then I want to help you in any way I can!" For the second time, she grabbed his hand and hauled him off the lifts. The duo made their way through the crowd of black-clad beings who were waiting at the doors. All eyes were upon them while they strode down the hallway to the right.

"What do you suppose that was all about?" one of the beings asked the others in the typically metallic-sounding voice. The voice appeared to belong to a female.

"Wasn't that Lord Nosfaren's apprentice?" another being asked.

"They were talking about the time of healing!" another masked male added.

"I think you must have misunderstood, iloni," the woman next to him offered.

"No, I don't think I did," the male responded.

The woman continued. "It's been onns since I've heard any being talk about the time of healing. Wasn't that kid the Silvarian whom Lord Nosfaren picked up from Earth?"

The last two beings finally made it through the lift doors, and the second male interjected, "I think so, though he looks a bit different than when I saw him the deronn he arrived."

"Wait! You didn't hear about his fight with Arisha in the pit!" The other three appeared to be in a relative state of shock. Then the doors closed.

Azala and Visage were a bit too far away to hear the beings' full conversation, but, from what Azala could hear, it made her smile despite herself. Visage, on the other hand, had no response, since he was too preoccupied with his own thoughts.

It wasn't long before Azala stopped in front of one of the doors in the hallway. Visage was so excited that he headed straight for it, pushing it open and walking right in. Azala did her best to stop him but to no avail.

＊＊＊

Riza, who was lying on her bed reading a book, looked up with a bewildered smirk on her face. Azala slapped her face with her open hand at Visage's blatant disregard for privacy. "Well, Azala, are you just going to stand in my doorway, or are you actually going to come in?" Riza asked. Though she was a bit embarrassed, Azala came in and the door automatically slid closed behind her.

"So what brings you to my room, Visage? Not that I'm complaining, but I wish you had come alone," she rather bluntly offered when she glanced at Azala. Azala had already felt uncomfortable, but now she felt even worse.

Visage looked around the room, and, though it resembled the one he and Azala shared, it was a dump. There were discarded garments lying about everywhere, and many half-read books lay face down, the pages well marked where Riza had apparently stopped reading before scattering them all over the unoccupied bed next to her own. Visage shook his head at the mess but tried to ignore it, for he was on a mission. "Riza, do you know where your cousin is?" he blurted. Though Riza was obviously taken aback by Visage's out-of-the-blue question, she quickly recovered and smiled.

"I'm sorry, Visage, but I have several cousins. To whom are you referring?" she asked.

"I need to find Chaos's wife!" He was so excited that he didn't notice Riza's expression going from her usual warm smile to a cold stare.

"Who told you about her!" Riza's voice now sounded colder than ice, causing Visage's over-the-top enthusiasm to vanish.

"He did." Visage felt as though he was confessing for having committed some unknown sin.

Riza's eyes went wide. "Did you see him again?" she asked. Her attitude had done another one eighty. Now even she seemed excited.

Visage cautiously nodded, indicating that he had.

"Not once, but now a second time? There are no such things as coincidences!" Riza then closed her book and got off her bed. "Visage, I need to know what you saw," she said while she walked over to him, got down on one knee, and peered into his eyes.

This time it was Visage who initiated the kiss, shocking both Azala and, even more so, Riza! Riza's eyes popped open as far as they could go, while at the same time she was being pulled into the void where Visage could privately share his memories. With her jaw agape, the demoness stood silently while Visage replayed the memory of his new encounter with Chaos. When the vision closed, she withdrew from him, stood up, and started to pace.

"Of course Eendril would make Visage the one who breaks that guy's chains." Riza shook her head at the irony. "I don't know if he really ilonis ironies or if He's getting me back for something," she muttered. "Ugh! And, of course, Vira and Nos need to know about this new development—right away!" She immediately turned to Azala, who jumped right when Riza's eyes fell upon her. "Azala, tell your master that he has to assemble the Council for an emergency meeting!" the demoness sternly demanded.

"Yes, Lady Riza, of course," Azala stammered. She immediately started fumbling with her U-gem in an attempt to get a hold of her master. Riza herself started racing about her room, getting ready to head to the Council Room. Visage had to move over by Azala in order to get out of her way.

Riza ripped off her trellgown. Visage couldn't help but notice that it looked very similar to the one Chirras had been wearing when he had run into her the other trell. The only real difference was that Riza's was cut low in the back in order to accommodate her wings. Visage closed his eyes and allowed Riza some privacy while she dressed. First, the demoness donned a pair of the same form-fitting pants that Ali'stia and Azala liked to wear. After that, she picked up a top. It covered only her chest, since her wings were in the way of her wearing much on her back. She fastened the clasps above and below her wings, picked up the belt she had slung over her chair, and quickly threaded it through the belt loops. Visage, who had slightly popped open an eye to check on Riza's progress, looked on with amazement as her blood sorjin flew off the shelf and into her open hand.

Azala had no sooner pressed her gem than it started to glow green. "Master, are you there?" she asked. There was a slight pause before she heard Nos's reply. "I'm here, my apprentice. Why are you calling me so early?" He tried not to sound groggy, but his attempt was unsuccessful.

"I'm sorry about the time, Master, but I'm contacting you on behalf of Lady Riza. She needs you to assemble the Council for an emergency meeting," Azala calmly explained.

"Riza? Why does she want an emergency meeting? What's going on?" Though he was still a bit groggy, he was awake enough to know that something was up—and the something wasn't good.

Azala paused a moment before asking, "Do you know anything about Chaos?" she asked.

Nos fell silent before sternly asking, "Azala, where did you hear that name!"

Riza rushed over and grabbed Azala's wrist, bringing the Twillan's gem to her face. "I'll explain everything when you summon the Council, Nos! Now get your crath in gear before I have Ali'stia stuff a blortworm up it!" she yelled into the gem.

Azala snickered. "I'd iloni to see that, Lady Riza."

Riza gave Azala a wink before ushering the two smaller beings toward the door. Once in the hallway, she gave a directive: "Visage, we are heading to the Council Room, and Azala, you should head back to class."

"Oh, do I have to? This sounds really fun!" Azala complained to the demoness.

Riza, whose face was strained from worry, stopped and peered at the Twillan. "Azala, the less you know about this the better. Trust me on this... You don't want to know too much."

Azala thought about Riza's words before lamenting, "I suppose you're right, though the whole thing sounds very intriguing."

Riza smiled at Azala before bending down and whispering, "Perhaps Visage..." Riza's eyes shifted to the young demon... "can fill you in later if you're really curious; just don't say I didn't warn you." At that, she left.

"Did she just give me permission to look inside your head, Visage?" Azala asked.

Visage shrugged. "That's what it sounded like to me."

Azala smiled mischievously, and her eyes narrowed. She then flicked Visage's forehead with her finger. "Come on, Visage, we don't want to keep your fiancée waiting." She then took off for the lift. Her two twills bounced playfully as she hurried on. Visage rolled his eyes and sighed. *I will never understand her.* He then took off after his fiancée and friend.

Once in the lift, Visage stood next to Riza. Though he sensed that she was distraught, he was hesitant to ask her what was wrong, so he stood in silence. Finally, Riza addressed him. "Visage, why did you close your eyes?" she asked, sounding rather demure.

Visage blinked, caught off guard at the question. "I don't understand," he asked, his expression indicating that her question had definitely flown over his head.

Riza bit her lower lip and clutched her left arm with her right hand. "When we were in my room and I started changing, you closed your eyes... Am I really that... unattractive?" She hung her head, causing both of her rather lengthy ears to droop.

Visage's eyes went wide. *Is that what she thinks?* Once he fully realized what Riza was implying, he emphatically waved his hands. "Oh no, Riza, that's not it at all!" he cried; *How can I ever explain this?*

Riza's ears popped back up, and she turned to face Visage, though now she was looking more puzzled than hurt. "I don't understand."

Visage rubbed the back of his head. *It's not that you're ugly or unattractive, Riza. It's just that back home, well, women don't like it when a guy stares at them when they're changing.* He hoped his thoughts would make their way to Riza.

Riza was taken aback. "Why is that? Didn't you say you ran around naked most of the time and even burned up your clothes because you didn't know how to control your indren'freth? And haven't you seen Azala naked before?"

Visage knew she had him there. "But Azala caught me off guard, and I was distracted by the bruises that Lord Nos had given her." Visage was embarrassed but continued. "I got really angry when I saw what he did to her." He lowered his head so Riza couldn't see his flushed face.

Riza started chuckling. "Still, it kind of hurt when you closed your eyes. I thought you didn't like the way I looked," she openly confessed. At this point, they were looking into each other's eyes. Riza had gotten down onto one knee, put her hand on his shoulder, and tilted his chin up. He knew that he was at fault for this misunderstanding. Then he had an idea. With her being so close, he easily kissed her.

Riza blinked and immediately appeared inside the void. She was touched when Visage let her sift through all of the memories from his time on Earth, starting from when he was very young. After he had shown her everything, they withdrew.

Riza was stunned. "Is that how the Earthlings are! I mean, from what you just showed me, it seems that a lot of the males act like Zor'ret!" she cried in disbelief.

"That's why nudity is frowned upon on Earth," Visage explained.

"But why would nudity suddenly become obscene when Earthlings reach adolescence?" She was struggling to figure out this enigma.

Visage shrugged. "I have no idea, Riza."

"That's the complete opposite of how the Marcisians are."

"Really? Then again, I've never met a Marcisian before."

"Yes you have!" Riza shouted so loudly that Visage winced. "Sorry about that, Visage. But practically every being in the Zaharaj is part of the Marcisian Empire!"

"And how are they opposite from Earthlings?" *Or do I even want to know.*

"All I can say is that Marcisian males are extremely dense."

Dense? Visage thought. *What does she mean by dense?*

"It means that Marcisian women, in order to even get noticed, have to practically throw themselves at the males. And, well, that kind of behavior has spread across the entire empire!"

Visage disappointedly commented. "It sounds like you don't really mind guys like Zor'ret then."

"No. I just wish that males would at give us *some* sign that they are interested," she started giving him a menacing glare.

"It's not that I don't like you, Riza. It's just that I'm more accustomed to the way things are done on Earth. Everything here is new to me you know!" The boy flashed a half-hearted smile.

"Earthlings are really strange." Riza removed her hand from Visage's shoulder and touched his nose with her finger. "Most Marcisian males are so preoccupied with work and seeking knowledge that they can't see past the noses on their faces." She smirked. "Not that Marcisians have much of a nose, anyway. Even the Twillan males have become apathetic when it comes to the fairer sex. However, their behavior has also made males like Zor'ret really stick out. I guess you could say the term 'pervert' has pretty much been erased from Marcisian society. I know it's different where you're from, Visage, but it hurt when you shut your eyes on me. Though I guess it's better than being ignored completely," she lamented.

Visage was still pondering Riza's comments when the doors opened; he responded while the pair walked towards the Council Room. "I can't argue with you on that one. I mean the part where you said, 'it's different where you're from'. My mi'thia always scolded me when I left the house without wearing anything. But my two older sisters, or sri'nas, didn't care at all—they dragged me off to the bathroom whenever they needed to take a bath. Even as young as I was, I didn't really like that." He shuddered at the memories.

Riza chuckled. "At least your family didn't seem to mind your nakedness—at least not when you were in your own home," Riza offered while she opened the doors to the Council Room and let Visage through first.

"I don't think they had much choice in the matter."

"It must have been tough trying to raise a demon on a planet full of humans."

Visage only nodded in agreement.

Now that the pair was finally in the Council Room, they took the time to enjoy the amazing view. Riza gazed upon it from the vantage point of her chair, but Visage was so mesmerized that he walked to the back of the room and stood near the middle of the three massive windows. As usual, asteroids were hanging about just outside Zharaj's atmosphere. Several of the giant rocks were glowing around their fringes, since the sun was just starting to rise in the west. *That's so strange. I wonder why Earth's sun rises in the East and Zharaj's rises in the west. And just look at those mountains.* The mountains in the distance were now lighting up with streaks of bright yellow color wherever the sunlight managed to filter through the cracks in the blanket of asteroids above. Though Visage couldn't yet see the sun, he closed his eyes, imagined its warmth, and reflected on the times he had stood with his father on the deck of his destroyer. Watching the sunrise over the ocean with his father and the other Navy guys was one of his fondest memories. He smiled as he remembered the first time he had flown—he was just over four years old. The carrier crew always welcomed him. The fighter pilots even tried to out-maneuver him while escorting him to the ship to meet the admiral. The 'Blue Bomber' was his call sign, since he looked like a small blue-and-white fireball streaking through the sky.

The Navy personnel were the only ones who didn't seem to mind that Tim's son was so different. And out of respect for his father and the Admiral, he was treated like one of the crew. The men even set a bunk up for whenever he dropped in for a visit. "Look out"—they would say —"we're about to receive a visit from Tim's little Blue Bomber!" Visage clutched his stomach and started laughing when he recalled how he had gotten his nickname from Iced Tea and Scorpion.

Riza adjusted in her chair. *I wonder what's so funny.* Feeling her curiosity, Visage let down his barrier and let her in. "Really?" "*The Blue Bomber?*" she questioned through her own laughter. "Why not *The Sapphire Streak?*"

"I guess your call sign would be *Over the Top*," he shot back.

Riza had an obvious aversion to the name. "Hmm, I'd prefer *The Crimson Comet.*" She put her finger to her chin and tilted her head back while thinking about other possible call signs. She was busy enjoying the exercise when the door suddenly opened. Visage and she were both startled but settled down quickly when they saw the culprits: Lord Nosfaren, Lady Ali'stia, Lord Baltrix, and Lord Forscythe. Lord Nos appeared groggy but managed to lumber over to his chair. "It's way too early for meetings," he grumbled.

"I second that," Forscythe added. "I was up most of the trell arguing with my apprentice about Chirras," he complained.

"Don't blame me." Nos pointed an accusing finger at Riza. "You have Riza to thank for this!"

"I guess even some demons aren't menronn beings," Visage muttered, causing Ali'stia, Riza, and Baltrix to chuckle a bit.

Nos countered, "It's not that we're not menronn beings, Visage. It's just that I haven't been able to sleep for several deronns, and even demons get tired."

"Don't mind me, Lord Nos. I'm with you on the early menronn stuff."

Visage peered down at his bare feet and wiggled his toes before making his way over to Riza's seat. After putting his hands onto the armrest of her chair, he leaned in and glared at his fiancée. "You know, Riza, you never returned my boots after my match with Arisha."

Riza looked shocked. "I didn't! Are you sure?" she asked, trying to sound innocent.

"Yes, I'm sure. You didn't," Visage pressed.

Wow, I don't know why he's so riled up over a pair of boots. "Fine. I'll give them back after the meeting... Happy?" Riza snapped back.

Visage gave Riza a hearty nod before shocking all of the meeting attendees: He plopped himself down into her lap! The being who was taken aback the most by his unexpected move was Riza herself. Once her heart returned to its normal rhythm, she spoke in a whisper. "Um, Visage, why did you do that?"

Visage tilted his head back so he could look into his fiancée's eyes. "Why? Do you want me to move?" Riza immediately responded with an emphatic shake of her head.

Lord Nos and Ali'stia were amused by the unfolding scene. Baltrix huffed and crossed his arms. "Demons," he muttered under his breath. Forscythe was so busy sleeping that he was oblivious to anything that had transpired.

"Visage, why did you decide to sit on my lap?" Riza was dying to know, since V had never acted like this before.

Visage fidgeted a bit before sharing his reasoning. "Well, you are my fiancée, Riza, and I love you. You're a really cool demoness, and you taught me how to control my power. Even though that seal Vira and you put on my back really hurt, it has also helped a lot," he said in a matter-of-fact tone.

Everybeing—and one in particular—was in a state of shock over Visage's comments. Ali'stia leaned over and whispered to her husband, "Did he just use the 'l' word, iloni?" Nos shot up from his reclining position in his chair. "I think he did!" Ali'stia was not expecting such a passion-filled outburst; she marveled at her husband's response,

"Visage, you mean you iloni me?" Riza asked, more hopeful than skeptical.

Visage, who looked totally innocent, tilted his head back and responded, "Does that mean love in the Marcisian language?" he asked.

Nos spoke before Riza could answer. "And in the demon tongue as well, Visage," he enthusiastically added; a wide smile adorned his face. *Nothing like waking up to a demon confessing iloni to his betrothed.* His thoughts were blocked from everybeing but his wife; she stifled a giggle before agreeing with Nos's telepathic communication. "Thanks, Visage. I'm wide awake now!" Nos smirked and winked before giving the demon child a thumbs up.

Visage shrugged. "I don't know what the big deal is. I only meant that Riza has a really pretty heart."

Riza and the others were puzzled. This time Ali'stia was the one who beat them to the punch. "What do you mean by that, Visage?"

"Wait! I thought all demons could see the same way I do," Visage shared. The three demons traded confused glances.

"I'm sorry, Visage, but apparently we don't," Nos replied.

"Oh. Well I guess that's alright." Visage slumped and frowned a bit. "It's kinda sad though, because most of the beings I've seen have really pretty hearts, too!" He glanced around the room at to peek at all of the beautiful beating hearts.

Baltrix's curiosity now kicked in. "Visage, could you explain that so we can understand what you're talking about. Apparently, you can see things that we can't?" He folded his arms and raised a quizzical eyebrow at the boy.

"Sure!" Visage was elated by Baltrix's extended invitation and proceeded to hop down from Riza's lap, much to her disappointment. Even *she* was curious about this newly revealed power.

Visage strutted to the middle of the room. Right when he was about to start, the Council Room doors flung open and in walked Michael, Zoric, Fenrir, Serishin, and Sharas. The Council members who were already seated glared at the newcomers as though they had just shattered a cherished piece of china. In response, the latecomers quietly hurried to their respective seats. However, though the council beings' looks had been imposing, they didn't deter the newcomers from wondering what on Zharaj was going on and why the Silvarian was standing in the center of the room. Lord Nosfaren sensed their angst and sent out a telepathic message in order to catch them up on what had just transpired.

"So his eyes are different from those of a Meserino?" Fenrirwondered aloud, making sure everybeing could hear him.

"Yes, he was about to tell us how his eyes work before all of you barged in and interrupted," Ali'stia harshly retorted. Lord Nos took over from there and ordered everybeing to remain silent. He then gestured for Visage to continue his explanation.

"Well," he began, "I focus on a beings' insides more so than their outsides."

"What does that mean?" Michael asked.

"I think he means he can see through a being—kind of like having constant infra-red or even xera-ray vision," Ali'stia guessed.

"Yes, kind of, but I can't see all the way through a being; I can only make out certain things, like muscle and tissue. However, the things I can see most clearly are a being's blood vessels and what his or her heart is like," Visage explained. He turned to Riza. "That's how I know that Riza is a good woman... err... demon. Her heart is really bright, and the way it beats is totally awesome!" Visage grinned from ear to ear. The parts on Riza's cheeks that weren't covered by her black biree patterns was turning bright red, she flushed in embarrassment.

The other council members were awe-struck. "Visage, can you tell me what you see when you look at *my* heart?" Zoric asked. Visage nodded and immediately walked over and stood in front of Zoric's seat. He stared at the Twillan and watched his blood vessels rush the liquid of life throughout his body. Though the red liquid seemed to be flowing very chaotically, it was actually completely organized. The inner workings of the body seemed, to Visage, to be an artistic masterpiece. *It would be amazing if everybeing could see the body the way I do.* His eyes were wide with wonder while he watched Zoric's beating heart. That bright muscle, which kept his life force from fading, seemed to Visage to be a magical instrument—one that God Himself had placed inside each of His creations. Watching Zoric's heart beating along with such a happy rhythm was giving Visage great joy.

The room fell silent; everybeing was fully focused on Visage. While the Silvarian continued to stare at the Twillan, his eyes filled with hope and wonder. Finally, the spell was broken, and he stared up into Zoric's eyes and pronounced, "It's really pretty... though it looks like it has been broken." Zoric's eyes widened at Visage's findings. "But it also looks as though it's healing," Visage quickly added, while emphatically waving his hands.

Zoric sat totally still. He was speechless. *How can he know that? I haven't told anybeing about that incident. But Visage can see it?* The Twillan's eyes started to become heavy, and tears rolled down his cheeks. Nosfaren, who had been intently watching the entire scene, understood full well what had just transpired. He was about to ask Visage about it, but the ever-observant Baltrix beat him to it.

"Visage, can you really see the state of a being's heart?"

Visage walked back into the center of the room and turned on his heels in order to face the Lord who had asked the question. "Yes, Vlad, I can," he pronounced with a bit of cheerful pride in his voice. "And I can clearly see how bright your heart is; it looks as though almost *all* of your scars have healed," he chimed with a bit of a laugh at the stunned look on Baltrix's face.

Many council members were now whispering to their neighbors. Fenrir was thoroughly confused. "His real name is Vlad?" I thought his name was Baltrix." His unbridled comment brought forth several nods, though Nosfaren, Riza, and Ali'stia seemed unfazed.

Nosfaren was about to approach Visage regarding a totally unrelated matter when the doors opened widely and the rest of the council members entered. Vira winked at Visage before strolling past and taking her seat. Barren was barely halfway seated before he burst out with his question: "so, what did I miss?"

Lord Nosfaren claimed the right of response. "The short version is that our Silvarian friend can see into a being's heart. He can tell if a being is good or bad as well as whether or not he or she is nursing old wounds."

Barren's interest was now piqued. "You're kidding me, right? I thought only gods could do that!"

Nosfaren shook his head and shrugged. "I thought so, too. Then again, since Visage is the first Silvarian I've met, I'm sure there will be many more revelations to come."

"Visage,"— Vira excitedly asked.—"can you really see into a being's heart! Can you tell me what mine looks like!"

Visage was happy to comply and immediately started the assessment. Everybeing waited with anticipation while he intently studied the Veserino demoness. "Your heart is just like Riza's, except it's a different color." He glanced at Riza. "But she's still a whole lot messier than you are..." he muttered under his breath. Vira smiled and snickered while Riza gasped and gaped before blushing in embarrassment.

I am not that messy, Riza silently cried behind a strong mental barrier.

Since Vira was a latecomer, she had missed the outcome of her friend's heart evaluation. Appearing a bit befuddled, she glanced at Riza in hopes of getting her input. Riza shook her head before blinking several times and then quietly responding. "He said that my heart is really pretty."

Vira was quiet for a moment before becoming flushed. Startling everybeing, she jumped up from her seat, scooped up the Silvarian, and spun around the room. "Really! You think my heart is pretty!" She was so excited that she nearly forgot where she was. Slowly, she lowered the confused-looking child back down to the floor and strode over to her seat. She used her wings to shield herself from the amused gazes of the other council members.

Everybeing's attention now turned to Lord Nosfaren. Nobeing had ever heard him speak with such soberness. "Visage, can you tell me what my heart looks like?" His eyes glowed with anticipation, though he was both fearful and hesitant. His fellow beings were shocked; he was literally shaking out of fear and anticipation.

Visage rubbed the back of his head before he faced the Dark Lord. "I'm sorry, Lord Nosfaren, but I can't."

Nosfaren's eyes immediately clouded over, and his countenance mimicked that of a being who was in great despair. Everybeing was on edge. Fortunately, the lord quickly cooled down and calmly asked the boy, "Why can't you tell me, Visage?"

Visage answered without missing a beat. "Because your heart is so bright, I can't focus on it for very long."

Nosfaren's eyes opened as widely as they could go. He shook his head, trying to clear his disbelief. He then spoke again. "Are you sure, Visage?"

Visage took several quick glances up at Nosfaren before starting to shuffle his feet and nod his head. "Uh, huh," he squeaked while all eyes turned to Nos and then back to the young demon.

Ali'stia finally couldn't take it anymore. "Visage!" she said a bit harshly, causing the child to snap to attention. "What do you mean by, Nos's 'heart is so bright' that you 'can't focus on it for very long?' "

Visage struggled to find the right words to clarify what he had conveyed, or at least tried to convey to them. "You see, everybeing's heart is different, and I can see when a heart has been wounded. It has a dark blotch—like what Zoric's has," he explained before he gestured towards Zoric. "But when the wound heals, that dark spot becomes really bright and shiny. That's why Lord Nos's heart is so bright. He was repeatedly and severely hurt in the past, but now all of his scars have healed." Visage glanced at Nosfaren again but had to look away almost immediately. "I'm sorry, Lord Nos, but I can't look at you for long; without my eyes starting to hurt."

Ali'stia peered on with amazement. She watched her husband's countenance transform before her eyes. His typically stern features softened, and tears welled up in his eyes as he gazed upon the child with awe. The awe, however, quickly turned to worry. Ali'stia was a bit saddened, but also relieved, when her husband's appearance returned to that of the demon she ilonied. "Visage, have you told anybeing about this ability of yours?" Nos's voice betrayed his grave concern.

"No. I mean, even if I had told the people back home, they wouldn't have believed me." He slumped a bit but quickly reverted to his more chipper self. "But you believe me, don't you, Lord Nos?"

Nosfaren nodded. Nevertheless, his voice took on a stern tone, one that he only used when he wanted to make sure that his message had been heard. "Visage, you can't tell anybeing outside this room about this ability of yours. Do you understand?" Nos glared at the shrinking Silvarian in an attempt to discern whether he understood or not.

Visage peered at other beings in the room before giving his firm answer: "Yes, Lord Nos, I understand." Convinced by Visage's reply, Nosfaren relaxed and slumped back into his chair.

"That's good, Visage. So, now that that matter is settled, just what is it, Lady Riza, that's so important that you needed us to assemble without the customary notice?"

Riza had been so caught up by the goings on that, for a moment, she forgot why she had called the assembly together. "Oh, yeah. How could I forget? She stood up from her chair, walked over to Visage, and knelt down to look him in the eyes. "Visage, can you show the rest of the councilors what you showed Azala and me?"

"Of course, Riza!" With that, the boy closed his eyes and opened his mind, pulling everybeing into the middle of some unknown universe. And there they all stood.

"What's going on?" Barren asked. He was beyond perplexed.

"Where in the universe are we?" Sharas marveled at the various spatial bodies surrounding her fellow intruders and her.

"Where have you taken us!" Michael angrily cried, throwing his hands into the air while he stared at the Silvarian.

"I'm sure he'll show us, so calm down!" Ali'stia unabashedly shouted. Soon after she had mouthed the words, a red road appeared under the group's feet. Without a moment's hesitation, Visage headed down the road. Riza positioned herself at his side, and Vira strode off behind them. The rest of the troop either shrugged their shoulders or shook their heads before falling in behind the three leading demons.

Straightaway the road stopped, and the group was facing a great, white-tiered platform.

"Back so soon, kid? I see you brought more friends this time. And here I thought nobeing iloned me anymore," the Dark God said facetiously while staring down at the visitors.

Unlike Riza, Ali'stia, Vira, Nosfaren, and Visage, the mortal beings in the group had dropped to their knees. The power of the bound God had washed over them like a great tide of darkness.

"Chaos, you're alive!" Riza was so happy that she spread her great wings and flew to the top of the platform. "By the Verse, what did Skath do to you!" The demoness was mortified. Before her was a pitiful being whose body was almost fully incased in a full black body-cast and then covered with great black chains.

"Hello, Riza; it's been a long time," Chaos calmly replied with a hidden smile. "Excuse me for not giving you a proper greeting, for, as you can see, I'm a little tied up at the moment," he quipped.

Vira had also flown up to see Chaos. "How can you make jokes when you're in such a state!" she cried before she knelt down and attempted to undo the chains.

"Don't touch them, Vira!" Chaos screamed with such force that he knocked both demonesses off the platform. Their wings beat vigorously in order to right themselves, before they hovered in the air.

Visage had been making his way up to the platform when Chaos had screamed, so he used his claws and talons to dig into the steps, narrowly averting being blown away by the powerful blast of dark energy. Once the danger was past, he resumed his ascent to the top tier and sat down just to the left of the chained-up God. He made sure that his two fiancées were alright, giving them a weak smile before lighting into Chaos. "Why'd you do that! Why'd you treat Vira like that! I wonder if you even deserve to be rid of those chains!"

Since Chaos's chains were preventing him from turning his head far enough to face the speaker, he simply proceeded on, attempting to justify his previous outrage. "I am bound by the chains of hate. Even though Vira is a powerful demoness, if she had actually been here—in her physical body—and had managed to touch the chains, she would have been seriously hurt!" Chaos peered up at the demoness and directly addressed her, this time showing a little more restraint and a bit of respect. "However, since you're not physically here, you would have only woken up—and I don't think you would have wanted that."

"You are right, Chaos." Vira pressed her hands to her waist and frowned down at him. "But, if I were physically here, it wouldn't have hurt to try!"

"Yes, it would have," Chaos retorted matter-of-factly. "And, though I am a Dark God, I still don't like seeing the beings I care about getting hurt!" Vira was shocked by Chaos's honesty.

At this inopportune time, Lord Nosfaren appeared, having made his way up the stairs. He was now within two steps of Chaos and was looking him in the eye. "Chaos, you have no idea how glad I am to know that you are still alive. I feared that Skath had killed you, like he did all the others who rebelled against him." Nosfaren sounded relieved; his voice carried undertones of remorse and compassion.

"Well, if it isn't the most intelligent of the Ze'therac clan," Chaos responded. "I'm rather surprised that you are friends with the one who ended your dar'nra," Chaos's eye went back-and-forth from the demon, disguised as a human, to the demoness who was still hovering above him.

Nosfaren waved his hand in a dismissive manner. "My relationship with Riza has nothing to do with my family's tainted past. Besides, I forgave her and her family a long time ago. However, what I'd like to know is why you chose Visage, of all beings, to be your apparent savior," Nos stated. He was obviously bewildered.

Chaos laughed. "I didn't choose him. He just showed up here a while ago. As a matter of fact, he said he was going to find my last living wife." Merely repeating Visage's words caused Chaos to close his eye and let out a muffled chuckle. After reopening his eye, he looked up at Riza. "Orran told me that you are his fiancée, Riza. Do you find that fact to be a coincidence, or perhaps He had something to do with it?"

"I wouldn't doubt but what He is involved with all of this, Chaos," Riza sarcastically muttered before she flapped her wings, landed near Nosfaren, and crossed her arms under her chest while she folded her wings over her shoulders turning them into a makeshift cloak. "After all, He was always several steps ahead of us!"

This made Chaos laugh again. "It's nice being omnipotent; you always know what everybeing is capable of achieving—for good or bad—before he or she is even born." He then attempted to look over at the Silvarian. "Still, there are beings who are outside the sight of even the greatest of gods."

Riza rolled her eyes. "Spare me," she whispered.

Chaos's eye then focused on Forscythe, who cowered a bit under the Dark God's soul-piercing gaze. "You! Forscythe! You'd best be cautious while you're putting that little plan of yours into motion." Everybeing balked at the God's warning.

"What are you getting at, Chaos?" Lord Nosfaren asked as the Dark God refocused his eye on him.

"That woman, Chirras, is more dangerous than even you know, Nosfaren,"— Chaos continued to glare at Forsythe who cowered under the chained and bound god's scrutinizing gaze. —"she has made many friends in very dark places."

All eyes but Visage's went wide. Chaos's other guests understood exactly what he meant. Sharas clenched her fists and bit her lower lip. "Even Chirras wouldn't fall that far, would she?"

Chaos responded. "Chirras's thirst for power is unquenchable. Though she has become desperate, she's by no means stupid," Chaos warned. The God then turned his attention back to Forscythe. "I give you this warning, Forscythe. I suggest you tread lightly, for it's not only you who will suffer, but—" He shut his eye and slowly reopened it— "your plan could become a catalyst that will spawn a being who's even worse than Skath!"

Visage jumped up from his sitting position. His eyes narrowed, and his anger erupted. "I am nothing like Skath!" he loudly declared in indignation.

Chaos tried to look over at the child. "At least not yet!" he shot back silencing the boy.

Visage would have continued his protest, but his eyes snapped open, and the entire group was back in the Council Room of the temple. Visage was still enraged. "I'm not like Skath! I'll never be like Skath!" He slumped to the floor, his tails wagging wildly behind him. The palms of his hands touched the mural of the galaxy. A myriad of white dots were inlaid into the smooth, black, moribite. When Visage peered at the masterpiece, he could see the reflection of his eyes peering back at him.

Vira sprang from her chair, dropped to her knees, surrounded her fiancé with her arms and wings, and hugged him tightly. Tears of frustration formed in his eyes, but the stubborn young demon refused to let them fall. "You know, sometimes one's worst enemy is one's-self," Vira whispered.

What in the verse does that mean? Visage wondered.

It means it's easier for a being to see the darkness in others than to see it in themselves, Nosfaren telepathically told him.

Lord Nos's explanation hit the Silvarian like a freight train. *That's the truth. When I saw my eyes reflected back at me from that polished door, I didn't like what I saw—at all!*

Vira spoke softly, interrupting Visage's train of thought. "Visage, have you ever used your eyes to look into your own heart?"

"No, I've been too afraid to do that," the child whispered before he shook his head and gritted his teeth, trying to come to grips with the unfolding scenario.

Lord Nosfaren arose from his chair, walked over to Vira, and put his hand on her shoulder. Vira immediately understood; she unwrapped her wings, let the child go, and got to her feet.

Lord Nosfaren knew that Chaos was pushing Visage, but, to what end, he couldn't guess. Though the council members could see that Visage meant well, he was a young demon with great power. That meant he had the potential to use that power for good or for evil—or both. Nosfaren was determined that he wasn't going to lose this one to darkness. "Visage?" The boy lifted his head in response. The expression on his face revealed that he was, without a doubt, in great turmoil. Nos, while attempting to remain calm, got to his knees and took up Vira's position. He returned to his question. "Visage, what is it that you fear most?"

"I'm afraid I might become like Skath."

"And why is that?" Nos prodded.

"Because of what Riza's mi'thia showed me... because of what Chaos said... and because of what I am," the boy replied.

"Oh. And what are you?"

"I'm a demon... a mons—" Nos stopped him before he could finish.

"Yes, Visage, you are a demon, but you still don't understand what that means, so Riza and Vira are going to teach you," he proclaimed. Vira was about to ask Lord Nos what he meant, but Nosfaren's piercing glare reached her in time for her to swallow her words and remain silent.

Nosfaren got up and helped Visage to his feet, then gestured for Vira to go back to her seat while he went to his own. "Fellow council members, I hereby propose that Lady Riza and Lady Vira take over ar'teth Visage's training." He then turned to Baltrix. "I'm sorry about this, old friend, but Visage will no longer be able to attend your classes." Baltrix conceded, though he was unhappy that Lord Nos had failed to consult him regarding the matter. However, since he understood that Nos's mandate was the best option for his highly gifted ar'teth, he graciously smiled at Visage and even added a nod.

"All those who approve of the demonesses taking over Visage's training, say 'aye,'" Nos directed.

"Aye!" Ali'stia heartily cheered while she raised her right hand.

"Aye!" Riza and Vira shouted out in unison. They still couldn't believe their good fortune at this sudden turn of events.

"Aye," Barren added before he half-heartedly raised his arm.

Sharas, Fenrir, and Glavian all gave their own resounding "Ayes" before enthusiastically raising their hands.

Zoric appeared disgruntled. "My kid's going to kill me," he mumbled before he too raised his hand and gave a half-hearted "Aye."

Serishin and Michael had to think a moment. "Lord Nos, a question before I give my consent," Lord Michael asked while eyeing Visage. Lord Nos nodded and gave him the floor. "What of the boy's weapons training?" The look in his eyes revealed that he would really like to be Visage's weapons instructor.

"I have no objection to your desire to take over the boy's sorjin training, Michael, but only on one condition: You must get Riza and Vira's approval to help with the training. If you can get it, then I will approve!"

Lord Nosfaren's conditional approval caused Lord Michael to smile widely and to throw in his own emphatic, "Aye!"

Only the Zebrecian, Serishin, was left. "Lord Nos, I'll give my consent on two conditions."

Nosfaren was hoping for a unanimous vote, so, after a nudge from his wife, he relented. "Fine, Lady Serishin, let's hear them." Everybeing could tell he wasn't too pleased.

Lady Serishin cleared her throat before proceeding. "First, I would like to know what Visage sees in my heart."

"And secondly?" Lord Nos prodded, since he really wanted to close the meeting.

"Secondly, Visage, would you be able to assist my apprentice and me in the library?" she asked.

Visage responded enthusiastically, "That sounds cool! I'd love to work in the library!" Serishin grinned a bit at his response. He then walked over to where she was sitting and focused intently on her beating heart. Everybeing was anxious to hear the results of the evaluation. "I'm sorry, Lady Serishin, but your heart seems normal to me," he half-heartedly announced with a slight shrug.

Everybeing was confused—especially Serishin. "What do you mean by 'normal'?" she asked, obviously disappointment.

"I mean it's pretty, but it's not like Vira's or Riza's or even Lord Nosfaren's. It's more like..." The boy paused and began assessing the hearts of the other beings in the room. Some started to blush when his gaze fell upon them. However, it wasn't long before his eyes fixed on Michael. "... like Lord Michael's—but, a bit different," Visage said with apparent satisfaction.

Michael jumped up. "And just what does *that* mean!" Lady Serishin appeared to share his sentiments.

Visage tilted his head to the side and folded his arms while he thoughtfully considered his response. "Well," he started, "Lady Serishin's heart is full of hope and wonder. I can tell she likes to seek knowledge." Serishin grinned a bit, appearing quite honored by Visage's assessment. "And, though Lord Michael's heart shines like Seri's, it seems that he likes learning different martial arts. He's more of a physical type. Oh, and he has a short fuse, but a strong sense of justice." Michael turned beet red, slumping in his chair. *How does he do that!* He was dumbfounded by Visage's spot-on assessment. The other councilors' moods brightened, and many began chuckling to themselves.

"He's certainly got you pegged, Michael," Zoric quietly offered.

Michael whipped around and glared at the Twillan, but Zoric seemed unfazed by his gaze.

The other councilors were taken off guard as Serishin jumped up and shouted, "Aye!" before relatively running over to the Silvarian and giving him a big hug. Riza and Vira were about to protest, but Serishin quickly sent them a telepathic message. *Sorry, but he's just so fraking cute!* The demonesses gave each other a quick glance before responding, "Absolutely!"

Serishin stood up and patted the top of Visage's head before returning to her seat. Lord Nos then announced, "The vote is unanimous! So, starting tendronn, Visage will be trained by Riza and Vira with the assistance of Michael and Serishin." Nos's celebratory tone was short lived. His whole demeanor suddenly changed: his countenance appeared strained and his voice took on a more somber tone. "Now that that's over with, I'd like to put a new measure to a vote. Considering the damming information that Chaos provided, I hereby recommend that Chirras be put under constant surveillance." An air of resolve came over the council members before they all raised their hands and shouted, "AYE!" Glavian, Michael, Barren, Fenrir, and even Zoric jumped to their feet when they made their proclamation.

"Very well." Nos then turned to Forscythe, who already knew what was coming. "Lord Forscythe, your plan from the last meeting has been suspended until further notice." Though it was obvious that Forscythe was crushed, he gave Nosfaren a nod and got to his feet.

"I'm not finished yet!" Lord Nos snapped. Forscythe, who was already heading for the door, turned to face the disguised demon again. "Lord Forscythe, I need you to continue working on your plan. It needs to be complete and foolproof. I mean... it needs contingencies upon contingencies. Do you understand?"

"You mean I'm not off the Council!"

Nosfaren balked before he shook his head. "Why would I take you off the Council when you were just placed on it last trell!"

Forscythe scratched the back of his head and shrugged. "I don't know. But why do you want to continue with the plan when Chaos himself said it would fail?"

Nosfaren rubbed the bridge of his nose in aggravation, with a hint of disappointment. "No, Chaos didn't say it would fail; he said you needed to tread carefully...So...do so!" Nos commanded.

Forscythe's eyes wandered around the room while he pondered Nos's words. Then he clenched his fists, and, with head held high, strode back over to his seat. "I'll make sure that the net we cast won't have so much as a pin hole that Chirras can wiggle through!" he declared. The members cheered. They were determined to support Forscythe in his quest to bring Chirras down.

"Then I hereby declare this council meeting adjourned!" Nosfaren felt relieved, having more confidence than ever that Forscythe could—and would—follow through with his promise. He also felt invigorated, fully committed to rooting out every Skath worshipper on the planet.

Barren yawned widely and stretched his arms. "I still say it's much too early to be holding council meetings, even if I did get to see Chaos," he muttered while he headed for the door. *I hope I can get back to my room in time to get another half-a-minronn of sleep. It's going to be a long deronn.*

Most of the council members had left; only five beings remained. Nosfaren was speaking to his wife and Vira, leaving Riza and Visage to themselves. Both conversations ended rather abruptly when Nosfaren's U-gem began to beep and blink. *I wonder who's calling me at this time of deronn.* After pressing the gem, a screen appeared with a lengthy message written inside the glowing box. Nos's facial expression quickly changed from his normally cheerful countenance to a look of bewilderment. By the time he finished reading the message, he was noticeably angry. Ali'stia, who was standing right next to her husband, was also reading the message. Her lengthy tail was starting to sway about faster and faster. She and Nos turned to Visage and stared at him; the stare caused Vira and Riza to quiver. Their anxiety only heightened when Nos gave both demonesses quick glances and asked Visage to leave the room. Visage immediately complied and headed out into the waiting area. Once the doors fully closed, Riza glared at Nos.

"All right, what's going on?" Riza was more demanding than usual. "I saw the look that you and Ali'stia were giving Visage."

Letting out a heavy sigh, Nos responded. "Did you know that we are going to be receiving an emissary from the Empire in a mcronn?" he asked.

Riza, who appeared drathed-off, was puzzled by Nos's question and gave the demon a rather confused look. "Yeah, so?"

"It seems they aren't coming in a mcronn, like we thought," he related, rather sheepishly, averting his eyes from the demonesses.

Vira was impatient; she put her hands on her hips. "All right, Lord Nos, spill!" She was also clearly annoyed at Nos for not immediately sharing his obviously important and recently discovered information. Ali'stia, sensing the tension in the room, gave Nos a quick kiss and made a hasty retreat.

Nosfaren, one of the most powerful demons in the galaxy, was rarely unnerved. However, being alone in the Council Room with two greater-demon princesses was one of the most anxiety-laden experiences he had ever had to face. *I wish I could be anywhere else in the universe but here,* he mused.

"What are you hiding from us, Nosfaren?" Riza pressed.

After throwing the two glowering demonesses a hesitant glance, Nos finally opened up. "Apparently, the Imperial delegation is going to be here tononn—and they found out about Visage, so they want to meet him!" He spoke fast and winced as he braced for the demonesses' sure-to-come outrage.

"Well, what's so bad about that?" Vira asked.

Nos was shocked! "I don't know. I just thought you might be upset that the Empire found out about Visage."

The demonesses glanced at each other, not understanding what Nos was trying to get at. "Why would we be upset about that?" Riza asked the now-confused Lord, who was in the middle of a stress-releasing sigh.

Vira chimed in: "Listen, Nos, we may be demons—and yes, our

galaxies are hidden inside a different dimension—but the Meserino and Veserino clans have been part of the Marcisian Empire for eons."

Riza then re-entered the conversation. "And we all knew we couldn't keep Visage hidden forever. Truthfully, I'm surprised it took this long for the Empire to find out about him."

Lord Nos looked on with unbelief while the demonesses headed for the door and then left. *That... was not what I was expecting,* he thought. He then made his way over to the central chair in the semicircle of thrones, slumped down into it and tilted his head up towards the ceiling. *Visage's arrival, the prophecy concerning the Dark God Chaos, the delegation of the Empire arriving in just one deronn, and Chirras—too many things happening at once.* After a bit more musing, Nosfaren pushed the majority of his concerns to the far recesses of his consciousness. However, one last thought lingered. "Eendril, if this is some kind of joke, I don't think it's funny. And they say that demons have a twisted sense of humor," he mumbled before he got up and headed for the door. Once there, he held the door open and took one last glance around the room, smiling while he reflected on everything that he and the other lords and ladies had accomplished in their hallowed meeting place. For a moment, he fell into deep thought. *Though our Council has the responsibility of deciding the fate of more than a million souls, our task is nothing compared to the tasks that Eendril faces on a deronn to deronn basis—having to decide the fate of trillions and trillions of souls scattered across innumerable galaxies. He watches over all of us, even His adopted de'taris and dar'taris... like me. He follows us along our paths of life no matter where they lead— whether too good or to evil.*

"This is no joke, Nosfaren. I'm sorry, but I need to push things along. There is another galaxy full of My children; they will soon need the power of the Empire. And that includes all of your Verse users. Though the War of the Gods is over, Skath's many worshipers still roam the mortal plane, and I am powerless to stop them. At this very moment, My children throughout several galaxies are being overrun by Skath's followers." Though Eendril was the Grand God of Light, even He could not hide His grief.

27

Hide and Seek

After stepping out of the lift, Vira and Riza took their places at Visage's flank, and the trio headed for the coliseum in the pit. The young Silvarian was nervous. He took quick glances at the pair of demonesses whose eyes were glowing brightly with a determination that was rarely seen. The beings remained silent as they made their way to the center of the ring. Though the place was empty, Visage felt as though many eyes were upon him.

Vira got to one knee, placed her hand on Visage's shoulder, and spoke with sternness. "Visage, Riza and I are going to teach you what it means to be a true Silvarian demon."

"A Greater Demon's power is on par with a Grand God, but the Vorihelcom seal prevents us from displaying all of the power we harbor," Riza added.

Vira nodded her head. "Not only is the Vorihelcom seal a restraint, but it helps a being focus as well," she related, picking up where Riza left off.

"You see, Visage, every point on your seal can be broken, and every time you break one of the points, you will lose more control over your power," Riza informed him. She then turned around and pulled her black and red hair out of the way so she could show him her own

Vorihelcom seal. The main part of the seal was emitting a soft red color, which was a pleasing contrast to her dark-red and black skin. Though it was partly concealed by her leathery wings, Visage could see that ten layers of runes led up to the central infinity sign, which was the color of gold. The infinity sign itself was located in the same area as Vira's was located. Before making her way over to Vira and Visage, Riza let go of her hair and allowed it to cascade down her back. "You see, Visage, we are so much more than monsters." Riza spread out her arms and wings while she spoke. "Like the gods, we celebrate life: We think, we feel, and, though some don't believe it, we care!" Riza folded up her wings, got to her knees, and placed a hand on Visage's chest. "Even demons have hearts," she softly uttered before arising. "Visage, like it or not, you are the last of the Silvarian race. Vira and I are here for you. We'll do all we can to help you carry this burden."

Vira now stood beside her friend. "My dar'nra was a Silvarian. He and my mi'thia taught me everything I needed to know. Since your parents on Earth are human, they could not possibly have known how to raise a being such as yourself. That's why we brought you here. So, let's get started! The first thing you need to know is that Silvarian demons have three forms. They can switch into or out of any of the forms just by desiring to do so."

"Wow! I can change forms?" The young demon's eyes began to shine more brightly.

Vira nodded her head, held up her index finger, and then continued. "The first form is the one you're in now." Then she raised her middle finger. "The second form is a combination of your first and third forms; my dar'nra called it the 'werren form.'" Then she raised her ring finger. "The third form is that of a giant wolf. Generally, once you know how to switch between the three forms, you'll be unstoppable!" Vira proudly and enthusiastically noted while at the same time putting her hand on her hip. "So, go ahead and try to change into your werren form."

Visage wanted to comply but was hesitant. Vira, on the other hand, was staring at him with giddy excitement.

Riza then challenged the demoness's request. "Vira, isn't he a bit too young for that?"

Vira's excitement instantly faded. *Yeah, I guess she's right.* "But my dar'nra always said that, from the time of birth, Silvarian demons know how to transform," she whined.

Riza curled up her tail and used it as a seat. After crossing her right leg over her left, she leaned onto her chin and placed her elbow on her knee. "Fine, Vira, I'll go along with this for now," she conceded. She then turned her attention to Visage. "Visage, all you have to do is to think of your other forms, though you shouldn't be too disappointed if you can't transform immediately." Riza glanced at Vira, whose expression kept shifting from a look of hopeful cheeriness to a look of defeat.

Visage was so anxious that he started twiddling his thumbs. Though he didn't want to dash Vira's hopes, he was, at the same time, itching to test out her dar'nra's knowledge regarding a Silvarian's innate powers. He mused over his options for a time before finally addressing the eager-looking demoness. "Um... Vira, I don't know if I can do this."

Immediately, Vira's shoulders slumped. Visage responded, frantically waving his arms in protest. "No, no! I mean—I'd like to try. Just don't expect anything!" After he had uttered the words, he caught site of Riza, who was smirking. *I think she knows more than she is letting on.* Though Riza was managing to keep her mouth shut, the smirk spoke volumes. And, despite Visage's heartfelt attempt to minimize her expectations, Vira gave him a hearty nod. *Great! This is just great! I have one fiancée who expects me to transform on a whim and another who is skeptical, to say the least. Oh, well, if I can't pull this off, one will be gloating over being right and the other will be elated. But... if I can pull it off... we'll all be celebrating. So, I may as well give it a shot.*

The Silvarian took a deep breath and cleared his mind. Almost instantaneously, he began to feel a tingling sensation coursing throughout his body. The seal on his back began to get warm, but not hot. He let his indren'freth flow, and, with all the intensity he could muster, he concentrated on his werren form.

Vira and Riza were spellbound as they watched the young Silvarian's transformation. The boy's arms and legs grew and the muscles bulged; his fingers grew; his claws not only lengthened but became much more curved. His feet didn't change much; they just got a bit bigger in order to help support his bulkier frame. However, the talons on his toes became much sharper and longer. His face changed the most. He grew a muzzle full of white, razor-sharp teeth, which gleamed in the dim-red light. His ears lengthened and moved from up towards the top of his head. They became fuzzier, since they grew a coat of black hair that was dotted with ugly purple patters.

With the change complete, he opened his eyes. "Well?" he asked expectantly, "did it work?" Riza sat on her tail, wide-eyed and with an awestruck expression. Vira was in a similar state with her hands hanging limply at her sides and her mouth hanging open. *What's wrong with them? Oh!* he thought when he looked down at his newly lengthened nose. He brought his hands up to touch his elongated face. *No way! This can't possibly be me!* His mind screamed in protest while he felt his face with his larger more menacing hands. Then he lost it! He slumped to the floor and peered at the image reflecting back at him from the smooth moribite surface.

This is fantastic; I look like a damned werewolf! For a moment, his conscience tried to straighten him out, telling him that it didn't matter what he looked like; he was still the same being on the inside. *I know that! But look at me! What if had turned into this... this creature when I was back home? I would have been hunted down by guys with silver bullets in their guns!*

Visage could have continued his conversation with his inner self, but fate—or God—intervened. The black skin and purple biree, which he had had since he used the Cloak of Darkness, fell away only to be replaced by his former pure-white skin and azure-colored biree. The hair on his head returned to its original silver color, and his hands reverted to normal. *Finally! It's about fraking time that Cloak of Darkness—or whatever it was—wore off.* After clenching his fingers a few times, he brought his sapphire eyes to bear on the two gawking demonesses.

Riza and Vira had been in a state of shock over the rapidity of

Visage's changes; Vira was the first to find her voice. "It's been a long time since I've seen a silver werren," she said while her face brightened and tears started to form in her eyes.

"Ugh—silver werren—like a silver werewolf? Or silverware?" His questions brought Riza out of her own daze, and she and Vira both appeared confused.

Visage shook his head in disbelief. "Seriously? Silverware?" he repeated, his eyes half-closed. "This would be hilarious back on Earth," he grumbled. *My sri'nas would never let me live this down... nor would the Navy guys for that matter.*

His thoughts were interrupted when Vira spoke again. "Now that you've figured out your warren form, Visage, try going into your full wolf form!" she urged, eagerly awaiting the results!

Visage put his hand where his now long mouth began and brought it down over his nose. *Well this is just great!* "And just how do I change back to normal?" Visage asked the pair of know-it-all demonesses.

Riza chuckled. "It's easy Visage; you simply have to think about what form you want to take, and your body will do the rest."

Vira piped up. "Along with telling me that Silvarians know how to change forms from the time of their births, my dar'nra also told me that once a Silvarian goes through the transformation process the first time, he can easily change forms with only a thought."

Visage wasn't completely convinced, but he felt he didn't have a choice, so he closed his eyes and concentrated. This time, the energy that flowed around and through him was much more intense than it was when he changed into his warren form. His arms and hands lengthened even further, and his legs became like those of a canine. He was forced to all fours and his body itself grew and lengthened. Now that the transformation was complete, the energy that enveloped him dissipated.

"Did it work?" Visage knew he had asked the question, but his voice sounded rather strange. It was much deeper and more menacing, and there was a strange kind of echo to it.

Vira could no longer contain herself. She gave Visage, who was now fully in his wolf form, a great big hug. His silver-and-blue, fur-covered body tickled her skin and made it tingle. "Wow, V, your wolf form is much bigger than that of a normal wolf. If you were a bit bigger, I'd be able to ride you!" Vira exclaimed after she pulled herself away, only to hug him again.

"So, Visage, how does this form feel?" Riza asked before she put her right leg down and crossed her left over it.

With his newly enhanced eyesight, Visage had to avert his gaze from Riza, since her whole body appeared to be on fire, and her heart was shining brilliantly. "Um"—Visage was momentarily at a loss for words—"it feels good, Riza." *I can't believe how gorgeous she is!*

Riza almost toppled over when she heard and felt what he was thinking! It didn't take long for Visage to figure out that his fiancée had heard his thoughts, and he responded by hanging his head in shame. *I'm sorry Riza, I didn't mean—*

"It's all right, V... And thank you for your compliment," Riza sheepishly offered. When she smiled, Visage swore he could see her heart skip a beat, but her entire aura was so blinding that he wasn't entirely sure.

Vira had pulled away from Visage and was now pouting. "What about me, Visage?" She spoke quickly and loudly. Visage attempted to look at the Veserino demoness, but she was in such close proximity that he had to cover his eyes immediately in order to protect them from the glowing light that was radiating from her entire body.

"Come on, Vira, I can't see you unless you turn off that blinding light of yours!"

"Am I really shinning?" Visage nodded. "Even more than Riza?" she persisted.

"I don't know, Vira... Maybe?" He gave an awkward shrug. And it was definitely awkward, considering that he had one hand on the floor while the other was busy shielding his eyes.

"I think you should go back to your more human form now, Visage," Riza suggested. The young demon couldn't agree more, so he concentrated and was instantly standing on two legs. "Well, that was definitely different!"

Vira took no time in getting her ar'teth reengaged. "So, V, now that you've gotten the hang of changing into your different forms, we will start training you on how to use them."

"But I'm not sure that I can master the training," Visage weakly replied, still unsure about all of this transformation business.

"That's why you need to practice, and the best way to practice is simply by doing." At that, Riza uncurled her tail and rose to her feet.

Visage wasn't all that enthusiastic, but he knew that his fiancée had made a good point. "Fine. What do I have to do now?"

The two demonesses gave each other a quick glance; both smirked as they said in unison, "You have to catch us!" Visage was taken aback by this.

"Wha—" Riza cut V off before he could finish.

"Listen, V, Vira and I are going to head into the catacombs." She pointed to a large hole in the wall at the furthest end of the coliseum. He couldn't really tell what was in there, but it didn't look at all welcoming. "We are going to hide in the catacombs, and all you have to do is use your forms while trying to find us."

"But you have to give us a head start, Visage," Riza added.

"So, we're playing hide-and-seek?" Visage unenthusiastically asked.

"Is that what Earthlings call it?" Vira asked. "We've always called it Zah'seric ard'ec." Judging from Visage's blank expression, Vira realized that he had absolutely no clue as to what she had just said, so she decided to translate. "It simply means, 'the dark sport.'"

"'The dark sport?'" Visage was still unconvinced of the need for all of this hide-and-go-seek type of stuff.

"More like the sport in the dark. There are lots of variations, but we are going with a more benign one where all you need to do is find us." Vira unfurled her wings and headed for the opening, patting the boy's head when she walked by.

Different variations? Does that mean the rules can change? While Visage was busy thinking, Riza popped into the conversation.

Yes, Visage, there are lots of different ways to play this game. Though some are, well, more dangerous than others. It is used as a training tool by the Zaharaj, after all.

Visage understood. "So all I have to do is find you?" He crossed his arms in front of him and waited for Riza's answer.

"Yes, that's it." Riza bent over and laid a kiss on the top of Visage's head, then ran to catch up with Vira.

"Wait! How long do I have to wait before I come after you?"

"Just do like you did on Earth," she suggested.

"You mean count to ten?"

"That sounds sufficient..." Her voice trailed off after she took off into the darkness.

"Isn't this wonderful... Well, I'd better get started. Annnd ten!" The Silvarian headed over to the hole at the far end of the coliseum, grumbling to himself with every step. *And to think I used to enjoy this game. Oh well, hopefully I can find those two in short order.* He rolled his eyes. *With the way that those to shine... this should be a cinch.*

✳✳✳

The opening to the catacombs was a lot bigger up close. Once inside, Visage was completely engulfed in darkness. Looking behind him at the grand coliseum, he shook his head, not at all aware of what was to come. After sighing heavily, he changed into his werren form, still surprised at how easily he made the change.

"I guess it gets easier the more times you do it," Visage said aloud, looking himself over and clenching his fingers a few times before taking a calming breath and heading into the gaping opening.

The catacombs were dark and cool, and Visage soon realized that the sound of rushing air, coming from multiple directions, was messing with his very sensitive hearing. The tunnel he was traversing was well constructed. It was wide as well as tall. Other tunnels were visibly branching off from this one, which appeared to be the main one. Though he didn't have time to stop and investigate, the other tunnels appeared to be actual catacombs. The entrances were ornately carved, and he caught glimpses of the stone tombs, which were lying inside the walls. He could sense that the entire place was sacred—even hallowed—a place where many Zaharaj had been laid to rest. Suddenly, an almost unbearable sadness overcame him—so much so that he started to fall. However, he was able to right himself, enabling his feet to hit the ground first. His talons, which had come out, threw sparks when they dug into the cavern floor.

With his enhanced vision, Visage could easily make out two brightly glowing forms heading down and away from him. He couldn't help but smile; his smile allowed his mouthful of fangs to be on full display. *This is going to be easier than even I had thought!* With that, he was off and running. His feet sped along so fast that, in no time, they were off the ground; he was actually flying! *Wow! I haven't done this since I was at home!* he marveled, quite amazed by his re-acquired skill.

The large wolf did -hundred-and-eighty-degree spin. Visage came to a halt in front of the entrance to one of the off-shooting rooms. Once his hand was on the entrance-way, he felt even more extreme sadness—this time accompanied by anger. *What the frak? This is so strange!* Once re-focused, he peered into the darkness, which was no longer as imposing as it first seemed.

Once again, Visage's highly sensitive visual acuity came in handy. It caused the tunnel-like room to appear as though it were basked in a dim light, though he knew the place was actually pitch-black. Swallowing hard, he glanced at the two glowing forms, which were now no more than dots far off in the distance. *I'll never catch Riza and Vira at this rate.* He immediately shook off the thought, knowing that the demonesses would have to stop eventually. *I think I might even have a little time to do some exploring,* he thought before he stepped into the large, wide, tunnel-like area. Four rows of caskets were laid into the opposing tunnel walls—eight rows in all; they seemed to go on endlessly. *I wonder how many beings are buried in here?* After walking over to the wall on his right, Visage placed his hand on the closest casket and closed his eyes. *Nothing. I don't feel anything! Seriously, where is that feeling coming from? There's a lot of sadness and anger coming from something in here, but where is it?* He removed his hand off the casket and proceeded further into the alcove. Balancing on the balls of his feet was awkward, but he was getting more used to it with every step. *It feels as though I've walked like this before,* he thought while continuing his investigation.

When the feeling of sadness morphed into an intense feeling of remorse, the demon became increasingly frustrated. "I don't like this place. I don't like feeling like this. And I don't like being separated from Riza and Vira. The longer I'm side-tracked, the harder it's going to be for me to find them." He was on the verge of giving up when he noticed that one of the caskets on the left side, third row up, was glowing a soft red. "Alright..." He blinked a few times to make sure he wasn't seeing things. "Now that's weird!" After coming to an abrupt halt, he stared at the offending casket.

"Is somebeing there?" Visage jumped back a few feet, startled at the voice he had just clearly heard—or felt. Still a bit unsteady on his feet, he stumbled backwards and started to fall. Utilizing gravity to assist him, he executed a nearly perfect back flip before approaching the glowing tomb. Once there, he was hesitant to reach out and touch the side of the cool, glowing stone slab that covered the tomb. But, an unseen force seemed to be guiding him, so he finally succumbed and touched the offending casket. Immediately, his eyes snapped open, and a rush of all-consuming guilt and anger washed over him.

Who is this? A feminine voice telepathically questioned. For a moment, Visage was too stunned to answer but finally managed to compose himself.

I'm Visage of the Zaharaj... and who is this? He thought back.

I'm Lady Xarani of the Zaharaj... You're just a child! The woman's thoughts caused the young demon to grit his teeth—a low growl escaping his now wolf-like muzzle.

So what if I am? he shot back at the corpse, which was definitely that of a woman.

No! This is all wrong! I was hoping I'd at least get the attention of a knight or lord—not some young ar'teth!

I can leave you know! Visage threatened the dead woman.

The woman fell silent for a moment. *No, don't leave. It's fine. It's just I was hoping... Never mind, you'll have to do!*

Visage rolled his eyes. *This is just my luck. I'm supposed to be playing hide-and-seek with Vira and Riza, get side-tracked by the spirit of some dead lady who needs help, and then she isn't happy that I'm the one who noticed her plight!*

What was that? How do you know Lady Riza and Lady Vira?

"Actually, they're my fiancées," Visage muttered, closing an eye and bracing for some kind of retort.

By the gods, you're a Silvarian, aren't you!

Yep... Visage got on his haunches and folded his arms across his chest. *Why, is that a problem?* he curtly responded with a slight fiery snort thru his canine nose. He was a bit startled by the small flames, but he shook his head and chose to focus on the dead woman.

No, this is fantastic! Visage was surprised at the dead woman's sudden change of attitude. He could sense that she was not only relieved but also very excited.

"All right, Lady Xarani, what is it that you need from me?" Visage asked, hesitantly placing his left hand back on the stone coffin. He was trying to hurry the situation along.

Actually, I was cursed and in order for my soul to be freed, I need you to take the holo-record that's with me in the casket and give it to one of the council members. Do you understand? Visage appeared disturbed after Lady Xarani told him that.

I don't like being a grave robber. His thought caused the woman to laugh.

I'm giving you my permission, Visage. Besides you're not grave robbing— you're doing me a very big favor. You see, I died before I could complete my mission, so I need you to complete it for me!

Though still reluctant, Visage acquiesced. As soon as he withdrew his hand, the top of the casket lifted up, all by itself. After levitating off the cavern floor, the boy peered into the now-open casket. He gasped. There lay nothing more than the skeleton of a woman. The woman was dressed in the attire of the Zaharaj.

Lady Xarani's mask covered her skull, and her bony arms were neatly crossed. In her hands, Visage beheld a large item, which appeared to be a big ornately decorated jewelry box. He gently reached into the casket and took the woman's skeletonized fingers off from the box and then he tucked the precious cargo under his right arm. The casket closed by itself, and Visage found himself standing on the cavern floor once again.

Well, Visage glanced down at the box in his arm and then at the resealed casket. *That was creepy! And now I'll probably never catch Riza and Vira. Oh, well, I'd better get back to the main tunnel. So much for side trips!* However, he had hardly had a chance to move before being waylaid by the appearance of a bright light. There in front of him stood a human woman, tall and fair. Her eyes were purple, and a warm smile adorned her lips. She was wearing the robes of the Zaharaj, but they were white as opposed to their customary black color.

"Thank you, Visage," was all the spirit said before she and the surrounding light vanished. Now alone in the dark once again, Visage's thoughts briefly focused on the mysterious box, which was still cradled under his arm.

"She's been waiting, who knows how long, for someone to come along and take this off her hands, skeletonized though they may be." He shook his now oversized head. "I'd better make sure I deliver it and its contents safely into the hands of a council member, no matter what!"

Once back in the main tunnel, Visage could barely make out the presence of two glowing, stationary dots that were below him. "The lady told me to get this to one of the council members, and here I have two... but which one is closest to me?" Visage muttered aloud. Weighing his options, he shifted the box from his right arm to his left and headed off in the direction of the dots.

He was making good time until he noticed a junction, immediately ahead. Without enough time to slow down, he threw the box into the air and charged at the wall. He attempted to quickly transform into his full wolf form, but he ran into some trouble. He tripped over himself and tumbled toward the cave's junction. In a desperate attempt to right himself from his end-over-end tumble, he brought his two hind legs down and dug his talons into the floor. This allowed him to break just enough to get his hands working properly. His mind wandered back to a wildlife show he had watched with his cousin and sri'nas at his uch'nra's house. He remembered the sleek and muscular running movements of the animals. Using his back legs, he launched himself forward, mimicking the gaits of the zebras and hyenas. He managed to get a rhythm going right before he neared the wall. The box he had thrown was still in the air but dangerously close to hitting the cavern floor. Since his two arms were occupied, he opened his mouth and, without thinking, let loose his tongue. With whip-like speed, it wrapped itself around the box and brought it to his awaiting jaws, which he quickly shut. His fangs clutched the cargo with amazing precision. *Please don't let me break it!*

The wall was awaiting the charging Silvarian, but the full impact never came. Visage's wolf-like form leapt at the wall before putting himself into a spin. All four feet met the hardened surface, breaking several chunks off from it. He used his new momentum to spring himself down the left passage.

Now that Visage was getting the hang of his new wolf form, he increased his pace, causing all of his feet to flair with white and blue flames. Since he was fully focused on the bright red light, which was becoming larger by the second, Visage failed to notice that his feet were not even touching the floor. *Riza, I'm coming! I need to give this box to you!* was all he was thinking while his now sleek, wolf-like body raced ahead. Suddenly the tunnel widened, and he found himself surrounded by a field of stalagmites. He had to skirt around or over them, utilizing every bit of the agility offered by his newly acquired form. *This form does have its uses,* he mused while veering around another one of the large structures. When he leapt to the top of yet another stalagmite, his silver and azure hair rippled. This stalagmite was fortuitously flat on top, enabling the wolf to use it as a springboard to launch himself up toward the ceiling.

Unfortunately, because the ceiling was laden with stalactites, which were all bearing down on him like the teeth of a giant monster, he had to instantaneously turn upside down and start running between them, just as he had done with the stalagmites. Visage felt so free in his wolf-like form that he almost grinned. But he resisted, since grinning would cause him to drop his precious cargo. He certainly did not want to drop the box in his muzzle. Instinctively, he knew he was getting very close to one if not both of the demonesses. In fact, he slowed his pace so abruptly that the flames on his hands and feet nearly sizzled and died.

Riza was hanging upside down on the cave's ceiling, hiding behind one of the bigger stalactites, while at the same time trying to peer out from behind her cover in order to see if what she was sensing was indeed Visage. All she saw was four fast-moving, white-and-blue flames lighting the stalagmites that were nearly a mile away and far below her. *Is that really Visage?* she wondered while she watched the flames leap into the air, clearing several of the natural spears on the floor. She stuck her head back behind her cover right before the flaming object neared her hiding place. The next thing she knew, a warm breath was hitting the back of her neck. When she cautiously turned around, she beheld a wolf-life creature, with two, burning, sapphire-colored eyes, staring back at her. The creature had a rather large maw, which was open on one side. Riza could only surmise that it was holding something with its teeth.

"Riva..." Visage tried to say Riza's name in order to not scare the demoness. Riza, on the other hand, didn't know whether to scream at the top of her lungs or to laugh herself out of her precarious perch. With only a moment's thought, she opted to let her fiancé off the hook.

"Congratulations, Visage! You found me!" The demoness was trying hard not to laugh when the wolf-demon in front of her tilted its muzzle to the side and blinked.

"Comf on, Riva, diff if imprtanf," Visage muttered; he used a clawed finger to point to the box he was holding in his maw. Sensing that something was amiss, Riza reached up and grabbed the curious-looking box, which was now dripping with Silvarian saliva. She didn't even seem to care, having immediately realized the nature of Visage's precious cargo.

"Visage, where did you get this!" The question made the upside-down Silvarian give Riza an awkward shrug.

"Um... would you believe me if I told you a dead lady— or woman's corpse— gave it to me?" *I'm not sure I even believe it myself.*

It was now Riza's turn to shrug. "It depends on the lady," she replied.

"I think her name was Xarin, Xirin... something like that" The Silver wolf sat on his haunches and put his claw to his muzzle. *What the frak was her name again?*

"Do you mean Lady Xarina or Xarani?" Riza inquired.

Visage eagerly got into Riza's face his tails wagging about behind him. "That's her—Xarani!" he cheered. He then changed back into his more human form, which was a big mistake! Immediately he was in a freefall and heading right towards the spikes below! With lightning speed, using his indren'freth, he managed to halt his fall and keep himself aloft.

When he flew over back up where Riza was and kissed her, she almost dropped the precious box. Now that they were both in the void, Visage showed her what had happened to him back in the catacombs. He was chatting excitedly after he ended their psychic link. "So Riza, who is she? Why is that box so important? Why"— Riza shut him up by clamping his lips closed. He was disheartened—putting it mildly—but she didn't have time to explain everything and wasn't sure if he should even know about the story behind the box.

"I'm sorry, Visage but this is something that only the Council should know about." The boy's eyes went wide with excitement.

"You mean it's like top secret stuff?"

"Something like that."

"That's so awesome!" Visage yelled. A fierce echo resulted. Riza actually winced from the noise and was certain that Vira must have heard it as well.

"Sorry, Riza," Visage whispered. "I didn't mean to yell like that."

Riza couldn't help but grin at the young demon's contagious enthusiasm. "It's all right, Visage... but next time you could think instead of actually shouting. However—that echo was pretty 'cool.'" Visage gave a toothy grin and an energetic nod.

I'm sorry, but if you don't mind Visage, I need to get this to the Council, Riza shared while she gestured to the box under her arm. *And you still have to go and find Vira. That is, unless she heard your little outburst and is on her way.*

Visage started to apologize again, but Riza waved him off, raised her wings, and began her flight to the coliseum and the lifts. Visage watched her go. After Riza's light faded, he decided to begin his search for Vira, so he stopped supporting himself with his indren'freth and began his rapid descent. When he was about to hit the top of one of the stalagmites, he changed back into his wolf form and took off, heading back to the junction. Within moments he was there. Now breathing heavily, his feet were aflame once again. Without the box in his mouth, his tongue was freely flapping about, and he was starting to pant.

Meanwhile, Vira had heard a voice echo throughout the cavern. It was a bit faint by the time it reached her, since she was hidden high up among the stalactites. *That sounds like Visage's voice. I wonder if he's alright.* Her worry outweighed her patience, so she flew down to the floor, beating her great wings in order to right herself in midair when she made her descent. Finally landing on one of the spiky stalagmites, she balanced on her right foot and listened closely, hoping to further pinpoint where the voice had come from.

If that was Visage, why did he yell the way he did? Maybe Riza spooked him—or maybe he's hurt. He may have smashed into one of the walls! Vira shook her head, hoping the answer was the former and not the latter. However, since she was now experiencing a great urgency regarding the entire situation, she jumped into the air, spread her wings, and flew off into the cavern. *I'd better find those two, and fast!*

Though several of the tunnels were relatively tight spaces, she continued to fly at maximum speed. She was still flying at a decent clip when she noticed a light coming from the other end of the tunnel. It got brighter and brighter—fast!

Visage charged around a sharp bend, heading for what was a very brightly glowing being. He gasped when he realized that he was running—or flying—right at Vira, and she was most definitely flying right at him! The two demons slammed on their breaks, desperately attempting to avoid a collision. Visage landed hard, digging both his talons and claws into the floor and sending out a torrent of sparks when he did so. Vira wrapped her wings around herself as she too dug her talons into the floor, attempting to put herself into a spin in order to slow her momentum. Both demons realized that their efforts were too little too late and collided—hard. They became a tumbling mess of fur and leathery wings, coming to an abrupt stop several yards from their point of collision. Vira worked to dislodge herself from the Silvarian, whose eyes were still rolling, even though he was no longer moving. Finally getting a grip on the situation, Visage vigorously shook his head a few times before he shifted back to his human form while Vira struggled to get to her feet. Once able to sit up, Visage put his hand on his head, hoping to stop the spinning. "Ugh. Vira, can we please not do that again?" he asked the demoness, who was now standing over him.

"I don't think we'll have to worry about that, V. Are you Alright?" After Visage responded in the affirmative, she reached down and lent him a hand to help him get up. Now that the excitement was over, she was dying to know what had happened. "So what was the rush? And why did you scream?"

"Yeah, Vira, I can't wait to tell you what happened! But I guess it would be quicker if I showed you." Since Vira was still holding onto his hand, he gave her a yank and brought her face close enough to kiss her. Vira was quite shocked that Visage hadn't seemed to give a second thought to his rather bold action. *He's come a long way,* she quietly mused. However, the musing was short-lived, since they were now inside the void. By the time Visage broke from the kiss, Vira was wide-eyed—seemingly frozen. A fair amount of time passed before Visage became worried. "Um... Vira... is everything alright?"

Vira blinked a few times. "Oh. Sorry. It's... Oh never mind! Let's get back to the coliseum."

They both walked side by side in silence until they got to the lifts.

Vira pressed the button to summon the elevator and then glanced down at Visage who was still grinning from all of the excitement. "Visage?"

"Yes, Vira?"

"Why did you do that?"

Visage started rubbing the back of his head. "I'm so sorry. I was trying to stop. I didn't mean to hurt you."

"No, not that," Vira quickly responded while turning to face him. She was about to ask about the kiss when the lift arrived and the doors opened. The timing of the lift's arrival agitated her, so she dejectedly trudged inside. Visage followed, looking her over to make sure she didn't have any injuries. When Vira noticed his worried expression, she quickly pressed two buttons, causing the lift to make its ascent. *This is going to keep bugging the slith out of me if I don't ask him.* She quickly took a knee and put her hand on Visage's left shoulder. "Visage, why did you kiss me like that?" As soon as the question escaped her lips, she started fearing the answer. The way he was now looking at her wasn't helping, either.

Visage suspiciously eyed his fiancée. "Are you sure you're alright, Vira? Did you hit your head?" He began looking her over again, making sure he had not missed anything.

Vira scowled. "I'm being serious, Visage!" She was now more agitated than before. Visage halted his inspection, his short-lived frown quickly becoming a smile.

"I kissed you because it was the quickest way to show you what had happened," he explained. Vira took this in, and then cursed herself for thinking that the kiss was anything more than that. With a relenting sigh, she stood back up.

"But you're also my fiancée, and I love you, Vira!"

Vira's eyes went wide and her lower jaw fell. *Did he just say what I think he said? Love—isn't that the Earth term for iloni?* Her mind could not catch up to her mouth. "What does love mean?" Vira didn't even realize she had uttered her thought until she was hearing Visage's reply.

"It means iloni... I think." Visage wasn't quite sure but hoped he had gotten it right. "And why wouldn't I love you? Your heart is very pretty." He then shook his head as if that wasn't quite right. "I mean—it's gorgeous!" That was the final straw!

If demons can have heart attacks, then I must be having one; my heart feels like it's going to beat right out of my chest! Vira thought. She then struggled to put forth her next question. "Is that how you feel about me?" she stuttered. Visage looked very bewildered.

"Why, Vira? Do you not want me to love you? I mean, it's not like I'd force you to marry me or anything. I am still a kid, after all. And I'm sure there are lots of guys out in the galaxy who would love to have a girl... err... woman... like you." His words stung a bit.

Vira got to her knees once again, but this time it was because she wasn't sure if she could even stand anymore. She wrapped her arms around the young demon and emphatically shook her head. "No, Visage," she whispered almost inaudibly. "When I carried your soul, I felt your warmth and knew you were the one for me." She pulled back, having tears in her eyes. "I've waited eons for you... And I'd wait even longer if I had to. But now... that you're here with me, and with what you've told me—the wait has all been worth it!"

Vira's words lay heavily on Visage. He didn't know what to say, so he gave up and simply said what he was feeling. "Thank you, Vira... for being my friend. I promise I'll try to not make you sad anymore." He wasn't sure if he got his point across, but, while he looked at his friend, he realized that she was very special to him. He couldn't help but notice her heart beating more rapidly in her chest and shining even more brightly than normal. He wasn't even surprised when she wrapped her arms around him, continuing the embrace until the lift doors opened.

Vira stood up and gestured for Visage to get off the lift. "This is the level where the library is located, so I'm sure you'll be able to stay out of mischief here." Visage was already halfway out of the lift, but turned in time for Vira to give him a quick wink before the doors slid closed.

<h1 style="text-align:center">28</h1>

The Blind Can See

The young Silvarian child was alone once again. He stood in front of the lifts for several dironns, watching the lights above the doors while the lifts stopped and started, ascended and descended. Startled by a hand patting him on the shoulder, he reacted without even thinking. After jumping to the side, he crouched, ready to spring on the being who had disturbed him. The black-clad man was gesturing with both hands, attempting to dissuade him from his intended course of action.

"Whoa, whoa, whoa! Calm down, kid!" The man's voice sounded surprised at the sudden hostility he was facing. "I didn't mean to startle you, but why are you here so early in the deronn?" His muffled, metallic-sounding voice downgraded from surprise to curiosity, and he slowly lowered his hands to his sides. Not liking the way the man was holding his hands in the folds of his robe, Visage didn't budge. Instead, he peered into the man's heart. *Is he just curious, or is he a being like Chirras?* After he ascertained from the examination that the result was the former, he relaxed.

"Sorry, um... mister. I was just brought here by Vira. She said that the library was on this level." The man started circling him, causing Visage's discomfort to re-spike a bit.

"Oh, yes, sorry." The man had halted and was now standing in front of the boy. "My name is Lord Harneth. And you must be the Silvarian kid whom Lord Nosfaren brought from Earth... Yes?"

Visage nodded. "Yes, Lord Harneth, I am. And my name is Visage."

"I sense that you're troubled, ar'teth Visage," Harneth said while he headed for two double doors, which had an inscription pad mounted between them. Harneth pressed on the pad. When he stopped, there were two resounding beeps, and the doors clanged, unlocked, and swung inwards. Harneth stood to one side and gestured for Visage to enter. "After you, my little demon friend."

Visage stepped into the room, which turned out to be the library. His jaw hung open while he took in the myriads of books and tomes. *Wow! They go on forever!*

After entering the room himself, Harneth rested his hand on Visage's shoulder and removed his mask. "Welcome, my friend, to the greatest library in the galaxy! Even the one on Marcisia doesn't compare to ours!" Harneth was beaming with pride. Visage responded with a hearty nod of agreement.

Now that he knew Harneth was a "friend," Visage did a little deeper assessment of his being. Harneth was a human male with short brown hair, which had streaks of red running through it. He looked rather young and appeared to have a pleasing personality. However, one thing that Visage found to be somewhat off-putting was the black band that was tied over his eyes; it was decorated with all sorts of red and purple symbols. "Is there something wrong with your eyes?" Visage asked before even thinking.

Harneth chuckled. "Did my blindfold give it away?" His facetious reply caused Visage to don a sheepish grin. Harneth then shook his head. "It would be easier if I showed you." He then set off into the library and beckoned the boy to follow. While he walked, he broke into an unexpected chant. "Darker than black, darker than pitch, darker than even the deepest abyss. There I feed, and there I grow, tugging at your heartstrings, just so. For you're so weak, I'll continue to hunt you even in your deepest sleep. When you let me in, your fate is sealed;

you're consumed by sin. For I am fear—I'm not your friend. Because of me, you'll meet your end." Harneth's words chilled the air.

Where did that come from? Visage wondered. Harneth halted, turned, and faced his visitor. "That is a verse from a very ancient script, and it has a lot to do with you." Harneth's imposing gaze caused Visage to cower. Though Harneth had no sight, Visage felt he was peering into the core of his very being. A little fearful, the young demon took several steps back. "What's going on? Why are you doing this to me?"

"That's easy, Visage. You see, I can read a being's mind, no matter how shielded it is. "And," he said while taking a knee, "I can also see into your heart... and what I see has me worried."

"You can see the same way I do? But I thought I was the only one!"

Harneth frowned. "I don't know how you see, Visage." He then moved his fingers up to his covered eyes. "But ever since the accident that took my vision, I've been allowed to see things that I had never before even imagined." His hand fell away from his face, and tears started to moisten his blindfold.

"I'm sorry you lost your vision, Harneth," Visage said, thinking that Harneth was reflecting on the pain from his injuries.

Harneth smiled. "No, Visage, I'm not crying because I lost my sight. I'm crying because of what I see inside of you." He pressed his hand to Visage's chest.

Visage rubbed the back of his head, unsure of what Harneth was getting at. *Is there something wrong with me?*

Harneth nodded his head. "Visage, I can see the seeds of fear in your heart."

Visage's eyes went wide. "But I'm not afraid—am I?"

"It looks as though you're afraid of what you might become," Harneth responded.

Visage frowned; he knew what Harneth had said was true. *If you had seen what Rashia showed me, you'd be afraid too.*

"I don't doubt it," Harneth said in response to Visage's unspoken words. "But the threads of fear have already begun to wind around your heart... And, if you're not careful, you'll become that which you fear, and I don't want that to happen." Harneth got back to his feet and headed for the far end of the library. "You have Riza and Vira; I can see that easily enough. You also have Lords Nosfaren, Baltrix, Barren, and even Glavian." Harneth turned his head but kept walking. "And now you have me." Though Visage couldn't see the grin on the librarian's face, he instinctively knew that it was there.

I wonder if he ever misses being able to see? Visage thought while he continued to follow the older boy.

Harneth laughed. "Nope. In fact, after I awoke from my accident, I could see everybeing for who he or she really was. Now that was a shock!" Harneth chuckled. "It took me a while to get used to not seeing, but now I can see better than ever!"

"Didn't the doctors try to fix your eyes? Le'Shara said the Marcisians fixed hers."

"Oh yes, they offered me the option... but I was afraid if I got my normal eyesight back, I wouldn't be able to see the way I do now—which, to me, is even better," Harneth replied.

"I guess that makes sense. Have you told anybeing else about your ability?"

"No, you're the first. Though most beings think I can still see, to some degree, only Lord Nosfaren and Lady Serishin have come close to discovering the truth," Harneth gloatingly stated.

Visage was surprised. *So, why did you tell me your secret?* he silently asked, realizing that his mental barrier was useless on this being.

Harneth shrugged. "It just seemed to be the right thing to do. I've never encountered anybeing who has the same visual ability that I do."

"Yeah, I know what you mean." Visage glanced up at the grinning blind man. "And I assure you, Lord Harneth, that your secret is safe with me."

The pair walked for several more dironns before reaching the back of the room, where there was another set of doors. But these doors were different. They were circular and had a diagonal slit running through them. *I've never seen doors like this before,* Visage thought. At the same time, Harneth accessed the inscription pad that was embedded into the wall to the right of the doors. After several keys were pressed in rapid succession, the doors opened, accompanied by the hiss of escaping gas.

"We keep the reliquary vacuum-sealed when it's not in use," Harneth offered before Visage could even utter his question. "Come on, there is something I want to show you." Visage could immediately tell, simply by the manner in which Harneth entered the room, how much the man revered it. Since he could sense a myriad of jumbled emotions emanating from the place, he was a little hesitant to enter. However, not wanting to disappoint Harneth, he made his way through the special doors and over to where the librarian was standing.

The library was grand, but the reliquary was even more so. There were two rows of shelves; the first lined all three of the far walls and the second was positioned several feet away from the first. The appearance, at the entrance, was of a box within a box, only with the tops cut off. Though the reliquary's architectural design was exquisite, it wasn't the primary reason why Visage was filled with wonderment. He was utterly enthralled by the ancient scrolls and artifacts that graced the shelves. He could literally *feel* the power exuding from these treasures. It was as though they were alive!

Harneth was standing in the center of the room in front of a large table, which was also blanketed with ancient artifacts. However, Visage quickly discerned that his attention was fully focused in on two, black, red-rune-covered, pyramidal objects. Though Visage could hear the librarian speaking, he was so short, even standing on his tiptoes, that he could barely see over the top of the table. Finally, he gave up and opted to use his indren'freth to levitate; he really wanted to see whatever it was that Harneth was so anxious to show him.

Harneth picked up one of the pyramidal objects and held it out for Visage to see. "Visage, do you know what this is?" The young Silvarian shook his head. Even though he had seen similar-looking things on Azala's desk, she hadn't explained what they were, nor had he asked.

"In the Marcisian tongue, they're called Imret'fethlen." Visage was completely confused. "And what does that mean?"

"Imret'fethlen translates into the common tongue as the image of souls, but they are more commonly referred to as holo-journals or holo-records."

That did not help, Visage thought as he looked from the two pyramids to Harneth, hoping for more insight.

"This isn't going very well." Harneth was obviously frustrated. In an effort to help the child understand what he was trying to share, he brought Visage's face close to his own with his free hand. Within moments, the two beings were inside the void, and Harneth started going through his memories. He showed Visage several things, but the most important one was how a holo-journal was made.

Visage winced at what he was seeing. A much younger Harneth was standing next to a black-clad being who was apparently his master. They were in a room much like the one he was sharing with Azala. Harneth's master was sitting at his desk with a black pyramid in front of him. After removing his glove from his hand, Harneth's master forcefully pressed his naked thumb down onto the point of the pyramid. Red blood flowed down the sides of the pyramid while, at the same time, he uttered a prayer or incantation in a language that Visage did not recognize. Once all of the runes were in place, The older man removed his still-bleeding thumb from the sharp point. He wrapped his thumb up with his gloved hand and sent a surge of dark energy through his thumb. The energy crackled and sparked before dissipating. When the man uncovered his thumb, it was completely healed! Visage was impressed! Then the vision faded, and Harneth released him. "Do you understand now, Visage?"

Visage thought for a moment before replying. "I'm still not sure."

"Think of it this way. These"—Harneth gestured to the holo-journals —"are created by using a combination of our blood, which is part of our own life force, and the Verse. You could say they contain a faux soul. That is why the Marcisians call them the 'image of souls'," he explained.

"That sounds really creepy and totally awesome at the same time! So why are these holo-journals so important?"

"Because these holo-journals belonged to my grandparents"—

Harneth picked up the second one from the table—"and I've decided to give them to you."

Visage was wide-eyed. "Can I really *have* these! Harneth, why you would ever give up such treasures?"

"Sorry but, I'm not really giving them up; I'm only lending them to you for a while. After all, they *are* part of the library. And I think you will find them very interesting." Harneth lowered his voice. "But you must treat them with great care. Do you understand?"

Visage responded in a reverential tone. "I understand, Harneth. I'll guard them with my life. And I promise to keep them in great shape!"

"I know you will, Visage. Oh, and take your time; my grandparents were both... well... chatter boxes, if you catch my drift."

"Yes, I do. And thank you so much, Harneth! I can't wait!"

At that point, Harneth escorted Visage out of the reliquary, put in the code, and locked the doors. Visage put the pair of holo-journals in his pocket since he didn't yet have a U-gem. Harneth started heading back to the library's entrance to prepare for new arrivals but was interrupted by another question from Visage. "Harneth, do you have any books on demons or Silvarian demons? I'd like to know...more about myself."

Harneth chuckled. "Kid, you are holding the Imret'fethlen that belonged to one of the greatest demonologists who ever existed. If you have questions about who you are, he's the one who can give you the answers."

"I sure hope you're right, because I have a lot of questions."

Suddenly, Harneth turned around and took off at a near run. He motioned for Visage to follow and yelled back, "Visage, come on! I have a book that might help you!"

Visage was hot on Harneth's heels when the librarian made a quick turn to the left and headed down one of the long isles. Stopping short, the man glared up at the shelf on his right. "I've managed to learn the resting places for most every book in the library. A great feat, even if I do say so myself. Now, let's see. Ah! It should be right up there." The book lifted off the second shelf from the top and floated gently down, landing in Harneth's hands. "Here," Harneth said, offering the book to Visage. "It's not much, but it will fill you in on the Marcisian Empire and the different species and races that have joined it in the last three hundred onns."

Visage was ecstatic! "I don't know how I'll ever repay you for all your help, Lord Harneth. Thank you! I'll start reading this the moment I get back to my room."

The two then headed back to the main entrance. Harneth took his place behind a desk, which was several yards long and located just to the left of the library entrance. Behind the desk were rows of shelves, which were packed with books and holo-journals. *That must be where they store the returns,* Visage thought.

"Visage, I have to sign out your items before you can leave the library." The boy was more than happy to oblige and made his way over to the desk. Harneth scanned the book and the two Imret'fethlen with his U-gem and handed them back to the boy. "Now, there really isn't any return date on the holo-journals, but the book has to be back in a mcronn."

Visage gave an emphatic nod. "Right—by next week." Harneth didn't understand what the word "week" meant, but trusted that his new friend had understood his directive.

"And, I almost forgot. This might come in handy." Harneth handed the boy a folded piece of paper.

"Oh, this is a map of the temple layout!" Visage beamed. "Thank you, Harneth!" I can really use this!" he enthusiastically replied before waving and heading off to the lifts. *Now I just have to figure out whether or not to go back to my room.*

Harneth eased his anxiety when he called out to him from the library entrance, "Don't worry Visage, if either Riza or Vira stops by, I'll let them know that you went to your room." *He'll definitely head straight to his room; there's no way he can resist getting into those journals.*

Visage grinned. *Harneth just met me, and he already knows exactly what I'll do.* He pressed the button to summon the lift, and while waiting, he opened his map; a three-dimensional image of the temple's interior popped up. By means of a small blue dot, the pyramid pinpointed his current location. The dot was blinking next to the lifts on the thirty-third level. Visage proceeded to think about where he wanted to go, and the map plotted the course! A red line went down the lift shaft, stopped on the twenty-fifth level, went down the hallway on the right, and stopped in front of the fifth room. *This isso cool!* Visage thought as the lift doors opened and he stepped in. When the doors closed, the map somehow communicated with the keypad, the buttons were automatically pressed, and he was on his way. His timing was perfect. Unbeknownst to him, the doors of the lift next to his opened just after his had closed, and a very perturbed-looking Chirras disembarked and headed for the library.

***

Harneth was busy logging in several books and Imret'fethlen, which had been dropped off by beings during the trell. He looked up to see who had entered, since he could feel a decidedly chilling presence.

"Why Chirras, gunrek menronn. You're up early." So far, Harneth had been able to hide the fact that he could see Chirras's blackened heart.

"Spare me your pleasantries, Harneth," the human female harshly complained. When she slammed the holo-journal onto the counter, a resounding bang echoed throughout the library. "I'm only here to drop this useless thing off and find some information." She had lowered her voice, but her tone was still harsh. Harneth shook his head, took the item from her, and logged it back into the system. Chirras put her elbow on the desk and leaned into it while crossing one foot over the other. "So, are you going to help me, librarian?" she sarcastically asked.

Harneth turned away for a moment, gritted his teeth, and swallowed hard before facing the woman again. "All right, Lad... sorry... Chirras, what is it that you need?" Unfortunately, he was unable to see Chirras's right eye twitch and a blood vessel bulge in her forehead—as though it were about to burst. However, through his unconventional gift of sight he was able to tell that his jab had obviously hit a nerve.

Chirras acted as though she had missed the librarian's cutting remark. "I need to find information about immortality," she hissed more than spoke through gritted teeth.

Harneth gaped at her request. "Do you need to know about gods... or demons?" he asked as his heart started to pound and several sirens went off in his head.

"No, I need to know how a mortal can become immortal!" She then leaned in so closely that Harneth thought she was trying to kiss him. He quickly backed up, not wanting the woman to see any of his recent thoughts. "Do I look like a fraking god worshipper!" Chirras bellowed.

Harneth shook his head. "No, you don't." He continued. "I'm sorry, Chirras, but there is only one way for a mortal being to become immortal: he—or she—must die." The embers in Chirras's eyes flared after hearing the truth. "I thought every being in the Empire knew that," Harneth muttered, ignoring the woman's rage and attempting to get back to work.

Chirras, however, was far from finished. She reached over the counter, grabbed Harneth by the front of his shirt, and pulled him in so closely that the pair could feel each other's breath. "I'm not playing games with you, blind boy. If you don't give me what I want, I promise that you won't live to see tononn." She spoke quietly, her evil-looking eyes narrowing to slits. Not yet finished with the librarian, she leaned over and whispered into his ear. "They'll never find your body, blind boy." Then she released the man and returned to her original position.

Harneth was frightened—and shocked. So much so that he broke out in a cold sweat and nearly lost his balance. He knew, considering the way her heart looked, that Chirras would actually do as she promised. After taking a moment to steady his nerves, he told her what she wanted to hear. "Listen, Chirras, there is one book that might have what you're looking for. However, another being has already checked it out."

Chirras narrowed her eyes again. "And just which being is it that has this book?" she asked Harneth in that sickeningly sweet threatening way of hers.

Harneth had to work to hold back a grin. "Lady Riza has it, and because she's on the Council, she can have it for as long as she wants."

He took great pleasure in seeing Chirras's face contort in anger. Right after she left the library, he thought, *don't let the door hit you in the crath on the way out, betrak!* After hearing the chime of the lift, he knew the coast was clear, but he still pressed his hand to his chest and let out a massive sigh of relief. "I'll have to report this to the Council." His heartbeat quickened at the sound of the lift doors opening once again. *Oh, frak, I hope she didn't hear me!* He breathed another sigh of relief when Cormack, the blue-skinned Twillan, came through the doors.

When Cormack entered the room, Harneth collapsed! Cormack ran to the counter and jumped over it, got to his knees, and peered at his blind friend. "Harneth, are you all right!"

"No, Cormack, I'm not."

The Twillan's anxiety level skyrocketed. He scrunched up his face and furrowed his narrow black eyebrows but calmed down right after he realized that his friend was alright. Though Harneth needed his help getting to his feet, the librarian was weak and had to lean against the counter for support. Cormack crossed his arms over his chest and glared at his friend. "Harneth, what's going on?"

Harneth was dying to tell his story but held back. "Cormack, I have to get to the Council Room immediately! The Councilors have to hear what Chirras is up to! Can you help me get there?"

At this point, Ferinin, a red-skinned Twillan female, sauntered in from the hallway and joined the pair. "Hi, guys, what's going on?" Immediately, she sensed the aura of anxiety—even fear—that was hanging heavily over the room.

Cormack turned to the older woman. "Feri, would you mind watching the library for a few dironns? It's really important."

Ferinin studied both beings before answering. "Nah, I don't mind. You guys go ahead." Though she was concerned about what had happened to her friends, she managed to force a smile onto her dark-gray lips.

"Thanks, Feri, I owe you one!" Cormack yelled back while at the same time assisting Harneth with rounding the counter and making his way over to the exit.

Feri, who still had her eyes on the pair, was unable to contain her curiosity. "Hey, guys, what happened?"

The two didn't stop, but Harneth did turn his head to answer. "Let's just say I had a little run-in with Chirras, and now I have to go and report it to the Council."

Fully aware of the Council's mandate for everybeing at or above the rank of a knight to keep tabs on the disowned Councilor, Ferinin was now extremely anxious for Harneth and Cormack to get on their way.

"You'd better hurry," Ferinin urged. "I heard that the Council already had one emergency meeting earlier tederonn, and few dironns ago, Riza called for another one. You can probably catch the Councilors if you get there soon!" she yelled. The Twillan then walked over to the counter, stood where Chirras had stood, and leaned back against the wood. She flopped her twills over her shoulder in order to protect them from being squished and then gazed up at the ceiling. *That woman will be the death of us all if we aren't careful. God help us all if Chirras turns out to be a Skath worshiper.*

29

Ik'thorian Puzzle Box

The Zaharaj Council members were gathered in their chambers once again. Lord Nos was intrigued, as were most others. Riza had brought in an Ik'thorian puzzle box, which had belonged to a Zaharaj woman who had died nearly three hundred onns ago. Zoric and Serishin were giddy with anticipation and wanted to open the box immediately. Lord Nosfaren rebuked the pair regarding their impatience and, to a degree, their irreverence. He informed them of the delicate nature of the situation that was now before the Council. However, Michael cavalierly brushed aside his admonishment.

"I'm getting tired of all of these meetings, Lord Nos," Michael unabashedly shared. He rested his chin on his fist and leaned so heavily into it that it created an indentation.

"The meetings can't be helped, Michael. After all, we are members of the Zaharaj Council, so this is our job," Barren countered.

Michael—who was obviously bored—scoffed in return. "Really! All of you are about to jump out of your skins because some old dead lady gave her little trinket to the Silvarian kid. Shouldn't we be training and preparing for when the Skath return—not wasting our time on ancient history!"

Fenrir offered a brash response to his pouting friend. "You really can be a downer sometimes, Lord Michael."

"I think you mean all the time," Sharas muttered under her breath, causing Barren to chuckle.

"In any case, I have to wonder why all of these issues are cropping up at this particular time," Lord Nosfaren frowned while glancing at the offending box in Riza's hands, briefly giving pause to the chattering of the other beings in the room.

"Does it really matter?" Michael interjected without as much as a hint of care in his voice.

"Of course it matters!" Lady Serishin shot back. "You should try using your head for something besides combat, Michael!" She jumped to her feet. "Take a look around you! Do you really think we should be spending every waking dironn preparing for a Skathic invasion? Do you think God feels that way? Do you honestly believe He would have us care about battle preparations—and nothing else?" She marched over to her fellow council member, grabbed him by his black mithril weave shirt, and got right into his face. Her eyes took on the appearance of fire, and she menacingly asked, "Well, Lord Michael!"

Michael was surprised at the woman's outburst, but deep down inside, he knew she was right. "I'll take that as a no!" She heard him grunt after she shoved him hard back into his chair. She then turned on her heels and marched back to her own seat. *I can't believe how much of an id'rth he can be at times!*

While the two Councilors finished their small sparring match, Riza was gingerly holding the puzzle box in her lap and rubbing her hand over the intricate design on the cover. Except for the area where the design was carved, the box felt as smooth as glass. "I agree with Nos on this one. It is rather strange that things appear to be moving at such a rapid pace." She peered over at Zoric, who frowned when he noticed her stare. "Perhaps you could consult your prophetess or seer on your home world for us, Lord Zoric? Could one of them ask Eendril why such haste? Or even what's going on?"

Zoric's brow furrowed while he closed his eyes and thought about her proposition. "No, Lady Riza. I don't think it wise for me to ask such questions." He shut his eyes once again and folded his arms. "It's unlikely that they would even see me, considering I'm a member of the Zaharaj; they really don't care much for beings of darkness."

"That's true, Zoric... but wait! What about the Marcisian prophets? Could they help us find out what's going on?" Riza had directed her question more at Lord Nos than any being else.

Lord Nos shook his head. "I don't know if that's such a good idea, either, Riza."

"Riza, you're a demoness; why couldn't you go to see Eendril and ask Him yourself?" Barren asked.

Riza rubbed the top of the puzzle box and gazed at the floor. "I can't," she replied.

Serishin then jumped into the conversation. "Why's that? I mean, aren't you Meserino demons like Eendril's children because of the war?"

"Yes we are, but that's not the reason." She was thankful when Nosfaren intervened.

"It's because demons in general aren't allowed to step foot inside Eendril's place of residence—at least not without an invitation." He sighed. "Unfortunately, Kolob is off-limits to us demons."

"Ah yes, good point," Serishin conceded.

"Perhaps not, iloni!" Ali'stia excitedly stated to her husband. Nosfaren raised a quizzical eyebrow. "I've heard that His Majesty has been invited to Eendril's court to celebrate the anniversary of the end of the war." She then looked hopeful. "Perhaps we could ask him if we could attend with him."

Everybeing in the room was astonished. "That might actually work!" Lord Nos exclaimed, but his excitement quickly waned. "Unfortunately, however, I don't think King Zareth would agree to ask Eendril anything."

"Are you joking! I don't think my ber'nan would even consider *going* to Eendril's gathering!" Riza cried.

Vira thought about the lazy demon who had somehow wound up becoming the Meserino king before chiming in, "That is so true, Riza."

"Just leave him to me," Nos confidently stated.

"Really, Lord Nos? Are you actually going to try to convince my lazy ber'nan to attend the Council of the Gods?" Riza was shocked. *I didn't think you wanted anything more to do with the Meserino.* Nos read the demoness's thoughts. He gave her a wry smirk and a wink.

Everybeing could see that Ali'stia was ecstatic at the prospect of returning home. She hadn't seen her family for eons. However, rather than shouting with glee, she suddenly developed a rather peculiar facial expression.

Ranic was a bit worried. "Is there something wrong, Ali'stia?"

Ali'stia was so deep in thought that she remained silent. She was hiding her thoughts behind such a strong mental barrier, not even her husband could read them. Every councilor was on edge, wondering what was going on inside her head. The tension reached its peak right before Ali'stia broke her silence.

"So, do you think this was part of Eendril's plan all along... in order to get my husband to return home?" Her question hung in the air.

Baltrix was the one who voiced the group's thoughts. "That's probably true, Ali'stia. It's very likely that this whole ordeal was part of His plan from the beginning!" Baltrix jumped up, walked to the center of the room, and gestured widely, holding out both arms. "Just think about it! First, Lady Riza sends Lord Nosfaren to Earth to pick up Visage! Then Chirras turns out to be a deser'rec! Then Visage receives an Ik'thorian puzzle box from a long-ago-dead Zah! And now Lord Nosfaren is being forced—or at least heavily influenced—into going back to Demeros! Then, to top it all off, the delegation from Marcisia is going to be arriving tononn!" Baltrix dropped his arms. "And you think all of this is simply mere coincidence?" he asked. His tone was solemn. Everybeing on the council agreed that his observations were sound.

"But why would Eendril do all of this—especially now that Skath is gone and his followers have long since retreated?" Vira asked. Every councilor struggled to come up with an answer.

Baltrix shook his head. "I don't know. But what I do know is that our God has a hand in all of our lives, whether we like it or not." His eyes fell on his friend. "Lord Nos, perhaps you could ask Him when you see Him." Falling silent once again, Baltrix returned to his seat. His words gave everybeing something to ponder.

Several dironns passed before Lord Nosfaren rose from his seat. "If there is no further business, I will end this meeting. Lord Fenrir, would you please lead us in our oath?"

"I'd be honored, Lord Nosfaren." Fenrir took out his blood sorjin and started the council members off. "Peace is fleeting, so I thirst for knowledge." After Fenrir finished the first verse, the others brought out their own sorjins and joined in on the recitation. Once the meeting was officially adjourned, the attendees started mingling about. Several of the councilors began to discuss the box, which had been entrusted to Riza—at least for the time being. Baltrix was busy telling Barren and Michael about his theory regarding Eendril's interventions. Serishin finished her conversations and was headed for the doors when, suddenly, they flew open. All talk ceased. A very grave looking Cormack walked in, accompanied by an extremely weakened Harneth.

"Of course!" Lord Michael rolled his eyes. "What now! What else can possibly happen!"

Cormack glanced around the council room, making sure that all of the councilors were present. "Sorry, Master, but you need to see this."

Harneth let go of his friend's supporting shoulder and stood, tentatively, on his own. "I have something to show you." He didn't even give the attendees time to get back to their seats before bringing them all inside the void.

"Now that's how a Silvarian should look!" Serishin almost shouted after viewing Harneth's meeting with Visage. Riza and Vira both gave Serishin sharp glances before having to admit that she was right.

Michael was the one who grumbled the most while he watched Harneth and the young Silvarian's exchange. "What's the big deal? We already know that Visage has limited knowledge regarding his heritage and history."

Momentarily out of the void, Harneth telepathically relayed, *What I really wanted you to see is yet to come.*

Michael's eyes narrowed when Harneth's thoughts commanded the attention of everybeing. The councilors all smiled while watching the happy Silvarian leave the library with two very precious holo-journals and one large book. However, the smiles quickly turning to scowls when Chirras arrived on the scene. After watching Harneth and Chirras's confrontation, Michael and Baltrix's hands moved to the hilt of their blood sorjins. Nobeing was happy. Right after Harneth released all of the beings from the void, Michael blatantly announced, "That does it! Lord Forscythe's plan be damned—we need to kill Chirras—now!" Fenrir, Serishin, and Glavian nodded in agreement. "Any being who defiles my library deserves death!" Glavian shouted angrily. "So I agree with Michael in this case!"

"I second!" Serishin exclaimed, giving the master librarian a quick nod.

Even Lord Nosfaren was taken aback by what he had just witnessed; he now realized that Chirras was a greater threat than he had previously surmised. While he was going over the whole scenario and the council's possible next steps, Ali'stia responded to the inflammatory suggestions that were already on the table.

"Quiet, all of you! We can't move on Chirras, yet!" She raised her hand, quickly silencing the onslaught of dissenting voices. "We will deal with Chirras, but we'll have to wait until after the visit from the Marcisian delegation." She gave Riza a quick glance and received an approving nod from her fellow Meserino. "Besides, Riza has the book that Chirras is after, which gives us the advantage." She then flashed a menacing smile, causing several of the councilors to shiver. Almost to a being, the councilors thought, *Chirras has drathed off the wrong being.*

Lord Forscythe piped up. "I've been working hard on my plan. But now I'm wondering if we should use the book as the bait instead of our Silvarian friend. What do you think about that?"

The newly proposed plan got Lord Nos's attention. "That sounds like it might work!" He glanced at the four councilors who had had the loudest complaints, smiled, and voiced his decision. "Lord Forscythe, I want you to work with Lords Michael, Baltrix, and Glavian, as well as with Lady Serishin. Your mission is to trap that deser'rec using the book as bait! I want no mistakes!" After giving the assignees a deathly glare, he continued. "We Zaharaj will not tolerate deser'recs in our organization!" The cheer from the council room was so resounding that it caught the attention of beings from other levels of the structure.

With their second meeting of the deronn adjourned, the members of the council started to disperse. However, Nos was not finished with Riza and Vira. "Riza, Vira, I need to speak with you for a dironn."

"Yes, Lord Nos, what is it?" Riza asked as she shuffled the box around and tucked it into the crook of her left arm.

Nos leaned back in his chair and studied the demonesses. His red eyes shifted back and forth from Riza to Vira several times before he firmed up his decision. His first directive was aimed at Vira. "Vira, I need you to look after our resident Silvarian."

Vira glanced at Riza and back at Nos. Honestly confused, she responded, "I don't know what you mean, Lord Nosfaren."

Nos let out a small sigh of frustration. "Weren't you paying attention, Vira?" He spoke again before she had the chance to answer. "Chirras is going after Visage. Therefore, I need you to keep your eye on your fiancé at all times." Nos's voice now took on a more commanding tone. "So he'll be your roommate starting tendronn. Do I make myself clear?" Vira's eyes went wide. She wanted to jump for joy! Riza, on the other hand, vehemently protested. "Hey! Why does he get to stay with Vira! Why can't he stay with me!" Her tail swayed rapidly behind her, clearly demonstrating the level of her discontent.

Nos was trying hard to come up with an answer to Riza's complaint when Vira came to his rescue. "Come on, Riza, how could you even ask that, considering the current state of your room?" Riza, who was borderline livid, glared at her friend, but Vira was not deterred. "Honestly, I'm surprised you can find anything in that mess!"

Riza made her rebuttal. "My room isn't a mess it's just... in a state of organized chaos!" she exclaimed with a triumphant smile on her face. Vira merely shook her head. Even Nos groaned.

"Riza, until you get your chaos under control and Chirras has been dealt with, Visage will be staying with Vira." Nos then turned to Vira. "So, Vira, I suggest you go and fetch your fiancé. And Riza, I suggest you do something about that room of yours. Even a blortworm would protest living in such conditions. Now, if you'll excuse me, I need to get back to my office."

Once Nos had departed, Vira turned to her sour-looking friend. *It pays to keep one's room clean,* she mentally chided. Riza shot back a glare that would have made any other being squirm. Vira quietly giggled to herself before heading out to convey the bad news to Azala.

Riza rolled her eyes. *It's not a mess; it's organized chaos!* she mentally whined before she chased after Vira. "I can still come over to see him, right Vira? Right?" Though her voice was raised, Vira ignored her. "Come on, Vira, I know you can hear me!" By this point, she was talking so loudly that beings several levels below could hear her.

After the lift doors opened, Vira turned and faced her fellow demoness. "I'm sorry, Riza, did you say something?" Riza didn't know if Vira had been too engaged in mulling over Nosfaren's bombshell of a decision to have heard her or if she was still messing with her. Stepping into the lift next to the still-beaming Veserino, she concluded that it was probably the former.

***

Vira was getting more and more nervous when the lift descended to the floor where Lord Baltrix was teaching his ar'teths. "What's wrong, Vira?" Riza had seen her fellow demoness anxiously clenching and unclenching her fists and was now starting to worry.

What do I tell him when I see him? Vira mentally pleaded as she stared at Riza through fear-filled eyes.

"What do you mean?" Riza was perplexed.

"I mean about how hard we had to fight in order to save his soul. Vira's thoughts made Riza uneasy, since she was able to recall the time to which Vira was referring as though it were yederonn.

***

Vira was closely holding her precious cargo, protecting it with one hand while wielding her weapon that took the shape of a spear and fending off attackers with the other. Riza was also fighting for her life—defending herself from several Meserino demons. At first, she attempted to plead with them, trying only to defend herself. However, their leader made the mistake of sneering at her and baring his fangs. This enraged the demoness. She clenched her teeth, held her great scythe over her head, tapped into her infinite indren'freth, and burst into flames of black and red.

"For Skath!" the leader of the Ze'therac clan yelled as the other traitors raised their own voices: "Send the abomination into nothingness!" This caused both the Meserino and Veserino's eyes to blaze; they knew all hope of negotiation was gone. As a result, six Ze'therac Meserino demons were erased from existence. Vira's weapon ate two of their souls, and Riza's great scythe devoured the other four.

***

After shaking off the memories and assuring Vira that she was 'Alright,' Riza exited the lift. However, Vira persisted, asking her fellow demoness again if she was all right.

"I'm fine, Vira!" she snapped. Now even more annoyed, Riza raised her eyes to the ceiling and peered at the Zaharaj architecture. "As for that other thing—don't tell Visage what happened." She turned her head to her friend. "It's in the distant past. I don't see any need to place such a burden on him now, do you?" Vira slowly shook her head in agreement. Riza sighed. "Soon Chaos will be freed, and the wounds of the war can finally begin to heal; all will be right with the universe in all of its infinite dimensions." She stretched her arms and interlocked her fingers behind her head. Both demonesses now smiled widely as they looked forward to a bright future.

***

When Vira opened the door to the lecture hall, Baltrix didn't seem surprised to see her—or Riza. He simply turned his head and glanced up at Azala, beckoning her to come to the front. "Azala, I believe that Riza and Vira are here to tell you something." Azala responded nervously. Her footfalls seemed to echo quite loudly, even though the stairs were carpeted. She was obviously perspiring while she stood in front of the two demonesses; they were imposing enough by themselves, but together they were a force that even God himself would have a hard time reckoning with.

Riza gazed down at the Twillan. "Azala," she said, crossing her arms under her chest, "we came here to tell you that Visage will be living with Vira from now on." The announcement was loud enough for every ar'teth to hear.

Azala stood motionless, as though she had not quite heard Riza's words. "Alright. Wait! What!" She was dazed. "But why!" she cried after she tried to make sense of Riza's pronouncement.

Vira stepped forward. "Chirras is after him!" she blurted, again speaking loudly. Instantly, murmuring was rampant amongst the ar'teths.

Ranic jumped up from his seat. "But why would Chirras go after a Silvarian!"

Baltrix grunted, and then responded. "That is something we can't tell you; we don't even have the answer ourselves."

"This fraking sucks!" Arisha shouted in frustration. "I'm losing my rival because of some Skath worshiping blortworm?"

Nate chimed in. "Hey, Arisha, that's an insult to all blortworms!"

"Frak me, Nate! Then what do you want me to call her?" Arisha snidely responded.

Azala clenched her fist. "She's a fraking deser'rec is what she is!" Every other being fell silent.

"Is what Azala just said true, Master Baltrix? Is Chirras really a deser'rec?" Ranic asked, cutting through the blanket of silence.

The trio of councilors had known that they could not keep Chirras's status as a traitor secret forever. In addition, Lord Baltrix knew that Azala had not purposely discussed Chirras in front of the entire class. Nevertheless, the feelings of anger and frustration exuding from the young demoness were palpable. Riza had already knelt down and was attempting to calm the girl.

"All right, ar'teths, I'm going to see how well you can keep a secret," Baltrix stated. He was the immediate recipient of a backlash of glairs from both Vira and Riza.

No, Baltrix! Don't do it! Vira mentally pleaded.

I'm sorry, Vira, but this is the only way, he messaged back, wearing a noticeable frown. After closing his eyes, Baltrix opened his mind and brought everybeing in the room inside his head. "I'm going to show you what happened to Visage on his way back to his room." He glanced at Vira and Riza who, though they didn't like having the young ones see Visage and Chirras's meeting, also knew that somebeing would confront Chirras if he or she was not fully aware of the situation. So, reluctantly, they gave their approval for Lord Baltrix to proceed. The ar'teths then observed the unfolding of the entire hallway scene. Many gasps and awes were expressed before the scenario ended as quickly as it had begun.

"My dar'nra is going to seriously kick Chirras's crath!" Arisha announced while she slammed her fist into her palm.

"Why hasn't the Council done anything about Chirras besides stripping her of her title, Master?" Ranic asked Baltrix. Baltrix responded with a shake of his head.

Riza piped up. "Because we don't know how many beings like Chirras there are! This whole mess is extremely frustrating."

"So, we're setting up a trap for Chirras and her friends," Baltrix adamantly related. He tightly gripped his blood sorjin and gave his listeners a wicked smile.

"Is there anything we can do to help!" Moonreth shot up from his seat and cried, his eyes gleamed with vigorous enthusiasm.

"I want to help, too," Le'Shara said more quietly than Moonreth. The councilors were humbled when all of the ar'teths stood and voiced their support.

Arisha jumped back into the conversation. "I'll have to tell dar'nra to hurry his plans! I want my fraking rival back! And I won't let some fraking deser'rec bakrath take him from me!" Riza and Vira were quite surprised by the young demoness's display of determination. She even defiantly crossed her arms under her chest.

"My my, Arisha, it sounds like you have feelings for my fiancé," Vira eyed her with a smirk.

Riza narrowed her eyes at her long time friend. "I think you meant to say *our* fiancé, right Vira?"

Vira rolled her eyes in answer.

"No! It's nothing like that!" Arisha protested ignoring Riza's blatant sarcasm. Everybeing in the lecture hall started laughing—definitely lightening the mood.

"I'm sorry, Lord Baltrix, but we have to leave," Vira said. "Come on, Riza; we've got to get going." Before getting Riza's response, the demoness headed for the door.

Riza grabbed Azala's arm and gave her a reassuring squeeze. When Azala winced, she quickly let go. "I'm so sorry, Azala, I forgot about your bruises."

Azala didn't seem to care. "Not a problem Lady Riza." Riza turned to leave, but looked back when Azala added, "Keep an eye on him for me. He can be a handful sometimes."

Vira smiled. "Don't worry, Azala, we've got it covered."

Once the doors closed, the conversation became all about Chirras and the possible reasons why she would be interested in the Silvarian demon. Baltrix threw his hands in the air in mock surrender. "Well, I've lost this one!"

***

Vira took a deep breath before entering Azala's room. When the doors slid open, she hesitatingly stepped forward. Her presence immediately caught Visage's attention, and he tore himself away from the book that Harneth had given him from the library. Though his mask was covering his face, his body language indicated he was a bit surprised to see her. "Hi, Vira... What's going on?" he asked in a sweet, metallic-sounding voice.

"I'm here to pick you up, Visage," Vira gingerly announced.

Visage slumped into the chair so hard that it rocked a bit. He then turned his head to the side and flashed an inquisitive look at Vira. "Am I in trouble again?"

Vira laughed. "No, you're not in trouble." She bent down and pressed the button on Visage's earpiece; she wanted the mask to vanish so she could see his face. Then, she dragged a chair over so they could talk. "Visage, the Council has suspended the plan involving you and Chirras." She started to explain, Visage went wide-eyed.

"Really! That's great! No! Wait... hold on a dironn!" After folding his arms in front of his chest, he uttered, with a hint of defiance, "There's a catch, isn't there?"

Vira meagerly nodded. "But don't worry, it's nothing bad," she added, attempting to downplay the actual gravity of the situation. "You see, the Council has decided that one of us should keep our eye on you, just in case Chirras gets any... ideas." Visage seemed confused by Vira's words. *What the frak is she trying to say?* He narrowed his now intensely glowing sapphire eyes at his fiancée. Vira continued on, seemingly unaware of Visage's unspoken concern. "So, you're going to be staying with me in my room!" Vira excitedly told him with a wide smile.

Visage balked—not sure what to think. Finally, he mustered the will to ask. "But what about Azala?"

Vira turned her head and glanced at the cluttered desk in the corner. Her voice lowered a bit, but she managed a reasonably upbeat reply. "She'll be fine Visage. It's only been a few deronns, so I'm sure she won't even notice that you're gone."

"Alright, Vira." Visage let out a lengthy sigh. "I guess you're right. So, when do I leave?"

"Right now!" The demoness relatively jumped up from the bed and began to gather up Visage's belongings—including the precious book borrowed from Harneth.

"Shouldn't we at least tell Azala that I'm leaving?"

"Don't worry, Riza and I already told her about the plan." Vira was silent for a moment before continuing. "She was upset at first, but, once she realized the logic behind Lord Nos's decision, she knew that this is the best way to keep you safe."

"It figures that she would be upset. I mean, when I arrived, she was one of my first friends," Visage emotionally offered, shifting the warm ball, which he was now cradling in his arms.

Vira felt his thoughts. "Don't worry, V, this arrangement is temporary."

"I know, but it still makes me sad."

After giving Visage a consoling hug, the demoness and her companion headed for her room. Within dironns, they arrived. The room was similar to the one Visage was sharing with Azala; the only real difference was the location of the desks and refresher. Vira's desk and bed were to the left of the room's door, and Visage's was to the right, near the refresher. However, Visage didn't care about the setup of the room; he was fully engaged in trying to process his mixed emotions about the whole mess. *This is great! First I get picked up by Lord Nos; then I get this Vorihelcom seal slapped on my back; and, to top it all off, I get some psycho, power mad, crazy bitch who wants me for who knows what reason after me! And now I have to live with Vira so said woman can't hurt me! Oh, and I still need to find Chaos's missing wife! How can all this have happened—and still be happening! I'm only a kid!* He silently complained when he entered the room. Once inside, he shook his head and ignored Vira, who was lying on her bed, chuckling about his inner thoughts. After carefully setting his precious ball down onto the empty bed and positioning it just right so it wouldn't roll off, he set the pair of holo-journals from his cargo pants' pocket onto his new desk. Finally, he could get back to doing what he'd been so anxious to do. He scooped up the book—the one Harneth had lent him—from Vira's bed. "Vira, are you all done having a chuckle at my expense... yet?"

"I'm sorry, Visage, it's just that what you were thinking was really quite amusing."

"Vira, you may think my thoughts were funny, but you're used to being around gods and demons... and... and... all of this stuff. But, to me, this is all pretty overwhelming—and scary!" He let out a grunt, fell into his chair, and spun it until he was facing her again.

Vira shuffled herself around, so she was sitting on the edge of her bed with her tail hanging down on her right side. *It's not so bad once you get used to it, Visage,* she telepathically shared, smiling widely.

"And how long does that take?"

"It's different from being to being. It could take anywhere from rinonns to eons. That's what's so great about being immortal; we have all the time in the universe!"

"I hope that's a good thing," Visage quipped. Vira followed up with another slight laugh. *Vira has such a great laugh and pretty voice—and Riza's is nice too.* At that, Vira's face turned a much brighter blue. *Damn it, I keep forgetting to put up my mental barrier!*

"Sorry, Vira, I didn't mean to embarrass you like that."

Vira aggressively shook her head in response to the boy's comments. "Visage, I don't mind you thinking of me that way. Trust me, when everybeing seals off his or her mind, things get really boring." She stared at him with a toothy grin. "Your mind is so open, and everything is so new to you. It's... well... like a breath of fresh air!" she exclaimed.

"I don't know about that. Some beings think I'm annoying—especially Arisha." Vira started laughing again at Visage's thought about the loud-mouthed demoness.

"That might be true, but I don't think you're annoying."

Visage smirked. "You're one of the few, Vira. I think even Baltrix has gotten tired of my questions. And Ranic seems a bit annoyed with me, too."

"I think it's ironic that Ranic, of all beings, could find *anybeing* annoying."

"Yeah, that's true; he definitely has an overzealous personality," Visage tapped his chin in thought. "I wonder where he gets it from. His dar'nra is so mellow."

"I don't know." Vira hid her snicker behind her hand. "That is one of our temple's greatest mysteries."

"Really?"

"Really." Vira quickly replied. "Zoric is definitely laidback, and his wife is even more laidback than he is. Nobeing has any idea where Ranic's overly affectionate and outgoing personality came from. For a time, Zoric was considering sending him to the Empire to be checked for a neurological problem—but he decided against it. The healers here couldn't find anything wrong with him, and Lord Nosfaren said it was best not to put him through any more tests." Vira then narrowed her eyes, cautiously looked around the room in order to make sure they were alone, and whispered, "But I heard Lord Nos say that Ranic was probably given to Zoric and Farina by God in order to provide them with a little excitement in their lives." She grinned and wiggled her eyebrows a bit.

Visage chuckled. "That's probably truer than everybeing thinks. Just look where God put me!" Vira had to agree. After contemplating for a moment over Vira's comments and his own situation, Visage asked, "Do all gods have a strange sense of humor, or is it only ours?"

Vira lay on her back and began to stretch. "I don't think there's a god out there who has the same sense of humor as Eendril. And He's definitely the kindest God that I know." She smiled widely as she thought about everything Eendril had done for her race. "Visage?" she asked.

"Yes, Vira?"

"Did you know that, after the war with Skath ended, it was none other than Eendril who took us in?" Visage had heard this before but could not remember who had told him. "Yes, I think so... Why?" Vira now had his full attention.

"Did you also know that Eendril was the only God who wanted us? I mean, there were lots of gods and angels who were involved in the war, but Eendril was the only God who not only decided He would deal with our kind but went so far as to adopt all of us." By now, tears had welled up in the demoness's eyes. "That's how much Eendril ilonied us, Visage. Even we demons are"— She couldn't continue. Sensing Vira's mind in such turmoil, Visage shocked her by walking over and getting up onto her lap. Though Vira was touched by his kind gesture, she continued to be overcome by thoughts from the past. She hugged him tightly and cried.

"It's all right, Vira," Visage whispered.

The demoness calmed down but didn't want to let Visage go. *It's been forever since I've held him, and now he's no longer just a soul—he has a corporeal form.* She clutched him a bit tighter, feeling his warmth flow through her entire being. *I have missed this feeling.* Her thoughts were interrupted by his whispered plea.

"Ugh. Vira, if you're all right now, would you please let me go?" Vira groaned a bit in protest before she reluctantly complied.

She watched, Visage head back to his chair, opened his book, and pulled out the mask from his pants pocket. The metal formed over his face, and he began to read. She continued to watch him for several dironns before deciding she needed to get her own work done. After reluctantly getting off her bed, she made her way over to her desk and shuffled several papers around. She then read and signed them and put them into proper order.

Even as advanced as the Marcisians are, they still preferred paper to the more convenient electronic format, especially when it came to official documentation. I'm glad paperwork like this is rare. At least I can use my U-gem to sign my name. She let out a long lamenting sigh. A narrow green beam emitted from the gem and burned her name into the top sheet of paper, precisely on the dotted line. Quite satisfied, she put the paper into her stack, took out her book, and started to read.

***

Visage finished the first twenty or so pages of his book. The title was written in small print along the top of every other page: *The Marcisian Empire: Its Development and the Adoption of Other Races.* He determined that the book, though it had a lot of valuable information, was actually rather dated, since it indicated that the Empire covered only fifty-two percent of the galaxy. In Baltrix's class, he had learned that the Empire now covered seventy-five percent of the galaxy. *Wow, the Empire surely has grown.* Visage thought in wonder before he turned back to the task at hand. *I guess I'd better skip through some of these pages and see if I can find the part where it talks about the different races.* The Silvarian was surprised to find that the races weren't even mentioned until he was close to the end of the book. "Oh! Here it is!"

Humans: People (beings as opposed to gods, animals, or machines) who comprise over ninety percent of the Empire and are referred to by the Marcisians as "Enrec'chendrel." In the common tongue, "Enrec'chendrel" translates into God's favored children. These beings are created in God's own image and are the largest group of His creations to be seeded. They are found in their own galaxy as well as throughout Eendril's universe. Human colonies can be found on most of the planets in the Firaxian galaxy, but their inhabitants are still in their fledgling stages and are not technologically advanced enough to join the Empire.

Humans are classified into different races, based on their physical/inherited characteristics like skin color, bone structure, etc. They are also grouped based on their ethnicity: religion, culture, and nationality. Age, gender, weight, and many other factors also separate humans from each other and prevent them from reaching the eternal goals that others within the universe have managed to obtain. If acrimony among the differing groups continues, the future of Eendril's most favored children will not be bright.

Visage had to agree with the author on that one. He smiled at the kindness that his family and his father's Navy friends had shown him, but the smile quickly turned into a grimace when he thought about the kids at school who had grabbed his tails, twisted them, and called him a freak and monster. *I guess the humans who joined the Empire are more like Dad and the other Navy guys. At least I hope so.*

After turning the page, Visage was shocked—almost elated—to see the sketch of a Twillan male in the upper right hand corner. Without hesitation, he dove back into what he expected to be the fascinating words to come:

Twillans: This race of bipeds has a very long history. Twillans were the first race in the Empire at large to travel in starships.

"That's amazing! Really?"

Twillan culture and society revolve around the worship of the same deity worshipped by the Marcisians and most human societies. However, the Twillans are part demon. The Empire first encountered them when exploring the far reaches of the Tetherl arm. At the outset, the encountered beings were thought to be some new form of demon, since they possessed several demon-like features. However, after much research, Marcisian scientists proved their theory to be true. They found that Twillans had trace amounts of either Meserino or Veserino genes—or both. Apparently, skin color is the one distinguishing characteristic. What's even more surprising is, even though red-skinned and blue-skinned Twillans intermarry, their offspring only have one skin color. Cases where blue-skinned and red-skinned Twillans have produced offspring with both skin colors are extremely rare! This phenomenon has baffled even the most renowned Marcisian scholars. To this deronn, no determination has been made as to which parent carries the dominant gene. The Twillans no matter their skin pigmentation have upbeat natures.

The other strange thing about Twillan society is its lack of any sort of government. Twillans run their territories like giant corporations. What is stranger still is that a laborer, through hard work, can progress to the point of managing an entire territory! Twillans vote the current territorial heads out if they don't keep the great gears of industry turning a profit. On Raxia, the Twillans' home world, or, as they call it, their capital (of finance), one of the industry heads had to step down when a couple of Twillan workers came forth with some bold and refreshing new ideas and were able to oust him from his position. Needless-to-say, the Twillans were thrilled when they received the offer to join the Empire. Joining provided them with the opportunity to expand their industries throughout the galaxy.

Visage tilted his head back. *The Twillan's are an amazing race! I bet Grandpa Do-Woon and Uncle John, would die if they knew the Twillans have industries throughout our entire galaxy!* He stretched a bit before continuing to read.

On one of the planets out on the fringes of the Galaxy. There are a group of Twillans who don't worship the same deity as the Marcisians or the humans. Instead, they worship the demons to whom they are related, even though the demon king, King Zareth, finds their behavior disturbing and has asked them to "cease and desist." However, Eendril is not concerned. He said He will teach them the truth after they leave their mortal lives. In the meantime, King Zareth will continue to get a grand headache from receiving the prayers from all of these wayward Twillans; he doesn't understand how Eendril survives this practice.

Vira's reading was interrupted by Visage's sudden outburst of laughter. "So what's so funny over there, Visage?"

"I... can totally... picture... King Zareth rubbing... his temples in frustration... whenever those Twillans... pray to him!" Visage found it hard to get the words out since he was still bear hugging his chest in an attempt to prevent a muscle strain from his hearty laughter.

I don't know what to make of him. Vira got up from her chair and stood over the Silvarian, who was just starting to settle down. She glanced at the book, quickly glossed over the page he had been reading, and frowned after she read what she thought had caused his hysterics.

"Visage, you shouldn't laugh at anybeing's religious beliefs... even if they are a bit misguided."

Visage got off the floor and shook his head. "No, Vira, that's not it. I... I could see Zareth on his throne and... Ugh. Never mind, I'll just show you!" With that, he jumped up, grabbed Vira around her neck, and brought her in for a kiss. Before Vira could react, they were inside the void. Vira could see the image of King Zareth lazing on his throne, using his fingers to rub his temples in circular motions and holding his eyes closed; he was wincing from the never-ending complaints that were being beamed into his head. Even Vira could not constrain herself from bursting into laughter.

"All right, I agree. That actually was pretty funny, but you should warn me before you start laughing your crath off." She gave Visage a light flick to his forehead.

"I have no idea how I can do that, Vira. When I think something is funny, I laugh. It's not like there's a warning system for laughter... is there?" Vira went to sit in her chair and turned it so she was facing him.

"Not that I know of—but there really should be," she added with a wink and a smirk.

Visage knew she was kidding, so he shrugged and went back to reading. "Sorry for disturbing you Vira. I honestly didn't mean to."

"Nah. It's fine. Don't worry about it. I'll get back to my book now."

Visage turned the page of his own book. Staring at him from the top right corner was the strangest looking creature he had ever seen. It was tall, standing upright on spindly-looking legs. Its body was long and slender. Very insect-like, it seemed to be a cross between an ant and a mantis. Its two eyes jutted out from its elongated head, which was adorned with two horns and a pair of antennae. It also had a pair of mandibles near its mouth. The insectoid appeared to be rubbing its upper set of limbs together as if it were washing them or perhaps praying; Visage couldn't decide which. A second pair of limbs jutted out from its body right under the first. The creature was holding an open book in one arm-like thing and a beaker in the other. And the oddest thing about it—it wore a lab coat! *I can't wait to see what this is!* He then returned to his reading:

Skelaxians: The Skelaxians are our galaxy's strangest race. These insectoids were one of the first races to be discovered by the Empire. They have rather large colonies, inhabiting practically every planet in their solar system. Imperial explorers were hesitant to make contact, fearing that the Skelaxians might be hostile. This was not the case; they were a highly developed society, and most of the workers or drones turned out to be extraordinarily intelligent. They were eager to join the Empire, for they, as we, were seeking further knowledge. After only a single meeting, their queen made the determination that the Skelaxians should become part of the Marcisian family. To this deronn, some of our top scientists are Skelaxians; they have opened several academies throughout the Empire. Professor Nic'rec was instrumental in designing the new cyber brain—now found in most of our mechanized dolls; the dolls themselves were designed by another Skelaxian: Dee'tix. The belief is that the Skelaxians, being pacifists, designed the dolls in order to boost the Empire's defenses against the Skathic.

Skelaxian society revolves around technology and engineering. However, Skelaxians do worship God—though His or Her name is unknown. They are very close knit and consider every other Skelaxian to be part of their family. The other odd thing is that the only female among them is their queen. However, though they are a sexless race, they do take on gender traits and refer to themselves in either a masculine or a feminine context.

The Skelaxians sound awesome! I hope I can meet them somederron, Visage thought before he turned the page. Since the sketch of a rather scantily clad female was located in the same corner where the other two sketches had been, Visage deduced that the next segment of the book was going to be about Night Elves:

Night Elves: The Night Elves of Devros are rather new to our galaxy. During the God Wars, when the Skathic were rampaging or, as his worshippers called it, "crusading," several universes had to be evacuated. The Grand Goddess, Elindil, brought as many of her children as she could to our galaxy; they were under Eendril's protection. Eendril created a new planet just for Elindil and her surviving children. Devros is that planet. It is one of the few inhabitable planets that doesn't use a star for a light source. Instead, it has five moons. Each moon represents one of Elindil's sister, or sri'na goddesses, who fell when her universe was overrun by Skath. I guess you could say that Devros is a world unto itself, since Eendril has left Elindil and her children to their own devices. Though Night Elves worship their goddess, they do pay homage to and are very grateful for Eendril and the sanctuary He had provided for them. Upon arrival on Devros, they immediately joined the Empire, pledging their forces to our defense if Skath's followers ever attack us again.

Night Elves are tall, slender creatures with skin color that is of varying shades of gray. Their hair color ranges from silver to pure white and their ears vary in length, though most seem to end at their shoulders. The women become priestesses to their goddess through a religious ceremony called The Attunement, sometimes referred to as The Joining. This ceremony bestows a beast of great strength and power into the care of the participating Night Elf. The beast is called a Night Mare. It looks like a large horse with a coat as black as midnight. Its mane and tail are made of fiery flames, which are red, orange, or, more rarely, blue. The creature's eyes match the color of its flames. Riding upon their Night Mares, the Night Elves vanquish the varying shades and fiends who appear on their planet, having traversed through temporal rifts, which, according to Marcisian scientists, trace back to the Night Elves' home universe.

Night Elf society is set up into seven united clans or houses. Each house has a high priestess as its leader or head. The high priestess receives revelation from her goddess and passes it along to the rest of the priestesses in her house. One high priestess is given the title of grand priestess, acting much like an emperor. The process for becoming a grand priestess is considered very sacred and therefore is not revealed in any Night Elvin writings. Only the Night Elf goddess and the selected grand priestess are aware of the details of the selection process. Once selected, the grand priestess watches over all of the houses, deals with off-worlders, and handles all imperial matters.

Night Elves, though appearing matriarchal, all work together for the betterment of not only their respective houses but of the entire empire. However, one must not be fooled into thinking that Night Elves are benign. To the contrary, they are skilled in all of the martial arts and, since their colonization of Devros, they have been successfully keeping it free of the fiends and shades that materialize there, as noted previously. Within their great forests, they have set up coliseums, which are used as centers for offensive and defensive training as well as arenas, which are used for settling disputes. The settling of disputes is called "The Trial of Sak'szen," which translates into, The Three Cuts. The rules for this trial are easy enough. A winner is declared when a combatant lands three blows on the other combatant's chest. The loser then has to complete whatever challenge he or she agreed upon prior to the outset of the match. Usually, the loser becomes a servant for the other combatant's family or house for a set period—generally no more than one or two onns.

Night Elves also use the Sak'szen as a means for honing their sorjin skills. Since the Marcisian Empire declared sorjin fighting to be a galaxy-wide sport, beings gather from across the Empire to Devros in order to test their own skills. Though Sak'szen is a violent sport, there have been no deaths reported. Beings have collapsed from blood loss, but the sport itself is about finesse and grace more than the savagery of true combat. Because of the lucrative prize offerings, so many beings from off-world joined the competitions, so the Emperor decreed the Sak'szen could only be held every five onns so they wouldn't overwhelm Devros's meager population.

Visage put his book down and stretched. He noted that Vira was still absorbed in her own

book. When he noticed that her tail was waving wildly, he considered going over to see

why she was so excited but decided not to disturb her and continued reading. He could

tell immediately that the author was now delving into the Zebrecian race, since, in the top

right hand corner of the page, there was a sketch of a being who looked very similar to

Vok'et.

The Zebrecians: These beings are related to the Vorihelcom demons, who have vanished. Zebrecians are usually tall, having varying shades of brown skin. Their hair is straight, long, and streaked with shades of dark brown or black. Their most distinguishing feature are their five horns. The central horn, which adorns the Zebrecian's head, is always the tallest and largest of the five. The smaller horns are almost covered by the being's hair, so they actually appear to be more like bumps than horns. Other than their strange horns and bent pointy ears, the Zebrecians (Zebrecs) are very much like humans. Their society is also very similar. Elected officials head each of their many colonized planets. They are also very family oriented—perhaps even more so than the

Night Elves. Though they haven't set themselves up into clans or houses, they do care about what their ancestors think of them. They are always trying to do the right thing, hoping to earn their place at Eendril's side when they move from this mortal life into the next realm. Zebrecians are kind and very intelligent. Because of their superior engineering skills, they run most of the imperial shipyards. They have also become the overseers of the facilities, since the Skelaxians don't like being in positions of authority. Skelaxians believe that only their queen should be in a position of authority. These two races complement each other and work together so well that the imperial fleet is performing like a well-honed machine.

I bet Grandpa Do-Woon and Uncle John would love to have a few Zebrecians and Skelaxians working for them! Amused by his own thought, Visage paused for a moment before flipping the page. However, once he did, the sketch from the corner seemed to jump right out at him! The being was like none other he had ever encountered. It looked even more otherworldly than a Skelaxian! "Wow, this ought to be good!":

The Marcisians: These are my own race. We are known for our height, white skin, glassy eyes, bony and pointy-ended dreadlocks—which I suppose pass for hair—our rather stubby noses, and, of course, our nonexistent mouths. We are capable of audible communication, since we do have lips. Though our lips appear to be sealed—they are covered by a mucous membrane—we can still move them. However, we do not use them for eating. Instead, we have several small tendrils, which we use for that function. These tendrils protrude from the bottoms of our chins, but we usually keep them retracted while in the presence of other beings. The only real problem with tendrils is that they have a tendency to flop about if we get overemotional—like if we become agitated or scared. The rest of our body is basically like that of the other species inhabiting our galaxy.

Visage's curiosity was piqued, so he quickly turned back to the title page of the book: The Marcisian Empire: Its Development and the Adoption of Other Races by Koft Marcis, Grand Imperator. *Grand Imperator? I wonder what that means.* Visage read the title and author once more before closing the book. Though he was tired from his long reading session, he got out his newly acquired map of the temple and headed out the door. As soon as he thought about the library, the holo image magikally produced a red line—one that would guide him directly to his destination.

"Where do you think you're going, Visage?" Vira's voice startled the young demon.

"Vira, please don't scare me like that." He held his chest and took a deep breath. "I'm only going to return this to the library and hopefully get a new one."

Vira glowered. All she could think of was Visage going happily on his way to the library and being abducted by Chirras. The thought was almost too much for her to bear—so she shook it off. "If you're going, then I'm going with you!" She was adamant.

"Seriously... I'm only going to the library; what are the odds of my running into that... woman!" Visage couldn't even say Chirras's name.

"Honestly... not high. But I'm going anyway," the demoness responded after she grabbed two of her own books from the pile on her desk that was closest to the door. "I should have returned these deronns ago, anyway."

"All right, let's go!" Visage was practically giddy with excitement about getting another book.

Vira couldn't help but feel that there was something very magickal about this Silvarian; he radiated cheerfulness! "Come on, Visage, we need to get back soon; it's already getting dark and tononn is going to be a real pain in the crath."

Visage tilted his head. "Why's that?"

"Because the Empire is sending one of its Imperators, along with several other delegates, to incorporate the Zaharaj into its organization."

Visage was flabbergasted! He came to a sudden halt, so Vira stopped too. "You mean the Zaharaj are going to officially join the Marcisian Empire... tomor—" He shook his head. "I mean tononn!"

"That's right."

"Why don't you sound enthusiastic, Vira? Don't you like the Empire?" Visage asked, noticing that her answer had sounded quite dispassionate.

Vira shook her head. "That's not it, Visage. I'm concerned because..." She closed her eyes and snorted "the visitors want to meet you."

I wonder if that's a good or a bad thing. "Why do they want to meet me?"

"That's what has me concerned"—

"Well, don't be!" the Silvarian chimed, interrupting the demoness. Vira appeared a bit surprised by his sudden outburst. "Vira, the Marcisians are good. They probably want to ask me a bunch of questions. But I won't be able to answer them because I wasn't raised by demons."

Vira did seem to breathe more easily. "You're probably right, Visage. Now, let's get to the library before they close it for the deronn!"

Visage's mouth gaped as he watched Vira leave him in the dust. He took off after her, yelling out, "You can't lose me that easily!"

"Who said I was trying to?" Vira joked. Visage caught up right after the lift doors opened.

***

It took some time for Vira and Visage to get back to their room. Visage had talked extensively with Glavian and Serishin. The librarian recommended several more books for him to read in order to catch up with the other ar'teths. Having such an insatiable appetite for learning, Visage chose to take every book. However, he was unable to carry the entire treasure trove, so Vira ended up having to utilize her U-Gem.

"That was awesome! Serishin and Glavian know everything!" Vira smirked at her roommate's comment.

"I wouldn't say that, Visage—but they do know a lot." Vira kept her eyes on the boy while she pulled six books out of her U-Gem and stacked them on his desk.

Wow! That thing is amazing! The distraction was short lived, and Visage got right back on topic. "Do you know more than they do, Vira?" He received only a sly smile in response. Thinking that that was all he was going to get out of his roommate, Visage lay on his bed and curled up around his ball.

"I don't know if I know more than they do—I've just been around longer. Annnd, you're asleep... It figures. It's strange having another being in the room with me. I haven't had a roommate since Riza, and, with her messy habits, I had to end that fast. Honestly, how can anybeing live like that?" Changing her train of thought, she picked up a book from the corner of her desk. With book in hand, she grabbed an ancient fountain pen from the top drawer of her desk. She then laid down on her bed, unbound the cord that was wrapped around the black-leather book, and opened it to where she had left the ribbon-like bookmark. *I should have recorded this a long time ago, but I can't procrastinate any longer, for Visage's sake. If anything ever happens to me, he will never know his full story.* "So, here goes."

I remember it as though it were yederonn. I ran down one of the hallways of the grand palace of the Silvarian demons. The sparkling white walls were made of pure thermite, as were the elaborately carved white pillars that lined both sides of the main hallway. The light streamed in from the decorated windows, which were placed in between each set of pillars from high up near the ceiling. However, not even the grand majesty of the palace could compare to my excitement—my heart felt as though it were going to thump right out of my chest! I still remember the whooshing sounds I heard when I ran past the majestic-looking pillars. My feet felt light as I sped along the soft blue carpet. It was as though I were flying!

Then, suddenly, there they were! Their backs were turned to me— the Silvarian Demon King with his gorgeous Keldras at his side. Their hair shimmered in the sunlight. Arnen's two, bushy, silver-and-blue tails swayed in time beside Keldras's own long glowing-white locks as they walked arm-in-arm towards the throne room. Keldras's long, shimmering, white gown, embroidered with the golden crest of her noble family, trailed behind her. Arnen, on the other hand, was wearing white pants, which had blue flames printed on the hems. The flames looked almost real, dancing with his every step.

By the time I caught up with the royal couple, I was almost breathless. Then, the couple turned, and Arnen's bright, sapphire-colored eyes felt as though they were staring deep into my soul. His light-blue lips greeted me with a warm smile. The queen's smile emanated graciousness and was equally as warm. It was adorned by her crimson-colored lips. "We're delighted to see you, Vira," Keldras offered. Her voice was melodic.

"Why are you in such a rush this morning?" Arnen asked with a raised silver-and-blue eyebrow.

For several moments, I was so overwhelmed with emotion that no words would come. I got to my knees and peered up at the two bright, albeit puzzled-looking, faces. After taking off my cloak, I began to bare my heart and soul to the dumbfounded king. "My life and heart belong to you, Your Majesty; please take me as your wife!" I knelt for what seemed like eons while I awaited Arnen's response.

Arnen knelt and gently placed my discarded robe around my violently shaking frame. I peered up at the king in anticipation, but he simply smiled and shook his head. "I'm sorry, Vira, but Keldras is the only wife I will ever want or need." His words pierced my heart and tears welled up in my eyes. My spirit was broken. I clung to the folds of my robe and wept. Arnen arose, appearing to be in deep thought. After a few moments, he spoke. "Vira, I am truly flattered by your sincerity and passion, but, considering that I am forever unavailable, I would like to propose another viable option. If I ever have a son, you can marry him." I was stunned but managed to peer up into Arnen's eyes with my still-pained expression, fully aware that Arnen was only making this generous offer in order to alleviate my suffering. With gratitude, I nodded in agreement. Even Keldras was graciously supportive of Arnen's proposal. She cautioned her husband that he could not go back on his word.

"My word is my bond," His Majesty said before offering me his hand. Once on my feet, though still a bit shaky, I bowed politely and headed for my room.

For a long time, I was under Arnen and Keldras's rule. It was a joy-filled time. I eventually became the captain of Arnen's Royal Guard, though, thankfully, those times were peaceful. However, the peace ended abruptly. The news of the Dark God Skath and His evil plans forced Arnen to rally his fellow Silvarians in order to come to the aid of the Gods of Light. Though I held a senior rank, Arnen ordered all of us Veserinos to stay out of the initial battles. He gave us strict orders to defend our own galaxy in the event that Skath broke through his defensive lines.

For what seemed like an eternity, my fellow Veserinos and I were on high alert. Then Arnen came home—alone and broken. He told us of his loss and of the ultimate sacrifice that was made by thousands of his fellow Silvarians. Keldras wept, for at this time of seemingly insurmountable despair, she had news to share with Arnen: they were going to have a child. The news was so bittersweet. Though Arnen was overcome with joy, he knew with every fiber of his being what he had to do—he had to destroy Skath. If Skath were to get wind of a child being born to a demon and a goddess, he would not rest until the child was destroyed. Soon thereafter, Arnen left—and never returned. Keldras, heartbroken, entrusted me with the spirit body of her precious son. She directed me to carry it to Eendril, for she knew Eendril would iloni and protect her son as though he were His own. Keldras's final act, before vanishing herself, was to share the name by which her son should be known: "Orran." The name was derived from the demon tongue as well as from the language of the gods. Orr, the shortened form of Orranth, is a demon term which means peace or peaceful. An is the shortened form of anneth, a godly term that translates into bring or bringer. Therefore, Orran means peace bringer or peacemaker. Wasn't that a wonderful name for your mi'thia to bestow upon you, Orran?

Accompanied by the Meserino demoness, Riza, and with your spirit cradled in my arms, I traveled to carry my precious cargo to Eendril. Keldras had known that this option offered you the best chance of remaining safe and eventually gaining your physical body. However, because Skath learned about your spirit birth He kept sending beings to annihilate you, it took eons for you to receive your body.

So tendronn, Visage, I have written this history for you and your progenitors—enabling you to know of your beginnings. But now I am going to 'speak' just to you. You are finally here! Visage (Didn't Lord Nosfaren bestow upon you a glorious name!). I can't believe that you are finally here! For the first time in all these eons, I am able to see and touch you in your physical form. Your body is so cute—and perfect! And you bear such a resemblance to Arnen—it's uncanny! I'm sure one of the reasons Keldras gave you up was because you reminded her so much of her beloved Arnen. Though we don't know for sure which god dealt Skath the lethal blow, whoever it was saved an infinite number of lives, born as well as unborn, through his or her noble sacrifice. And, thanks to that being, I'm now able to see the one I fell in iloni with so many eons ago—when Keldras placed you in my arms.

After taking a quick glance at the sleeping form in the bed across from hers, Vira finished writing and slowly closed her journal. She was emotionally exhausted. Using telekinesis, she levitated her book and pen back onto her desk, flipped onto her back, and closed her eyes. A smile adorned her face, and she drifted off to sleep. Her dreams filled her soul with renewed hope.

***

Visage awoke with a start and bolted upright. He held tightly to his ball. As usual, there was no way he was going to let it fall. Vira was sitting on the edge of his bed.

"Is there something wrong, Vira?" Visage groggily asked. He was a bit puzzled.

The demoness quickly turned her head away and quietly uttered an awkward sounding "No." Visage then noticed the second being in the room.

Riza was present. She was standing at the foot of his bed, peering at him. An amused smirk was adorning her face. "I told you that you wouldn't get away with it, Vira." Riza put her hand on her hip and eyed her blue-skinned friend.

Visage glanced from Riza to Vira and back. "What's going on? What didn't Vira get away with?"

Riza smirked. "Vira was going to"—

Vira's head whipped around, revealing the bright-blue blush on her face. She jumped up from her comfortable position at the foot of the bed and belted, "Riza, you don't have to say it!"

Riza ignored her friend and blurted out the rest of her cut-off sentence, "try to sneak into bed with you!" Vira's face fell; she now looked more depressed than embarrassed. Visage closed his eyes, placed his ball down next to him, and, once satisfied it wouldn't roll away, turned to Vira.

"Is that what this is all about? I don't understand what the big deal is, Riza." Back home, my sri'nas would sometimes come into my room and sleep with me—especially when there was a storm. They hated the sound of thunder, though I don't understand why. Visage then turned to Vira. "Is there something that's scaring you, Vira?"

Riza had a conniving grin on her face. "Yeah, Vira, is there something you're afraid of?" she mocked. Vira didn't even bother with Riza; she was too busy staring at Visage.

"I'm afraid of losing you the same way Keldras lost Arnen." After hearing Vira's heart-wrenching response, Riza couldn't help but regret her spiteful-sounding remark. She had made the remark in jest— never dreaming she would be adding to Vira's pain.

Visage smiled. "Don't worry, Vira, I'm not going anywhere," he announced while at the same time giving her a big hug. Vira was more than happy to accept the hug and gave a hearty one in return.

"You'd better not, iloni," the demoness whispered.

"All right, all right! That's enough, Vira!" Though Riza sounded annoyed, Vira sent only a silent message to the agitated Meserino: *The benefits of having a clean room.* Riza drew a blank on a decent comeback.

Vira moved quickly, grabbing the still groggy and somewhat confused Silvarian up into her arms. "Come on, Riza, we don't want to be late!"

"Wait up!" Riza yelled out, attempting to catch up with the other two demons.

Visage was disgruntled and clearly irritated, about his mistreatment.

"Vira, I can walk on my own! I'm not some stuffed animal, ya know! Put me down!"

"Do I have to—you're so soft," Vira whined back, rubbing her face against the Silvarian's hair.

"Put him down, Vira!" Riza ordered. Vira gave a menacing glare. She was reluctant but finally let the boy down. Once everybeing had settled down, the demonesses flanked Visage and they all walked along together in relative peace. However, the quietude was short lived.

"Well, if it isn't the trio of demons," Chirras snidely quipped when she snuck up behind them, having entered their route from another corridor. As usual, she was sporting a menacing smile. Realizing that they had to act cheerfully around the woman, the demons donned the calmest look they could muster before turning to face her.

Vira spoke first. "Gunrek menronn, Chirras. Why are you up so early?" *At least she's wearing her uniform,* Riza thought, causing Vira to give her a sideways glance and Visage to stifle a laugh. Apparently, either Chirras had not heard what Riza was thinking, or she chose to ignore it, since she responded as if nothing out of the ordinary was going on.

"I'm heading for the landing area to wait for the Marcisian emissary. Looks like everybeing else is doing the same," Chirras grumbled. Visage's hand went to Riza's, and he shuffled over as closely as he could to his fiancée. She gave his hand a reassuring squeeze.

"Chirras, did you know that Silvarians can see into a being's heart?" Riza asked with a sneer.

Vira was completely shocked! *What are you doing, Riza! Are you crazy!* she telepathically screamed at the Meserino.

I know what I'm doing, Riza quietly responded, attempting to ease Vira's concern. Chirras herself, in response to Riza's bombshell, was not looking too hot. She stared daggers at the demoness, an obvious look of panic blanketing her countenance.

Riza persisted. "So, Visage, what does Chirras's heart look like?"

Visage gritted his teeth before looking up into Riza's eyes. *What! Riza you're seriously crazy! Do you have any idea what you're asking me to do!* He telepathically shouted. Riza ignored his loud complaints, though she did tighten her grip for an instant. *I don't understand. Are you testing her... or me? I really don't know what I'm supposed to tell her!* Riza tightened and loosened her hand again. Visage wasn't pleased at, what he perceived to be, Riza's plan. *Riza, why are you forcing me into this, this... situation!*

Chirras was surveying the area, apparently considering her options for escape. Riza and Vira's demon eyes narrowed when she took a step backwards. "Is there something wrong, Chirras?" Vira calmly asked. By now, she was all in with Riza's plan.

"You seem... rather uptight, Chirras; it's not like his eyes can melt you or anything." Riza was seemingly trying to reassure the jittery-appearing woman.

Almost jovially, Visage stepped forward. "I'm sorry, Chirras, but your heart is normal." Chirras's eyes went wide.

"Well, that's to be expected." Chirras managed to reply as though nothing of any significance had happened. "Now, if you'll excuse me." Hoping not to have tipped the trio off about how shaken she really was, she turned on her heels and headed down the hallway as fast as she could. She was elated when the lift chimed and the doors opened.

"So, what's her heart really like?" Vira anxiously asked, confident that Visage's previous diagnosis was far from the actual truth. Riza was also staring expectantly at the boy.

"If you must know, her insides are completely black. I don't think there is a bright spot in her entire body." Visage got quiet for a moment before continuing. "And her heart is like an endless abyss; it's as though all of the light inside of her died a long time ago."

Riza closed her eyes and crossed her arms under her chest. "hmm, it's not like she hadn't already revealed her true self," she dryly stated.

Vira gave Visage, a reassuring smile. "Don't worry, Visage, we'll deal with her right after the Marcisian delegation leaves." She squatted down. "And that's a promise!" She smiled when she offered her pinky finger to him.

Visage's eyes widened in wonder and excitement. He couldn't believe that Vira knew how to pinky swear. He eagerly wrapped his own pinky finger around hers.

Riza was a bit puzzled, but she was also very intrigued at the two demon's strange exchange.

Vira and Visage were both smiling wide while they shook their pinkies.

30

New Plan

The temple stood empty. Everybeing was outside in the landing area. Thousands of beings stood in hundreds of rows while they awaited the arrival of the Marcisian shuttle, which had to break through the asteroid belt before landing. Tension was high. Everybeing on Zharaj knew that this time the emperor wanted an answer. The Marcisian representative would not leave without one.

Within the crowd, mixed emotions were rampant: excitement, joy, fear—all were prevalent as heads rose to peer at the rust-colored sky. The crowd looked on with anticipation when a small metal dart cleared the last of the oversized rocks that were hanging in the atmosphere. In what seemed like mere moments, the dart-shaped ship was hovering just above the onlookers' heads. It turned its back and landed with a groan, its feet touching down on the black moribite landing area. The rear of the ship opened with a hiss. One door swung up and inward while the second slid out and downward. The feet of the latter reached the ground and enabled the beings inside to disembark.

Two T.A.Ds led the procession. The black long-limbed robots marched in time, and their feet clanged loudly while they made their way down the ramp. Another pair of beings, clad in white robes, followed closely behind the T.A.Ds. Next in line was a Marcisian female.

The crowd came roaring to life and greeted the female with a deafening cheer. A pair of armor-clad beings, whose rifles were shouldered, flanked the Marcisian woman.

Rows of Zaharaj ignited blood sorjins, turned on their heels, faced the group, and cleared an aisle for the visitors. The aisle led up to the temple's entrance where all thirteen members of the Zaharaj Council were less-than-eagerly awaiting the delegation's arrival. Visage, who was standing behind Riza and Vira, was so anxiously anticipating the arrival that he nearly fell over.

I can't believe you're this nervous Visage, Riza glanced down at the jittery Silvarian standing behind her and Vira. *You faced the Dark God Chaos by yourself, and now you're nervous about meeting the Marcisian delegation? Really?*

Visage had been totally focused on the procession, but, having received Riza's sarcastic message, he now snapped his head up and glared at the demoness. *Riza, Chaos is tied up!* He telepathically retorted.

Several of the other councilors overheard the telepathic give-and-take and snickered. "The kid's got you there, Riza!" Glavian flashed Visage a sly grin and followed up with a quick nod of approval.

Quit the chatter, all of you! The onlookers responded immediately to Lord Nosfaren's harsh warning and abruptly ended their telepathic conference—and none too soon, since, immediately thereafter, the imperial representatives reached their destination.

Right after Lord Nosfaren stepped forward to greet them, the T.A.Ds halted, did an about face, and took two steps before turning on their heels and facing each other. The beings in the white robes did the same and allowed the Marcisian woman to pass in front of them; her own guards followed closely behind. The crowd fell dead silent, and everybeing shut off his or her own blood sorjin.

Lord Nos gave the woman a slight bow. "Imperator Kala, on behalf of the"—

"I care not for such pleasantries, Lord Nosfaren," Kala said, outspokenly disinterested in Nos's greeting. Though the woman's surprisingly curt behavior was disconcerting to Nos, he was given little time to bemoan the issue, since she continued unabated. "I am here, on orders from His Majesty Barren Marcis the Third, to receive your answer. Is your group going to officially join the Empire?" Though she was attempting to follow at least a semblance of proper protocol, considering the serious nature of her mission, Imperator Kala could not constrain herself. She bent her head down and strained to get a glimpse of the rumored Silvarian, who was continuing to hide behind Riza and Vira. "You there!" she cried, pointing her finger at Visage. "Step forward!"

Everybeing on the Council grimaced, except for Riza and Vira who had full-blown scowls on their faces.

Lord Nosfaren sidestepped, abruptly cutting the Imperator off before she could interrogate the child. "We are not yet part of your empire, Imperator Kala," he sternly stated while at the same time glancing back at Visage; he wanted to see how the child was faring. *Don't worry, Visage, she can't touch you.* After sending his silent communication, he snapped his head back around. "Where is the Grand Imperator? I was told he would be here to make our transition official!"

The Councilors nodded their approval of Nos's statements. Kala took a step back, so did her guards. "He's... very busy dealing with the Ja'Shari." Kala voice was shaky under the intimidating Lord's glaring gaze. "But he'll arrive here later this deronn," Kala quickly finished, attempting to ease the tension.

Lord Baltrix stepped forward and stood next to Lord Nosfaren. He was extremely upset about the whole "joining the Empire" situation and was not too keen about having to wait for the Grand Imperator's arrival. Wondering why Kala had even come, he snapped, "So why are *you* here?" His unwelcomed question only added to the palpable anxiety of the crowd. Murmuring, both silent and audible, was widespread throughout the throng of Zaharaj.

One of the visiting dignitaries was cloaked in white robes and assumed the role of Kala, who was not eager to speak. The man (Athrin) was human. He threw off his hood and revealed his black spiky hair, which spilled out from the top of his head and fell down to the level of his shoulders; more than several strands were obscuring the left side of his face. After making his way past Nos and Baltrix, he got to one knee. His intention was to get the attention of Lord Nos, while under the guise of speaking to the half-hidden Silvarian. "We came here to see if the rumors of a living Silvarian were true, and, if they were, to invite him to join the Ja'Shari."

Visage peeked out from behind Riza. He was too shocked to speak, as was everybeing else. Athrin's amaranth-colored eyes dimly glowed even while he gave the child a warm smile. Lord Nosfaren glowered at him, grabbed him, and held him up by his collar. "Is there a problem, Lord Nos?" The man appeared undaunted by Nos's unexpected eruption.

"It appears that your memory has totally failed you, Grand Master! Let's see if I can jog it a bit!" Nos dropped Athrin before continuing his tirade. "First, you cajoled the Emperor into allowing a visit to Zharaj so you could see if the rumors of a Silvarian demon were true. And now that you have your answer, you want to recruit him for *your* order!" Nos crossed his arms before glaring at Kala and then at Athrin. "Do I have that right?" He defiantly folded his arms across his chest. "Grand Master?" His words dripped with venom and sarcasm.

Athrin took his sweet time before responding to the angry demon. "It doesn't hurt to try, now does it, Lord Nos?" He smiled slyly at the still-hiding child.

Though Nos remained irate, he turned to Visage. "Visage, it's really up to you... We can't force you to stay here." The demon muttered under his breath—"especially now that Chirras is interested in you."

Vira and Riza stood aside, allowing Visage to step fully into the open. The crowd found him to be cute as well as entertaining, since he was now fiddling with one of his silver-and-blue bushy tails. On the other hand, Visage was extremely perturbed by the many expectant eyes that were glaring his way.

Out in the crowd, Cormack, Moonreth, Le'Shara, Arisha, and Zoric were beyond troubled about Visage's possible exit from the Zaharaj. *Do you think Visage will want to join the Order?* Cormack was the first to start a telepathic conference.

No, he can't leave! My parents won't let him leave! Arisha silently cried.

It's not your parents' decision to make, Arisha. It's Visage's decision, Cormack retorted. *But I don't want him to go any more than you do.*

"What if he does go?"Le'Shara asked, surprising everybeing in the group.

"Sorry, sri'na... It's his choice, like Cormack said," Moonreth offered in a consoling tone.

"What does it matter to you, Elf! Aren't you leaving the Zaharaj and going back to your home-world to become a priestess to that goddess of yours!"Arisha shot an accusing glance at the albino, causing Le'Shara to twiddle her fingers before responding.

I haven't decided... yet, the Night Elf hesitantly replied.

Ranic threw his hands in the air and shook his head, causing both of his twills to flop about. He couldn't believe what he was hearing! "This is just great! Now I may be losing two friends." He barely had time to complete his thought before Visage's voice pierced the banter.

Finally addressing the Grand Master's offer, Visage firmly, responded. "I'm sorry..." He glanced up at Vira and then Riza who both smiled back at him. "but my place is here." Though only those closest to him could hear his decision, word spread through the crowd like wildfire. His friends let out a great cheer! Vira picked the young demon up and started spinning him around! Riza was so happy that all she could do was breathe a sigh of relief.

"Well, I can't say I didn't try." Athrin offered a manufactured smile while he watched Vira reluctantly release the demon back onto his feet. Though the demoness didn't want to let Visage go, she knew she had to, since Riza was standing by to give him a hug.

Ali'stia dampened the mood a bit. She came up behind Visage and put her hand on his shoulder, causing the boy's stress level to soar. "I know you mean well, Athrin, but he *is* a demon of light." She then narrowed her eyes. "And I don't care if you *are* a Light Warrior, if you ever try to take my friend's fiancé and my de'tari's rival away again, I'll feed your soul to my blade! And that's a promise!" As soon as her point was made, the demoness made her way over to her husband's side.

I know there are plenty of evils in the universe... but that *woman really scares me,* Athrin hid his thoughts with a powerful mental barrier before swallowing. After watching the Councilors congratulate the Silvarian on a decision well made, the Grand Master turned to his God. *So, Eendril, it seems I've lost this one.* Immediately, his temperament mellowed. Somehow, he now knew that this loss wasn't really a loss.

He is still *a demon, after all.* The thought gave Athrin pause, since he realized it wasn't his own. He peered up into the asteroid-filled sky, fully aware of Eendril's hand in all that had transpired.

Returning to the moment at hand, Athrin spoke. "Since we're here, Lord Nos, why don't we get on with the vote." Nos nodded and gestured for the Imperial delegation to follow him inside.

***

The doors to the empty room slid open, and Chirras strode right in. The dim overhead lighting came on, triggered by the motion detector, and Chirras was able to gaze with disgust at the mess laid out before her. "Ugh! How could anybeing live like this!" she scathed with a scowl.

Books were strewn everywhere, so it was hard for her to decide where to start. She finally settled on the book closest to her—the one lying face down on the bed. A quick glance at the contents told her it was not the right one. Then she picked up another and another. "This is getting me nowhere fast." Though she had tried to make things easier by putting all of the books into a grid and rifling through them in a left to right order, she was coming up empty handed. Time was fleeting by, and she couldn't afford to go through the same book twice. Her anger was mounting. "I've already gone through nineteen books! Where the frak is it!" Although her hope was waning fast, she was determined to find *the* book, so she picked up number twenty. "Finally!" Her anger dissipated the dironn she caught sight of the book's title: *The Three Greater Demon Races.* "This is it! This is the one I need!" Fearing discovery, Chirras activated her U-gem, scanned the book, returned it carefully to its place on the bed, and exited the room. "While those fraking fools celebrate the arrival of the Imps, I can come and go as I please." After taking a quick glance back at the room, she thought, *Still, it's a good thing that Riza is such a slob, or I probably wouldn't have been able to pull this off.* She let out a hearty and contemptuous laugh before heading to her room.

***

Ranic, Moonreth, Le'Shara, Cormack, Arisha, and Azala were walking together, heading for the cafeteria. Nate was trailing several steps behind.

"I knew he'd stay," Arisha told her small group of friends.

"No, you didn't," Ranic retorted, pointing his finger accusingly at her while walking beside her in the hallway.

"Who cares!" Moonreth exclaimed. "I only want to get this voting thing out of the way so we can get back to our every deronn lives!"

"What's going to happen to us if every being decides to vote for joining the Empire?" Le'Shara asked, directing her question towards her ber'nan, Moonreth.

"I don't think anything will change," Cormack shrugged before giving her a smirk.

"Does it even matter, Le'Shara? I mean, since you're going back to Devros to become a priestess, why do you even care?" Azala added, glancing up from her book just long enough to see the Night Elf siblings walk by.

Le'Shara blushed a bit at Azala's comment. "I don't know what I want to do, Azala."

Moonreth frowned, sensing how conflicted his sri'na was, considering that she was facing a life-changing decision. He thought back to when Visage had told Le'Shara that she wasn't cursed. *Thanks to Visage, Le'Shara had had lab work that proved his original assertion—that her albinism was due to a genetic disorder and not to a curse.* Moonreth slowly and subtly shook his head.

Moonreth's parents were overjoyed, though at the same time embarrassed and ashamed that their very own genes had turned out to be the culprit—the cause of his sri'na's white skin and crimson-colored eyes. With the evidence in hand, they had gone to the high priestesses and informed them of the genetic disorder. As a result, the law was changed. Night Elves who were suffering from the disorder could no longer be considered cursed and treated like outcasts. Moonreth was thrilled when he heard that Le'Shara and other albinos could now become priestesses. He was even more thrilled that scientists from the University of Marcisia—once they caught wind of Le'Shara's case—traveled to Devros in order to study the parents of the few children who were afflicted with the disorder. Finally, Moonreth's thoughts drifted back to the present, and he continued to contemplate the current state of Zharaj. *So much has happened since Visage's arrival. What would this place be like without him?*

"I don't get it, Le'Shara. All you've ever talked about is your dream of becoming a priestess!" Ranic had stopped to turn around and confront his younger Night Elf friend.

"That's true. I mean, come on Le'Shara, you can't go and throw this opportunity away!" Nate yelled out from behind the group. When everybeing suddenly focused on him, he threw his hood over his head.

"What's going on?" Envine, the blond human, asked when he came from an adjoining corridor and linked up with his friends. He, like Azala, was holding a book in his hands so he could read and walk at the same time.

"Hey, Envine!" Ranic exclaimed. He ran over and threw his right arm around his now-disgruntled friend, causing him to drop his book. Envine glared at the hyperactive Twillan until he took his arm away. "Sorry, Envine." Ranic proceeded to fill Envine in on what had been going on. "The Night Elves have offered Le'Shara a chance to become a priestess! Isn't that great!"

Le'Shara was within hearing distance; her face turned a deep shade of red.

Envine glanced over at the Elf. "So what are you going to do?" The still-stunned girl merely shook her head, so Azala voiced an answer in behalf.

"She doesn't know yet."

"Ah," was Envine's big response. Ranic found the halfhearted response to be a little puzzling.

"Come on, Envine, can't you be more excited than that? I mean, Le'Shara is about to make a life-changing decision, and all you can say is, "Ah!" Ranic was attempting to get his friend to open up a bit more.

Envine didn't look up from his book. Nevertheless, he did comment. "I think you're excited enough for the both of us."

The red-skinned Twillan fell silent. "I guess he's got a good point there."

"Don't worry about it, Le'Shara. I'm sure whatever you choose to do will be the right thing," Cormack offered. Le'Shara perked up at this and gave her friend a sharp nod.

Once at the lifts, the group had to split up; the lift was too small. Le'Shara and Moonreth graciously offered to wait for the next lift. Azala decided to join them in order to escape Ranic, who had been pestering her about losing her roommate. When she began stepping into the lift, Nate offered for her to stay in his room, but Azala was not thrilled about the invitation. "No thanks, Nate. As much as I like you, your pet stinks so badly that nobeing can be around him for more than a dironn without wearing a mask."

Nate frowned and let out a lamenting sigh. "I know... But my dar'nra asked me to watch Stinky until he gets back from his tour in the Twill sector." The lift door closed and ended the little chat.

"You simply don't want to give up on Visage returning, do you Azala?" Moonreth pointedly asked.

Azala hid her face behind her book. "I don't know Moonreth... Visage puzzles me." Her sheepish answer revealed her embarrassment. Moonreth smirked, Le'Shara giggled, and Nate remained silent. The doors of the lift opened, and the four friends headed to the cafeteria to meet up with the rest of the group.

31

A Room with a Veserino

The Council plus one assembled in its chambers. Visage climbed up onto Riza's lap. Vira was a bit jealous, but, since Visage was staying in her room, the demoness felt obligated to allow her friend this courtesy.

"The Emperor wishes to know if Visage is truly a Silvarian," Kala related to Lord Nosfaren, who was the Zaharaj's spokesbeing for the negotiations.

"Of course he's a Silvarian," a disgruntled Nosfaren quipped in response. He was becoming bored with this run around. "I've told you three times now he is… and you still haven't told us why the Emperor has such an interest in the child."

"And I told you that I don't have the authority to answer that for you, Lord Nosfaren." The Imperator managed to keep her cool.

Visage liked looking at the woman. She was shorter than Riza or Vira. Her skin was like his, the color of fallen snow. Her eyes looked like highly polished mirrors, reflecting everything while at the same time having a noticeable glow behind them. She didn't have much of a nose—it looked like a small bridge with a pair of nostrils. Her lips were small and slim and covered by a transparent fleshy membrane. Her dreadlocks were off-white and appeared to be interlocking bones rather than hair. They were very long, hanging down below her waistline. Visage couldn't tell what her ears looked like, since they were hidden beneath her hair. The silver dress she was wearing was quite low cut, and a chain with a ring attached hung down into her ample bosom. Visage guessed that she was married; she occasionally played with her ring. Overall, she was quite stunning.

Eventually, the Silvarian's attention turned from Kala to the doorway. Grand Master Athrin and a blue-skinned Twillan were leisurely leaning against the wall on opposite sides of the doors. Athrin was smirking at the whole situation while simultaneously the Twillan was staring at Visage; his eyes were filled with wonder. Visage didn't mind the staring, since he was captivated by the Twillan's aqua-colored eyes. He gave the being a toothy grin, and the Twillan gave a hearty laugh in return. Visage then tuned back in to the ongoing conversation.

Ranic asked Kala, as politely as he could, "Why can't you tell us the reason behind His Majesty's interest in Visage?"

Kala turned to him and grimaced before she frowned, "I've already told you, I can't tell you!"

Several Zaharaj groaned, and Baltrix let out a grunt of frustration. "We're not getting anywhere with this!"

Visage decided to act. He jumped off Riza's lap—she was shocked and disappointed—walked over to Kala, and waited. When Kala realized that he was standing right in front of her, she almost tripped while trying to put some space between them.

"So why does the Emperor want to see me?" Visage asked, smiling broadly.

Kala peered over at the seated Zaharaj and silently pled for help but to no avail. "He's got you now, Kala. You have to answer the question because it concerns him." Lord Nos gave the woman an impatient grin. Every councilor was now awaiting her response.

"Uhhh... he wanted to know if you really are a Silvarian."

Visage tilted his head and folded his arms. "Until I came here, I had no idea I was a Silvarian. All I know is, that's what everybeing here has told me." Visage glanced behind him; Riza, Vira, and Nos, were all nodding their heads.

Kala began to fidget. "Yes, I understand that that's what you've been told, Visage. But the Emperor would like you to have some tests—just to make sure."

Riza shot up from her chair. "You're not taking him anywhere!" she screamed.

"If the Zaharaj vote to become an official part of the Empire, he'll have no choice in the matter!" Kala countered.

"That's blackmail!" Ranic yelled, pointing an accusing finger at the woman.

Michael jumped in. "This is treachery!"

Visage glared at his fiancées and his friends. His eyes glowed icy-blue. He surveyed the room before refocusing on Kala. "Imperator Kala, could you please kneel down so I can talk with you a little more easily."

Kala swallowed hard and dropped to her knees. "I'm sorry, Visage… but this is how the Empire does things," she whispered.

Strangely, Visage appeared to be preoccupied. Ranic and Baltrix, who understood exactly what the demon child was doing, returned to their seats. The two grandmasters from the Order exchanged inquisitive glances, unaware of what was transpiring.

Visage scowled and slowly started walking backwards towards Riza. "You're lying about something, Kala!" None of the Councilors seemed shocked when what little color she had started to drain from Kala's face.

"How do you know that!"

"I can see inside of you," Visage nonchalantly said while he climbed back up onto Riza's lap. Of course, Riza was more than happy to accommodate him. "I saw your heart rate increase every time Lord Nos asked his question. And it increased even more when I pushed you for an answer."

Lord Nos got up and narrowed his eyes. "Kala, what are you going to do with Visage?" Then his voice took on a threatening tone. "And, just so you know, if I don't like your answer, you might not leave here alive!"

Lord Nos towered over the now-sweating Kala, since she was still on her knees. Humbled, the Imperator plead with Athrin and his companion.

Athrin was the next to speak. "Sorry, Kala, you're on your own. I'm not about to start a war with the Zaharaj over something I know nothing about." The Imperator then turned to Nos. "However, I'm curious how the child knew that Kala was hiding something in the first place—we've been trying to read her mind ever since we left Firax."

Nos appeared to be oblivious to Athrin's question, since he was focused on Kala. "Please don't hurt me, Lord Nosfaren," Kala pleaded. "Listen! We heard a rumor that there was a Skath worshipper hiding somewhere in the Zaharaj. So the Emperor decided, after much deliberation, that we should try to protect the Silvarian by taking him to Firax or Marcisia. I swear that's the truth! Please believe me!" She was now sobbing.

Lord Nos was taken aback. When he surveyed the room, he could tell that he wasn't the only being who was shocked by what Kala had just revealed. He proceeded to offer the poor woman a hand to help her get back to her feet. She hesitated, but once she realized that her life was no longer in danger, she accepted Nos's generous offer. When Nos made his way back to his seat, his expression was depicting the gravity of the situation.

"Unfortunately, the rumors are true." Kala and the pair of Ja'Shari gaped at Nos's unexpectedly forthright confirmation.

Athrin stood up straight. "You mean to tell me there really *is* a Skath worshipper here!" This horrifying development seemed to have caught Athrin totally off guard. In response to his heart-felt concern, Nos nodded sharply.

"Though she's not really a Skath worshipper... per se,"— Now the three beings were puzzled, but Barren continued before they had a chance to ask what he meant—"she's a fraking deser'rec!"

Kala was the first of the trio to recover enough to speak. "How in the universe did a deser'rec manage to wheedle her way into your ranks!"

Sharas now jumped into the conversation. "Let's just say that this woman is a master at hiding her true self." She crossed her arms under her chest and huffed. "She's managed to fool me for onns," the human female muttered, her voice dripping with disdain. "The mere thought of having befriended her makes me sick."

Athrin and his blue-skinned Twillan friend made their way over to the center of the room and stood at Kala's side. "I assume you have a plan to deal with this deser'rec, Lord Nos?" Athrin questioned the ancient demon.

"Of course we have a plan!" Baltrix interjected.

"So, let's hear it!" the Imperator shot back at the not-so-enthusiastic-looking Councilors.

Lord Nos was less than excited about involving the Ja'Shari in Zaharaj business, but he also knew that the Ja'Shari, more so than the Zah, had a lot more experience dealing with Skath worshippers. *I guess I have no choice.* After telepathically polling the Council members about their wishes regarding sharing the plan with the visitors, the outcome came as quite a shock. Everybeing agreed! Even Michael gave his consent! "Fine then," Nosfaren said and proceeded to explain his plan to the two Ja'Shari and the Marcisian representative.

"It's an ingenious plan, for sure." Athrin nodded his head approvingly. "But"—he added—"it could use some refinements. If you'll allow it, Lord Nosfaren, I'd like to send for a Skelaxian friend of mine to help you monitor Chirras's activities."

"What do you mean, Athrin?" Glavian asked while drumming his armrest with his fingers.

The blue-skinned Twillan, Mirth, whom Athrin had introduced before Nos had begun to explain the plan, spoke up. "Trust me; you'll be grateful to have his help. When it comes to monitoring transmissions, he's one of the best." Mirth's twills were dancing about wildly. He couldn't contain his excitement about being part of the plan to catch Chirras.

"The Skelaxian's a hacker!" Visage yelled excitedly.

"What does that mean?" Riza asked.

"You don't know what a hacker is?" Visage was quite shocked that Riza was unaware of the term, even though the Zaharaj had far more advanced technology on Zharaj than his grandparent's Corporation did back on Earth. "Well," he elaborated, "a hacker is a being who hacks or cracks into a computer system and steals information, or takes down servers, or even changes the software."

"Oh, yes, we have beings like those, but we call them splicers." *Though 'hacker' seems more appropriate term, now that I think about it,* Athrin mused.

Lord Nos seemed upbeat. "That's an excellent idea, Athrin. We were just going to monitor Chirras, but we should also be keeping an eye on her transmissions."

Lord Barren then jumped into the conversation. "How soon can you get in touch with your Skelaxian friend, Athrin?"

Athrin pondered a moment. "I'd say he could be here in a deronn—two at most. It depends on how involved he is in his current work. Though, I believe he'll jump at the chance to work for the Zaharaj."

Kala was obviously nervous. "Would it be all right if I informed the Emperor about this Chirras woman?"

The council members proceeded to engage in a telepathic discussion. *I have to learn how they do that,* Athrin thought.

Ali'stia spoke for the whole group. "We won't mind if you tell the Emperor. This is, after all, an Imperial matter—especially with the up-coming vote go'trell." As soon as she finished, the Marcisian woman started beaming.

"Thank you, my Lords and Ladies!" Kala gave them all a slight bow. "I will inform the Emperor as soon as I get back to the ship."

"Make sure you use a secure channel," Lord Nosfaren warned. He glanced around the room, assuring himself that every being was satis-fied with what had been discussed. "If that is all, I suggest we adjourn till the votes have been counted." With all in agreement, Lord Nos rose and led the Zah in their traditional mantra. They were a bit surprised when Athrin and Mirth joined in, igniting their own blood sorjins. Visage couldn't help but notice that Athrin's blood sorjin glowed in the same dark blue hue as the one Vira had.

With the council adjourned, the councilors headed for their rooms to await the start of the vote. Lord Nosfaren, still in the conference room, was stressed. "I wonder if joining the Empire is such a good idea." Ali'stia wrapped her arm around her husband and reassured him that everything would be fine no matter how the vote turned out.

***

Baltrix managed to catch up with Kala and her guards, who were all waiting for the lifts. "Imperator Kala, could I have a word?" he excitedly asked. Kala's two guards saluted him and took two steps back. Baltrix gave them a slight nod for their courtesy right after Kala started speaking. "Yes, Lord Baltrix, what is it?"

"I wonder if you can tell me what will happen to the Treaty of Firax if we *do* join the Empire."

Kala appeared amazed that Baltrix had even ventured to pose such a concern. "You mean you don't know! Why, it will be abolished—didn't Lord Nosfaren tell you?"

Baltrix's eyes went wide and his mouth hung agape. "Really? You mean we'll be able to get more ar'teths if we join?" he asked with hope-filled eyes.

"The short answer is, yes. It's also the reason why Grandmasters Athrin and Mirth came along with me. I'm sure they will be able to provide you with detailed information on how the transition process will work." She paused. "Of course, everything is based upon the outcome of the vote, so we'll have to wait and see how that turns out, Lord Baltrix." At that point, Kala and her guards walked into a lift and left the area.

Baltrix was savoring the possibility of having more ar'teths. *I hope the vote goes the right way—whatever the right way is,* he mused.

Kala pressed her hand to her chest after the lift started moving. Her two guards were snickering at how flushed she was. "What," she snapped at her two guards, who quickly averted their gazes. "You saw how he was looking at me so intently with those eyes of his." She took a deep breath. If only I was a bit younger and wasn't already married, she thought. Her two guards snickered again.

32

She Won't Get Away
With This

Riza stepped forward, causing the doors to open with a hiss. Upon entering her room, she glanced over her organized chaos. "Wait a minute... Something's not right here."

"Is there something wrong, Riza?" Visage asked, wondering why the demoness was so diligently surveying the room.

"What?" Riza abruptly asked the worried-looking Silvarian. "Oh. Sorry, V. It's..." She closed her eyes, but they narrowed after she re-opened them. "I believe that some being has been in my room."

Visage scanned the messy room. "Uhh, your room is such a mess, how can you even tell?"

"I just can," Riza unhesitatingly quipped before going over to her book-covered bed. She picked up the closest book, turned it over, and showed him the open pages. "See! This proves it!"

Visage shrugged. "What's the matter with it, Riza?"

"I left this book open to page one hundred fifty-six, but now it's on page one hundred and twenty-one!" Her voice was dripping with ire.

"But who would be dumb enough to come into your room? And what could they possibly want?" Visage asked while stepping over several pieces of discarded clothing. It was nearly impossible for him to find a spot on the floor that wasn't covered by one article of clothing or another.

Riza ignored Visage and proceeded to rifle through all of the books on the bed. "They've all been tampered with!" She put the last book down so hard that its impact made the mattress jiggle. After picking up one of the books in the center of the bed, she headed back to the door, motioning for Visage to follow. He started shaking his head and then trotted behind her. "I'm going to have to speak to Vira about touching my things!"

Visage was quick to jump to Vira's defense. "But Vira wouldn't have touched your things. Besides, she was with us the whole time," Visage cried in alarm before he and Riza walked into Vira and his room.

Vira was rather puzzled, having caught the tail end of the conversation. "What wouldn't I do?" she asked, now looking up from her book.

"Riza thinks you messed with her books, but I told her you wouldn't do that."

Vira didn't mince words. "Because I wouldn't! Riza your room looks like you were riding a solar storm, pummeled it into a black hole, and left everything where it had fallen when the gravitational pull stopped. So why would you think I'd even set foot in there!"

Vira's question gave Riza pause. "I don't know... But I know that somebeing was definitely in my room."

Vira's initial eye rolling quickly turned into a look of panic. "I have an idea whom it might have been!" She stood up, grabbed Riza by the arm, and tore back to the demoness's room. Visage, who was a little bewildered, eventually caught up to the duo.

Vira turned to Riza. "Alright Riza, what was disturbed?"

Riza pointed to the books on the bed. "Only those."

Vira scanned the books on the bed. "And which one is *The Three Greater Demon Races*?"

Riza now understood where Vira was going with this. She raced over to the far wall and picked up the third book in the last row. "It's this one!" she announced, proudly holding up the book. After glancing through it, she noticed it was also turned to the wrong page. She tossed it to Vira, who scanned it with her U-gem. A glowing screen popped up and displayed the scan results.

"That fraking woman took advantage of the Imperator's arrival and copied your book!" She tossed it back to Riza who caught it with a serious scowl on her face.

"I'm going to kill her!" Riza scathed. She slammed the book closed and threw it back onto the bed.

Vira pressed the gem on her fingerless glove and Lord Nos's voice patched through. "Yes, Vira, what is it?"

"We've been had, Nos. Apparently Chirras decided to forgo the welcoming ceremony so she could come to Riza's room and copy the book about the greater demons." Vira took a breath and added, "So please tell me you confiscated her mask so she can't read it!" For a moment, all three demons held their breath, awaiting Nos's reply.

"I did. How long will it take Chirras to translate the book?" Before answering, Vira and Riza both let out extremely audible sighs of relief.

"The book was written in the ancient language of the demons, so without her mask I'd say at least a rinonn... maybe more," Vira guessed.

"That buys us a little time. I'll have to tell Forscythe and the others to speed up their timetable."

Riza leaned over and spoke to Nos via Vira's U-gem. "What do you want us to do, Lord Nos?"

"Neither of you can let Visage out of your sight. Chirras doesn't fear many beings, but she does fear us. If you're both with Visage, she won't be able to touch him." Lord Nos's voice became stern. "And that's an order! Nos out!"

Once Vira's gem stopped glowing, the demonesses faced Visage. "uh, oh... Am I in trouble?"

"No, but if Chirras gets a hold of you, then you will be!" Riza warned.

"What does she want with me anyway?"

The demonesses glanced at each other before answering. "It's because you're a Silvarian demon," Riza started. Then Vira took over.

"You're the only demon who can grant immortality to mortal beings."

Visage's eyes opened widely. "How do I do *that!*" Both demonesses started to blush.

"Do you really want to know?" Vira hesitatingly asked.

"Did you have to ask?" Riza added. Now it was Visage's turn to blush.

"You're kidding... right?" The boy was really hoping they were, but his hopes were dashed when his fiancées shook their heads. "Isn't that just peachy," he sarcastically remarked.

Considering the obviously confused looks on their faces, he knew the demonesses had no idea what he was trying to say. "Come on! This is seriously dumb! First, I'm some kind of extinct demon; secondly, I have powers I can't control without that Vorihe... majigger—the thing you put on my back; next, I meet Rashia and Chaos who say I'll turn into some kind of Dark God or something; and, to top it all off, I have some black-hearted bitch after me because I can grant her immortality! Where on Zharaj is the being in charge! I want to file a complaint!" Visage was panting when he finished, having paced throughout his entire tirade. Vira and Riza were amused.

"That would be Eendril... though I don't think He'd see you. But He *can* hear you," Riza offered. Visage glared at her, slumped forward, and hung his head.

"Eendril, please get me out of this mess. Just kill me if You have to!" Visage pressed his back to Riza's bed, slunk to the floor and groaned into his hands. He was completely disheartened and frustrated.

"I hate to say this, Visage, but you're immortal, so that's not going to happen," Vira nonchalantly replied.

"Yeah, great, whatever. Can we go back to our room now before my head explodes?" The demonesses had to cover their mouths so the Silvarian wouldn't hear their giggles. He shook his head before getting back to his feet, kicking one of Riza's sets of pants off his foot when he did.

Once Vira regained her composure, she remarked to Riza, "If nothing else, he is quite entertaining."

"He's way more entertaining than my ber'nan, that's for sure," Riza replied before she headed for the door. Vira nodded and followed after her glum fiancé.

***

Visage was sitting on Vira's lap, but he was not amused. He glanced over at Riza, who was now occupying his chair. "How did this happen? Why are you *both* here?"

"Lord Nos ordered us to keep you in our sight at all times,"— Vira responded. —"at least until we deal with Chirras."

Visage frowned; he was trying hard to make sense of the whole situation. *An order is an order, but why does Riza have to be here? I mean, her room is right next door for crying out loud!*

Riza slightly turned her head, having overheard the boy's psychic rant. "It's because Chirras is powerful. After all, she was a member of the Council, V. She might try to pull something if Vira is alone, but she's not id'rthic enough to take us on when we are together." Riza winked at the boy before flashing him a conniving grin and wiggling her eyebrows at him. "So, deal with it."

Visage couldn't argue, so he gave up. "Is 'V' going to be my new nickname, Riza? I mean, couldn't you come up with something better than that?"

Vira chuckled. "It suits you," Riza replied with a smirk.

And I'm going to be marrying *her in the future?*

"Don't worry, Visage, she's only playing with you," Vira whispered.

"I know, but she acts more like a kid than even Jun does." Vira thought about his comment for a dironn.

"When you're ageless, I suppose you could say there really isn't a grown up among us—except maybe Eendril."

"So, the gods are the mature ones, and demons act like immature kids." He frowned. "Go figure."

Riza piped up in protest. "Not all of us demons act like that, V... I hate to tell you but we demons aren't all goody, goody like the gods are. Even Eendril has a sense of humor, though some beings hate to admit it. Anyway, He still ilonis us, despite our... deviances?"

"I think you mean delinquency," Visage offered.

"Hmm. I guess." Riza wasn't too sure, but she smiled widely and conceded the point.

The blinks and beeping noises coming from Vira and Riza's U-gems interrupted the conversation. "You know what that means—it's time to vote!" Riza enthusiastically chirped. Then she pressed her gem. A window appeared with several lines of text and two symbols: one represented yea and one represented nay. She pressed the one that stood for yea.

Visage looked on as Vira brought her hands in front of him and also pressed the one for yea. Then the screen reset. He was a bit bewildered at this. "Do you get *two* votes, Vira?" he asked, but she shook her head.

"You mean I get a vote!" the boy excitedly asked, hoping for Vira's confirmation.

"Of course you do, V." Visage ignored the fact that Vira had called him by his new nickname and pressed the symbol for yea. The image blinked, and "Thank you for your vote" appeared across the screen.

"Now all we can do is wait for the results," Riza muttered before she got up from the chair and headed for the refresher. Vira, however, was scowling.

"Riza, if you're going use the rinser, please do so in your own room."

"But I have orders to keep an eye on V," Riza retorted.

"I don't think Chirras will make a move while we're in our room," Vira told her with a slight frown.

Riza pouted before shooting back, "You really don't like me using your stuff!"

"That's right," Vira replied without even having to think.

Riza moaned but knew Vira's point about Chirras was probably a valid one. "Fine," she huffed, "but I'll be back soon!" Then out the door she went.

"Don't you like Riza, Vira?"

"No, I like her just fine—but her attitude towards tidiness really gets to me."

"I couldn't agree more. If I had kept my room the way she does, my oma... I mean mi'thia... would have killed me."

"That's the reason I requested that the Council give me my own room," Vira offered while turning the page on the book she was reading.

"Thank the verse you did. I iloni this room—it's so clean and neat. I'm so glad I get to stay here instead of in Riza's room!" Vira couldn't help but chuckle.

Riza came back in the room right in time for their gems to activate. A message appeared informing the demons that the votes were in and counted, so the trio excitedly headed for the lifts.

***

The temple atmosphere became more and more electrified; the arrival of the Grand Imperator was imminent. The Marcisian was bringing news that would affect the lives of everybeing on the planet.

The Council was standing in front of the crowd of Zaharaj. The black mass of beings intentionally created a path from the landing area all the way over to the temple grounds. Kala, her two guards, and the representatives from the Ja'Shari were standing beside the Zaharaj councilors. Visage was standing between Riza and Vira, eagerly awaiting the Marcisians' arrival. The crowd came to life with a grand roar when the small ship emerged from the asteroid field and made a hasty descent.

It didn't take long for the ship to land and the rear hatch to open. A Marcisian male started running down the ramp before it even reached the ground. He jumped from the edge and ran past the grand statues, his dreadlocks fluttering behind him. Within moments, he was standing in front of the Council, trying to catch his breath as he spoke. "Greetings to you, Lord Nosfaren. I have to say, it's an honor to be here with you—"

"Yes, yes, Nar'gal, you can dispense with the pleasantries; just get on with it would you please," Lord Nos impatiently requested.

Nar'gal, who appeared unfazed by Nos's rather sharp comment, smiled widely, took a long look at the Council of the Zaharaj, and turned to face the crowd. The huge gathering became deathly silent as he brought his U-Gem up to his mouth. "Members of the Zaharaj, greetings. I am Grand Imperator Nar'gal, Emissary of the Marcisian Empire. I have come here to inform you of the results from your vote." Nervous tension was thickly present while the Imperator peered over the crowd. Per Lord Nosfaren's request, he immediately dispensed the news: The vote was overwhelmingly in favor of the proposal, with only three nays and two abstentions!" The crowd roared loudly—blood sorjins ignited and hugs and congratulations were exchanged.

Lord Nosfaren stepped forward and inserted himself into the pandemonium. "Zaharaj! Silence!" His voice boomed and everybeing quickly hushed.

Nar'gal gave a thankful nod before resuming his comments. "I have a message for all of you from His Imperial Majesty." He then took a disk-like object from his pocket and threw it on the ground. The red-colored gem in the disk's center began to glow before projecting a giant hologram of a male Marcisian.

The being glanced out over the gathering. "My fellow beings, I am Barren Marcis the Third, the current Emperor of the Marcisian Empire. I welcome you wholeheartedly into our fold. Though some beings have been part of the Empire for what seems like eons, the rest of your organization has now joined us—and I extend a hearty welcome to all of you!" The crowd roared for so long that the Emperor finally had to gesture for them to quiet down. He then continued. "Of course, there will be a few changes within your organization." Though the crowd began to murmur, he proceeded. "First, I am happy to report that the treaty of Firax is now officially dissolved!" Everybeing went wild—even more so than before.

Lord Baltrix was overjoyed. He now envisioned the currently empty seats in his classroom. *They'll soon be filled with ar'teths!*

Emperor Marcis was so flattered by the crowd's enthusiastic reception to his message that he allowed the cheers and congratulations to go on a bit longer before continuing. "As you are probably aware, two representatives from the Ja'Shari are already there. They will assist you in setting up a plan that will enable the two organizations to freely exchange their knowledge of the Verse." The crowd appeared pleased with the pronouncement, exchanging cordial waves with Athrin and Mirth. Attendees then turned their attention back to the Emperor, steeling themselves for whatever was to come.

"Lastly, both of your organizations will take on new names." The crowd reacted with total silence. "The Ja'Shari shall henceforth be known as The Order of the White Hand." The Emperor paused while Athrin and Mirth respectfully bowed. "And the Zaharaj will now be known as The Marcisian Shadow Knights!" For a moment, the crowd seemed stunned. However, once the "Shadow Knights" had had enough time to process the information, the crowd as a whole erupted into cheers of glee. The Emperor actually seemed a bit taken aback by the borderline raucous behavior of the new inductees. Lord Nos appeared to share the crowd's sentiments, even cheering a few times himself. *That's a damned good name. It's fitting for my Zaharaj, he thought*, internally applauding the Zaharaj's approval.

Bah! If you ask me, our name should be The Firaxian Shadow Knights," Michael disdainfully thought, folding his arms and looking sour-faced.

"Who gives a crath what we're called! I'm just happy that that fraking treaty has been trashed! Now we'll have more ar'teths than ever before!" Baltrix's excitement fully overshadowed Michael's negative thought.

"I guess you have a point," Michael replied after contemplating the positive effects that having new ar'teths would bring.

All beings were discussing the new changes, but the Emperor was not finished. "As for your oaths, I have decided not to change them. However, I would like both the Order and the Shadow Knights to study each other's teachings and techniques. By doing so, you can all gain much." The Emperor bowed and then arose. A warm grin adorned his membrane-covered lips. "I bid you all a go'trell... and may God continue to watch over us."

At this point, the giant image of the Emperor vanished back into the gem on the disk. For a moment, the crowd remained silent. Then some being began chanting the oath of The Marcisian Shadow Knights:

"Peace is fleeting, so I thirst for knowledge." Those with blood sorjins kept them lit while the entire crowd joined the chant, including Athrin and Mirth.

"Through knowledge, I gain power; through power, I gain strength; through strength, I gain wisdom; through wisdom, I become enlightened and will become one with the universe!" With the final word said, the crowd cheered once more.

Marcisian Shadow Knights... I wonder which god gave the Emperor that idea, Lord Nosfaren mused. With a broad smile, he shut off his blood sorjin and peered up at the asteroid-filled sky.

33

Back at Home

Tim sat hunched over his desk. He reached over, picked up one of the pictures, and wiped off the dust that had settled on the frame. A feeling of melancholy washed over him after the images of three men, all wearing flight suits, were revealed. The men were grinning from ear to ear while the man in the center held his son, Orran, on his shoulders. Tim chuckled at Orran, who was wearing the Admiral's hat. The hat was much too big and hung down, covering up one of the boy's sapphire-blue eyes. Orran himself was smiling and showing off his fangs while he waved at the camera with both arms, causing the sleeves of the blue, oversized, Navy shirt to flap around.

Tim's eyes had welled up with tears when he had gotten the news that Orran had burst into flames, burned his mother, and taken off. When he told the Admiral about the incident, the commander tried to reassure him that Orran was fine. "He probably just flew somewhere to cool his heels."

Tim frowned after the memory faded. "It's been three months. Orran, where are you?" His eyes began to blur. Small teardrops hit the picture, rolled down, and pooled at the bottom of the frame. After wiping his eyes and putting the picture back, a surprise knock came at the cabin door. He quickly straightened his disheveled shirt before responding with a half-hearted, "Come in." The door crept open and an unrecognized officer entered and immediately stood at attention.

"Captain Sang-Ai?" the officer questioned.

"Yes?" Tim questioned back, struggling to put a name to the face. "Are you one of my crew?"

The man shook his head. "No, Captain, I'm here to tell you that your son is fine." Tim balked at the news, not daring to hope that it might be true. A moment later, he was bolting from his chair.

"How do you know about my son! Where is he! What have you d"— The man raised his hand to silence the outraged father.

"I have only been sent here to tell you that Orran is safe and that you don't have to worry about him." Tim lowered his head, struggling to comprehend what was going on. When he looked up, he was determined to ask more questions, but the man was gone. He ran to the open door, looked down the hallway, and saw two of his petty officers walking and talking, their backs to him.

"Hey! Gorman! Harrison!" The pair halted, turned, and saluted their captain. He quickly saluted back while exiting the cabin and heading their way.

"Is there something wrong, sir?" Gorman, the youngest of the pair, asked.

"Did you see an officer leave my quarters just now?" The two men glanced at each other before Harrison answered.

"No, sir, we didn't see anyone exit your quarters." He paused, then repeated officer Gorman's question. "Is there something wrong, sir?" At this point, Tim started glaring at the two men, as though his piercing eyes would force them to cough up the information he so desperately wanted to hear.

"Are you sure you didn't see an officer leave my quarters just now?" After vigorously shaking their heads and seeing the captain's expression soften, they simultaneously breathed a sigh of relief.

"That's fine, then. Carry on." The men gave a brisk salute before heading down the hallway; Tim turned and headed back into his quarters.

"What was that about?" Harrison thought aloud. Gorman was too bewildered to respond. Harrison took off his cap and ran his fingers through his dirty-blond hair before continuing. "Orran's disappearance is obviously weighing heavily on the Captain. Do you think we need to report this to the Admiral?"

"Absolutely not!" Gorman glanced at his friend. "The Captain is really worried. We're in the middle of a war, and his son is flying around— somewhere. Even the carrier squadron is worried. I know you're new here, so you haven't met the Blue Bomber... but everyone who has is worried." He stared at Harrison. "But no one is more worried than the boy's own father. So, cut the man some slack before you go and report him to the Admiral."

Harrison shoved his hands into his pockets, fully aware that he had lost this one. "Fine, but if the Captain sees any more phantom officers, I will report him," Harrison threatened.

Gorman smirked before half-heartedly nodding. "Fair enough." He then turned and retreated from the conversation. He could hear Harrison's words following him while he proceeded down the hallway.

"Don't worry, Captain Gorman, I'm sure we'll find him. After all, we are the United States Navy!"

Gorman muttered to himself. *I hate to think that Orran may have been captured by one of our enemies. He could be in some kind of lab somewhere being—*He cut himself off, shaking his head in an attempt to break loose from such a horrible thought.

"Don't worry, Gorman, he's in good hands."

Gorman halted and surveyed the immediate area in an attempt to locate the speaker, but no one was there. "So, he's in Your hands. Thank you, Father."

"As you all are," came the response. Gorman went on his way, his faith and vigor renewed.

***

Kim sat at the dining table. Though she wasn't hungry, she had agreed to accompany her boss to his dinner appointment. Her mind drifted from the conversation. She rubbed her burned hand. It had been three long months since the incident. Though the pain was gone, the scars from her third-degree burns remained. The only good thing was that her dressings were now off.

Kim had relived that fateful night, the night when Orran had run away, a million times. She remembered the incident as though it were yesterday and had a picture-perfect image of Orran's fire-engulfed form running out into the rain-filled night. *It's been months. Orran, where are you!*

Kim's thoughts drifted back to reality right when John and his dinner guest had shaken hands and the well-dressed executive had taken his leave. John, an American-looking Korean, sat back down, his cheery mood quickly fading. "Kim, are you all right? You haven't said a word all evening." His blue eyes were focused on her, and she could tell by the look on his face that he was worried.

"I'm fine, John, it's just—"

"I know. You're worried about Orran."

Kim responded with a nod. "Where could he be?"

John knew that Kim was talking more to herself than to him, but he replied anyway. "I don't know, but I'm sure that wherever he is, he's fine." *I'm not sure what I can say to help her feel better.*

Kim had been John's secretary since she had gotten out of college, and, by what he and Kim both believed to be fate, she had ended up marrying his half-brother, Captain Sang-Ai. "I don't know how I'd feel if I lost one of my kids," John consolingly offered.

Kim was about to respond when a man walked up to the table and prevented her from doing so. "Excuse me. Kim Sang-Ai?"

"Yes. I'm Kim. Is there something I can do for you?" The man shook his head.

"No, I'm only here to tell you that you don't need to worry; Orran is safe." Kim's eyes literally bulged!

"How do know my son! Where is he! What have you done with him!" She bolted from her seat, knocking the chair over in the process.

The man chuckled. "Your husband asked me pretty much the same thing."

Kim and John were both in a state of shock! *How can he know Tim? He is in the Persian Gulf with his task force,* they both thought. The man was unphased.

"I was sent to give you both the message that Orran, or should I say Visage, is just fine." At this, Kim didn't know whether to feel overwhelming relief or paralyzing fear.

"Visage?" John questioned, but the man was gone. A quick look around the dining area yielded no mysterious stranger and no answered questions. Kim raced down the aisle, nearly knocking over a waiter and relatively shot out the exit door.

"Kim, wait for me!" John called. He had lost time, having briefly stopped to check on the waiter who returned his credit card and receipt. By the time he made it through the door, Kim was standing in the middle of the street, frantically looking around for the elusive man. His reassuring hand on her shoulder only served to startle her and cause her to jump.

"John, who was that, and what did he mean by 'Visage'?"

"I have no idea, Kim "I wish I could be of more help."

"Be at peace. Orran is learning what he needs to learn in order to fulfill a promise from long ago." Kim and John's eyes went wide—they had heard the very distinct voice. A feeling of calm washed over them, and their eyes turned towards the source of the voice—the heavens.

"Do you think?" John whispered, prompting Kim to cry.

"I don't know, but..." she trailed off. Together, the long time friends stood in the road for a while, realizing that Orran was apparently on a mission that was far beyond their mortal understanding. "Do you think he'll ever come back?"

"We can only hope and pray so," John said before they got into the back seat of their black sedan.

"So, where to?" the driver asked.

"I need you to drop Kim off at her apartment, *Ha-Yung.*"

The man tipped his hat to his boss. "Very good, sir." Within moments, the passengers were on their way home.

My daughter, the future has not yet been written. Orran may very well return to you— at some point in time.

Kim looked questioningly over at John. "Did you say something?" she asked.

"No," he stated, a bit bewildered. Noticing Kim's demeanor, he again asked, "Are you alright?"

"I'm fine, I'm a little... stressed I guess. Hearing about Orran is really bringing the pain back to the surface. Right then, I thought I heard a voice telling me that Orran may return in time! I want to believe, but do you think it's true?"

John's interest was piqued at the possibility of another heavenly intervention, but he was not sure how to answer Kim's question. "I don't know for sure, Kim, but sometimes you really need to have faith that everything will work out in the end."

34

Foes Among Friends

Chirras hunched over her desk and groaned in frustration. She was having a hard time making any sense out of the demon language in her stolen book. Since the Council had confiscated her mask, she was unable to use it for instant translation, so she was on her own.

"Would you like some help with that?" an energy blob asked from its safe space behind a containment field.

Chirras was almost giddy! "Don't tell me you can read this ancient scribble!"

"I can do much more than that, my dear," it chided. Chirras raised a quizzical eyebrow.

"Tell me, how much paper do you have?" the energy blob asked.

"Why?"

"Because, if you fetch me some then, I can translate the book into a language you can actually read."

Chirras got up from her desk and marched over to the containment unit. "And why would you do that?"

"After listening to all of your groaning, I'd do anything if only to shut you up."

Chirras was livid. She was about to stab the energy being in order to ease her own frustration, but she thought better of it. Instead, she headed out to go get some paper.

"Where are you going? You know the Zah have their eyes on you."

Chirras smirked. "I'm only going to get some paper my blobby bodiless friend." In next to no time, she was back, carrying a small bundle of paper. "Now what?" she demanded, speaking to the blob through its containment unit (cage).

"Now, stick your hand with that gem of yours through the containment field."

Chirras didn't like the sound of the blob's proposal. "What are you going to do, bite my hand off!"

"No! But, I need to be able to read that book so I can translate it for you."

Chirras was still leery. "For the iloni—Look, do it or don't! Just quit your whining; it's really starting to become irritating," the unborn gripped.

"Fine!" With that, Chirras shoved the hand with the U-gem into the containment field. Immediately, it began to glow while the blob of energy absorbed the information. Chirras was in awe while she watched the unborn finish the process. She withdrew her hand, grateful that it was still intact.

"Now what?" she asked with slightly less irritation in her voice.

"Now give me those papers," the unborn ordered. Chirras immediately complied, shoving the whole stack into the containment field. The first page floated from the top of the stack. The unborn then focused a beam of energy onto the page, and words miraculously appeared! Once that page was full, another page levitated, and the procedure was repeated. Chirras waited impatiently, tapping the top of her desk while watching the stack of finished pages grow and the stack of blank pages diminish.

"This is the final page," the unborn gleefully boasted, pleasing Chirras to no end. She immediately ran to the containment unit, reached in, and pulled out the translated book.

"Now that wasn't so bad, was it my goddess?"

Chirras felt free to scoff at the energy blob, now that the precious book was safely in her possession. "Looks like you're good for something," she sarcastically remarked after inspecting the book and verifying that it was indeed translated into the common tongue. The mass of energy actually gleaned some pleasure from the remark, snide though it was.

35

Training is the Pits

Clack, clack, clack. The sound of wooden blade meeting wooden blade echoed off from the cavern walls. Once Visage landed on his back, Michael positioned his faux sorjin over the boy's right shoulder and held him down. "Not bad. Not bad at all," Michael commented.

However, Visage wasn't quite sure about Michael's optimistic assessment. "Ugh... I don't think I'm cut out for this," Visage whined. Though Michael offered him a hand getting back on his feet, he graciously refused; instead, he did a forward handspring, landing upright.

"Nah, Visage, you're actually quite the natural, though it does surprise me that you're more adept at the Fremmin and Elven styles as opposed to the Marcisian or Hyperion."

"I don't even know what all of that means, but I'll take your word for it."

"How many times do I need to go over this?" Michael drooped and sighed. "Listen, V, the Elvin and Fremmin techniques are based on quick strikes and pierces, which keep your opponent off guard. The Marcisian technique, like most others, is based on powerful swings. The first strike isn't necessarily a killing blow; it's used more to throw your opponent off balance. Then, through the use of precise footwork, you adjust the angle of the attack and finish the opponent off before he or she gets the chance to recover."

Visage didn't hesitate to speak his mind. "I understand all that. But, I don't understand why you're so keen on the stronger forms."

"I guess it's because of my home planet. However, because of your physique, you're more suited to the quick, more agile forms than the more common stronger ones." Michael smiled widely. "Either way, your skills are coming along nicely. I'll make a sorjin master out of you yet! You'll see!" He directed the last couple of words towards the pair of demonesses, who were watching with bemused smirks on their faces. "Visage will be the first sorjin master of The Shadow Knights," he added. Vira and Riza didn't bother to answer; they knew they'd only be adding to the man's already overinflated ego.

"Are you going to stand there and boast? Or are you going to continue to beat my young fiancé senseless?" Riza asked.

"Uh... well, I wouldn't say that, Vira." He glanced at Visage. "I mean, sure, he's a demon, so he can take a lot more punishment than most beings I've trained. So, I guess I have been kind of hard on him. But I can't deny that I am enjoying myself."

At that point, Cormack hesitatingly entered the ring. Not wanting to interrupt the debate, he turned around to leave. "Cormack, you're as punctual as ever."

Cormack winced when he heard Riza mention his name. He cautiously turned back around and faced the Meserino demoness. "Eh... yes, Lady... I mean..." Cormack stammered. "Judicator Riza... I'm here." His embarrassment quickly dissipated after Visage ran up and gave him a big hug. The boy didn't realize his own strength and almost knocked the wind out of the Twillan's lungs.

"Cormack!" Visage cried.

"Oof. Hi, Visage. Um, could you please let go? That hug of yours is actually starting to hurt," the Twillan whispered. Visage immediately let go, releasing the pressure on Cormack's chest. After a few weak coughs, the Twillan indicated that, "I'm okay." He then directed his attention to Riza. "So why did you need to see me, Riza? My master told me that it was important."

"It's nothing, I only need you to strip is all," Riza replied, completely catching the Twillan off-guard.

"Come again?"

Visage caught his friend's attention and explained. "Riza wants me to be able to take all of the forms of the Empire's inhabitants so I can disguise myself and... blend in?" He turned to get confirmation from Riza. She nodded and Cormack visibly relaxed.

"Well, why didn't you say so?" He smiled and took off his cloak. "I'm always happy to help!" *I wonder why they didn't ask Ranic?*

"It's because he'd be too excited," Vira interjected. "Besides, he's a red-skinned Twillan, so he wouldn't work as well since Visage is more like a Veserino than a Meserino."

"So, that's the reason why I'm here instead of Ranic... Makes sense," Cormack responded while pulling off his shirt, folding it up, and placing it on top of his cloak while he gave Visage a knowing smirk. "I was rather shocked to see you running around as a Night Elf, V."

"I have Moonreth to thank for that." Visage recalled how his Night Elf friend nearly jumped out of his skin when he saw Visage standing before him in Night Elf form. "It kinda sucks that, whenever I take on a new form, Riza and Vira want me to stay in that form for a mcronn." Visage glanced over at the two amused demonesses.

"It helps you keep that form in your mind," Vira stated. "That way you can use the forms of the different races whenever you need to."

"I still think all of this disguising and transforming business is strange."

"Psh. You're a demon, V, so things like changing your race and such should be second nature to you. Not to mention that you can hide from women like Chirras," Michael told him with a nod.

Visage grimaced at the sound of Chirras's name before halfheartedly responding to Michael's comment. "I guess so."

Cormack spoke up while folding his pants and adding them to his pile of clothing. "No, Visage, Lord..." he sighed and shook his head a few times. "Judicator Michael is right! Now that you're officially a member of the Empire, you need to be able to hide your demon nature as much as you can!" *I can't believe that we'll have to start calling each other by those new titles...*

Michael, Vira, Riza, Cormack and even Visage all lamented.

"I've been wondering... why is that, exactly?"

The beings seemed perplexed. Michael even slapped his face with the palm of his hand. *Boy is this kid dense,* he thought, only to be quickly corrected by Vira.

It's not that he's dense, Michael; he just doesn't understand that he's an endangered species. Few beings have ever even seen a living Silvarian. Even I haven't seen one since my dar'nra and our king were killed in the war.

"Okay so, I'm disrobed; now what?" Cormack asked, breaking into their silent banter.

"All right, V, it's just like you did with Moonreth," Riza told him while folding her arms under her chest.

"Yeah, yeah, I know," he retorted after he closed his eyes and began focusing his indren'freth. "Cormack, could you please raise your arms out and spread your legs a bit more?" Though a bit leery, Cormack complied with the request. Within moments, Visage burst into flames of white and varying shades of blue.

"Don't worry, he isn't going to hurt you," Vira informed the very worried Twillan with a reassuring tone.

Easy enough for you to say. Cormack shook his head and frowned. *You are an immortal demon, too. I, on the other hand, am standing here completely naked with a Silvarian demon, bristling with his inner fire, standing right in front of me.*

"Cormack, it's hard to concentrate while you're thinking so loudly," Visage complained. His friend responded immediately, quieting his mind before putting up a mental barrier and looking on with wonder when Visage pressed his hands together and caused sparks of energy to bounce from one to the other. The boy then knelt down and pressed both of his palms against the moribite floor. Cormack could see several blue-glyph-filled rings form under his feet. A warm breeze-like tingling sensation arose from the same area and traveled upwards, causing his twills to rise high above his head. *Is this what a demon's energy flow feels like?* Right after the thought abated, the tingling died and the glyphs beneath his feet faded back into the black moribite stone.

"Now, was that so bad?" Riza quipped at the awestruck Twillan.

"No, it actually felt surprisingly good." Cormack was too shocked to go on after he noticed the Silvarian had turned into a Twillan and was now standing before him.

"So, how do I look?" Visage excitedly asked. His two blue twills bounced a bit whenever he moved his head.

That is unbelievable! He looks just like a Twillan. Minus the white biree patterns. Cormack remained speechless, gaping at his friend's new form.

"Looking good, V. I kinda like the reverse coloring." Vira put her hand to her chin, walked around the newly formed Twillan, and admired his new look.

"At least this time, he got it right in the first attempt." Riza was so impressed that she let out a low whistle when Visage looked her way.

Visage proceeded to look himself over. His assessment: "I wouldn't say I got it that right. This color is a much darker blue than the softer azure color of my biree. And these biree are more of an off white than pure white." However, once the assessment was completed, he wiggled his fingers for a moment before smiling. Generally, he was satisfied with the outcome.

The group couldn't help but laugh when Visage attempted to grasp one of his very evasive twills. Cormack finally took pity on him and came to his rescue. "Here." He gently clutched Visage's right-sided head twill and placed it into the boy's eagerly awaiting hands. Cormack was grateful by the fact that Visage was so eager to learn and so packed with enthusiasm.

"Ow!" Visage cried out; he had grabbed his new twill a bit too tightly.

"What did you expect!" Cormack was critical, then instructive. "A Twillan's twills are very sensitive, especially in the tips."

Visage glared at his critic. "Couldn't you have said something sooner, Cor?"

Cormack chuckled after briefly reminiscing about the time when Visage himself had nicknamed him. "You didn't really give me a chance to warn you," Cormack shook his head before he retorted.

Yeah, he's right, I didn't. But, even though they're sensitive, they're still really cool! His excited thoughts drifted out for every onlooker to hear.

"Thanks, V. I like mine too!" Cormack smiled widely, overjoyed that his friend not only liked to study as much as he did but now looked like him as well!

The conversation was interrupted by blinking and beeping from Vira, Riza, and Michael's U-gems. "Oh, great!" Michael grumbled.

Riza was openly perturbed. "Why is it that every time we start training V, Lord Nos summons us to the Council Room?"

"And I was waiting for you guys to finish up so we could all head for the library together." Cormack's heart sank. He had been looking forward to spending time with Vira and Visage. He wasn't too happy about being around Riza.

That woman scares me sometimes, Cormack thought behind a mental barrier while he took a few quick glances at the irritated Meserino Demoness.

"Sorry, Cor, but duty calls." Vira muttered in a dejected tone.

"Hopefully, this meeting won't take long," Michael huffed before he started heading for the lifts.

Riza chimed in. "What do you think the Emperor wants now?"

"I don't care!" Michael shouted over his shoulder. "Just so long as it's not about the integration of our two organizations, again."

Everybeing nodded and expressed frustration over the fact that there were more white-and-black-cloaked beings roaming the halls than ever before.

"Those White Handers are really nosey," Cormack declared, defiantly crossing his arms.

"'In order for us to learn how to better combat the Skath and the Fallen, we must learn to share our resources,'" Riza said in a mock impression of Grand Master Athrin.

"I'm starting to think that they're only here to use us! If I have to listen to them go on again about the Zah'harrim and why I choose to use it instead of the Jah'harrim, I'm seriously going to lose it!" Cormack blurted.

All three councilors could relate to his sentiment. The goody, goody White Handers were continuing to ask why the Zaharaj were learning about the same Verse power that's used by Skath's followers. Even Cormack's own master, Lady Serishin, was agitated. "Those White Handers have pretty much overrun our library."

"At least Glavian doesn't let them take anything from the reliquary," Vira frowned and groaned before adding a rather sarcastic, "yet!"

Visage sighed. "And I'm... caught in the middle."

Cormack was almost dressed. He gave his friend a supportive nod. "Don't worry, V, the Council has your twin tails covered."

Visage managed halfhearted smile. "Thanks Cor, and thank you for helping me with my training too!"

Cormack donned his last boot, threw his cloak around his shoulders, and ran after the other four beings, two of whom were already at the lifts. He patted Visage on the head and walking beside him. "I don't think those White Handers will stay for long. The ones I talked to told me that staying on our planet makes them sick."

"That's what happens to those who have lived in the Jah for a long time and then try to dwell in the Zah." Michael couldn't help but smirk because he relished the idea of sick White Handers. The lift arrived and the group filed through the doors.

Visage was curious. "But how come I didn't get sick when *I* first got here?"

Cormack responded. "That's because you're a demon. Your kind can tolerate both great darkness and great light. Even I still have a hard time if I go too deeply into the caverns."

"Is that why you don't go exploring with Ranic and Moonreth?" Cormack nodded in the affirmative.

"That is why we demons are both feared and revered, V," Riza explained. "It's because we are immune to all forms of the Verse." "You could say that we're even scarier than the gods," Vira gloated, taking over for her friend. "We demons can go either way—Zah or Jah; it doesn't really matter to us. But gods, they can only be one or the other—"

Michael was so enthralled with the conversation that he interrupted Vira and completed her thought—"either completely light or totally dark—for them there is no in between. It sucks to know that I can only play with the Zah'harrim while I'm in this mortal life, because, once I die, that's it!"He finished with a grunt.

"Wait! You mean to say that after you die you can't use all of the totally awesome, spectacularly incredible, techniques you've shown me, Lord Michael?" For a moment, Michael's countenance glowed; he was overcome with a feeling of pride. However, the feeling soon waned, and he gave an affirming nod.

"That's right, V." Michael chuckled at the looks that both Visage and Cormack were giving him. "Once I kick the glort, I'm all done dabbling in the damned darkness."

Visage wasn't sure if the tall blond man's statement about being done with "dabbling in the damned darkness" indicated that he was depressed, or angered by the thought. However, he did know that most beings had a hard time figuring him out.

The lift stopped and the door opened. "Here's my floor." Cormack stepped out, turned to his friends, and gave them all a slight bow. He received smiles and nods in return.

***

Cormack frowned when he walked inside his beloved library and saw a bunch of white-and-black cloaked beings milling about. More than a dozen were also sitting at the long tables reading from his precious books.

"Oh, Cormack, thank the Verse you're here!" Harneth called out from behind the counter.

"What's going on, Harth?" Cormack asked, using the nickname Visage had bestowed upon the blind man.

Harneth desperately plead, "Can you please go and guard the reliquary?"

"Why, what's happening?" Cormack whispered, feeling that he had stumbled across a delicate situation, and he wasn't sure if the White Handers should overhear the conversation.

Harneth took note of Cormack's approach and also started whispering. "I'll try to keep it short. Apparently, one of our new Order friends has decided to... shall we say... try to break into our vault." Cormack's mood transformed from shock to outrage so fast that Harneth was surprised his twills didn't fall off. "Calm down, Cor. He's gone. Lord Glavian and Lady Serishin stopped him and escorted him out of the temple."

Cormack's rage eased. "So *that's* why they summoned the Council!" Harneth flashed a firm nod.

"I guess I'm now on guard duty." Cormack strode off towards the reliquary.

At least until the others get back, Harneth silently imparted to the still-perturbed Twillan. Cormack waved his right hand, indicating he had gotten the message.

With him here... the reliquary will be safe, for now, Harneth thought before he looked up at the ceiling. *I hope the Council will be civilized. I know Lord Nosfaren and the others will not take this lightly.*

✳✳✳

The Council Room was a torrent of shouts. Vira, Michael, Riza, and Visage were standing right outside the door. "Um... is it only me... or is that Lord Nos I hear?" Michael asked. He wasn't looking forward to entering the room.

"Yeah, when Nos is like this, it's not a good sign," Vira bluntly added. Then, unexpectedly, the doors shook; some being had apparently slammed into them from the other side. Vira quickly removed her hand from the door handle. She was scowling and wincing.

Riza had no sooner said, "That didn't sound good," when the sound of moaning penetrated the door.

Visage was a little creeped out. "I don't think I want to go in there right now." The group understood where the child was coming from and shared his concern. Everybeing was worried about what-on-Zharaj was happening behind the big doors! Before Vira could remove her hand off the door handle, the nearing sound of footfalls further escalated the beings' trepidation. Could the goings on behind the doors feel more sinister? Indeed, they could—and did. They were completely terrified when they heard somebeing getting dragged, accompanied by the sound of heavy footfalls.

Vira assumed that whoever was the source of the moaning was now being dragged into the center of the room. *We'd better get in there!* Cautiously, she cracked open the door.

"Vira, Riza, Michael—get in here! Now!" Lord Nosfaren sternly ordered. Four beings hurried in, walked past the semiconscious form of Grand Master Mirth, and took their seats. Visage sat on Riza's lap, both sitting right next to the enraged Lord. Riza was hoping that Visage's close proximity might help calm Lord Nos down a bit.

"We just came from the pit—so what the frak is going on!" Michael boldly cried while glancing from the unconscious Twillan in the center of the room to the outraged Councilors.

Glavian jumped to his feet and pointed an accusing finger at the now half-conscious Twillan. "This Skath-sucking scum had one of his subordinates use his blood sorjin to try to break into our reliquary!" The Grand Master's compatriot, Athrin, feared to make a move; he simply stood and watched the scene unfold. Riza held Visage more closely when she felt everybeing's anger rise.

"Shouldn't we do something?" Visage whispered.

Riza shook her head. "No, we wait," she whispered into his audio cone, giving him a weird feeling. Glavian returned to his seat.

Lord Nos was still fuming. "So, Grand Master Athrin, what are you going to do about this situation!"

Athrin pondered for a moment, not wanting to create a rift between the Marcisians and their newly adopted Zaharaj; they had not even had a chance to bond. "I'm going to send Mirth back to Firax, along with any others who were involved. Not even I can tolerate beings who break the rules." Mirth, though still groggy from his sudden impact with the door, got tentatively to his feet.

"I protest! I was told by one of your own that we could use the reliquary!" he exclaimed. The anger in the room subsided while the councilors contemplated Mirth's accusation.

"Who told you that?" Lord Ranic yelled in anger at his fellow Twillan.

"I think she said her name was Dereth... Dearth—"

Lord Baltrix interrupted. "You mean Dreth?"

"Yes, that's it... Lady Dreth!" Mirth snapped his fingers and shouted in recognition. The mood in the room instantly soured.

"Fool! Didn't you know that Lady Dreth was kicked off the Council and stripped of her title!" Lord Michael shot up from his chair, startling both of the Grand Masters and shouted, "Lady Dreth is none other than Chirras!" Mirth and Athrin's eyes went wide when they recognized the name.

"Oh, Frak me!" Mirth shouted while his aqua eyes widened. "You mean that she's the deser'rec bakrath who's after the young Silvarian!"

Visage scowled.

Lord Barren was fuming. "That does it! Lord Nosfaren, I say we put that woman away for good!"

"Knight's of the Empire... we must stay the course!" Judicator Nosfaren took a deep breath. "Judicators Forsythe, Baltrix, Michael, Glavian, and Serishin." The beings mentioned snapped to attention after Nosfaren sounded off their names. "Seeing that our book plan has failed, I need all of you to focus on the library, especially on the reliquary." Everybeing enthusiastically agreed. "Athrin, I need you to keep a closer eye on your Order. If you even think a being might be a problem, send them back to Firax. That includes you too, Mirth!" Lord Nosfaren glared at the Twillan, who began to protest.

"But I—oh never mind, I'll go," Mirth conceded.

"And Athrin..."—Nos was a little calmer now—"I need you to assist your Skelaxian friend with monitoring all of Chirras's transmissions. I want to be informed about everything that woman says or does!" Lord Nos stood up. "Do you understand? This isn't Firax. This is Zharaj, the planet of darkness, and though the Emperor changed our name, he hasn't changed our nature, and we deal with traitors in our customary way!"

"I understand completely, Lord Nosfaren. And, in order to ensure that we don't cause you added distress, I'll send all of the White Handers back home until Chirras has been brought to justice. Only I will remain. Will this suffice?" Athrin was concerned, knowing full well that the treaty with the Zaharaj, already tentative at best, was now close to collapse. He was grateful and relieved to see Lord Nos nod his head in agreement.

Mirth limped to the door. "I'll tell the others to gather at the landing area. If we hurry, we can be off world before trell fall," he said, then closed the door behind him.

"Vira and Riza, I want the two of you to continue keeping a close eye on your fiancé. Is that understood?"

The two demonesses burst out in unison, "Of course, Lord Nos!"

"If that is all, then we are dismissed."

✱✱✱

Chirras sat hunched over in her chair. The last several deronns had been a mess. She was under constant surveillance, so she had to create the illusion that she had not noticed the eyes, constantly tracking her every move. Still, she had managed to get out from under surveillance for a short time—time enough to convince one of the gullible White Handers that anybeing in the Order could go into the reliquary and borrow anything they wanted.

Her deceit had bought her some time, though not enough. She now read the passage on the page in front of her. "Silvarian demons have the ability to turn the women they iloni from mortals to immortals." For a fleeting moment, the passage drove Chirras into a state of sheer euphoria. However, her elation was short lived. "But it doesn't tell me how! How does a Silvarian turn a mortal into an immortal! Where the frak is the rest!" she screamed. She turned her sights onto the bubbling mass of dark energy stored safely behind the shielding of its containment unit. "You didn't translate the rest of it!" She grabbed her sorjin and held it menacingly in her right hand.

The blob started to laugh. "I translated all of it, my queen."

"But it doesn't tell me how! If you know something, you'd better tell me, or I'll"—

"You'll what," The unborn mockingly accused her. "Chirras? Kill me? Just how many times have you tried… and failed? I'll tell you what. If you accept my gracious offer, I'll tell you exactly what you want to know," the blob taunted. Chirras let out another blood-curdling scream before starting to pace and loudly vent.

"Wait a minute! This is impossible! How does a male Silvarian turn a being into an immortal?" She suddenly halted. "Were Silvarians really all males?" She spun around, literally ran to her desk, and grabbed the page of the book pertaining to Silvarian demons.

"Everybeing should know that," the blob of energy gloated.

Chirras ignored the blob's sarcastic remark. Instead, she ruminated over what she had learned so far. It took a few moments, but a smirk gradually formed and then… then the power-hungry woman all but rolled on the floor with laughter! The energy ball bounced around inside its prison, annoyed and disappointed that the deser'rec had apparently gotten her answer. "Now I'm grateful I was born a woman, even if it wasn't my choice! Otherwise, this information would have been completely worthless!" Chirras resumed her hysterical laughter.

"So now what are you going to do, Chirras, ask the nice demonesses to let you borrow their precious fiancé for a deronn or two? They'll kill you before you get anywhere near him." Chirras stopped laughing; she knew the smart crathed thing had a point.

"Yes, but that's just it—they care so much about him that they will do anything to keep him safe. And I have friends who can help. All I really need to do is get him off planet," she cackled—"in pieces if necessary!"

The mass of energy was actually startled by Chirras's obvious disregard for life. Perhaps I was wrong about her. We dwell in darkness, but even we preserve life when we can. There is no way I can allow her to become our goddess, nor anybeing else's for that matter. I know she doesn't have the ability to kill me, at least not yet. But if she gets a hold of the Silvarian, there will be no hole black enough to hide me. For the first time in its existence, the energy blob was terrified.

***

Chirras moved quickly to her desk and pulled out the bottom drawer on the left side. Sitting there was the item she had hoped never to have to use. However, she was very much a fan of an old saying: desperate times call for desperate measures. The box she now held was very much a replica of an Ik'thorian puzzle box but with one slight difference—it wasn't layered with trap runes, so she was able to open it without any form of incantation or even trial—something the original were known for. She merely focused her power, and the lid snapped open. Carefully, she sat the box down on her desk and pulled out the transmitter, which was able to transcend all space and time in order to communicate with a being from a far distant galaxy. She didn't like to think about the being she was about to contact, but with grim determination she pressed the button on the metal disk, and its dark green gem began to glow. Almost instantaneously, the gem projected the foot tall holographic image of a cloaked figure hunched over in his throne. The figure studied Chirras for a few moments before even recognizing her existence. "I must say, Chirras—I'm impressed." He spoke in a voice that was low, menacing, and ominous.

"Don't patronize me!" Chirras slammed the palms of her hands down on top of her desk. She then leaned in and sneered at the image. "Unlike you, I don't worship that pathetic, fraking, Dark God."

"Which is the reason why I'm quite intrigued, my daughter," the being responded, leaning back in his throne. His identity was all but concealed under his massive robe.

Chirras gritted her teeth. "I don't think, even for a moment, that I've ever considered you to be my dar'nra!" she furiously spat.

The being ignored her obvious disdain. "So, why did you contact me, Chirras, since you're obviously not thinking about taking Skath as your God?"

"I don't worship anybeing! There is only one thing I worship, and that's power!"

Her announcement made the man laugh. "Good. Very good. At least we have one thing in common."

Chirras actually cracked a smile at her dar'nra's witty comment, and then proceeded. "The reason I'm here is to tell you that all of your little scouts have been converted!" She thoroughly enjoyed the show when her dar'nra cursed in several languages before settling back down.

"Pathetic weaklings! Chirras, I want you to hunt all of those traitors down and kill them!"

Chirras laughed so hard that she had to clutch stomach. "They're not *my* problem—they're *yours*!"

The man's reaction was even worse than his previous outburst. This time, it took him much longer to calm down, only adding to Chirras's pleasure. "So, if you're not joining us and you're not going to take care of those traitors, then why *did* you contact me?"

"I need you to help me escape from this galaxy," Chirras coolly answered.

The man was intrigued. *I wonder if she actually wants to come home.* His lengthy pause aggravated Chirras.

"So, are you going to assist me or not!"

"Very well, Chirras, I'll arrange for a transport to meet you at the Selorn Sector's Hunter's Guild... Will that suffice?"

"It will. However, there is one small issue. I won't be alone. Will that be a problem?"

"It shouldn't be. Why? Did you actually manage to find an apprentice among those heathens?"

Again, Chirras erupted with laughter, much to the man's ire. "Frak no!" Then she whispered, "But the one I bring will be mine alone."

"Really now. How strange for you to claim a being. Perhaps you've become a slaver, or perhaps you've decided to get yourself a plaything?" the man goaded.

Chirras's anger flared. "How dare you make such accusations!" She got her face as close to the holo image as she possibly could. "If you must know, I've found a way to become immortal—without divine intervention!"

The man balked at Chirras's declaration, though, at the same time, he wanted to know more. However, Chirras ended the transmission, slamming her fist down so hard on the device that it shattered. She was elated! *Frak the gods—light and dark. I've found another way! But, what if I drathed-off that Skath worshipper so much that he doesn't send me any help! No. I'm sure he'll send help. He's curious to know whom I have, and he'll want to know how to obtain immortality. Oh well, he can't get in on this one; he's male. He'll never be able to taste immortality without first tasting death.* She reveled in the thought. *Without a god to care for his soul, he is quite literally damned. So sad.* She smirked before she picked up her sorjin and headed for the door.

"Where do you think you're going?"

Chirras flicked the hood of her cloak over her head. "I'm going to find my fiancé," she brashly shot back at the thing in the containment unit before gleefully exiting the room for the very last time.

36

Kidnapping a Demon

The Shadow Knights were busy escorting the White Hand rabble to the landing area where Chirras's ticket off planet was awaiting her arrival. But the woman still needed one more thing before she could leave Zharaj—a Silvarian demon. Chirras knew Visage was roaming the temple somewhere, and she needed to find him—fast! When a group of Shadow Knights headed her way, she lowered her head, hoping to conceal her identity. "Frak Nos for confiscating my mask," she muttered, though the Knights were too busy talking among themselves to take notice of her passing. "If I had my mask, I could more easily find that little imp," she cursed under her breath. Another group of Shadow Knights passed by. One of them caught Chirras's attention when he mentioned the name "Visage" and the word "library." *So, that's where you are!* "Wow, that was close," she softly muttered, having quelled an audible outburst just in time. Now she had to back track to the stairwells. "I wish I could use the lifts, but I'd probably get spotted." She needed to climb up three flights of stairs. However, after climbing up the first flight, she decided to jump the last two using her indren'freth.

***

The library doors were wide open. Chirras thought the Zah'harrim was with her this deronn, since nobeing was in sight. She walked past the abandoned counter where "that blind boy"—as she referred to Harneth—usually hung out. She passed several aisles before spotting the being she was looking for. *So, they're trying to disguise him as a Twillan. Well, they actually did a really good job. That off-white biree surely stands out against the dark-blue hue of his skin. I don't have much time.* Chirras wasn't bashful. She strode right up to Visage, grabbed his arm, and caused him to drop his book.

"Hey! Watch it!" Visage tried to bend over to recover his book, but the woman held his arm fast. "Chirras!" he screamed out in alarm, alerting his true Twillan friend, Cormack.

Cormack immediately telepathically shouted as loud as he could, *Chirras has Visage! Riza, Vira, everybeing—hurry!* Chirras winced at the telepathic scream. She wrenched Visage much closer and ignited her blood sorjin. The inky-black blade came to life right before a pair of drathed-off demonesses and several other beings blocked her escape route.

"Back off!" the woman warned as she held her blade dangerously close to Visage's neck. "Or we'll see just how immortal a Silvarian truly is!" Her tone was so cold and threatening that even the more powerful demonesses moved out of her path. Chirras sneered at them while slowly backing up.

"Come on, Chirras, let me go!" the young demon screamed. Chirras ignored the plea and started making her way over to the lifts, dragging her hostage along. The others, horrified, followed.

"You! Press the button for the lifts!" Chirras commanded. Cormack didn't move, so she added. "If you don't, then your Silvarian friend will lose his head!" Cormack was mortified, but he had no choice. He marched over to the button and slammed it with his fist.

"Good Twillan," Chirras sweetly chided. Though Cormack had carried out the mad woman's order, he proceeded to clench both fists and to attempt to kill the betrak with his thoughts. She scoffed at his pathetic psychic intrusions, right after the doors opened. "Get out!" she commanded the stunned passengers.

At first, the three occupants glared at the crazed-looking woman, but all thought twice about trying to resist her command and opted to exit without protest. With hostage in tow, Chirras climbed in, and, using the Zah'harrim, she telekinetically pressed the button for the ground floor.

Riza screamed with rage and flared out her wings, nearly knocking Cormack over in the process. Vira, acting more calmly, activated her U-gem and informed the other members of the Council what had just transpired.

***

Lord Nosfaren was sitting at his desk when Nic'telec burst into the room. "Ssssir, I have ssssomething you ssssshould sssse," the Skelaxian chirped excitedly through his mandibles. Nos motioned for him to continue. The oversized bug—a cross between an ant and a mantis—placed a holo emitter on Nos's desk. He then pressed the red gem in the center, bringing the disk to life.

The recorded transmission of Chirras ranting to the Skath worshipper played out in front of Nos. Nos was shocked but also pleased. "So they did send others... but they were all converted. That means the onlybeing we have to deal with is Chirras herself." The Meserino demon was grinning widely when he stood up. "Thank you for your invaluable service, Nic'telec."

The insectoid appeared embarrassed; his green face took on a lighter tint. "It wasssss my p-pleassssure, Masssster Nossssfaren." Nos came around his desk and shook the insect's claw-like appendage, flustering the poor being even further.

"Nic'telec, could you please transmit this to the Imperators on Marcisia. We need to find the beings the Skath sent so we can protect them and, hopefully, gain some useful information from them."

The Skelaxian made a buzzing sound, indicating that he supported Nos's plan and would gladly comply with his request. "I will do sssso!" Nic'telec cheerfully agreed.

Lord Nos lost no time in escorting his visitor through the door.

"Oh, Nic'telec, could you also send a copy to our friends in the White Hand?" Nic'telec nodded in affirmation and headed back to the communications annex. Nos re-entered his room right before his U-gem lit up and started beeping. Right after he pressed it, he heard a familiar but greatly distressed-sounding voice.

"Lord Nos, we have a problem! Did Vira's message get to you! Chirras has taken Visage hostage in the library! Please lock down all transports in the landing area! We can't let her get away!" Cormack blurted in a single breath.

Nos was seething! "I'll see to it, Cormack! I'm on my way!"

The transmission ended, and Nos activated his U-gem in order to make a temple-wide announcement. "This is Lord Nosfaren of The Marcisian Shadow Knights. This is a level five alert! This is not a drill! Chirras, formerly Lady Dreth, has taken a hostage and is heading for the landing area. She cannot leave this planet! All craft must be locked down, and I am authorizing the use of deadly force! Nosfaren out!"

Several thousand beings heard Nos's message and scrambled to comply with his orders. Judicator Nosfaren met up with Ali'stia while making his way to the lifts. "Is this really happening, iloni?" Ali'stia asked, knowing full well the answer. Her husband quickly confirmed her fears, giving her first the look then the nod.

37

Duel of the Fates

It was as though Chirras were in a sea of black. She was surrounded by Shadow Knights along with a few beings from the Order of the White Hand. The only thing keeping the defenders at bay was the blood sorjin she was holding to the neck of her captive. "Get back!" she warned, bringing her inky-black blade even closer to her captive's neck. "If you don't, then your precious little Visage will lose his head!"

Vira and Riza were beyond livid; they were crazed with anger. Several beings had to back up after both the demonesses tapped into their indren'freth and burst into red and black or, blue and black flames. "I swear, Chirras, you won't leave here alive!" Riza screamed.

"Correction, Riza… we're leaving!" Chirras shot back.

"I hate you, Chirras!" Visage cried while he struggled to get away from his captor.

Chirras chuckled. "For now, Visage, but soon you'll only belong to me!" she scoffed. At this, Vira and Riza clenched their teeth so hard that their gums began to bleed.

"My sentiments exactly, ar'teth Visage," Baltrix announced when he burst through the crowd of black-cloaked figures. He was headed straight for Chirras, his blood sorjin lit and ready for battle.

"I'm warning you Baltrix—back off!"

Baltrix utilized his own telekinetic powers causing Chirras's blood-sorjin-bearing hand to be racked with pain. Her fingers bent and twisted at odd angles, several of them audibly snapping and popping. When Chirras dropped her blood sorjin, Visage took the opportunity to stomp down hard on her foot. Chirras, who was now suffering from pain in both her hand and her foot, let her guard down. Miraculously, this allowed Visage just enough time to wiggle free and escape unharmed. He was shocked when Baltrix used telekinesis to lift him off the ground and fling him right at Vira and Riza. Since the young Silvarian had landed in their arms, the demonesses had to calm their inner fires.

Knowing that Visage was safe, Baltrix was now on the move. When several other beings in the crowd ignited their blood sorjins and headed towards the disarmed woman, he flung them out of the way. "She's mine!" he shouted. "Nobeing is to interfere!" The surrounding crowd was obedient. Everybeing immediately shut off their blood sorjins and prepared to watch the horrifying scene that was about to unfold. That is, everybeing but one.

Michael emerged. He glanced at Visage, gave him a nod, and proceeded towards Judicator Baltrix. "Are you sure you don't need help, Master Baltrix?" Michael pled, hoping the man would let him in on the fun. The crimson eye sockets on his mask were burning brightly in anticipation of the battle to come. However, Baltrix glared at him and gave him a curt answer.

"No! I've wanted to do this for a long time!" Michael backed down without so much as a word.

Chirras had used a Zah'harrim technique to mend her fingers. She immediately levitated her blood sorjin back to her hand and reignited it. "You're no match for me, Lord Baltrix!" she screeched.

"Ha! Like I'd ever fear a fraking deser'rec like you, Chirras!" Baltrix shot back before he let out such a blast of energy that it sent the woman flying back several yards—nearly knocking over several beings the crowd. Though Baltrix's hand still billowed with smoke, he clutched his sorjin with both hands and charged at the still-disoriented woman.

Baltrix has this in the bag! one of the beings in the crowd telepathically cheered. The crowd howled its agreement.

"Kick her crath back to the pit from whence she came!" another being yelled out, causing another great cheer to rise from the onlookers. At the very moment the cheer was reaching its crescendo, Lord Nosfaren arrived at the scene. His countenance spoke for itself—he wasn't pleased.

Silence! All of you! Let the man concentrate on his opponent! The crowd cowed under the powerful Meserino's intense mental might.

With everybeing now silent, Lord Baltrix was better able to concentrate on Chirras. She had managed to get up and take a defensive stance; the betrak was holding her sorjin in both hands, awaiting Baltrix's attack. She was shocked when, instead of landing a blow, Baltrix went airborne. By the time he landed in a crouch in front of her, he had shifted his sorjin to his right hand and was holding it in a reverse grip. Without enough time to reorient her own blade, Chirras could only tighten her stomach muscles, hoping to withstand the kick that was inevitably coming. Baltrix did not disappoint. He exploded upward from his crouching stance and into a wide spin; his left leg shot out, delivering a hard kick to the center of Chirras's abdomen. The deser'rec grunted and again flew several feet backwards before landing with a thud. After rolling around on the floor, she finally managed to get up on her hands and knees.

"If this is all you're capable of, Chirras, I'm very disappointed," Baltrix taunted as he brought his leg down and calmly walked over his still downed opponent. The woman sneered, rose up, lifted her hand, and sent a fierce blast of red-and-white lightning his way. In a flash, Baltrix surrounded himself with a shield of pure indren'freth energy. The swirling, crimson and white fire absorbed most of Chirras's lightning, reflecting the rest against the walls, ceiling, and floor of the hallway. Chirras stopped her attack. Though she attempted to create several energy spheres to hurl at the oncoming fire engulfed Judicator. Chirras's eyes widened in panic when she discovered that she was blocked from tapping into her own indren'freth.

Baltrix began to laugh. "Don't you know that if you drath off the gods enough, they punish you by sealing away your inner fire?" Chirras's eyes looked past her formidable opponent and glared at the Silvarian. In her rage, she let out a blood-curdling scream, having deduced that Visage was at fault for her current predicament.

Baltrix wasted no time charging his hands with his own lightning, but didn't stop there; he added the fire swirling around him to his lightning and shot the flame-blanketed bolts towards his weakened adversary. Without her indren'freth, Chirras had no choice but to tap into the arcane arts in order to put up a glyph shield of her own. She only managed to get three glyphs fully materialized before Baltrix's storm of lightning and fire slammed into the first of her arcane shields. The lethal storm instantly shattered the first barrier, causing the purple glyph to burst into shards. The second barrier wasn't faring any better, when Baltrix let his built-up energy flow down his arms and out his fingers. Once his massive energy blast shattered her second barrier, Chirras dropped to her knees and held out her hands in a desperate attempt to save the last defensive glyph. Her efforts were futile; the last glyph exploded and fractured into a myriad of shards. Baltrix's offensive efforts had succeeded—but only for a moment. Chirras was not done yet. She peered at Baltrix with hate-filled eyes before letting out another spine-chilling scream. She then jumped to her feet and ran full force at her opponent, her blade held high above her head. When she thrust the blade down towards him, Baltrix merely stepped aside. Within a moment, Chirras stumbled forward. Baltrix, seeing an opportunity, stuck out his foot and tripped the demonic woman, causing her to slam her face down into the floor.

"Pathetic. And you claim to be a Councilor?" Baltrix spat. Chirras stood up and wiped the black blood away from her left nostril.

"And what of you, Baltrix? Or should I call you Vlad the Impaler!" Baltrix's eyes went wide and his face contorted from anger to pure panic that quickly turned into rage. Chirras had brutally revealed his long-held secret. A din erupted from the crowd, not so much because of Chirras's revelation about Baltrix's past but rather from Chirras's entire demeanor—a demeanor that indicated just how blood thirsty and power hungry she really was.

"How dare you—"

Chirras did not let up. "How dare I? Don't you mean how dare you! You're sooo much blacker than I am, Vlad. And yet, here you are, acting like some pristinely pure champion of justice!"

The dual of the fates of both combatants began again. The two beings squared off and began circling each other. While their blades pulsed loudly, they planned their next moves. Chirras, yet again, attempted her overhead slice, but this time Baltrix brought his own blade up to intercept. The two blades collided, emitting an eerie hissing sound and the scent of boiling blood wafted out over the crowd making a lot of them put their masks on in order to filter out the vial smell. With blades now locked, Chirras and Baltrix again began again to move slowly in a circle, neither willing to give up his or her position.

"Do you think that God of yours will ever accept a being as dark as you, Vlad?" Chirras scathed through gritted teeth. Baltrix's anger raged. He took a step forward, then another and another, pushing the smaller woman back with every step. Chirras was gritting her teeth so hard that her gums began to bleed. "What's the matter, Vlad? Are you going to impale me, too?" she chided.

Baltrix's momentum slightly slowed while he mused over Chirras's disclosure. He was flabbergasted. *How? How does she know?* For mere moments, Baltrix delved into old, painful memories. However, his brief lack of focus provided Chirras with some critically needed time. The Fallen woman put all of her weight on her left foot before springing forward and breaking the stalemate. She sent Baltrix stumbling backwards, then jumped back herself in order to create more distance between them.

Nosfaren, who had been intently watching the fight from the sidelines and noticed that Baltrix was obviously being distracted by Chirras's cutting remarks, intervened. *Baltrix, don't let her get to you! Your past doesn't matter! Now finish this before I do!* Baltrix briefly flashed a smile, having felt Nos's supportive directive.

"At least I'm not such an id'rth that I believe in a being who no longer exists!" Baltrix screamed at Chirras.

Chirras had had a chance to revise her strategy and was once again charging Baltrix, using the same overhead chop. "I don't believe in ANY god! I only believe in—POWER!" she yelled. When she brought her blade down, Baltrix once again stepped aside, but this time he didn't trip her; instead, he spun around while she was passing him and tried to sever her head with his blade. Chirras had seconds to rescue her blade from its downward trajectory and get it back up over her head. Right when Baltrix's blade was about to reach her neck, she blocked it, but the force of his blow still drove her forward. Baltrix did a reverse spin on the ball of his right foot, having decided that, since her back was blocked, he'd attempt a frontal attack. Realizing that Baltrix's blade was now in front of her, Chirras did the only thing she could do: she shut off her blade and, with the assistance of gravity, dove to her knees. Miraculously, she arched her back and barely avoided Baltrix's second attempt at slicing off her head with his crimson-colored blade. Shooting forward, Chirras reignited her blade, but Lord Baltrix caught her in his telekinetic vice-like grip. Everybeing was watching expectantly when Chirras's form rose from the floor. The woman dropped her blood sorjin and struggled for air, grasping at her throat with both hands.

"I grow weary of this," Baltrix announced. He then used the verse to slam the gasping Chirras against the floor. When Chirras rolled onto her side, he kicked her back onto her back, twirled his blade, and readied himself for the final blow. "This ends now!" He gripped the hilt of his weapon with both hands, and then raised his blade over his head.

It's going to end all right, Baltrix my friend. In no more than a flash of time, the wicked woman executed her plan. She reached out and brought the hilt of her weapon to her hand, snapped it on, and thrust it with all her might upwards into Baltrix's chest. The beings were all silent; they watched in absolute horror when Chirras's black blade emerged from Baltrix's back.

"Finish it, Baltrix!" Lord Nosfaren yelled.

Lord Baltrix's eyes narrowed. With every bit of strength he could muster, he let out a primal roar and brought his own blade down into the chest of the woman beneath him. And there they lay, body slumped over body, for what seemed to the crowd to be an eternity. Miraculously, Baltrix was still alive and slowly crawled off Chirras's body and slowly rolled onto his back. And even more miraculously, Chirras sat up! She was gasping for air. Baltrix's blade had plunged through her right lung, causing it to partially collapse. Despite her severe pain and shortness of breath and driven by her unquenchable thirst for power, she continued to cling to life. *The key to immortality is right there in front of me*, Chirras gasped while black blood poured from her mouth. She slowly got to her feet and reached out toward the Silvarian while she stumbled over to where Visage was hiding behind Vira. Riza was in motion before any other being could move.

"Visage, you should cover your eyes!" Riza yelled right before she tore into Chirras's neck, biting down hard with her fangs sending out a nice plum of black mist. After she withdrew her fangs, Chirras was staring at her, her eyes wide in dazed bewilderment. Riza then produced her scythe out of thin air and twirled it over her head, leaving a trail of red and black mist in its wake. The scythe's blade made a sickening sound when it pierced the now broken Chirras. Immediately, the weapon started consuming Chirras's blood, body, and soul. Riza's scythe seemed beyond giddy while it happily devoured the Fallen woman, a black oozing energy came out of her body and traveled down the blade and into the length of the scythe's shaft. Only a pile of white powder and empty clothes remained where Chirras was. Riza swung her scythe, causing it to vanish in a spray of red and black sparks and mist.

"You didn't have to do that Riza," Nosfaren yelled while he went over to help the fallen Baltrix.

"Yes, I did!" she retorted before she too, made her way over to Baltrix's rather still body.

"That was magnificent, Riza," Baltrix weakly offered.

"Id'rth, save your strength!" Nos commanded after he knelt down and took his friend's offered hand in his own.

Baltrix shook his head. "My friend, I thank Eendril that Riza got to finish that deser'rec off—and that I got to see the whole thing. But now, I don't have much time left." The fatally wounded man was struggling to hang on. He had one more thing he wanted to do. "So, can somebe-ing please get this mask off?" Ali'stia was holding Baltrix's head on her lap, so she pressed the button, causing the mask to disappear into his earpiece. Amazingly, Baltrix was wearing a weak smile as he looked up at all of the beings, masked as well as unmasked, who were standing over him. "Ar'teth Visage, are you here?" Though Visage was severely shaken by everything that had transpired, he managed to make his way over to Baltrix's side.

"I'm here, Lord Baltrix," Visage said as he dropped to his knees beside the dying man. He began to sob when he saw the blood flowing from Baltrix's wound. Lord Nos was pressing down on the wound in an attempt to stem the blood flow but with minimal effect. However, through the use of the Zah's healing power, he was able to give his friend a few more moments of life.

Baltrix's eyes fell on Visage. "Don't waste your tears on me, my young friend," but Visage couldn't stem their flow.

"Here." Baltrix, with Ali'stia's help, managed to raise his blood sorjin up. "I want you to have this, Visage. Take it." Visage gingerly and grate-fully accepted the sorjin from the dying man. "Use it wisely."

Still overcome with emotion, Visage held the hilt of the weapon close to his chest. He struggled to offer even a quiet, "I promise." Baltrix gave him one last weak smile before turning to Nosfaren.

"This is goodbye, Master." Baltrix's hand, which Nos had continued to clutch, suddenly went limp and slipped from Nos's grasp.

"A great man has left us this deronn," Lord Michael whispered before he reverently bowed his head and silently wept.

"We'll never forget you, my friend," Ali'stia emotionally added.

"But his work wasn't yet complete," Riza stated while Chirras's blood continued to drip down from both sides of her mouth.

"Not now, Riza." Nosfaren turned to the demoness with a despon-dent look on his face. "We must lay our friend to rest. Then we can deal with what you've discovered." Riza wasn't looking too pleased but nodded that she understood. Judicators Nosfaren, Ali'stia, Michael, and several other beings hoisted the body of Lord Baltrix off the floor and headed for the lifts.

"What are they going to do with him now?" Visage weakly asked Vira, who had come over to stand at this side.

"They're going to the catacombs to lay him to rest," she dolefully replied. "Come on, V, let's go back to our room. I don't really like dealing with the dead." Visage was a bit taken aback by this, but, while he watched the morbid procession, he understood where Vira was coming from. "I want to remember Baltrix in life… not in death," the demoness added.

"I wish I could have known him longer." Visage's voice cracked as he struggled with the loss of his friend.

Vira peered down at the heartbroken boy. "I'll tell you all about him, if you want me to."

Visage thought for a moment, then shook his head. "No, Vira, I'd rather remember him as Lord Baltrix the teacher—not as Vlad the Impaler."

"You know, Visage, Baltrix bestowed a great honor upon you when he chose to give you his sorjin. He must have believed you to be a very special being—one with endless potential."

"I hope I'll be able to live up to his expectations," Visage responded before he clutched the cold metal cylinder a bit more tightly in his hands.

Vira put her hand on his head. "I know you will, my young iloni. I know you will." The grieving pair walked the rest of the way to their room in silence.

***

Vira dropped in and found Riza lying on her bed. Her feet were crossed and her legs were pumping back and forth while she casually turned the pages of her book. Vira, who was surprised by Riza's aloof-appearing attitude, rapidly tapped her left foot on the floor while observing the Meserino. "Visage is at the library, so I thought I'd check to see how you are doing. That was a really traumatic deronn. Are you alright, Riza?"

"Life is life," Riza responded. "We have to take the good with the bad. That fraking deser'rec had to be taken out! It's only too bad that Baltrix had to suffer the consequences for her fraking life choices! But, to your question, I'm okay. I appreciate your concern, Vira, I really do. You're a really good friend." The two friends embraced with tear-filled eyes.

Once composed, Vira offered, "I've been thinking about a passage used by prophets from other parts of the galaxy. It goes something like this: '...from little things great things can be accomplished. Line upon line, precept upon precept small works turn into wondrous feats...'

Riza's eyes narrowed. She struggled to relate the quoted scripture to what had so recently and painfully transpired. "So, what does that quote have to do with us?"

Vira smugly responded. "Well, it's true, isn't it?"

"Yes, I agree it's a true concept, but I still don't see how it applies to our current situation."

"Don't you get it, Riza! Visage has only been with us for a few ri-nonns, and look what he's already been through. If he's eventually going to free Chaos, not only does he have a lot to learn, but he also needs the experience required to fulfill his mission—the mission that Eendril has so graciously bestowed upon him. And, whatever he has suffered—and will yet suffer—will be for his benefit and learning." *And the same goes for all of us.*

Unbelievable. Not only is Vira right, but even Eendril's wretched Earthlings get it right occasionally. I would never have thought that those kids could make such a ludicrous prophecy sound... somewhat sane... 'Precept upon precept... line upon line.' "You may be right, Vira. Eendril wouldn't just throw such a huge task at Visage without some sort of preparation... would He?"

Vira shook her head. "No, Eendril isn't that kind of God."

38

The End of the Beginning

The man's eyes slowly opened. A soft breeze ruffled the hair of his beard and made his thick black hair flutter. *Where am I?* He stared in wonder, taking in his surroundings. He was lying on the grassy bank of a lake. The field around the lake was framed with tall trees whose bright-green leaves were casting shadows as they swayed and danced about in the breeze. Vlad got to his feet and fully assessed his condition. He was no longer wearing the uniform of The Shadow Knights; his clothes having been magickally replaced by a simple pair of white pants and a long-sleeved shirt that shimmered in the sunlight.

"Where on Zharaj is my sorjin!" Vlad panicked and frantically searched the ground for his weapon. "No. Wait. I gave it to Visage—" Suddenly, the sight of his reflection in the water interrupted his thoughts. He moved closer to the pool and dropped to his hands and knees. He gazed in awe of what he saw. "My eyes... they're... blue?" The zah'harrim, which had tainted his eyes for so long, was gone. "How long has it been since they've been that color?" He also noticed that he looked younger. All of the age lines and wrinkles he used to have had vanished. "I even feel younger!" He couldn't resist putting his hand into the lake of cool water and touching his reflection. Of course, when he touched it, the water rippled and distorted the wonderfully young-looking image, so he quickly withdrew his hand.

All of a sudden, Vlad could feel the presence of a being approaching him from the wooded area to his rear. Not knowing what to think, he did all he knew to do—sat and waited. *Who is that?* He didn't want whomever it was to know he was aware of his or her presence. *This being is a very powerful Jah'harrim user. A White Hander perhaps? No. This being is much more powerful than any of those glorts.*

Vlad's short-lived peaceful thoughts were abruptly hijacked by memories of his horrific confrontation with Chirras. He put his hand to his heart, expecting to feel the gaping stab wound caused by Chirras's blood sorjin. However, there was no wound to be found! "Wait a dironn! Am I dead!"

"Yes you are, my son." The powerful being had made His way over to Vlad and was now standing directly behind him.

Vlad slowly turned to face the being who had spoken. *This is impossible!* He thought when the being put a reassuring hand on his left shoulder, Vlad, the near invincible Earthling—who had been both feared and hated—transformed into nothing more than a child. The last of the shell that had been protecting his heart for eons shattered in an instant. He couldn't remember the last time he had cried, but warm liquid now poured from his cool-blue eyes when his very own God smiled down upon him. The holy being patiently waited before offering him a hand and helping him to his feet. "Vlad Tepes... welcome home," Jehovah smiled, speaking to Vlad as though he was an old friend whom He hadn't seen in a long time. Vlad was so humbled that all he could do was nod, drop back to his knees, and continue to weep. "Come now, my son, there are many who have been eagerly awaiting your return." Jehovah lovingly motioned for Vlad to follow. Though his vision was still blurred by tears, Vlad grasped Jehovah's offered hand, and the two then walked side by side into the woods.

"Father, may I ask where we are?" Vlad meekly questioned.

"All in good time, my son," Jehovah reassured him as the pair broke through the tree line. There in the clearing was a large group of beings who had been patiently awaiting Vlad's arrival.

"Oh, dear Lord, it's my wife!" Vlad was overcome with joy, and the pair eagerly and emotionally embraced. It was such a long awaited and touching reunion that it took a few moments before Vlad could focus his attention on the other members of the group. In his rush to reunite with his wife, he had overlooked the most important and magnificent being in the universe—Jehovah's Father and his adoptive Heavenly Father, Eendril Himself! The celestial light surrounding the heavenly being was almost blinding. *How did I overlook His presence!* For the third time, Vlad wept uncontrollably. "Father, please have mercy on my soul. I have been an egregious sinner—" Vlad's words trailed off amidst his heart wrenching sobs.

"Vlad, my son, I sent my only begotten Son to suffer, bleed, and die for you. Through repentance, those sins of yours can be totally washed away and you can become an eternally celestial soul. Please rise, Vlad Tepes."

Though he had just regained the vigor of his prime, Vlad now experienced a total loss of strength. He stumbled forward and was once now within the embrace of his Heavenly Father. I missed you, my son. Welcome home. For several moments, no further words were spoken.

Vlad experienced the depths of despair and the heights of celestial joy—all in mere moments of time. However, his joy was not yet full. For there before him, amongst the crowd of heavenly beings, Vlad spotted another being. "This can't be true!" Nevertheless, it was true. For there before him stood none other than a silver haired Silvarian with swishing tails!

"Vlad, I believe you know Arnen," Eendril said with a wide smile while gesturing to the grinning Silvarian.

Vlad was again speechless. Since he was so overcome with emotion that he couldn't move, the Silvarian took the lead and placed his hands on his shoulders. With his sapphire-colored eyes wide open with eager anticipation, Arnen managed to utter a few emotionally charged words: "Vlad, please tell me about my son."

Though another bout of shock was now coursing through his body, Vlad was somehow able to turn to Eendril. *Father, is what I'm seeing really real?* Eendril gave a confirming nod. Vlad then peered deeply into Arnen's expectant-looking eyes. The Silvarian's face lit up while he thought of the joy he had felt when Keldras told him that she was going to bear a soul and of the pain that followed—pain from the war and from knowing that he would never again see his family in the mortal plane. Arnen shook his head a few times to clear it. He awaited Vlad to tell him about the boy he'd thought he'd never get to see.

By this time, a crowd of onlookers had gathered around and was eagerly awaiting the story of Arnen's precious son. "And so," Vlad began, "Nosfaren had gone to Earth to pick up Orran and fly him back to Zharaj."

END

Word Definitions and Pronunciations

Mi'thia(Mĭ-thē-ǎ): Marcisian for mother
Dar'nra(där'nrä): Marcisian for father
De'tari(dāy-tär-ē): Marcisian for daughter
Dar'tari(där-tär-ē): Marcisian for son
Sri'na(Srē-nä): Marcisian for sister
Ber'nan(bər-nän): Marcisian for brother
Ari'thia(ă-rē-thē-ǎ): Marcisian for aunt
Uch'nra(ŭch-nrä): Marcisian for uncle
Onn(äwn): approx. 2.9 years

Rinonn(rĭ- näwn): approx. 2.5 months
Mcronn(mĭk-räwn): approx. 1 week 6 days
Deronn(dē-räwn): approx. 72 hours
Minronn(mĭn-räwn): approx. 2.4 hours
Dironn(dī-räwn): approx. 3 minutes
Veronn(vē-räwn): yesterday
Tendronn(tĕn-dräwn): today
Tononn(tō-näwn): tomorrow

Go'trell(gō-trĕll): Marcisian term meaning to have a good night. Can also mean tonight, depending on the context
Len'trell(lĕn-trĕll): Marcisian for last night
Gunrek denonn (gōōn-rĕk-dē-nŏn): Marcisian greeting meaning good evening
Gunrek menronn (gōōn-rĕk-mĕn-rŏn): Marcisian greeting meaning good morning

Zah'harrim(zä-här-rēm): dark power
Jah'harrim(jä-här-rēm): light power
Indren'freth(Ĭn-drĕn-frĕth): inner fire or the power within. Equivalent to Chakra or Ki

Imret'fethlen(ĭmrĕt-fĕth-lĕn): Marcisian term for holo-journal, a recording device that contains a faux soul. It literally translates to image of souls

Ik'thorian(ĭk-thōr-ēē-ăn)**puzzle box**: an ornate box, which usually contains a Zaharaj's blood sorjin and Imret'fethlen

Ar'teth(är-tĕth): student, disciple, learner

Betrak(bē-trăck): usually it means brat. Could also mean bastard

Bakrath(băk-răth): the closest thing is like calling someone a bitch

Deser'rec (dĕs-ēr-rĕk): Marcisian word meaning non-believer or godless. It sometimes has a more sinister context. In some cases, it means one who wants to overthrow God

Iloni(ĭl-ōwn-ē): love/lover

Id'rth(ĭd-rĕth): idiot

Crath(krăth): derogatory Marcisian word for ones behind or buttocks

Frak(frăk): most people can figure this one out

Drath(drăth): upset, angry, pissed

Moribite (mōr-ĭ-bīt): cool black stone that is both sturdy and strong

Slith(slĭth): derogatory Marcisian word for excrement

Ze'therac(Zĕ-thĕr-răk)**Clan**: Meserino demon clan that joined Skath when he declared war on all of the Gods of Ja

Demeros(dē-mēr-ōs): Meserino home world

Orran(Ŏr-ĕn): last of the Silvarian race. Born to human parents on Earth, and then taken to Zharaj to learn more about himself. In order to keep his race a secret, the Zaharaj Council changed his name to Visage (Vĭ-săwj)

Nosfaren(Nŏs-fär-rĕn): Meserino demon and head of the Dark Counsel. He is one of only two surviving founders. He is worried about the rift that is starting to form within the ranks of the Zaharaj

Baltrix(Bŏll-trĭx): member of the Dark Council. Human male from Earth, though most beings don't know this. Discovered by Lord Nosfaren while Nos was looking for a lost ship, which had crashed on Earth onns ago

Riza(Razz-ă): member of the Dark Council. Meserino demoness. Born in Demeros, the Meserino capitol. Fiancée of Visage.

Vira (Vēr-ă): member of the Dark Council. Veserino demoness. Born on the Silvarian home world of Forthien. Fiancée of Visage.

Chirras (Chēr-răs): formerly Lady Dreth and council member. Though she acts like a decent being most of the time, she has tried to persuade several other council members to see things her way, which has infuriated both Lord Nosfaren and his wife. The Council stripped Chirras of her title and place on the Council when she came back alone from a mission. She then tried to prevent Visage from arriving on Zharaj. She's a master manipulator who will do anything to gain more power, no matter how deep into the darkness her ambitions take her. She doesn't worship any being and is desperately seeking a way to become immortal so she won't have to rely on any deity.

Ali'stia(Ă-lēēs-tē-ă): member of the Dark Counsel, Meserino demoness, and Lord Nosfaren's wife. Joined Lord Nos in exile when his clan allied with the Dark God Skath.

Ranic(Răn-ĭk): red-skinned Twillan. A bit overzealous when it comes to befriending beings.

Azala(Ă-zăl-ă): female Twillan, Lord Nosfaren's apprentice and Visage's reluctant roommate.

Arisha(Ă-rē-shă): demoness know-it-all and prude. She loves the spotlight, good or bad. She usually is the antagonist who gets the trio of trouble into mischief but always seems to evade the blame. Nosfaren and Ali'stia's de'tari.

Moonreth(Mōōn-rĕth): gray-skinned Night Elf from Devros; friends with Ranic and Envine.

Le'Shara(Lă-shăr-ă): Moonreth's younger sri'na. She was called cursed because of her white skin. Very shy around most beings. She hated Zor'ret for what he did to her.

Envine(Ĕn-vīn): a human male from Theros. Likes Ranic despite his overly friendly nature.

Cormack(Kōr-măk): blue-skinned Twillan. Still isn't used to the Zah form of the Verse. He likes being around the trio of trouble. Enjoys reading in the library more than training or exploring the caverns. Apprentice to Serishin.

Glavian(Glāv-ē-ăn): member of the Dark Council. Human male who oversees the great library, including the massive reliquary. Enjoys seeking knowledge more than engaging in the martial side of the Verse.

Serishin(Sēr-ĭ-shēēn): member of the Dark Counsel. Zebrecian female. Her ancestors go back to the founding of the Zaharaj. Like Glavian, she'd much rather be in the library, learning from the many books and holo journals, than be on missions out in the galaxy. She gets along well with her apprentice, Cormack.

Zoric(Ză-rĕth): member of the Dark Council. Twillan male. Dislikes conflict, but does enjoy the martial side of the Verse. Is a master of weapons and lore. Continuously worries about his son, Ranic, who, with his friends, is constantly causing trouble.

Michael(Mī-kŭl): member of the Dark Council. Human male from Theros. Very martial in nature. Would much rather settle issues with a blood sorjin than open discourse. Though he was tempted to join the Ja'Shari, he decided he was more attuned to the Zah form of the Verse.

Fenrir(Fĕn-rēēr): member of the Dark Council. Human male. His grandparents were refugees from Renos Four. He is similar to Michael, since he is also very martial, though he is better natured. He passionately hates Skath's followers because of the devastation they caused on his planet.

Barren(Băr-rĕn): member of the Dark Council. Human male. His ancestors were also refugees who came from the Skath-devastated fringe. His parents named him after the Marcisian Emperor, and he tries very hard to live up to his namesake.

Sharas(Shăr-ăs): member of the Dark Council. Human female from Zharaj. She is a seventh generation Zaharaj. Her ancestry goes all the way back to two of the original founding members. She looks up to both Nosfaren and Ali'stia, the last surviving original members. She is very concerned about the actions of her childhood friend, Chirras.

Harneth(Hăr-nĕth): mostly human, though with trace amounts of Twillan. He lost his eyesight in an accident when he was just an apprentice. However, though he tries to hide the fact, he can now see beings like the gods or Silvarian demons can see them. Because of his apparent disability, the Council decided he was unfit for missions, so they made him one of the librarians under Serishin and Glavian.

Nar'gal(Năr-gāl): Marcisian male and a Grand Imperator. He heads up the negotiations with the Zaharaj and the Ja'Shari about whether or not the Zah should join the Empire. He is very intelligent and patient, unlike some of the council members who have extremely short tempers.

ABOUT THE AUTHOR

The author was born in New Hampshire. From a young age, he learned not only to read books but also to write them. As early as age eight, he was filling notebooks with his work.

After 9/11, the author's patriotism materialized in the form of an inspirational work, *Poems for Patriots,* which contains poems based on historic battles engaged in by the colonies and then the newly formed country from 1776 through the war in Afghanistan.

After earning degrees in Criminal Justice and Information Technology, the author's lust for writing resurfaced, and he became, essentially, a full time author. His latest endeavor came to fruition with the publication of *Demon Chronicles: The Chaos Prophecy.* This science fiction/fantasy is replete with imaginative, relatable characters and complex, smooth-flowing plots. It is centered in a fictional world where justice prevails and mercy is truly bestowed upon the weak, where mystical powers are combined with spiritual beliefs, and where magick and technology are embraced and normalized. *Demon Chronicles,* the first in a series, is destined to become a favorite amongst young and old alike.

www.ingramcontent.com/pod-product-compliance
Lightning Source LLC
Chambersburg PA
CBHW062105290726

48975CB00001B/118